F. W. Draper

Thirty-Second Report to the Legislature of Massachusetts

Anatiposi

F. W. Draper

Thirty-Second Report to the Legislature of Massachusetts

Reprint of the original, first published in 1875.

1st Edition 2024 | ISBN: 978-3-38283-174-5

Anatiposi Verlag is an imprint of Outlook Verlagsgesellschaft mbH.

Verlag (Publisher): Outlook Verlag GmbH, Zeilweg 44, 60439 Frankfurt, Deutschland
Vertretungsberechtigt (Authorized to represent): E. Roepke, Zeilweg 44, 60439 Frankfurt, Deutschland
Druck (Print): Books on Demand GmbH, In de Tarpen 42, 22848 Norderstedt, Deutschland

THIRTY-SECOND

REGISTRATION REPORT.

1873.

THIRTY-SECOND REPORT

TO THE

LEGISLATURE OF MASSACHUSETTS

RELATING TO THE

Registry and Return

OF

BIRTHS, MARRIAGES, AND DEATHS,

IN THE

COMMONWEALTH,

For the Year ending December 31, 1873.

PREPARED UNDER DIRECTION OF THE
SECRETARY OF THE COMMONWEALTH.

WITH EDITORIAL REMARKS
BY F. W. DRAPER, M.D.

BOSTON:
WRIGHT & POTTER, STATE PRINTERS,
79 MILK STREET (CORNER OF FEDERAL).
1875.

Commonwealth of Massachusetts.

SECRETARY'S DEPARTMENT, BOSTON, January 1, 1875.

To the Honorable Senate and House of Representatives.

In conformity with the requirements of the General Statutes of the Commonwealth, I have the honor to submit herewith the annual Report concerning the BIRTHS, MARRIAGES, and DEATHS, occurring in Massachusetts during the year 1873—being the Thirty-second Registration Year,—and returned according to law from the several cities and towns.

Since the publication of the last Registration Report, this Commonwealth and the cause of Sanitary Science in general have sustained a severe loss, in the decease of Dr. GEORGE DERBY, late Secretary of the State Board of Health, and for several years past editor of these annual registration reports. His labors in these directions have been an honor to the State, and of continually increasing interest and value to the friends of sanitary science.

For the present registration year, the editorial remarks and observations which follow, and the tables connected therewith, have been furnished by Dr. F. W. DRAPER, of Boston, favorably known in his editorial connection with the Boston Medical and Surgical Journal, and as author of several valuable papers, in the Reports both of the State and City of Boston Boards of Health; his experience, moreover, as associate and co-laborer with the late Dr. DERBY in the preparation of previous statistical and sanitary reports, has given him special advantages for the present work.

In the preparation and transmission of the registration returns of the year, commendable accuracy and punctuality have been manifested. Some deficiencies have occurred, requiring for their correction correspondence with the delinquent town clerks. But such defects have appeared, almost exclusively, in the returns of town clerks newly in office, and hence not well familiarized with the printed "Instructions" issued from this department for securing correctness in the Registration Returns from the towns of this Commonwealth.

Respectfully submitted,

OLIVER WARNER,
Secretary of the Commonwealth.

CONTENTS.

B

ERRATUM.

Page xxiii. — At end of note read as follows :—also, one case of triplets occur Berkshire County ; all males, and of foreign parentage.

THIRTY-SECOND REGISTRATION REPORT.

(1873.)

The accompanying tables are the thirty-second annual contribution to the vital statistics of Massachusetts. The utility of accumulating such a mass of figures from year to year is no longer questioned. Registration supplies an array of facts from which reliable conclusions can be drawn, for the benefit of the whole people. The growth and renewal of population; the inroads of disease and physical decay; the wave-like succession of epidemic diseases; the more constant and uniform operation of the wasting maladies that are always with us; the conditions, preventable or inevitable, affecting the mortality from the great class of zymotic disorders, — all these find their most significant illustration in the statistics available through the agency of the registration laws.

It is to be remarked, in general, concerning the statistics for the year 1873, that in many respects they present satisfactory and encouraging features as compared with former years. While the general tendency with regard to births, marriages and deaths is maintained in all the essentials, and while there are scarcely any startling contrasts to note in our comparison with the deductions published in previous reports, in several directions there is proof of progressive improvement in the conditions pertaining to the vitality of the people of the State.

During the year 1873, 44,481 births, 16,437 marriages and 33,912 deaths were recorded in Massachusetts. The aggregate of these numbers is 94,830, or 434 more than the total registry for 1872.

If we make a comparison with the previous year in each of these divisions of births, marriages and deaths, we find that—

The births have increased by   .   .   .   1,246
The marriages have increased by   .   .   295
The deaths have decreased by .   .   .   1,107

The natural increase of population, or excess of births over deaths, is 10,569, or 2,353 more than in 1872.

The daily natural increase averages 28·96.

One living child was born to every 32·76 persons, one person in every 44·33 was married, and one person in 42·97 died.

The daily average of living births was   .   121·87
The daily average of marriages was .   .   45·03
The daily average mortality was   .   .   92·91

The rates of births, marriages and deaths* are as follows :—

Births,   .   .   .   30·52 to 1,000 of population.
Marriages,   .   .   22·56   "   "
Deaths,   .   .   .   23·27   "   "

Excess of Birth-rate over Death-rate, 7·25 in a thousand, or ·725 of one per cent.

* Based on the population according to the Census of 1870.

TABLE showing the number of BIRTHS, MARRIAGES and DEATHS
Registered in Massachusetts during the past fifteen years.

YEARS.	Births.	Marriages.	Deaths.	Excess of Births over Deaths.	Births to 100 persons.	Deaths to 100 persons.	Excess of Births in 100 persons.
1859,	35,422	11,475	20,976	14,446	2·92	1·73	1·19
1860,	36,051	12,404	23,068	13,983	2·93	1·87	1·06
1861,	35,445	10,972	24,085	11,360	2·86	1·96	·90
1862,	32,275	11,014	22,974	9,301	2·62	1·86	·76
1863,	30,314	10,873	27,751	2,563	2·42	2·22	·20
1864,	30,449	12,513	28,723	1,726	2·42	2·28	·14
1865,	30,249	13,051	26,152	4,097	2·38	2·06	·32
1866,	34,085	14,428	23,637	10,448	2·61	1·81	·80
1867,	35,062	14,451	22,772	12,290	2·61	1·69	·92
1868,	36,193	13,856	25,603	10,590	2·62	1·85	·77
1869,	36,141	14,826	26,054	10,087	2·54	1·83	·71
1870,	38,259	14,721	27,329	10,930	2·62	1·81	·81
1871,	39,791	15,746	27,943	11,848	2·73	1·92	·81
1872,	43,235	16,142	35,019	8,216	2·96	2·40	·56
1873,	44,481	16,437	33,912	10,569	3·05	2·33	·72

POPULATION.

In making the calculations requisite for the analysis of the accompanying tabular returns, we are obliged to use as a basis the population of the State which was determined by the census of 1870. It is to be regretted that this is necessary; but if it is remembered that the resulting error is a constant one, carried throughout all the computations, and applied equally to all the conclusions, the objection loses nearly all its weight, for the comparisons are valid and reliable.

In the Report for 1869, it was found that, taking a series of five years, 1865–69, at the extremes of which the population was known by means of the census, the estimated annual increase throughout the State was at the rate of 2·848 per cent. This rate may be regarded as a close approximation to that obtaining during the series of years 1870–74. The population of the State in 1870 was 1,457,351. The estimated population in 1872 was 1,541,542. If we presume the rate of increase to be uniform, we find the estimated population for 1873 to be 1,585,445.

BIRTHS.

The following table shows the number of births annually during the last twenty years. A progressive increase will be noticed :—

YEARS.			Born alive.	Still-born.	YEARS.			Born alive.	Still-born.
1854,	.	. .	31,997	558	1864, .	.	.	30,449	856
1855,	.	. .	32,845	725	1865, .	.	.	30,249	859
1856,	.	. .	34,445	695	1866, .	.	.	34,085	1,046
1857,	.	. .	35,320	739	1867, .	.	.	35,062	1,007
1858,	.	. .	34,491	747	1868, .	.	.	36,193	1,050
1859,	.	. .	35,422	733	1869, .	.	.	36,141	1,094
1860,	.	. .	36,051	1,062	1870, .	.	.	38,259	1,019
1861,	.	. .	35,445	1,017	1871, .	.	.	39,791	1,390
1862,	.	. .	32,275	907	1872, .	.	.	43,235	1,283
1863,	.	. .	30,314	903	1873, .	.	.	44,481	1,246

The *Birth-rate* for 1873 was 3·05 for every one hundred persons. Including the still-born, a child was born to every 32 persons.

The whole number of births (still-born included) was 45,727, or 1,209 more than in 1872.

The birth-rate is higher than it has been in any previous year of the last fifteen years ; and, as we shall notice farther on, the recruits do not come entirely from the classes which give the highest mortality-rates. The disturbing influences wrought by the civil war on the birth-rate, due to the withdrawal from their homes of many thousand husbands, have ceased to leave their impress, and the rate is fully restored to its place before 1861.

LIVING BIRTHS, and numbers living to one Birth, in the different Counties in 1873.

COUNTIES.	Population—1870.	Living Births.	Numbers living to one Birth.
Barnstable, ...	32,774	615	53·29
Berkshire, ...	64,827	1,653	39·22
Bristol, ...	102,886	3,328	30·91
Dukes and Nantucket, . . .	7,910	111	71·26
Essex, ...	200,843	5,686	35·32
Franklin, ...	32,635	733	44·52
Hampden, ...	78,409	2,527	31·03
Hampshire, ...	44,388	1,111	39·95
Middlesex, ...	274,353	8,605	31·88
Norfolk, ...	89,443	2,517	35·54
Plymouth, ...	65,365	1,549	42·19
Suffolk, ...	270,802	10,254	26·41
Worcester, ...	192,716	5,792	33·27
Whole State, ...	1,457,351	44,481	32·76

The table illustrates a fact long since determined, namely, that the centres of population are comparatively the more fruitful; for Suffolk, Bristol, Hampden, Middlesex, Worcester and Essex, the counties containing the thickly settled communities, maintain their places as the more prolific in the list; while Plymouth, Franklin, Barnstable, Dukes and Nantucket—the rural counties—are at the other extreme. The island counties present an unusually small birth-rate this year; they have for many years been at the foot of the list in point of fecundity.

BIRTHS in Massachusetts.—*Quarterly Rates.*

PERIOD.	Numbers.	Percentage.
Quarter ending with March, ...	10,195	2·79
June, ...	10,132	2·78
September, . . .	11,839	3·25
December, . . .	12,315	3·38
Whole year, ...	44,481	3·05

The foregoing table supposes the birth-rate to have been maintained uniformly throughout the year. The relatively increased percentage of the last two quarters of the year is very noteworthy. In England the order is reversed, and more births are registered in the first half of the year. Social customs, and not natural law, must afford an explanation of this discrepancy in the two instances.

The next table presents a similar comparison, by periods of six months, and carried through a series of years.

BIRTHS arranged in Periods of Six Months.—*Thirteen Years.*

YEARS.	Two First Quarters.	Two Last Quarters.	Difference.
1861, ...	16,644	18,756	2,112
1862, ...	15,308	16,938	1,630
1863, ...	14,338	15,952	1,614
1864, ...	14,052	16,366	2,314
1865, ...	14,136	16,113	1,977
1866, ...	15,218	18,867	3,649
1867, ...	15,971	19,091	3,120
1868, ...	16,728	19,465	2,737
1869, ...	16,238	19,903	3,665
1870, ...	18,066	20,393	2,327
1871, ...	18,387	21,404	3,017
1872, ...	19,994	23,241	3,247
1873, ...	20,327	24,154	3,827
Average, ...	16,569	19,280	2,711

Proportion of the Sexes.—*Twenty-two Years.*

		1 8 7 3.	1852-1872.
Born alive,	Males, ...	22,974	370,417
	Females, ...	21,485	350,264
	Not stated, . . .	22	2,122
Males to 100 Females,	. . .	106·9	105·7
Still-born,	Males, ...	715	10,328
	Females, ...	455	7,011
	Not stated, . . .	76	2,484
Males to 100 Females,	. . .	157·1	147·3
Illegitimate,	Males, ...	294	2,268
	Females, ...	293	2,389
	Not stated, . . .	–	34
Males to 100 Females,	. . .	100·4	94·9

The proportion of males to females, among those born alive, does not vary greatly from that during the last twenty years. Among those still-born, the relative number of males is considerably in excess of that in former years.

BIRTHS by Counties in 1873.—*Proportion of Males to Females.*

COUNTIES.	Males, per cent.	Females, per cent.	Males to 100 Females.
Barnstable, ...	58·4	41·6	140·2
Berkshire, ...	51·9	48·1	108·3
Bristol, ...	52·6	47·4	110·9
Dukes and Nantucket, . . .	50·5	49·5	103·7
Essex, ...	51·6	48·4	106·5
Franklin, ...	53·5	46·5	115·
Hampden, ...	52·1	47·9	108·9
Hampshire, ...	52·6	47·4	110·8
Middlesex, ...	51·9	41·1	108·8
Norfolk, ...	51·	49·	104·5
Plymouth, ...	51·8	48·2	107·5
Suffolk, ...	50·4	49·6	101·6
Worcester, ...	51·9	48·1	107·9
Whole State, ...	51·6	48·4	106·9

All the counties, without exception, illustrate the observation made long ago, not only in Massachusetts but in other States and in other countries, that the excess of male children over female children is a constant and almost uniform one.

EXHIBIT OF THE PARENTAGE of the Children born alive, in several classes, which were Registered in the several Counties of Massachusetts during the year 1873.

BIRTHS.	State	Barnstable	Berkshire	Bristol	Dukes and Nantucket	Essex	Franklin	Hampden	Hampshire	Middlesex	Norfolk	Plymouth	Suffolk	Worcester
Totals,	44,481	615	1,653	3,328	111	5,686	733	2,527	1,111	8,605	2,517	1,549	10,254	5,792
Aggregates, { Males,	22,974	359	859	1,749	56	2,933	392	1,316	584	4,468	1,284	802	5,168	3,004
Females,	21,485	256	793	1,576	54	2,753	340	1,208	527	4,184	1,228	746	5,085	2,785
Unknown,	22	—	1	3	1	—	1	3	—	3	5	1	1	3
PARENTAGE.														
American,	17,647	493	720	1,270	93	2,615	461	958	508	3,174	1,061	1,025	2,750	2,519
Foreign,	21,293	80	708	1,724	10	2,345	217	1,298	503	4,370	1,111	362	5,820	2,745
American Father and Foreign Mother,	2,139	23	78	128	7	339	15	109	36	427	150	52	597	178
Foreign Father and American Mother,	3,062	19	137	190	—	353	33	155	58	622	189	73	894	339
Not stated,	340	—	10	16	1	34	7	7	6	12	6	37	193	11

2

Exhibit of the Parentage of the Children born alive—Concluded.

PLURALITY CASES (included above).

BIRTHS.		STATE.	Barnstable.	Berkshire.	Bristol.	Dukes and Nantucket.	Essex.	Franklin.	Hampden.	Hampshire.	Middlesex.	Norfolk.	Plymouth.	Suffolk.	Worcester.
Totals,	Aggregates,	832	2	39	79	6	113	20	44	14	166	54	32	147	116
	Males,	422	2	25	37	3	63	12	17	6	71	31	18	71	66
	Females,	410	—	14	42	3	50	8	27	8	95	23	14	76	50
American,	Males,	168	2	8	19	3	27	7	5	—	30	13	14	18	28
	Females,	158	—	8	23	3	19	7	8	4	39	7	10	16	14
Foreign,	Males,	212	—	17	18	—	28	5	10	6	30	16	4	47	31
	Females,	205	—	6	17	—	30	1	17	4	45	12	4	40	29
Am. Father,	Males,	23	—	—	1	—	6	—	1	—	3	2	—	4	6
	Females,	22	—	—	1	—	1	—	1	—	7	2	—	8	2
For. Father,	Males,	19	—	—	5	—	2	—	1	—	8	—	—	2	4
	Females,	25	—	—	1	—	—	—	1	—	4	2	—	12	5

ILLEGITIMATE BIRTHS (included above).

		587	11	14	27	2	39	3	13	10	62	12	42	322	30
Totals,	Aggregates,	587	11	14	27	2	39	3	13	10	62	12	42	322	30
	Males,	294	5	10	11	–	17	–	6	6	32	7	24	166	10
	Females,	293	6	4	16	2	22	3	7	4	30	5	18	156	20
Am. Mother,	Males,	152	5	7	10	–	13	–	4	6	8	5	12	74	8
	Females,	154	6	4	15	1	15	2	3	3	12	5	8	64	16
For. Mother,	Males,	184	–	3	1	–	3	–	2	–	22	2	12	87	2
	Females,	185	–	–	1	1	7	1	4	1	17	–	10	89	4
Not stated,	Males,	88	–	–	–	–	1	–	–	–	2	–	–	5	–
	Females,	44	–	–	–	–	–	–	–	–	1	–	–	3	–

Percentage of American and Foreign LIVING BIRTHS *in each of the past Ten Years.*

YEARS.			American.	Foreign.	One parent Foreign.
1864,	. . . .		44·91	47·62	2·47
1865,	. . . .		44·53	47·40	8·07
1866,	. . . .		44·42	47·30	8·28
1867,	. . . .		42·36	48·75	8·89
1868,	. . . .		43·05	47·60	9·35
1869,	. . . .		42·07	48·01	9·92
1870,	. . . .		41·01	48·33	10·66
1871,	. . . .		40·17	48·61	11·22
1872,	. . . .		39·45	49·21	11·34
1873,	. . . .		39·98	48·24	11·78

Certain very suggestive features are shown in this table. During the ten years, there has been a progressive decrease in the number of purely American births, and a corresponding increase in the number of those from a mixed parentage. The births from wholly foreign parentage have maintained a singular uniformity, comprising nearly half of all the births. In 1873, there was a slight re-action in the number of native births, the American element showing a little tendency to re-assert itself. We are hardly justified, however, in prophesying that this change is more than temporary; it is too much to expect that the relations of American to foreign parentage which were observed in Massachusetts twenty-five years ago, as shown in the following table, will ever again be realized.

Percentage of American and Foreign LIVING BIRTHS, *in the past Twenty-five Years.*

	Average. 1849-53.	Average. 1854-58.	Average. 1859-63.	Average. 1864-68.	Average. 1869-73.
American, ...	63·02	50·38	46·06	43·85	40 54
Foreign, ...	35·96	44·12	46·89	47·73	48·48
One parent Foreign, . .	1·02	5·50	7·05	8·42	10·98

The excess of foreign over native parentage is 3,646, or 544 less than the excess reported in 1872. Foreign births were more numerous than those of native parentage in Bristol, Hampden, Middlesex, Norfolk, Suffolk and Worcester. The counties which are the most fruitful are likewise most fruitful in children of imported stock, and for the obvious reason that they contain the densely populated sections wherein those prone to multiply the fastest generally congregate.

Comparing 1873 with 1872, we note that American births have increased by 725 ; Foreign births have increased by 181 ; and the births from mixed parentage (one parent being foreign) have increased by 337 ;—thus showing in another way that this year was favorable to American nativity.

Plural Births.—Four hundred and thirteen women in Massachusetts gave birth in 1873 to eight hundred and thirty-two children. Four hundred and seven bore twins and six had triplets. The number of cases of triplets is three more than in 1872.

Illegitimates.—Five hundred and eighty-seven are reported, two hundred and eighty-four more than in the previous year, and two hundred and ninety-nine more than the average annual number during the last fifteen years. This increase is very noteworthy ; its cause is not apparent, but the coincidence of this sudden rise with the stringent financial experiences through which the community has been passing during the last two years is at least worthy of consideration in this connection.

This explanation gathers some strength from the fact that a large proportion (54 per cent.) of all the illegitimate births occurred in Suffolk County, where, in seasons of stress, there would be a relatively greater tendency to this kind of immorality than in more rural sections, in which the sensitiveness to financial fluctuations would be less acute.

The sexes were almost equally divided, the males exceeding the females by a single one. In former years, the females have almost uniformly and largely exceeded the males.

The larger share of the births fell to the latter half of the year, there being 44 per cent. of the whole number in the first six months and 56 per cent. in the second.

Still-born.—Of these, 1,246 were recorded, 37 less than in 1872. The males were much more numerous than the females, there having been 715 of the former to 455 of the latter. The percentage of still-births to the whole number of births was 2·72, or one still-born to every thirty-seven births. This proportion is very near that found in previous years.

MARRIAGES.

The whole number of marriages recorded in 1873 was 16,437, or 295 more than in 1872.

The following table will show the steadily increasing number of marriages, annually, during the last ten years.

MARRIAGES registered in Massachusetts, *Ten Years*, 1864–73.

YEARS.	Marriages.	Persons Married.	YEARS.	Marriages.	Persons Married.
1864, . . .	12,513	25,026	1869, . . .	14,826	29,652
1865, . . .	13,052	26,104	1870, . . .	14,721	29,442
1866, . . .	14,428	28,856	1871, . . .	15,746	31,492
1867, . . .	14,451	28,902	1872, . . .	16,142	32,284
1868, . . .	13,856	27,712	1873, . . .	16,437	32,874

One person in every 44·33 was married in 1873.

The following table exhibits a very remarkable uniformity as regards the season of the year preferred by people in Massachusetts for entering the married condition. The rule has become one without exception, that the last three months of the year are the season when most marriages occur; the spring and early summer are deemed the time having the second degree of propitiousness; while the first quarter and the third quarter of the year are the least acceptable. November and March witnessed the greatest and the least number of weddings, respectively, the year 1873 adding another to the long series of years in which the same fact has been observed in this State.

MARRIAGES in Massachusetts.—*Quarterly Aggregates and Percentages.*

EIGHT YEARS.	1st Quarter.	2d Quarter.	3d Quarter.	4th Quarter.
1866, ...	3,047	3,751	3,151	4,441
1867, ..., .	3,252	3,658	3,137	4,404
1868, ...	3,085	3,395	3,004	4,372
1869, ... ꞏ .	3,007	3,854	3,401	4,564
1870, ...	3,277	3,625	3,259	4,560
1871, ...	3,421	3,800	3,616	4,909
1872, ...	3,423	4,157	3,711	4,851
1873, ...	3,600	4,269	3,738	4,830

PERCENTAGES.

	1st Quarter.	2d Quarter.	3d Quarter.	4th Quarter.
1866, ...	21·23	26·05	21·88	30·84
1867, ...	22·50	25·31	21·71	30·48
1868, ...	22·27	24·50	21·67	31·56
1869, ...	20·28	25·99	22·94	30·79
1870, ...	22·26	24·62	22·14	30·98
1871, ...	21·72	24·13	22·96	31·18
1872, ...	21·21	25·45	22·99	30·05
1873, ...	21·90	25·97	22·74	29·39

MARRIAGES in Massachusetts.—Rates by Counties.

COUNTIES.	MARRIAGES TO 100 LIVING.				PERSONS LIVING TO 1 MARRIAGE.			
	1866-1870.	1871.	1872.	1873.	1866-1870.	1871.	1872.	1873.
Barnstable,	0·941	1·001	1·001	0·906	107	99	99	110
Berkshire,	0·956	0·797	0·822	0·791	103	125	122	126
Bristol,	1·048	1·029	1·254	1·399	96	97	79	71
Dukes,	0·769	0·898	1·083	0·898	136	111	92	111
Essex,	1·155	1·117	1·114	1·095	87	89	89	91
Franklin,	0·910	0·919	0·855	0·928	112	109	117	107
Hampden,	1·226	1·150	1·164	1·174	82	87	86	85
Hampshire,	1·101	0·915	0·799	0·770	91	109	125	129
Middlesex,	1·087	1·079	1·171	1·132	92	92	87	88
Nantucket,	0·863	0·873	0·728	0·873	121	114	137	114
Norfolk,	0·773	0·763	0·751	0·894	130	131	133	112
Plymouth,	0·892	0·910	0·864	0·982	113	109	116	102
Suffolk,	1·445	1·406	1·401	1·459	69	71	71	68
Worcester,	1·074	0·973	1·016	0·959	93	103	98	104
Whole State,	1·111	1·080	1·108	1·128	90	92	90	89

3

It will be observed that these rates show marriages to be most numerous in the counties where cities and prosperity abound; while the counties from which young people tend to emigrate—the agricultural and sparsely settled sections — show that the disposition to matrimony is relatively less prevalent.

The rate for the whole State is larger than that observed in any year since 1869. It does not appear from this that there is such a growing disinclination among people to marry as has recently been asserted.

The following table exhibits the ages and social condition of those who were married in 1873, so far as stated in the returns :—

AGES at Marriage of 16,415 MEN and of 16,397 WOMEN.

	Under 20	20 to 25	25 to 30	30 to 35	35 to 40	40 to 45	45 to 50	50 to 55	55 to 60	60 to 65	65 to 70	70 to 75	75 to 80	Over 80
Men,	313	6,564	4,989	2,015	971	545	392	259	199	112	65	35	15	1
Women,	3,380	7,232	3,266	1,191	621	352	176	82	42	36	17	1	1	—

AGES at Marriage of 13,879 BACHELORS and 14,657 MAIDS.

	Under 20	20 to 25	25 to 30	30 to 35	35 to 40	40 to 45	45 to 50	50 to 55	55 to 60	60 to 65	65 to 70	70 to 75	75 to 80	Over 80
Bachelors,	313	6,492	4,685	1,564	515	173	85	32	8	7	4	2	—	—
Maids,	3,367	7,069	2,908	823	284	131	41	19	8	5	2	—	—	—

AGES at Marriage of 2,527 WIDOWERS and 1,731 WIDOWS.

	Under 20	20 to 25	25 to 30	30 to 35	35 to 40	40 to 45	45 to 50	50 to 55	55 to 60	60 to 65	65 to 70	70 to 75	75 to 80	Over 80
Widowers,	—	69	302	450	454	372	308	227	131	104	61	33	15	1
Widows,	10	162	354	368	337	221	135	62	34	31	15	1	1	—

The average age of all the men married in 1873 was . . . . 28·7 years.
average age of all the women married in 1873 was . . . . 24·8 "
average age of men marrying for the first time was . . . . 26·3 "
average age of women marrying for the first time was . . . . 23·5 "

Social or Conjugal Condition of Persons Married in Massachusetts, 1873.

MALES.		Whole No. of Marriages.	FEMALES.				
Number of the Marriage.			First Marriage.	Second Marriage.	Third Marriage.	Fourth Marriage.	Unknown.
Whole Number,		16,437	14,679	1,521	218	1	18
1st Marriage,	.	13,888	13,136	591	161	–	–
2d Marriage,	.	2,314	1,438	836	40	–	–
3d Marriage,	.	202	99	85	17	1	–
4th Marriage,	.	12	4	8	–	–	–
5th Marriage,	.	2	1	1	–	–	–
6th Marriage,	.	1	1	–	–	–	–
Unknown,	.	18	–	–	–	–	18

The percentages of first and subsequent marriages during the past ten years are shown in the following table :—

		First Marriage.	Second Marriage.	Third Marriage.	Fourth Marriage.	Fifth Marriage.	Sixth Marriage.	Not stated.
1864,	Males, .	81·78	15·71	1·78	·12	·02	–	·59
	Females,	87·26	11·50	·60	·05	–	–	·59
1865,	Males, .	81·10	16·37	1·76	·14	·01	–	·62
	Females,	86·14	12·70	·52	·02	–	–	·62
1866,	Males, .	82·25	15·82	1·25	·10	·01	–	·57
	Females,	87·39	11·67	·36	·01	–	–	·57
1867,	Males, .	83·25	15·04	·95	·18	·01	–	·57
	Females,	87·51	11·57	·30	·04	·01	–	·57
1868,	Males, .	83·63	14·62	1·41	·12	–	·01	·20
	Females,	87·95	11·54	·29	·02	–	–	·20
1869,	Males, .	83·81	14·38	1·42	·15	·01	·02	·20
	Females,	88·70	10·57	·47	·03	·01	–	·20
1870,	Males, .	83·97	14·12	1·41	·19	·01	–	·29
	Females,	89·06	10·22	·41	·02	–	–	·29
1871,	Males, .	84·21	14·14	1·39	·13	·01	–	·11
	Females,	89·37	10·07	·43	·01	–	–	·11
1872,	Males, .	84·96	13·39	1·46	·06	·01	–	·12
	Females,	89·15	10·27	·45	·01	–	–	·12
1873,	Males, .	84·48	14·08	1·23	·08	·01	·01	·11
	Females,	89·30	9·25	1·33	·01	–	–	·11

Certain Marriages.—1873.

	TOTALS.	AGES OF FEMALES.									
		14	15	16	17	18	19	21	25	26	32
NUMBER OF FEMALES, .	791	7	47	174	439	61	58	1	2	1	1
16, .	2	-	-	-	1	1	-	-	-	-	-
17, .	11	-	-	1	3	1	3	1	2	-	-
18, .	44	1	1	7	13	14	7	-	-	1	-
19, .	143	-	5	15	29	45	48	-	-	-	1
20, .	59	-	9	16	34	-	-	-	-	-	-
21, .	129	1	8	33	87	-	-	-	-	-	-
22, .	100	1	6	28	65	-	-	-	-	-	-
23, .	83	2	4	18	59	-	-	-	-	-	-
24, .	66	1	6	15	44	-	-	-	-	-	-
25, .	28	-	1	10	17	-	-	-	-	-	-
26, .	30	1	2	12	15	-	-	-	-	-	-
27, .	24	-	2	7	15	-	-	-	-	-	-
28, .	14	-	-	3	11	-	-	-	-	-	-
29, .	10	-	1	-	9	-	-	-	-	-	-
30, .	14	-	-	3	11	-	-	-	-	-	-
31, .	6	-	-	1	5	-	-	-	-	-	-
32, .	5	-	-	1	4	-	-	-	-	-	-
33, .	5	-	-	2	3	-	-	-	-	-	-
34, .	4	-	-	-	4	-	-	-	-	-	-
35, .	5	-	1	-	4	-	-	-	-	-	-
36, .	1	-	-	-	1	-	-	-	-	-	-
37, .	1	-	-	-	1	-	-	-	-	-	-
39, .	2	-	-	1	1	-	-	-	-	-	-
40, .	1	-	-	1	-	-	-	-	-	-	-
42, .	1	-	-	-	1	-	-	-	-	-	-
44, .	1	-	1	-	-	-	-	-	-	-	-
54, .	1	-	-	-	1	-	-	-	-	-	-
61, .	1	-	-	-	1	-	-	-	-	-	-

(AGES OF MALES)

Marriages.

First Marriage of both Parties. Ages.		1st Male. 3d Female. Ages.		2d Male. 1st Female. Ages.		3d Male. 1st Female. Ages.		3d Male. 2d Female. Ages.	
Ma.	Fe.	Ma.	Fe.	Ma.	Fe.	Ma.	Fe.	Ma.	Fe.
18	14	27	23	24	15	39	17	52	23
23	14	22	25	44	15	47	18	49	24
26	14	26	32	21	16	50	19	30	27
18	15	28	32	24	16	35	21	53	28
19	15	29	32	28	16	29	22	39	29
20	15	26	33	40	16	30	22	36	30
21	15	32	33	47	17	35	22	40	30
22	15	24	38	20	24	36	25	38	33
23	15			60	46	37	25	70	39
24	15					36	30	55	52
25	15					36	31	76	63
26	15					35	35		

1st Male. 2d Female. Ages.		3d of Both. Ages.		2d Male. 3d Female. Ages.		4th Male. 2d Female. Ages.	
Ma.	Fe.	Ma.	Fe.	Ma.	Fe.	Ma.	Fe.
22	17	46	31	28	24	41	28
19	32	32	33	44	29	63	39
60	35	55	39	36	31	60	40
21	36	66	41	29	36	63	40
67	47	73	63			43	43
		75	64			54	47
		80	67			62	53

Remaining entries of First Marriage of both Parties:

Ma.	Fe.
27	15
17	16
18	16
19	16
30	16
32	16
33	16
16	17
17	17
63	17
18	26
19	32
22	40
59	52

Remaining entries of 3d Male. 1st Female.:

Ma.	Fe.
28	36
60	57
60	62

2d of Both. Ages.	
Ma.	Fe.
31	20
22	21
32	22
26	25

4th Male. 1st Female. Ages.		3d Male. 4th Female. Ages.		5th Male. 1st Female. Ages.		5th Male. 2d Female. Ages.		6th Male. 1st Female. Ages.	
Ma.	Fe.	Ma.	Fe.	Ma.	Fe.	Ma.	Fe.	Ma.	Fe.
48	24	55	60	57	24	62	54	67	44
43	29								
56	32								
58	46								

During the year 1873, the number of females married at the age of 17 was 439, an excess of 89 above the average number for the last seven years.   One hundred and seventy-four were married at the age of 16, forty-seven at 15, and seven at 14. Among the males, two were married at 16, eleven at 17, forty-four at 18 and one hundred and forty-three at 19.   Of the males above named who married at 18, three took for wives girls aged 16, 15 and 14, respectively; while one young man of 16 became the husband of a maiden of 17.   A bachelor of 63 was accepted by a maid of 17; and a bachelor of 22 was united to a maid of 40.   A couple, aged 59 and 52 respectively, were married, it being their first venture.   A widower of 48 took for his fourth wife a maid of 24; and a widow of 23 was married to a bachelor of 27, her third husband.   A widower of 19 found favor with a spinster of 32.   The oldest parties married during the year were a widower of 80 and a widow of 67, it being the third marriage of each.   There were three fifth marriages of males during the year, at the ages of 62, 57 and 54.   One widow became a bride for the fourth time, her bridegroom being a widower of 55, her own age being 60.   Among those who had been twice widowed was one who, at the age of 23, was married to a bachelor of 22.   A widow of 17 married a bachelor of 22, and a widower of 20 married a maid of 22.

One case may have special mention here, because of the unusual aptitude manifested by the individual to contribute to the vital statistics of the State, especially in the departments of births and marriages.   The facts stated are well authenticated. A man died at Lowell, April 7th, 1873, at the age of 75.   His death was caused by consumption.   "He was the father of thirty-four children, fourteen by one wife, seventeen by a second, and three by a third."   His third marriage occurred when he was 70 years old.

NATIVITY OF PERSONS Married in the several Counties of the State.—*Numbers.* 1873.

	WHOLE STATE.	Barnstable.	Berkshire.	Bristol.	Dukes.	Essex.	Franklin.	Hampden.	Hampshire.	Middlesex.	Nantucket.	Norfolk.	Plymouth.	Suffolk.	Worcester.
TOTAL MARRIAGES,	16,437	297	513	1,440	34	2,200	303	921	343	3,106	96	800	642	3,952	1,850
American,	8,755	259	320	720	28	1,280	240	480	230	1,637	34	470	506	1,449	1,102
Foreign,	5,115	27	107	540	3	586	30	313	69	936	1	209	79	1,780	485
American Groom and Foreign Bride,	1,079	5	25	80	–	170	13	50	23	210	–	42	22	352	87
Foreign Groom and American Bride,	1,477	6	61	98	3	163	19	78	21	320	1	79	35	421	172
Nativities not stated,	11	–	–	2	–	1	1	–	–	3	–	–	–	–	4

MARRIAGES according to Nativity.—*Percentages.*

YEARS.	American.	Foreign.	Am. Groom and For. Bride.	For. Groom and Am. Bride.	Not stated.
1862, ...	62·38	26·56	4·54	4·08	2·44
1863, ...	61·34	27·85	4·44	5·14	1·23
1864, ...	60·53	28·32	4 52	6·08	·55
1865, ...	59·58	29·29	4·49	6 16	·48
1866, ...	58·81	27·84	5·32	6·51	1·52
1867, ...	58·39	28·96	5·40	6·31	·94
1868, ...	58·10	29·08	5·41	6·94	·47
1869, ...	57·48	29·26	5·24	7·58	·44
1870, ...	56·79	29·01	6·12	7·98	.10
1871, ...	55·71	29·37	6·24	8·50	·18
1872, ...	53·89	30·76	6·85	8·42	·08
1873, ...	53·26	31·12	6·56	8·99	·07

A progressive diminution in the relative number of marriages of purely American couples is shown in the above table, in marked contrast with the increase in the percentages of the other classes. A degree of caution should be exercised in forming inferences here, however, for it is an open question when persons proposing marriage appear to themselves, or to the registrars, to cease to be of foreign nationality and to become American. If we could carry the comparison back one degree farther and have the parent-nativity of persons married, the conclusions formed would be of more value. One feature of the foregoing table may be noted with satisfaction—the gradually lessening proportion of cases in which desirable facts were " not stated."

The following table presents in another way the comparison between the percentages of marriages among natives and foreigners in Massachusetts, in the last ten years.

4

NATIVITY OF PERSONS MARRIED during Ten Years.—*Numbers.*

	1864.	1865.	1866.	1867.	1868.	1869.	1870.	1871.	1872.	1873.
WHOLE NUMBER OF MARRIAGES, .	12,513	13,051	14,428	14,451	13,856	14,826	14,721	15,746	16,142	16,487
American, ...	7,574	7,776	8,485	8,438	8,051	8,522	8,360	8,772	8,699	8,755
Foreign, . . .	3,544	3,823	4,017	4,186	4,030	4,338	4,271	4,625	4,966	5,115
One party Foreign, .	1,332	1,390	1,706	1,692	1,711	1,900	2,075	2,321	2,465	2,556
Not stated, . .	163	62	220	135	64	66	15	28	12	11

Percentages of those stated, equally dividing the Half Foreign.

	1864.	1865.	1866.	1867.	1868.	1869.	1870.	1871.	1872.	1873.
Whole number, . .	100·00	100·00	100·00	100·00	100·00	100·00	100·00	100·00	100·00	100·00
American, . .	66·18	65·22	65·73	64·85	64·58	64·17	63·89	63·19	61·57	61·08
Foreign, . .	33·82	34·78	34·27	35·15	35·42	35·83	36·11	36·81	38·43	38·92

DEATHS.

The whole number of deaths recorded in Massachusetts in 1873 was 33,912. The number in 1872 was 35,019. The difference between the two years, and in favor of 1873, was 1,107. Although there is this marked improvement where comparison is made with 1872, yet the mortality was larger in 1873, by 6,912, than the average annual mortality during the previous ten years (1863–72).

The death-rate for the State during the last nine years is given in the following table. The population is estimated, except for the years 1865 and 1870, when the census gave us more exact numbers. It will be noted that the death-rate for 1873, though less than that for the previous year, is still considerably in advance of that recorded for the years between 1867 and 1871. This difference may be accounted for in a measure by the presence of epidemics in the years 1872 and 1873. A high death-rate is a "cautionary signal" of unusual local or epidemic influences at work. If the sanitary officer uses this signal as the guide to his operations, and analyzes the conditions of which the registration of deaths furnishes him a comprehensive formula in the death-rate, he will assuredly come, sooner or later, upon hygienic problems which will stimulate investigation and demand patient practical handling.

DEATH-RATE for Nine Years.

YEARS.	Population.	Deaths to 100 living.	No. living to one death.
1865, ...	1,267,031	2·064	48
1866, ...	1,303,116	1·815	55
1867, ...	1,340,229	1·691	59
1868, ...	1,378,398	1·852	54
1869, ...	1,417,654	1·838	54
1870, ...	1,457,351	1·875	53
1871, ...	1,498,856	1·864	54
1872, ...	1,541,542	2·272	44
1873, ...	1,585,445	2·139	47

The following table shows the death-rate in six geographical divisions of the State. These divisions possess more distinctive natural characters than if they took the county boundaries as limits :—

MORTALITY of Massachusetts in Six Geographical Divisions.— 1873.

DIVISIONS.	Population— 1870.	Deaths.	Deaths to 100 living.	No. living to one death.
1. Metropolitan (City of Boston),	250,526	7,868	3·14	32
2. North-Eastern (Essex and parts of Suffolk and Middlesex), .	465,116	10,882	2·34	43
3. South-Eastern (Dukes and Nantucket, Barnstable, Plymouth, Bristol and Norfolk), . .	298,378	6,564	2·19	45
4. Midland (Worcester and part of Middlesex), ...	223,072	4,201	1·88	53
5. Valley (Franklin, Hampden and Hampshire), ...	155,432	3,286	2·11	47
6. Western (Berkshire), . .	64,827	1,111	1·71	58

In all of the divisions above represented, there was a greater or less improvement in the death-rate, with one exception : the South-Eastern section which, in 1872, had a death-rate of 2·07 per cent., in 1873 showed a rate of 2·19. Two of the divisions (the Western and the Midland) present a rate closely approximating that established in England as the normal mortality-rate — 1·70 per cent.

DEATH-RATE in the Counties.—1873.

COUNTIES.					Population—1870.	Deaths to 100 living.	Persons living to one death.
Barnstable,	.	.	.	.	32,774	1·76	57
Berkshire,	.	.	.	.	64,827	1·71	58
Bristol,	.	.	.	.	102,886	2·83	35
Dukes,	.	.	.	.	3,787	1·53	65
Essex,	.	.	.	.	200,843	2·21	45
Franklin,	.	.	.	.	32,635	1·74	57
Hampden,	.	.	.	.	78,409	2·44	41
Hampshire,	.	.	.	.	44,388	1·81	55
Middlesex,	.	.	.	.	274,353	2·38	42
Nantucket,	.	.	.	.	4,123	2·57	39
Norfolk,	.	.	.	.	89,443	1·87	53
Plymouth,	.	.	.	.	65,365	1·89	53
Suffolk,	.	.	.	.	270,802	3·07	33
Worcester,	.	.	.	.	192,716	1·89	53
Whole State,		.	.	.	1,457,351	2·32	43

The order of mortality is as follows, beginning with the lowest :—Dukes, Berkshire, Franklin, Barnstable, Hampshire, Norfolk, Plymouth, Worcester, Essex, Middlesex, Hampden, Nantucket, Bristol, Suffolk. The order of relative mortality changes considerably from year to year ; there is, however, one constant feature ; namely, that the counties containing the large cities take their place at the foot of the list.

Seasons.   Dᴇᴀᴛʜꜱ by Quarters of the Year.

	Deaths.	Percentage.
Deaths registered in Quarters ending with—		
March, ...	8,257	24·35
June, ...	7,520	22·17
September, ...	10,451	30·82
December, ...	7,684	22·66

The year 1873 illustrates an observation made long ago, that the season of midsummer is unfavorable to life. The greatly increased mortality among children at that season is sufficient to determine the preponderance in that direction.

Sex.—The deaths of males exceeded those of females in 1873 by 600.

PROPORTIONS of the Sexes when distinguished in the annual Deaths.—*Twenty-two Years.*

	Annual Aver-age. 1852-61.	Four Years of War. 1862-65.	1866.	1867.	1868.	1869.	1870.	1871.	1872.	1873.
Males, ...	10,487	13,602	11,601	11,350	12,871	12,777	13,699	13,985	17,717	17,242
Females, . . .	10,602	12,748	12,003	11,869	12,695	13,291	13,598	13,931	17,256	16,642
Number of males to each 100 females, . .	98·9	106·7	96·6	99·8	101·4	96·6	100·7	100·4	102·1	103·6

DEATHS in Massachusetts in 1873.—*Ages, Sex, Rates.*

SEX.	Under 1 Year.	Under 5 Years.	20 to 30.	All others.	Totals.
Number of deaths, { Males,	4,391	6,635	1,744	8,877	17,256
Females,	3,520	5,739	1,805	9,112	16,656
Totals,	7,911	12,374	3,549	17,989	33,912
Per cent of deaths { Males,	25·45	38·45	10·11	51·44	100
for each sex, . { Females,	21·13	34·46	10·84	54·70	100
Per ct. of all deaths { Males,	12·95	19·57	5·14	26·18	50·89
for each sex, . { Females,	10·38	16·92	5·32	26·87	49·11
Totals,	23·33	36·49	10·46	53·05	100
Females to 100 Males, 1873, .	80·2	86·5	103·5	102·6	96·5
Females to 100 Males, 1872, .	84·4	87·5	101·2	104·9	97·4
Females to 100 Males, 1871, .	78·9	86	117·4	105·6	99·6
Females to 100 Males, 1870, .	79·9	84·9	126·8	105·1	99·3
Females to 100 Males, 1869, .	86·5	90·5	120·7	109·7	103·5
Females to 100 Males, 1868, .	83·6	85·2	114	106·2	98·6
Females to 100 Males, 1867, .	82·5	86·3	115·5	107·1	100·1
Females to 100 Males, 1866, .	81	87	110·4	113·2	103·5

AVERAGE AGE at Death.—1866–73.

	Of all who Died.	Of all above 20 years old.
1866, ...	30·92	52·08
1867, ...	30·05	52·58
1868, ...	29·92	53·44
1869, ...	30·38	53·20
1870, ...	30·26	52·42
1871, ...	31·36	55·75
1872, ...	28·27	51·83
1873, ...	27·96	52·13

A somewhat younger age is ascertained to be the average at which death occurred in 1873, if all the decedents are included, while the mean age of all above twenty years old maintains a nearly constant place during a series of years. The uncertainties attending the use of these averages as an indication of the health of any community and the fallacies into which those are led who take the mean age at death to be the same as the mean duration of life, have been ably pointed out in previous Registration Reports. We have only to compare the figures set down opposite towns having, so far as can be seen, precisely the same local characteristics, to find what wide contrasts can be found in this direction. Certain broad facts are, indeed, apparent; as, for example, that in cities and in manufacturing villages which attract a larger proportion of young people of both sexes, the average age at death is less than in the small towns from which these same young people have emigrated. But, on the other hand, we have an illustration of the very fallacies to which we have alluded, in the figures given the present year as the average age of those who died in the county of Dukes. The mean age at death, for the whole county, was 48·05 years, or more than twice that recorded for Suffolk; the county contains only five towns, and of these, Chilmark buried four of its people, whose ages at death averaged 68·50 years, while Gosnold lost a single inhabitant, whose age was four months. An inference that the situation and climate of Chilmark are necessarily favorable to long life should have as its counterpart a conclusion that the people of Gosnold are all infants whose expectation of life does not extend beyond the first year of their existence.

The estimated average age at death acquires significance and value in proportion to the numbers of people included in the calculation. If we wish, however, to study the statistics of small communities in regard to the mean age at which their people die, we can only arrive at reliable inferences by extending our comparisons through very long series of years.

The following table presents the record of eighteen persons who died in 1873, in Massachusetts, after having lived beyond a century :—

5

AGED over One Hundred Years.—*Died in 1873.*

Date of Death.	NAMES.	Age.	Place of Death.	Birthplace.	Whether previously Married, or Single.
1873.					
Jan. 10,	Dean H. Gabriel,	105	Pittsfield,	Pittsfield,	Married.
15,	William Hulett,	101	Lee,	Belchertown,	Married.
19,	Honora McGuire,	100	Boston,	Ireland,	Married.
Feb. 4,	Chloe C. Henson (colored),	100	Boston,	Salem,	Married.
Mar. 6,	James Moran,	104	Lynn,	Ireland,	Married.
7,	John Collins,	109	Charlestown,	Ireland,	Married.
Apr. 3,	Jane Gordon,	104	Sharon,	Ireland,	Married.
May 24,	Harriet Brown (m. n. Crosby),	100	Amesbury,	Ireland,	Married.
June 13,	Beulah Hunt (m. n. Littlefield),	104	Randolph,	Braintree,	Married.
Aug. 1,	Nancy Cady,	105	Oxford,	Oxford,	Married.
20,	Bridget Hayes,	100	Salem,	Ireland,	Married.
24,	Joseph Goslan,	100	Millbury,	France,	Married.
25,	Jeremiah Crowley,	103	Marlborough,	Ireland,	Married.
31,	John O'Hare,	101	Cambridge,	Ireland,	Married.
Oct. 9,	Margaret Father,	102	Northbridge,	Canada,	Married.
29,	Anna Hughes,	103	Russell,	Unknown,	Married.
31,	Elihu Emerson,	102	Leicester,	Westfield,	Married.
Dec. 17,	John Duff,	100	New Bedford,	Ireland,	Unknown,

Nativity of those whose *Deaths* were registered in the year 1873.

Nativity	Sex	State	Barnstable	Berkshire	Bristol	Dukes and Nantucket	Essex	Franklin	Hampden	Hampshire	Middlesex	Norfolk	Plymouth	Suffolk	Worcester
Totals	Whole number,	33,912	576	1,111	2,912	164	4,429	568	1,915	803	6,539	1,677	1,235	8,924	3,659
	Males,	17,242	313	556	1,524	80	2,270	270	978	400	3,236	808	616	4,930	1,861
	Females,	16,642	255	555	1,387	84	2,149	298	936	403	3,299	868	616	3,994	1,798
	Unknown,	28	8	–	1	–	10	–	1	–	4	1	3	–	–
	Percentage,	100.00	100·00	100·00	100·00	100·00	100·00	100·00	100·00	100·00	100·00	100·00	100·00	100·00	100·00
American	Whole number,	27,435	549	894	2,233	168	3,604	524	1,497	654	4,969	1,392	1,111	5,881	2,979
	Males,	13,466	296	429	1,179	76	1,851	247	762	325	2,451	662	546	3,111	1,531
	Females,	13,943	245	465	1,054	82	1,743	277	735	329	2,604	729	562	2,770	1,448
	Unknown,	26	8	–	–	–	10	–	1	–	4	1	3	–	–
	Percentage,	80·90	95·31	80·47	76·68	96·34	81·37	92·25	78·17	81·44	75·84	83·06	89·95	70·65	81·41
Foreign	Whole number,	6,198	23	182	653	6	798	39	375	139	1,518	269	111	2,414	671
	Males,	3,618	16	104	390	4	395	19	194	74	756	137	60	1,205	324
	Females,	2,579	7	78	322	2	403	20	181	65	762	132	51	1,209	347
	Unknown,	1	–	–	1	–	–	–	–	–	–	–	–	–	–
	Percentage,	18·28	3·99	16·38	22·42	3·66	18·02	6·87	19·68	17·31	23·21	16·04	8·99	29·00	18·84
Not stated	Whole number,	279	4	35	26	–	27	5	43	10	62	16	13	29	9
	Males,	158	1	23	15	–	24	4	22	1	29	9	10	14	6
	Females,	120	3	12	11	–	3	1	20	9	33	7	3	15	3
	Unknown,	1	–	–	–	–	–	–	–	–	–	–	–	–	–
	Percentage,	·82	·70	3·15	·80	–	·61	·88	2·25	1·25	·95	·90	1·06	·35	·25

NATIVITY of Persons deceased during Twenty Years.—1854-73.

	AVERAGES		1866.	1867.	1868.	1869.	1870.	1871.	1872.	1873.
	Six Years. 1854-59.	Six Years. 1860-65.								
WHOLE NUMBER,	20,996	25,459	26,637	22,772	25,603	26,054	27,329	27,943	35,019	33,912
American,	16,880	21,243	18,499	18,278	20,522	21,098	21,513	21,862	27,817	27,435
Foreign,	3,246	3,772	4,708	4,126	4,761	4,713	5,417	5,951	7,100	6,198
Not stated,	870	444	430	968	320	243	399	130	102	279

Percentages of those stated.

			1866.	1867.	1868.	1869.	1870.	1871.	1872.	1873.
American,	83·88	84·92	79·71	81·58	81·17	81·74	79·88	78·63	79·67	81·57
Foreign,	16·12	15·08	20·29	18·42	18·83	18·26	20·12	21·37	20·33	18·43

The comparison of the relative percentages found the present year in the nativity of those who died, shows a noteworthy change.   There is a marked increase in the proportion of those designated as American, and a corresponding decline in the percentage of the foreign element.   It should be remembered, however, that this distinction of the nativity of decedents is open to one important objection; namely, that every person born in America is reckoned as American, even though both his parents were foreign.   This consideration somewhat modifies the apparent significance of the contrasts shown in the foregoing table.   The following table seeks to avoid this difficulty, by carrying the comparison one generation farther back :—

PARENT-NATIVITY of all Deceased in 1873.—Arranged by Counties, Sex, and Age.

STATE AND COUNTIES. — WHOLE STATE.

PARENTAGE.	Sex.	Whole Number.	Under 1	1 to 5	5 to 10	10 to 20	20 to 30	30 to 40	40 to 50	50 to 60	60 to 70	Over 70	Not stated.
Whole Number,	Totals,	33,912	7,911	4,463	1,328	2,078	3,549	2,811	2,220	2,219	2,634	4,419	280
	Males,	17,242	4,377	2,243	720	960	1,744	1,302	1,121	1,194	1,360	2,003	218
	Females,	16,642	3,507	2,219	608	1,118	1,805	1,509	1,099	1,025	1,274	2,416	62
	Unknown,	28	27	1	—	—	—	—	—	—	—	—	—
American,	Totals,	15,792	2,849	1,318	440	855	1,626	1,288	1,061	1,247	1,741	3,303	114
	Males,	7,876	1,631	645	226	393	742	541	587	660	914	1,506	81
	Females,	7,900	1,203	672	214	462	884	697	524	587	827	1,797	33
	Unknown,	16	15	1	—	—	—	—	—	—	—	—	—
Foreign,	Totals,	16,110	4,192	2,749	778	1,100	1,814	1,500	1,108	917	831	1,000	121
	Males,	8,309	2,282	1,400	434	514	936	721	560	498	413	449	102
	Females,	7,794	1,903	1,349	344	586	878	779	548	419	418	551	19
	Unknown,	7	7	—	—	—	—	—	—	—	—	—	—
Half-Foreign,	Totals,	1,665	795	383	102	108	79	44	90	85	32	50	7
	Males,	851	429	192	54	46	42	21	10	21	13	19	4
	Females,	812	364	191	48	62	37	23	20	14	19	31	3
	Unknown,	2	2	—	—	—	—	—	—	—	—	—	—
Not stated,	Totals,	345	75	13	8	15	30	29	21	20	30	66	38
	Males,	206	35	6	6	7	24	19	14	15	20	29	31
	Females,	136	37	7	2	8	6	10	7	5	10	37	7
	Unknown,	3	3	—	—	—	—	—	—	—	—	—	—

BARNSTABLE COUNTY.

		1	2	3	4	5	6	7	8	9	10	11	Total
Totals,	Totals,	4	153	60	33	38	45	71	36	14	36	86	576
	Males,	3	78	38	18	22	20	39	15	6	25	49	313
	Females,	1	75	22	15	16	25	32	21	8	11	29	255
	Unknown,	–	–	–	–	–	–	–	–	–	–	8	8
American,	Totals,	4	146	57	29	35	43	62	32	12	28	67	515
	Males,	3	74	35	16	21	18	35	12	4	19	37	274
	Females,	1	72	22	13	14	25	27	20	8	9	22	233
	Unknown,	–	–	–	–	–	–	–	–	–	–	8	8
Foreign,	Totals,	–	6	2	1	3	2	8	2	1	6	17	48
	Males,	–	4	2	1	1	2	3	2	1	5	10	31
	Females,	–	2	–	–	2	–	5	–	–	1	7	17
Half-Foreign,	Totals,	–	–	–	3	–	–	1	2	1	2	2	11
	Males,	–	–	–	1	–	–	1	1	1	1	2	7
	Females,	–	–	–	2	–	–	–	1	–	1	–	4
Not stated,	Totals,	–	1	1	–	–	–	–	–	–	–	–	2
	Males,	–	–	1	–	–	–	–	–	–	–	–	1
	Females,	–	1	–	–	–	–	–	–	–	–	–	1

BERKSHIRE COUNTY.

		1	2	3	4	5	6	7	8	9	10	11	Total
Totals,	Totals,	5	207	112	72	73	74	112	65	45	128	218	1,111
	Males,	2	94	53	44	41	31	51	25	26	59	130	556
	Females,	3	113	59	28	32	43	61	40	19	69	88	555
American,	Totals,	3	159	82	54	38	33	74	25	18	61	104	651
	Males,	1	72	34	33	16	11	32	8	8	32	70	317
	Females,	2	87	48	21	22	22	42	17	10	29	34	334
Foreign,	Totals,	2	35	28	15	35	40	36	31	20	52	83	377
	Males,	1	17	18	10	25	20	18	15	14	24	44	206
	Females,	1	18	10	5	10	20	18	16	6	28	39	171

PARENT-NATIVITY of all Deceased in 1873.—*Arranged by Counties, Sex, and Age*—Continued.

COUNTIES.	PARENTAGE.	Sex.	Whole Number.	Under 1	1 to 5	5 to 10	10 to 20	20 to 30	30 to 40	40 to 50	50 to 60	60 to 70	Over 70	Not stated.
BERKS.—Con.	Half-Foreign,	Totals,	45	19	14	6	3	1	—	—	1	—	1	—
		Males,	20	11	9	4	—	1	—	—	—	—	1	—
		Females,	25	8	11	2	3	—	—	—	1	—	—	—
	Not stated,	Totals,	38	12	1	1	6	1	1	—	2	2	12	—
		Males,	13	5	—	—	2	—	—	—	1	1	4	—
		Females,	25	7	1	1	4	1	1	—	1	1	8	—
BRISTOL COUNTY.	Totals,	Totals,	2,912	708	452	151	194	279	205	152	171	213	364	28
		Males,	1,524	424	222	94	86	138	104	65	98	119	162	12
		Females,	1,387	283	230	57	108	141	101	87	73	94	202	11
		Unknown,	1	1	—	—	—	—	—	—	—	—	—	—
	American,	Totals,	1,194	201	96	35	65	119	86	76	99	139	266	12
		Males,	599	124	32	14	25	59	45	31	59	79	124	7
		Females,	594	76	64	21	40	60	41	45	40	60	142	5
		Unknown,	1	1	—	—	—	—	—	—	—	—	—	—
	Foreign,	Totals,	1,585	451	323	113	119	151	111	72	71	68	96	10
		Males,	850	266	169	78	58	75	53	34	38	37	37	5
		Females,	735	185	154	35	61	76	58	38	33	31	59	5

	Bristol—Con. Half-Foreign (T, M, F)	Not stated (T, M, F)	Dukes Totals (T, M, F)	American (T, M, F)	Foreign (T, M, F)	Half-Foreign (T, M, F)
	1, –, 1	–, –, –	–, –, –	–, –, –	–, –, –	–, –, –
	2, 1, 1	–, –, –	58, 30, 28	55, 28, 27	1, 1, –	2, 1, 1
	6, 3, 3	–, –, –	26, 15, 11	24, 13, 11	2, 2, –	–, –, –
	1, 1, –	–, –, –	23, 8, 15	23, 8, 15	–, –, –	–, –, –
	3, –, 3	1, –, 1	10, 2, 8	10, 2, 8	–, –, –	–, –, –
	6, 4, 2	2, 2, –	11, 7, 4	10, 7, 3	–, –, –	1, –, 1
	8, 3, 5	1, 1, –	9, 3, 6	8, 3, 5	1, –, 1	–, –, –
	10, 3, 7	–, –, –	5, 3, 2	4, 3, 1	1, –, 1	–, –, –
	?, 2, 1	–, –, –	3, 3, –	3, 3, –	–, –, –	–, –, –
	33, 21, 12	–, –, –	5, 2, 3	4, 2, 2	1, –, 1	–, –, –
	55, 33, 22	1, 1, –	14, 7, 7	9, 4, 5	4, 2, 2	1, 1, –
Totals	128, 71, 57	5, 4, 1	164, 80, 84	150, 73, 77	10, 5, 5	4, 2, 2

Totals, · · ·　Males, · · ·　Females, · · ·

Half-Foreign,　Not stated,　Totals,　American,　Foreign,　Half-Foreign,

BRISTOL—Con.　DUKES AND NANTUCKET COUNTIES.

6

PARENT-NATIVITY of all Deceased in 1873.—Arranged by Counties, Sex, and Age—Continued.

ESSEX COUNTY.

COUNTIES	PARENTAGE	Sex	Whole Number	Under 1	1 to 5	5 to 10	10 to 20	20 to 30	30 to 40	40 to 50	50 to 60	60 to 70	Over 70	Not stated
	Totals	Totals,	4,429	1,005	532	157	280	413	344	261	279	364	635	159
		Males,	2,270	569	269	80	130	185	145	129	149	170	291	153
		Females,	2,149	427	262	77	150	228	199	132	180	194	344	6
		Unknown,	10	9	1	—	—	—	—	—	—	—	—	—
	American,	Totals,	2,419	454	198	72	129	220	191	145	179	276	502	53
		Males,	1,213	255	102	34	66	97	80	74	94	132	229	50
		Females,	1,201	195	95	38	63	123	111	71	85	144	273	3
		Unknown,	5	4	1	—	—	—	—	—	—	—	—	—
	Foreign,	Totals,	1,686	445	276	72	128	173	139	109	88	72	108	76
		Males,	876	253	187	38	59	75	58	53	46	30	52	75
		Females,	805	187	189	34	69	98	81	56	42	42	56	1
		Unknown,	5	5	—	—	—	—	—	—	—	—	—	—
	Half-Foreign,	Totals,	247	101	56	12	18	15	9	4	7	8	13	4
		Males,	128	57	30	7	3	8	2	2	5	2	5	2
		Females,	124	44	26	5	15	7	7	2	2	6	8	2
	Not stated,	Totals,	77	5	2	1	5	5	5	3	5	8	12	26
		Males,	58	4	—	1	2	5	5	—	4	6	5	26
		Females,	19	1	2	—	3	—	—	3	1	2	7	—

												Totals
FRANKLIN COUNTY.												
Totals,	1	124	70	50	35	41	59	43	20	42	83	568
Males,	—	52	30	31	14	15	24	20	10	23	51	270
Females,	1	72	40	19	21	26	35	23	10	19	32	298
American, Totals,	1	120	62	39	25	36	48	29	11	27	50	448
Males,	—	51	27	25	7	12	19	11	5	14	28	199
Females,	1	69	35	14	18	24	29	18	6	13	22	249
Foreign, Totals,	—	4	7	11	10	5	10	13	8	12	28	108
Males,	—	1	2	6	7	3	4	9	5	8	19	64
Females,	—	3	5	5	3	2	6	4	3	4	9	44
Half-Foreign, Totals,	—	—	—	—	—	—	1	1	1	3	5	11
Males,	—	—	—	—	—	—	1	—	—	1	4	6
Females,	—	—	—	—	—	—	—	1	1	2	1	5
Not stated, Totals,	—	—	1	—	—	—	—	—	—	—	—	1
Males,	—	—	1	—	—	—	—	—	—	—	—	1
Females,	—	—	—	—	—	—	—	—	—	—	—	—
HAMPDEN COUNTY.												
Totals,	11	205	138	98	99	146	204	156	97	288	473	1,915
Males,	7	101	68	50	50	71	108	78	48	147	250	978
Females,	4	104	70	48	49	75	96	78	49	141	222	936
Unknown,	—	—	—	—	—	—	—	—	—	—	1	1
American, Totals,	4	150	95	64	55	75	97	57	30	93	141	861
Males,	4	74	42	30	28	36	52	33	15	40	64	418
Females,	—	76	53	34	27	39	45	24	15	53	77	453
Foreign, Totals,	5	45	40	33	40	66	105	88	59	172	291	944
Males,	2	25	23	20	19	32	55	40	29	99	161	505
Females,	3	20	17	13	21	34	50	48	30	73	130	439

PARENT-NATIVITY of all Deceased in 1873.—*Arranged by Counties, Sex, and Age*—Continued.

Counties	Parentage	Sex	Whole Number	Under 1	1 to 5	5 to 10	10 to 20	20 to 30	30 to 40	40 to 50	50 to 60	60 to 70	Over 70	Not stated
HAMPDEN—Con.	Half-Foreign,	Totals,	82	36	21	5	9	2	4	2	1	1	1	—
		Males,	41	24	6	2	4	1	2	1	—	1	—	—
		Females,	40	11	15	3	5	1	2	1	1	—	1	—
		Unknown,	1	1	—	—	—	—	—	—	—	—	—	—
	Not stated,	Totals,	28	5	2	3	2	—	1	2	—	2	9	2
		Males,	14	1	2	2	1	—	1	2	—	2	2	1
		Females,	14	4	—	1	1	—	—	—	—	—	7	1
HAMPSHIRE COUNTY.	Totals,	Totals,	803	168	77	17	50	75	72	50	54	76	160	4
		Males,	400	92	45	8	22	37	35	24	28	44	64	1
		Females,	403	76	32	9	28	38	37	26	26	32	96	3
	American,	Totals,	483	82	19	8	24	43	38	29	39	64	135	2
		Males,	239	48	14	3	9	21	20	15	19	38	52	—
		Females,	244	34	5	5	15	22	18	14	20	26	83	2
	Foreign,	Totals,	310	81	57	9	23	31	34	21	15	12	25	2
		Males,	155	40	31	5	11	16	15	9	9	6	12	1
		Females,	165	41	26	4	12	15	19	12	6	6	13	1
	Half-Foreign,	Totals,	10	5	1	—	3	1	—	—	—	—	—	—
		Males,	6	4	—	—	2	—	—	—	—	—	—	—
		Females,	4	1	1	—	1	1	—	—	—	—	—	—

MIDDLESEX COUNTY.

Totals, Totals,	6,539	1,593	844	266	365	687	562	432	437	531	789	93
Males,	3,236	819	416	185	174	307	251	230	241	274	370	19
Females,	3,299	770	428	131	191	380	311	202	196	257	419	14
Unknown,	4	4	—	—	—	—	—	—	—	—	—	—
American, Totals,	2,912	590	260	78	152	303	226	196	240	330	522	15
Males,	1,428	329	124	41	77	115	88	98	135	169	244	8
Females,	1,484	261	136	37	75	188	138	98	105	161	278	7
Foreign, Totals,	3,232	804	523	173	193	355	326	224	188	195	243	8
Males,	1,620	400	264	88	89	174	157	124	102	103	113	6
Females,	1,611	403	259	85	104	181	169	100	86	92	130	2
Unknown,	1	1	—	—	—	—	—	—	—	—	—	—
Half-Foreign, Totals,	313	171	59	15	20	17	5	4	7	4	9	2
Males,	147	81	27	6	8	9	3	2	4	1	4	2
Females,	166	90	32	9	12	8	2	2	3	3	5	—
Not stated, Totals,	82	28	2	—	—	12	5	8	2	2	15	8
Males,	41	9	1	—	—	9	3	6	—	1	9	3
Females,	38	16	1	—	—	3	2	2	2	1	6	5
Unknown,	3	3	—	—	—	—	—	—	—	—	—	—

PARENT-NATIVITY of all Deceased in 1873.—*Arranged by Counties, Sex, and Age*—Continued.

NORFOLK COUNTY.

PARENTAGE	Sex	Whole Number	Under 1	1 to 5	5 to 10	10 to 20	20 to 30	30 to 40	40 to 50	50 to 60	60 to 70	Over 70	Not stated
Totals	Totals,	1,677	358	200	62	101	156	133	104	119	135	302	7
	Males,	808	200	86	36	47	69	55	56	61	68	127	3
	Females,	868	157	114	26	54	87	78	48	58	67	175	4
	Unknown,	1	1	—	—	—	—	—	—	—	—	—	—
American,	Totals,	941	154	85	21	48	78	70	60	80	96	245	4
	Males,	439	84	44	15	21	32	20	30	36	52	104	1
	Females,	502	70	41	6	27	46	50	30	44	44	141	3
Foreign,	Totals,	626	149	100	30	48	73	57	41	38	36	52	2
	Males,	314	83	38	18	24	33	32	25	24	15	21	1
	Females,	312	66	62	12	24	40	25	16	14	21	31	1
Half-Foreign,	Totals,	95	48	15	11	4	4	4	3	1	—	5	—
	Males,	46	29	4	3	1	3	2	1	1	—	2	—
	Females,	48	18	11	8	3	1	2	2	—	—	3	—
	Unknown,	1	1	—	—	—	—	—	—	—	—	—	—
Not stated,	Totals,	15	7	—	—	1	1	2	—	—	3	—	1
	Males,	9	4	—	—	1	1	1	—	—	1	—	1
	Females,	6	3	—	—	—	—	1	—	—	2	—	—

PLYMOUTH COUNTY.

		1	2	3	4	5	6	7	8	9	10	11	Totals
Totals,	Totals,	4	262	141	82	79	89	121	70	45	121	221	1,235
	Males,	2	119	79	43	34	33	64	30	23	63	126	616
	Females,	2	143	62	39	45	56	57	40	22	58	92	616
	Unknown,	—	—	—	—	—	—	—	—	—	—	3	3
American,	Totals,	4	247	107	69	58	66	94	44	26	72	147	934
	Males,	2	110	62	36	23	20	52	16	15	32	79	447
	Females,	2	137	45	33	35	46	42	28	11	40	66	485
	Unknown,	—	—	—	—	—	—	—	—	—	—	2	2
Foreign,	Totals,	—	13	28	12	18	20	24	22	18	44	63	262
	Males,	—	7	13	6	11	12	12	13	8	29	38	149
	Females,	—	6	15	6	7	8	12	9	10	15	24	112
	Unknown,	—	—	—	—	—	—	—	—	—	—	1	1
Half-Foreign,	Totals,	—	1	2	—	2	2	2	4	1	5	11	30
	Males,	—	1	2	—	—	—	—	1	—	2	9	15
	Females,	—	—	—	—	2	2	2	3	1	3	2	15
Not stated,	Totals,	—	1	4	1	1	1	1	—	—	—	—	9
	Males,	—	1	2	1	—	1	—	—	—	—	—	5
	Females,	—	—	2	—	1	—	1	—	—	—	—	4

PARENT-NATIVITY of all Deceased in 1873.—*Arranged by Counties, Sex, and Age*—Concluded.

COUNTIES. — SUFFOLK COUNTY.

PARENTAGE.	Sex.	Whole Number.	Under 1	1 to 5	5 to 10	10 to 20	20 to 30	30 to 40	40 to 50	50 to 60	60 to 70	Over 70	Not stated.
Totals,	Totals,	8,324	2,175	1,273	339	459	998	813	645	563	473	579	7
	Males,	4,330	1,186	646	189	217	554	421	331	300	239	244	3
	Females,	3,994	989	627	150	242	444	392	314	263	234	335	4
American,	Totals,	2,395	554	236	86	121	289	221	200	196	200	283	4
	Males,	1,296	331	119	51	63	154	121	121	105	110	119	2
	Females,	1,099	223	117	35	58	135	100	79	91	90	164	2
Foreign,	Totals,	5,312	1,390	893	213	313	682	570	429	348	261	275	3
	Males,	2,705	707	446	114	137	383	289	202	181	125	120	1
	Females,	2,607	623	447	99	176	294	281	227	167	136	155	2
Half-Foreign,	Totals,	552	275	139	37	24	22	11	11	12	7	14	—
	Males,	287	138	78	21	16	12	6	3	8	2	3	—
	Females,	265	137	61	16	8	10	5	8	4	5	11	—
Not stated,	Totals,	65	16	5	3	1	5	11	5	7	5	7	—
	Males,	42	10	3	3	1	5	5	5	6	2	2	—
	Females,	28	6	2	—	—	—	6	—	1	3	5	—

Totals,	Totals,	3,659	809	465	112	264	365	276	242	238	295	581	22
	Males,	1,861	474	240	62	113	165	114	123	123	163	271	13
	Females,	1,798	335	225	50	141	200	162	119	115	132	310	9
American,	Totals,	1,889	296	139	40	125	186	143	134	136	208	473	9
	Males,	939	179	73	19	50	71	63	71	64	121	225	3
	Females,	950	117	66	21	75	115	80	63	72	87	248	6
Foreign,	Totals,	1,610	446	290	62	119	170	130	106	97	80	97	13
	Males,	829	259	150	36	57	88	48	50	55	37	39	10
	Females,	781	187	140	26	62	82	82	56	42	43	58	3
Half-Foreign,	Totals,	137	66	35	10	10	5	2	1	2	4	2	—
	Males,	75	35	17	7	6	3	2	1	1	2	1	—
	Females,	62	31	18	3	4	2	—	—	1	2	1	—
Not stated,	Totals,	23	1	1	—	—	4	1	1	3	3	9	—
	Males,	18	1	—	—	—	3	1	1	3	3	6	—
	Females,	5	—	1	—	—	1	—	—	—	—	3	—

WORCESTER COUNTY.

7

By the foregoing table, it appears that the deaths of those whose parents were both American, have decreased, in 1873, by 963, when comparison is made with the previous year ; and that the deaths of those of foreign parentage have also diminished, the number in 1873 being less by 126 than the number in 1872. On the other hand, the deaths of those of mixed parentage, one parent being American, and the other foreign, have increased by 119. Of the number of "not stated," there were 47 less the present year than in 1872.

The following table, based upon the foregoing, shows, in a more striking way, the comparison with regard to the parent-nativity of those who died, and carries the contrast through a series of years. In calculating the percentages, those of half-foreign parentage are divided equally.

One fact is very plainly shown in this table ; namely, that nearly three-fourths of the population, beyond the middle period of life, continues to be of native stock, although there is a progressive diminution in the proportion of deaths of Americans at all ages.

It must also be noted, that the deaths among children of foreign parents are relatively much more numerous ; the percentage of these deaths (of children under five years old, whose parents were foreign) was higher, in 1873, than in any of the previous six years. This result should be studied in connection with the progressive increase in the number of births of foreign parentage. Without attempting to speculate upon the correlative conditions and causes, the fact is a most suggestive one, that while the stock of foreign parentage continues to multiply much faster than the purely native population, the equilibrium is in a great measure preserved by the large proportion of deaths among children of foreign extraction.

		Under 5 years.	5 to 20	20 to 50	Over 50
1867,	American parents, . . .	2,947	1,197	3,182	4,958
	Foreign " . . .	4,432	987	2,536	1,393
	Half-Foreign " . . .	504	101	100	58
	Percentages.				
	American parents, . . .	40·6	54·6	55·5	77·8
	Foreign " . . .	59·4	45·4	44·5	22·2
1868,	American parents, . . .	3,501	1,189	3,280	5,248
	Foreign " . . .	5,067	1,193	2,763	1,855
	Half-Foreign " . . .	667	110	82	69
	Percentages.				
	American parents, . . .	41·5	49·9	54·2	73·6
	Foreign " . . .	58·5	50·1	45·8	26·4
1869,	American parents, . . .	3,538	1,250	3,337	5,492
	Foreign " . . .	4,854	1,194	3,018	1,922
	Half-Foreign " . . .	721	110	90	81
	Percentages.				
	American parents, . . .	42·8	51·1	52·5	73·8
	Foreign " . . .	57·2	48·9	47·5	26·2
1870,	American parents, . . .	3,601	1,107	3,474	5,645
	Foreign " . . .	5,284	1,171	3,462	2,082
	Half-Foreign " . . .	799	104	84	82
	Percentages.				
	American parents, . . .	41·3	48·7	50·1	72·8
	Foreign " . . .	58·7	51·3	49·9	27·2
1871,	American parents, . . .	3,386	1,109	3,456	5,765
	Foreign " . . .	5,191	1,364	3,647	2,296
	Half-Foreign " . . .	824	99	107	75
	Percentages.				
	American parents, . . .	40·4	45·1	48·7	71·3
	Foreign " . . .	59·6	54·9	51·3	28·7
1872,	American parents, . . .	4,779	1,463	3,986	6,405
	Foreign " . . .	7,551	1,752	4,489	2,471
	Half-Foreign " . . .	1,150	155	146	93
	Percentages.				
	American parents, . . .	39·7	45·7	47·1	71·9
	Foreign " . . .	60·3	54·3	52·9	28·1
1873,	American parents, . . .	4,167	1,295	3,925	6,291
	Foreign " . . .	6,491	1,878	4,422	2,748
	Half-Foreign " . . .	1,178	210	153	117
	Percentages.				
	American parents, . . .	38·7	41·4	47·1	69·3
	Foreign " . . .	61·3	58·6	52·9	30·7

CAUSES OF DEATH.

In many respects, this is the most important subject which we have to study in connection with registration. We are here introduced to the direct causes of the deaths, whose relations, in other respects, we have discussed elsewhere. We are enabled here to see what diseases and what classes of disorders make the greatest inroads into the lives of the people of the State, at what seasons they are most fatal, and whether they bear more heavily on the young, the old, or the middle-aged. It has been a subject of regret, frequently alluded to in previous Reports, that greater accuracy could not be attained in this department of registration,—in the primary record of the causes of death. It is obvious that there are many avenues by which errors may enter the registry of the specified diseases; but there is good reason to believe that these errors are annually diminishing in number and in importance, although a long way yet from being reduced to the lowest degree possible.

It has been the custom to introduce a table showing the monthly meteorological variations for the year. The record of the weather, as made at Cambridge and Amherst, in 1873, is as follows :—

MONTHS.	CAMBRIDGE.		AMHERST.	
	Mean Temperature.	Rainfall.	Mean Temperature.	Rainfall.
January, ...	22·8	5·97	20·5	5·01
February, ...	24·	4·04	24·	2·17
March, ...	30·7	3·36	30·6	3·17
April, ...	42·4	3·08	43·2	1·73
May, ...	55·3	4·09	54·5	3·91
June, ...	66·1	·50	67·4	1·59
July, ...	71·6	3·67	71·3	2·92
August, ...	67·2	5·07	67·	3·46
September, ...	60·8	3·22	60·3	4·76
October, ...	51·	4·28	49·9	6·35
November, ...	31·4	4·89	29·6	3·50
December, ...	30·4	4·64	29·2	3·30
Mean temperature for the year, .	48·1	—	45·6	—
Total rainfall in inches, . .	—	46·81	—	41·93

The percentage of deaths from *zymotic* diseases in 1873 was 28·7; from *constitutional* diseases, 23·8; from *local* diseases, 27·9; from *developmental* diseases, 15·2; and from *violence*, 4·4. Zymotic diseases were relatively less numerous in 1873 than in 1872, but all the other classes show a slight increase in their percentage.

The following table gives a comparative view of the mortality from the most destructive zymotic diseases during the past ten years :—

YEARS.	Dysentery.	Typhus.	Whooping Cough.	Croup.	Diphtheria.	Measles.	Scarlet Fever.
1864,	1,186	1,344	235	'768	1,231	320	1,503
1865,	1,548	1,694	363	504	672	136	807
1866,	949	1,091	287	431	399	109	385
1867,	658	965	297	356	251	194	828
1868,	685	896	247	485	297	287	1,369
1869,	481	1,205	320	473	296	222	1,405
1870,	471	1,333	330	434	242	269	683
1871,	389	1,116	243	473	274	131	867 '
1872,	564	1,703	363	480	273	428	1,377
1873,	435	1,406	264	435	310	180	1,472

We note in this table the fact that the deaths from scarlet fever attest by their number the presence of the disease in the State to an unusual degree in 1873. We must add, what does not appear in the table, that the deaths from small-pox in 1873 amounted to 668—a marked decline as compared with the number reported in 1872, but still greatly in excess of the mortality registered in previous years. These two diseases, scarlatina and small-pox, were the only contagious diseases which manifested extensive prevalence in 1873.

During the year, one hundred and twenty-six persons were killed in railroad accidents, thirty died by poison, eighty-eight perished from burns and scalds, four hundred and thirty-two (an unusual number) were drowned, one hundred and seventeen committed suicide and twenty-six were murdered. There were two judicial executions. Vaccination is assigned as the cause of five deaths, three of which occurred in persons between sixty and seventy years of age. It is gratifying to note that there were no deaths from privation in the State in 1873; although thirteen are reported as having perished from exposure. Twenty-two died from the effects of heat, and two were frozen to death. There were fifteen deaths from angina pectoris.

Order of Succession of Ten Principal Diseases.—Ten Years.

1864.	1865.	1866.	1867.	1868.
Consumption,	Consumption,	Consumption,	Consumption,	Consumption,
Pneumonia,	Typhus,	Pneumonia,	Infantile,	Pneumonia,
Scarlatina,	Dysentery,	Infantile,	Pneumonia,	Cholera Infantum,
Old Age,	Pneumonia,	Old Age,	Old Age,	Scarlatina,
Typhus,	Old Age,	Typhus,	Cholera Infantum,	Old Age,
Infantile,	Infantile,	Cholera Infantum,	Typhus,	Heart Disease,
Diphtheria,	Cholera Infantum,	Dysentery,	Heart Disease,	Apoplexy and Paralysis,
Cholera Infantum,	Heart Disease,	Heart Disease,	Scarlatina,	Typhus,
Dysentery,	Scarlatina,	Apoplexy and Paralysis,	Paralysis and Apoplexy,	Dysentery,
Apoplexy and Paralysis.	Diphtheria.	Croup.	Dysentery.	Infantile.

Order of Succession of Ten Principal Diseases.—Ten Years.—Concluded.

1869.	1870.	1871.	1872.	1873.—Numbers.	
Consumption,	Consumption,	Consumption,	Consumption,	Consumption,	5,556
Pneumonia,	Cholera Infantum,	Pneumonia,	Cholera Infantum,	Cholera Infantum,	2,553
Cholera Infantum,	Pneumonia,	Cholera Infantum,	Pneumonia,	Pneumonia,	2,097
Scarlatina,	Old Age,	Old Age,	Typhus,	Old Age,	1,672
Old Age,	Typhus,	Heart Disease,	Old Age,	Scarlatina,	1,472
Typhus,	Paralysis and Apoplexy,	Typhus,	Scarlatina,	Typhus,	1,406
Paralysis and Apoplexy,	Heart Disease,	Paralysis and Apoplexy,	Heart Disease,	Paralysis and Apoplexy,	1,289
Heart Disease,	Infantile,	Scarlatina,	Paralysis and Apoplexy,	Heart Disease,	1,252
Infantile,	Scarlatina,	Infantile,	Cephalitis,	Infantile,	774
Cephalitis.	Cephalitis.	Cephalitis.	Small-pox.	Cerebro-Spinal Meningitis,	747

The foregoing table, presenting the numerical relation of the ten most destructive diseases during the last ten years, is only measurably useful, because of the unsatisfactory terms applied to certain classes of diseases. Thus typhus is not sufficiently distinctive, since it should be made more clearly to represent all the class of continued fevers; if paralysis and apoplexy were grouped with cephalitis and "brain diseases," we should have a distinct class of affections whose aggregate fatality would express the brain-work and brain-worry of our generation. In one respect, we have an improvement in nomenclature the present year; for the first time, the name, cerebro-spinal meningitis, appears in the tables, and the extent of its prevalence is shown in the fact that it has a place in the list presented in the foregoing table.

8

The NUMBER of Deaths from several Specified Causes, of each Sex, in each Month, and at Different Specified Periods of Life, which were registered during the year 1873.

		Diphtheria.	Dysentery.	Typhus.	Measles.	Scarlatina.	Erysipelas.	Croup.	Cholera Infantum.	Teething.	Consumption.	Pneumonia.	Small-pox.
SEX	Totals,	310	435	1,406	180	1,472	235	435	2,553	348	5,556	2,097	663
	Males,	160	205	742	88	710	116	227	1,340	175	2,543	1,126	431
	Females,	150	230	663	92	762	119	208	1,212	173	3,011	971	232
	Not stated,	—	—	1	—	—	—	—	1	—	2	—	—
MONTHS.	January,	37	5	97	6	109	23	63	7	19	544	230	324
	February,	33	5	58	7	98	20	47	6	12	416	259	182
	March,	27	5	90	7	148	25	54	12	23	551	273	55
	April,	19	3	72	9	166	30	30	11	17	462	237	38
	May,	15	8	51	26	108	22	30	15	17	498	192	30
	June,	15	15	60	37	109	25	23	53	25	402	147	30
	July,	19	83	93	38	96	20	12	673	50	469	79	99
	August,	20	162	116	17	100	16	9	1,079	57	488	65	10
	September,	37	94	203	12	102	9	20	478	63	420	77	2
	October,	45	37	210	3	120	8	31	180	49	434	115	2
	November,	27	8	206	8	149	12	61	28	11	417	182	1
	December,	16	10	150	10	167	25	55	11	11	455	241	—

Ages.												
Totals,	663	2,097	5,556	348	2,553	435	235	1,472	180	1,406	435	310
Under 5,	179	805	357	348	2,553	381	69	991	135	132	219	164
5 to 10,	46	65	49	—	—	47	2	337	18	88	24	74
10 to 15,	27	24	105	—	—	6	8	83	5	105	5	20
15 to 20,	52	58	515	—	—	—	9	20	8	207	1	11
20 to 30,	193	127	1,514	—	—	1	21	22	7	389	11	9
30 to 40,	71	141	1,076	—	—	—	26	10	1	145	13	13
40 to 50,	40	158	702	—	—	—	15	3	2	102	19	4
50 to 60,	21	160	484	—	—	—	28	3	1	78	34	3
60 to 70,	14	216	435	—	—	—	23	1	1	83	38	9
70 to 80,	4	240	247	—	—	—	24	—	1	56	44	1
Over 80,	2	95	55	—	—	—	14	—	1	18	27	1
Not stated,	14	8	17	—	—	—	1	2	—	3	—	1

The PERCENTAGES *of Deaths from several Specified Causes, of each Sex, in each Month, and at Different Specified Periods of Life, which were registered during the year 1873.*

		Diphtheria.	Dysentery.	Typhus.	Measles.	Scarlatina.	Erysipelas.	Croup.	Cholera Infantum.	Teething.	Consumption.	Pneumonia.	Small-pox.
SEX.	Totals,	100·00	100·00	100·00	100·00	100·00	100·00	100·00	100·00	100·00	100·00	100·00	100·00
	Males,	51·61	47·13	52·77	48·89	48·23	49·36	52·18	52·49	50·29	45·77	53·70	65·01
	Females,	48·39	52·87	47·16	51·11	51·77	50·64	47·82	47·47	49·71	54·19	46·30	34·99
	Not stated,	—	—	·07	—	—	—	—	·04	—	·04	—	—
MONTHS.	January,	11·93	1·15	6·90	3·33	7·40	9·78	14·48	·27	5·46	9·79	10·97	48·87
	February,	10·64	1·15	4·12	3·89	6·66	8·51	10·80	·24	3·45	7·49	12·35	19·91
	March,	8·71	1·15	6·40	3·89	10·06	10·64	12·42	·47	6·61	9·92	13·02	8·30
	April,	6·13	·69	5·12	5·00	11·28	12·77	6·90	·43	4·88	8·32	11·30	5·73
	May,	4·84	1·84	3·63	14·44	7·34	9·36	6·90	·59	4·88	8·96	9·16	4·53
	June,	4·84	3·45	4·27	20·56	7·40	10·64	5·29	2·08	7·18	7·23	7·01	4·53
	July,	6·13	19·08	6·61	21·10	6·52	8·51	2·76	26·36	14·37	8·44	3·77	5·88
	August,	6·45	37·24	8·25	9·44	6·79	6·81	2·07	42·26	16·38	8·78	3·10	1·50
	September,	11·94	21·60	14·44	6·66	6·93	3·83	4·60	18·72	18·11	7·56	3·67	·30
	October,	14·52	8·51	14·94	1·68	8·15	3·40	7·13	7·05	12·36	7·81	5·48	·30
	November,	8·71	1·84	14·65	4·44	10·12	5·11	14·02	1·10	3·16	7·51	8·68	·15
	December,	5·16	2·30	10·67	5·56	11·35	10·64	12·64	·43	3·16	8·19	11·49	—

	100·00	100·00	100·00	100·00	100·00	100·00	100·00	100·00	100·00	100·00	100·00	100·00
Totals,	52·90	50·34	9·99	75·00	67·32	29·37	87·58	100·00	100 00	6·43	38·39	27·00
Under 5,	23·87	5·52	6·26	10·00	22·89	·85	10·81	—	—	·88	9·10	6·94
5 to 10,	6·45	1·15	7·47	2·77	5·64	1·28	1·38	—	—	1·89	1·14	4·07
10 to 15,	3·55	·23	14·72	4·44	1·96	9·83	—	—	—	9·27	2·76	7·84
15 to 20,	2·90	2·53	27·67	3·89	1·50	8·94	—	—	—	27·25	6·06	29·11
20 to 30,	4·20	2·99	10·31	·55	·68	11·07	·23	—	—	19·37	6·73	10·71
30 to 40,	1·29	4·37	7·26	1·11	·20	6·38	—	—	—	12·63	7·55	6·04
40 to 50,	·97	7·81	5·55	·56	·20	11·91	—	—	—	8·71	7·62	3·17
50 to 60,	2·90	8·74	5·90	·56	·07	9·78	—	—	—	7·83	10·30	2·11
60 to 70,	·32	10·11	3·98	·56	—	10·21	—	—	—	4·44	11·44	·60
70 to 80,	·32	6·21	1·28	·56	—	5·96	—	—	—	·99	4·53	·30
Over 80,	·32	—	·21	—	·14	·42	—	—	—	·31	·38	2·11
Not stated,												

Ages.

The NUMBER of Deaths from several Specified Causes, of each Sex, in each Month, and at Different Specified Periods of Life, which were registered during the Eleven Years, 1863–73.

		ELEVEN YEARS.	Diphtheria.	Dysentery.	Typhus.	Measles.	Scarlatina.	Erysipelas.	Croup.	Cholera Infantum.	Teething.	Consumption.	Pneumonia.	Small-pox.
SEX.		Totals,	5,665	8,522	14,195	2,417	12,095	1,920	5,703	17,984	3,088	53,304	19,390	3,081
		Males,	2,614	4,264	7,383	1,246	6,091	977	2,951	9,436	1,587	24,308	10,009	1,828
		Females,	3,047	4,249	6,809	1,170	6,001	949	2,750	8,524	1,499	28,987	9,379	1,200
		Not stated,	4	9	3	1	3	—	2	24	2	9	2	3
MONTHS.		January,	606	66	900	117	1,351	185	674	81	149	4,522	2,265	442
		February,	481	82	730	182	1,241	215	569	74	136	4,176	2,358	265
		March,	444	79	845	239	1,419	205	580	96	158	4,946	2,728	247
		April,	419	98	770	294	1,286	215	447	109	135	4,589	2,244	235
		May,	355	101	697	329	1,174	211	370	143	147	4,737	1,780	262
		June,	351	228	628	321	947	163	257	414	158	4,013	1,071	182
		July,	377	1,212	857	382	731	116	218	4,712	391	4,299	766	171
		August,	348	2,902	1,513	240	591	88	233	7,082	591	4,608	624	113
		September,	491	2,413	2,005	91	553	111	347	3,733	578	4,483	810	145
		October,	608	982	2,308	66	689	96	582	1,211	345	4,313	1,137	209
		November,	596	250	1,692	86	940	147	731	237	153	4,262	1,614	287
		December,	586	105	1,238	119	1,169	166	745	90	146	4,336	1,989	473
		Not stated,	3	4	12	1	4	2	—	2	1	20	4	—

Acres												
	5,065	8,522	14,195	2,417	12,095	1,920	5,703	17,984	3,088	63,304	19,390	3,031
Totals,	2,815	4,680	1,329	1,931	8,016	543	4,945	17,984	3,086	3,419	7,825	955
Under 5,	1,529	628	898	206	2,956	51	674	—	2	583	582	205
5 to 10,	501	190	1,084	35	608	35	48	—	—	978	235	100
10 to 15,	230	148	2,022	55	221	53	9	—	—	4,518	461	259
15 to 20,	249	306	3,374	82	177	158	6	—	—	14,291	1,177	822
20 to 30,	156	321	1,573	29	51	181	6	—	—	10,013	1,281	326
30 to 40,	59	322	1,098	28	15	142	3	—	—	6,821	1,422	133
40 to 50,	40	419	902	10	18	191	—	—	—	4,824	1,621	95
50 to 60,	46	501	908	12	7	214	—	—	—	4,337	2,064	56
60 to 70,	22	582	670	14	3	235	—	—	—	2,664	2,079	28
70 to 80,	1	372	261	5	1	109	1	—	—	571	1,053	17
Over 80,	17	41	81	7	20	8	11	—	—	255	90	35
Not stated,												

The PERCENTAGES of Deaths from several Specified Causes, of each Sex, in each Month, and at Different Specified Periods of Life, which were registered during the Eleven Years, 1863–73.

ELEVEN YEARS.	Diphtheria.	Dysentery.	Typhus.	Measles.	Scarlatina.	Erysipelas.	Croup.	Cholera Infantum.	Teething.	Consumption.	Pneumonia.	Small-pox.
SEX.												
Totals,	100·00	100·00	100·00	100·00	100·00	100·00	100·00	100·00	100·00	100·00	100·00	100·00
Males,	46·14	49·86	52·01	51·55	50·36	50·89	51·74	52·47	51·39	45·61	51·62	60·31
Females,	53·79	·50·08	47·97	48·41	44·62	49·11	48·22	47·40	48·54	54·38	48·37	39·59
Not stated,	- ·07	·11	·02	·04	·02	—	·04	·13	·07	·01	·01	·10
MONTHS.												
January,	10·70	·77	6·34	4·84	11·17	9·63	11·82	·45	4·82	8·48	11·68	14·58
February,	8·49	·96	5·14	7·53	10·26	11·20	9·97	·41	4·40	7·83	12·16	8·74
March,	7·83	·93	5·95	9·89	11·73	10·68	10·17	·53	5·12	9·28	14·07	8·16
April,	7·39	1·15	5·42	12·16	10·63	11·20	7·84	·61	4·37	8·61	11·57	7·75
May,	6·27	1·19	4·91	13·61	9·71	10·99	6·49	·80	4·76	8·89	9·18	8·64
June,	6·20	2·68	4·43	13·28	7·83	8·50	4·51	2·30	5·12	7·53	5·52	6·00
July,	6·66	14·22	6·04	13·74	6·04	6·04	3·82	26·20	12·66	8·07	3·95	5·64
August,	6·14	34·05	10·66	9·93	4·89	4·58	4·09	39·38	19·14	8·65	3·22	3·73
September,	8·67	28·32	14·13	3·77	4·57	5·78	6·08	20·76	18·72	8·41	4·18	4·78
October,	10·73	11·52	16·26	2·73	5·70	5·00	9·33	6·73	11·17	8·09	5·86	6·90
November,	10·52	2·93	11·92	3·56	7·77	7·66	12·82	1·32	4·96	8·00	8·33	9·47
December,	10·35	1·23	8·72	4·92	9·67	8·64	13·06	·50	4·73	8·13	10·26	15·61
Not stated,	·05	·05	·08	·04	·03	·10		·01	·03	·03	·02	—

Ages												
Totals	100·00	100·00	100·00	100·00	100 00	100·00	100·00	100·00	99·93	100·00	100·00	100·00
Under 5	49·69	55·02	9·36	80·02	66·28	28·28	86·71	100·00	·07	6·41	37·78	31·51
5 to 10	26·99	7·37	6·33	8·52	24·44	2·66	11·82	–	–	1·09	8·00	6·76
10 to 15	8·84	2·23	7·64	1·46	5·08	1·82	·84	–	–	1·83	1·21	8·90
15 to 20	4·06	1·74	14·24	2·27	1·88	2·76	·16	–	–	8·53	2·38	8·55
20 to 30	4·40	3·59	23·77	3·39	1·46	8·23	·10	–	–	26·81	6·08	27·12
30 to 40	2·75	3·77	11·08	1·20	·42	9·43	·10	–	–	18·79	6·61	10·76
40 to 50	1·04	3·78	7·70	1·16	·13	7·39	·06	–	–	12·80	7·33	4·39
50 to 60	·71	4·92	6·35	·41	·15	9·95	–	–	–	9·05	8·36	3·12
60 to 70	·81	5·91	6·40	·50	·06	11·14	–	–	–	8·14	10·64	1·85
70 to 80	·39	6·83	4·72	·58	·02	12·24	–	–	–	5·00	10·72	·92
Over 80	·02	4·36	1·84	·21	·01	5·68	·02	–	–	1·07	5·43	·56
Not stated	·30	·48	·57	·29	·17	·42	·19	–	–	·48	·46	1·15

6

Small-pox.—The mortality registration in 1873 affords us the statistics of the declining stages of an epidemic which will long be remembered in Massachusetts as a very wide-spread and fatal pestilence. The long-continued immunity of the people had engendered a sense of security which was deceptive. Vaccination had come to be regarded as a comparatively needless precaution, in the absence of the disease against which it is protective ; so that, at length, the poison which had shown itself, through a series of years, to be relatively inert or in reserve, and which manifested itself in a few sporadic or imported cases, found, in 1871, the conditions ripe for a progressive and rapid development. The material was abundant, and the contagion was active. In 1872, the disease reached the climax of its epidemic activity ; preventive measures were diligently and effectively employed in that year, and in 1873, to stay the pestilence, and at the beginning of the latter year it became apparent that the virulence of the affection was beginning to decline.

The whole State was included within the limits of the epidemic ; and all the evidence tends to show that the disease was not only unusually fatal, but that the non-fatal cases presented an uncommon type of severity.

We are now in a position to study the entire mortuary statistics of this remarkable epidemic, and to compare the number of deaths recorded in the account of this special incursion with the reports of previous years. The following table presents the total mortality from small-pox during fifteen years, with the percentage of deaths from this disease, as compared with the mortality from all causes. One instructive feature is here made manifest ; namely, that the disease moves in a wave-like periodicity through a series of years ; the years 1860, 1864 and 1872 mark the maximum of activity, while the years immediately following those named show a distinct remission. The progressive rise in the mortality,—from 20 deaths in 1868, to 1,029 in 1872,—is especially suggestive.

DEATHS from Small-pox in Massachusetts.—Fifteen Years.
Numbers and Percentages.

YEARS.	Total Annual Mortality, from all Causes.	Deaths from Small-pox.	Percentage of Deaths from Small-pox to Deaths from all Causes.
1859, ...	20,976	255	1·22
1860, ...	23,068	334	1·45
1861, ...	24,085	33	0·14
1862, ...	22,974	40	0·17
1863, ...	27,751	42	0·15.
1864, ...	28,723	242	0·84
1865, ...	26,152	221	0·84
1866, ...	23,637	141	0·59
1867, :	22,772	196	0·82
1868, . • . . .	25,603	20	0·08
1869, ...	26,054	59	0·22
1870, ...	27,329	131	0·48
1871, ...	27,943	294	1·05
1872, ...	35,019	1,029	2·94
1873, ...	33,912	668	1·97

The following table exhibits a comprehensive view of the rise
and decline of the epidemic. The beginning of the invasion
may be set down in the month of October, 1871, inasmuch as
with that month there was a distinct accession in the number of
deaths, the previous months having shown very nearly the average mortality of the same months in the previous year. If we
mark the inception of the epidemic at this point, we note a
nearly regular increase in the monthly mortality until December,
1872, when the highest mortality was reached. From this
climax we observe the regular retrogression of the disease, the
number of deaths diminishing steadily, until, in November,
1873, only a single death was recorded.

The same accession, development and decline are shown also
in the quarterly mortality and in the quarterly mortality-rates.
It will be observed that the total mortality set down to the
account of this epidemic, by this schedule, amounted to 1,755 :—

YEARS AND MONTHS.					Monthly Mortality.	Quarterly Mortality.	Quarterly Rates.
1871,	October,	.	.	.	37		
	November,	.	.	.	10	70	8·9
	December,.	.	.	.	23		
1872,	January,	.	.	.	10		
	February,	.	.	.	23	82	4·7
	March,	.	.	.	49		
	April,	.	.	.	49		
	May,	.	.	.	45	134	7·7
	June,	.	.	.	40		
	July,	.	.	.	38		
	August,	.	.	.	24	116	6·6
	September,	.	.	.	54		
	October,	.	.	.	117		
	November,	.	.	.	210	690	89·3
	December,.	.	.	.	363		
1873,	January,	.	.	.	324		
	February,	.	.	.	132	511	29·1
	March,	.	.	.	55		
	April,	.	.	.	38		
	May,	.	.	.	30	98	5·6
	June,	.	.	.	30		
	July,	.	.	.	39		
	August,	.	.	.	10	51	2·9
	September,	.	.	.	2		
	October,	.	.	.	2		
	November,	.	.	.	1	3	0·2
	December,.	.	.	.	–		
Totals,	.	.	.	.	1,755	1,755	100·00

In the table which follows, we have presented the mortality
throughout the epidemic, analyzed with reference to the ages of
those who died. The disease bore most heavily on the young
children and on those between twenty and thirty years old :—

DEATHS from Small-pox.—*Ages.*

		Under 5 years.	5 to 20	20 to 30	30 to 50	Over 50
1871,	Numbers, . . .	109	81	66	21	17
	Percentages, . .	37·1	27·5	22·5	7·1	5·8
1872,	Numbers, . . .	256	180	342	182	62
	Percentages, . .	25·1	17·6	33·4	17·8	6·1
1873,	Numbers, . . .	179	125	193	111	41
	Percentages, . .	27·	18·9	29·1	16·7	8·3
Whole period,	Numbers, .	544	386	601	314	120
	Percentages,	27·7	19·7	30·6	15·9	6·1

By the following table, we learn in what parts of the State
the disease was most rife during the three years. The counties
of Dukes and Nantucket were, happily, exempt from fatal cases,
although the contagion did not wholly avoid those isolated locali-
ties. The record of Suffolk County is particularly interesting,
since the great majority of the towns and cities in other counties
traced their infection to Boston; the fact is here brought out,
that Suffolk County registered more than half the total mortality
for the whole period, and that when the epidemic was at its
height,—in 1872,—the proportion of deaths falling to the same
populous section, amounted to 73·27 per cent. of the mortality
for that year. In 1871, the prevalence of small-pox in Lowell
and Holyoke determined the disproportionate mortality set down
to Middlesex and Hampden in that year:—

DEATHS from Small-pox in the Counties.—*Numbers and Percentages.*

COUNTIES.	1871.		1872.		1873.		WHOLE PERIOD.	
	Numbers.	Percentage.	Numbers.	Percentage.	Numbers.	Percentage.	Numbers.	Percentage.
Barnstable,	–	–	9	·88	4	·59	13	·65
Berkshire,	1	·34	10	·97	3	·45	14	·70
Bristol,	1	·34	15	1·46	10	1·50	26	1·30
Dukes and Nantucket,	–	–	–	–	–	–	–	–
Essex,	12	4·06	39	3·79	52	7·79	103	5·17
Franklin,	1	·34	2	·20	1	·15	4	·20
Hampden,	49	16·61	23	2·23	109	16·32	181	9·08
Hampshire,	1	·34	4	·39	6	·90	11	·55
Middlesex,	191	64·75	114	11·08	115	17·22	420	21·08
Norfolk,	3	1·02	22	2·14	16	2·40	41	2·06
Plymouth,	1	·34	6	·58	5	·74	12	·60
Suffolk,	24	8·13	754	73·27	315	47·15	1,093	54·90
Worcester,	11	3·73	31	3·01	32	4·79	74	3·71
Whole State,	295	100·00	1,029	100·00	668	100 00	1,992	100·00

Measles.—This disease was much less fatal in 1873 than in the previous year. There were one hundred and eighty deaths, two hundred and forty-eight less than in 1872. The number of deaths varies greatly from year to year; but, in 1873, the number was much below the annual average of the past thirty years. One hundred and thirty-five (seventy-five per cent. of the whole number) were those of children under five years of age. All the counties shared in the mortality, except Dukes and Nantucket. The months of May, June and July have the record of fifty-six per cent. of the deaths; this statement is not in accordance with the general impression that the fatality of measles depends mostly on the pulmonary complications, and that these complications are aggravated in the colder months.

Scarlatina was fatal in 1,472 cases, an increase of ninety-five upon the mortality from this disease in 1872. Nine hundred and ninety-one, or sixty-seven per cent., were the deaths of children under five years old; and ninety per cent. (1,328) were those of children under ten years of age. The four months, March, April, November and December, contributed forty-three per cent. of the mortality. None of the counties escaped. Suffolk County reported the largest number of deaths from the disease,—thirty-four per cent. of the whole,—and Middlesex follows next, with twenty per cent. If the comparison be made according to the relative numbers living instead of the actual number of deaths, Bristol County had the largest fatality to report, having 2·1 deaths to the thousand of population, while Suffolk had 1·8, and Middlesex 1·7.

Diphtheria.—The year 1873 presents a slight increase in the registered mortality from this justly dreaded disease; there were 310 deaths, against 273 the year previous. The average annual number of deaths, during the past five years, was 279. We are still very far from the alarming mortality recorded in the years from 1860 to 1865, when diphtheria took an unwonted place in the list of the ten most fatal diseases, standing, in 1863, the fourth in order. Of those dying in 1873, 164, or 53 per cent., were under five years old, and 238, or 77 per cent., were under ten years old. January, February, September and October were the most fatal months; the least mortality

was in May and June. Dukes and Nantucket Counties were
spared. The mortality was quite evenly distributed among the
other counties. The fact that diphtheria causes more deaths of
females than of males, has been frequently observed and com-
mented on. The present year is an exception to the rule, the
deaths of males exceeding, by ten, those of females.

Typhus Fever.—It is necessary to reiterate the explanation
that this term is used to include the class of continued fevers,
and is not understood in its narrow and distinctive sense. Inasmuch as the disease commonly called typhoid fever compre-
hends by far the larger portion of the cases under the above
title, in the Registration Reports, it might be well to substitute
that term to designate the entire class. We find also included
under the head of typhus fever, one hundred and thirty-two
deaths of children under five years old. These cases of so-called
" infantile fever " can hardly represent actual zymotic cases.

The mortality from the generic disease called typhus was
1,406 in 1873. This number is less, by 297, than the number
reported in 1872. The number of males exceeded the number
of females among the decedents by 79,—very nearly the usual
proportion. In one year (1864), the sexes suffered in very
unequal proportions; the percentage of the deaths of males was
60·75, while that of the females was 39·18. Forty-two per cent.
of the deaths in 1873 occurred among persons between fifteen
and thirty years of age; and forty-four per cent. of the mortality
was recorded in September, October and November. Suffolk
County reported the largest number of deaths (283), and Middlesex comes next, with 186. If, however, we make the comparison, with the population as a basis, Hampden stands at the
head of the list in point of relative mortality, having a death-
rate, from typhus, of 2·18 to the thousand of population;
Bristol is next, with a rate of 1·26, while Suffolk shows a rate
of 1·05. It thus appears that the observation is confirmed, that
the country has more cases of autumnal fever than the city.

Dysentery.—From this cause, there were 435 deaths reported,
a considerable reduction from the number registered in 1872.
Seventy-eight per cent. of the mortality was in the months of
July, August and September, August having a record of 37·24

per cent. Fifty per cent. of the deaths were those of children under five years old; and thirty-three per cent. were of persons over fifty years old. The largest number fell to Middlesex County.

Cholera Infantum.—The mortality from this summer scourge of children amounted, in 1873, to 2,553, a decided reduction from the registry of the previous year. There were 1,340 males, and 1,212 females. The mortality from cholera infantum comprised 7·6 per cent. of the deaths from all specified causes; this exceeds the average percentage for the last thirty-two years and eight months, by 3·3 per cent. Deaths were reported in every month; but the months of July, August and September contributed 2,230 (87·34 per cent.) of the deaths, the month of August standing at the head, with 1,079 deaths on its record,— 42·26 per cent. of the total mortality. The following table will show that the counties containing the cities and thickly-settled communities contribute most of the mortality from cholera infantum :—

DEATHS from Cholera Infantum, 1873.—*Percentages.*

COUNTIES.	Numbers.	Percentages.
Barnstable, ...	8	1·5
Berkshire, ...	51	4·9
Bristol, ...	211	7·3
Dukes and Nantucket, ...	5	3·1
Essex, ...	384	8·7
Franklin, ...	19	3·5
Hampden, ...	210	11·3
Hampshire,.	52	6·8
Middlesex, ...	563	8·7
Norfolk, ...	93	5·6
Plymouth, ...	60	4·9
Suffolk, ...	627	7·1
Worcester, ...	270	7·6
Whole State, ...	2,553	7·6

10

Consumption.—The number of deaths in 1873 was exactly
the same as that registered in 1872,—5,556. This number is
16·4 per cent. of the total mortality from all specified causes.
The disease maintains its traditional place as the most destructive
of life in Massachusetts. The deaths of females exceeded those
of males by 468, the percentages being 45·77 and 54·19
respectively.

The following tables show how slight an influence the seasons
have in promoting the fatality of consumption. The largest
number of deaths occurred in March, a month which has
repeatedly had the same fact recorded concerning it in former
years. Besides the fact that the month itself is proverbially
very trying, on account of its changeable temperature and its
dampness, its relation to the season which it follows must be
remembered, in seeking for an explanation of the larger mortality attributed to it ; for the month comes at the end of winter,
during which season invalids take out-door exercise less regu-
larly, and suffer, in consequence, a loss of vigor, whereby they
are ill-prepared to endure the various depressing conditions of
early spring :—

First Quarter,	.	.	. 1,511	Third Quarter, . . . 1,377
Second Quarter,	.	.	. 1,362	Fourth Quarter, . . . 1,306

If we make the comparison according to the recognized
seasons, essentially the same relation appears :—

Spring,	.	.	. . 1,511	Autumn, ... 1,271
Summer,	.	.	. . 1,359	Winter, ... 1,415

The following table, carrying a comparison, with reference to
ages, through a series of six years, shows that the mortality
from consumption bears most heavily upon the middle-aged.
In 1873, twenty-seven per cent. of the deaths from this disease
were of persons between twenty and thirty years old :—

DEATHS from Consumption at certain ages.—*Six Years.*

		Under 15	15 to 50	Over 50
1868, {	Numbers, ...	413	2,912	1,095
	Percentages, ...	9·34	65·88	24·78
1869, {	Numbers, ...	443	3,060	1,134
	Percentages, ...	9·55	65·99	24·46
1870, {	Numbers, ...	459	3,364	1,163
	Percentages, ...	9·21	67·47	23·33
1871, {	Numbers, ...	443	3,467	1,160
	Percentages, ...	8·74	68·38	22·88
1872, {	Numbers, ...	596	3,721	1,239
	Percentages, ...	10·73	66·97	22·30
1873, {	Numbers, ...	511	3,807	1,238
	Percentages, ...	9·19	68·52	22·29

We have, in the next table, a comparison of the counties with respect to the mortality from consumption :—

DEATHS from Consumption in the Counties, 1873.—*Percentages.*

COUNTIES.	Population—1870.	Number of Deaths.	Percentage to Deaths from all Specified Causes.	Persons living to one Death.
Barnstable, . . .	32,774	134	24·6	245
Berkshire, . . .	64,827	155	14·9	418
Bristol, ...	102,886	503	17·5	204
Dukes and Nantucket, .	7,910	34	21·1	233
Essex, ...	200,843	722	16·4	278
Franklin, ...	32,635	110	20·	297
Hampden, ...	78,409	251	13·5	312
Hampshire, . . .	44,388	128	16·7	347
Middlesex, . . .	274,353	1,090	16·9	252
Norfolk, ...	89,443	279	16·7	321
Plymouth, ...	65,365	245	20·2	267
Suffolk, ...	270,802	1,268	14·4	214
Worcester, . . .	192,716	637	18·	303

It will be seen by the foregoing table that certain rural
counties, as for example, Barnstable, Franklin and Plymouth,
appear to have a disproportionate number of deaths from consumption as compared with other causes, while the percentage
set down to Suffolk, Essex and Hampden is much smaller. It
should not be inferred from this that there is less consumption
in the cities than in the country, but rather, as we have pointed
out previously, that other diseases, as cholera infantum and
small-pox, make comparatively greater inroads upon the urban
population.

The following table will show more clearly the relation of
the counties to each other in regard to mortality from consumption, as compared with the mortality from all causes :—

ORDER of Mortality by Counties, 1873.

By all Diseases.	By Consumption alone.	By Consumption compared with all other Diseases.
Suffolk.	Bristol.	Barnstable.
Bristol.	Suffolk.	Dukes and Nantucket.
Hampden.	Dukes and Nantucket.	Plymouth.
Middlesex.	Barnstable.	Franklin.
Essex.	Middlesex.	Worcester.
Dukes and Nantucket.	Plymouth.	Bristol.
Worcester.	Essex.	Middlesex.
Plymouth.	Franklin.	Norfolk.
Norfolk.	Worcester.	Hampshire.
Hampshire.	Hampden.	Essex.
Barnstable.	Norfolk.	Berkshire.
Franklin.	Hampshire.	Suffolk.
Berkshire.	Berkshire.	Hampden.

The table which follows exhibits the fact, that there is a
gradual improvement as regards the destructiveness of con-

sumption, when a long series of years is included in the comparison.

In previous reports, greater intelligence on the part of the people in the matter of self-preservation, and on the part of physicians as regards the management of the disease, has been assigned as an explanation of this progressive improvement. To this we would add another condition which appears to deserve consideration. In an instructive essay recently read before the New Hampshire Medical Society, Dr. J. R. Ham presented a careful analysis of the meteorological changes as observed in the United States during a long course of years. He concludes that our climate has undergone a change in its humidity as the result of man's agency in felling the forests, in agriculture, in the building of canals and railroads, and in more general attention to drainage; and that, as a consequence of this increased dryness of the atmosphere, diseases of the respiratory organs are less prevalent than formerly.

MORTALITY from Consumption in Massachusetts.—*Twenty-one Years.*

YEARS.					Population.	No. of Deaths from Consumption.	Deaths from Consumption to each 100,000 living.
1853,	.	.	.	.	1,075,007	4,593	427
1854,	.	.	.	.	1,103,351	4,611	418
1855,	.	.	.	.	1,132,364	4,750	419
1856,	.	.	.	.	1,151,455	4,701	408
1857,	.	.	.	.	1,170,862	4,625	395
1858,	.	.	.	.	1,190,592	4,574	384
1859,	.	.	.	.	1,210,656	4,704	388
1860,	.	.	.	.	1,231,066	4,557	370
1861,	.	.	.	.	1,238,110	4,522	365
1862,	.	.	.	.	1,245,310	4,269	343
1863,	.	.	.	.	1,252,500	4,667	372
1864,	.	.	.	.	1,259,710	4,733	376
1865,	.	.	.	.	1,267,031	4,661	368
1866,	.	.	.	.	1,303,116	4,600	353
1867,	.	.	.	.	1,340,229	4,362	325
1868,	.	.	.	.	1,378,398	4,437	322
1869,	.	.	.	.	1,417,654	4,659	328
1870,	.	.	.	.	1,457,351	5,003	343
1871,	.	.	.	.	1,498,856	5,070	338
1872,	.	.	.	.	1,541,542	5,556	360
1873,	.	.	.	.	1,585,445	5,556	350

Pneumonia was the cause of 2,097 deaths in 1873.   In 1872, there were 2,295 deaths.   There were 155 more deaths of males than of females in 1873.   The greatest mortality occurred in March; the least, in August.   Nearly one-half the deaths were registered in the first four months of the year.

Eight hundred and five of the deaths (38·39 per cent. of the whole number) were of children under five years old; and seven hundred and eleven were deaths of persons over fifty years of age.   Thus it is seen that while pneumonia attacks all ages, its fatality is greatest at the extremes of life when the strength and vigor are less able to endure the disease.

It will be seen by the following table that as a rule, fatal pneumonia was more prevalent in the inland counties than on the seaboard :—

DEATHS from Pneumonia in the Counties, 1873.

COUNTIES.	Number.	Percentage to Deaths from all Specified Causes.
Barnstable, ...	24	4·4
Berkshire, ...	84	8·1
Bristol, ...	159	5·5
Dukes and Nantucket, ...	7	4·4
Essex, ...	267	6·1
Franklin, ...	49	8·9
Hampden, ...	104	5·6
Hampshire, ...	53	6 9
Middlesex, ...	421	6·5
Norfolk, ...	113	6·8
Plymouth, ...	64	5·3
Suffolk, ...	515	5·8
Worcester, ...	237	6·4

Cerebro-Spinal Meningitis.—This year, for the first time, we have a registry of deaths from this cause. The disease is now so well recognized, and at times prevails so extensively, that a special record of the mortality caused by it is of great advantage. In the Report for 1872, it was shown that the want of a distinctive nosological term to designate the deaths hitherto set down indiscriminately to "cephalitis," "cerebro-spinal meningitis," "spotted fever," "meningitis," and "spinal disease," led to considerable confusion. This difficulty will be less important in future.

In 1872, the number of deaths believed to have been caused by cerebro-spinal meningitis was 173. In 1873, there was a record of 747 deaths. Even if we make a considerable allowance for mistakes in the diagnosis of a somewhat unfamiliar disease, and for a tendency in times of epidemics to attribute to the prevailing affection many cases simulating it in certain respects but difficult of recognition otherwise, we still have occasion to observe, in the largely increased mortality, the fact that the malady in question was both wide-spread and fatal. In fact we find that all the counties shared in the effects of this much-dreaded disorder; the largest mortality was registered in the counties of Suffolk, Middlesex, and Essex, the numbers being 236, 157, and 106, respectively. The fact so often noted with reference to the zymotic diseases—that populous communities favor their development and fatality—is again illustrated here.

The progressive destructiveness and subsequent decline of the disorder are shown in the following table, which gives the number of deaths and the percentage for each of the four quarters of the year :—

	Numbers.	Percentage.
Quarter ending with—		
March, ...	145	19·41
June, ...	408	54·62
September, ...	130	17·40
December, ...	64	8·57

The largest mortality (185) fell in the month of April; the smallest number of deaths (13) was recorded in January.

The fatality bore the most heavily on childhood; after middle-life, the number of deaths diminished rapidly. There were 315 deaths of children under five years old—forty-two per cent. of the whole number. Only sixty-eight deaths are recorded of persons over forty years old.

(TABLES)

XXXIInd

ANNUAL REPORT

OF

BIRTHS, MARRIAGES, AND DEATHS,

REGISTERED IN

MASSACHUSETTS,

FOR THE YEAR ENDING DECEMBER 31, 1873.

TABLE I.—POPULATION, 1870.—BIRTHS,

General Abstract, exhibiting in connection with the Population according
Deaths registered in each County and Town in Massachusetts during
Born, the Nativity of Persons Married, and the Sex and aggregate

THE STATE AND COUNTIES.	Population. United States Census, 1870.	Whole No.	BIRTHS.							
			SEX.			PARENTAGE.				
			M.	F.	U.	Am.	For.	Am. Fa. and For. Mo.	For. Fa. and Am. Mo.	U.
MASSACHUSETTS, .	1,457,351	44,481	22974	21485	22	17647	21293	2,139	3,062	340
BARNSTABLE,	32,774	615	359	256	–	493	80	23	19	–
BERKSHIRE, .	64,827	1,653	859	793	1	726	708	78	137	10
BRISTOL, .	102,886	3,328	1,749	1,576	3	1,270	1,724	128	190	16
DUKES,. .	3,787	56	29	26	1	47	7	1	–	1
ESSEX, . .	200,843	5,686	2,933	2,753	–	2,615	2,345	339	353	34
FRANKLIN, .	32,635	733	392	340	1	461	217	15	33	7
HAMPDEN, .	78,409	2,527	1,316	1,208	3	958	1,298	109	155	7
HAMPSHIRE,.	44,388	1,111	584	527	–	508	503	36	58	6
MIDDLESEX,.	274,353	8,605	4,468	4,134	3	3,174	4,370	427	622	12
NANTUCKET,	4,123	55	27	28	–	46	3	6	–	–
NORFOLK, .	89,443	2,517	1,284	1,228	5	1,061	1,111	150	189	6
PLYMOUTH, .	65,365	1,549	802	746	1	1,025	362	52	. 73	37
SUFFOLK, .	270,802	10,254	5,168	5,085	1	2,750	5,820	597	894	193
WORCESTER,	192,716	5,792	3,004	2,785	3	2,519	2,745	178	339	11

MARRIAGES, AND DEATHS, 1873.

to the United States Census of 1870, the Births, Marriages, and the year 1873,—distinguishing the Sex and the Parentage of Children and average Ages of the Number who Died.

| | MARRIAGES. | | | | | | DEATHS. | | | | | |
| | | NATIVITY. | | | | | | SEX. | | | | AGE. |
Couples.	Am.	For.	Am. M. and For. Fe.	For. M. and Am. Fe.	Unk.	Persons.	M.	F.	U.	No. whose ages are registered.	Agg'te.	Average.
16437	8,755	5,115	1,079	1,477	11	33912	17242	16642	28	32969	921,718	27·96
297	259	27	5	6	–	576	313	255	8	574	·21,913	38·18
513	320	107	25	61	–	1,111	556	555	–	1,106	38,276	34·61
1,440	720	540	80	98	2	2,912	1,524	1,387	1	2,885	77,453	26·85
34	28	3	–	3	–	58	32	26	–	58	2,787	48·05
2,200	1,280	586	170	163	1	4,429	2,270	2,149	10	4,300	128,882	29·97
303	240	30	13	19	1	568	270	298	–	567	22,509	39·79
921	480	318	50	78	–	1,915	978	936	1	1,904	48,965	25·72
343	230	69	23	21	–	803	400	403	–	800	26,873	33·59
3,106	1,637	936	210	320	3	6,539	3,236	3,299	4	5,189	166,523	28·61
36	34	1	–	1	–	106	48	58	–	106	6,070	57·26
800	470	209	42	79	–	1,677	808	868	1	1,670	55,000	32·93
642	506	79	22	35	–	1,235	616	616	3	1,228	46,056	37·50
3,952	1,449	1,730	352	421	–	8,324	4,330	3,994	–	8,318	166,432	20·01
1,850	1,102	485	87	172	4	3,659	1,861	1,798	–	3,634	113,979	31·36

TABLE I.—*Births, Marriages, and Deaths,*

Counties and Towns.	Population. United States Census, 1870.	Whole No.	M.	F.	U.	Am.	For.	Am.Fa. and For. M.	For.Fa. and Am. M.	Unk.
			SEX.			**PARENTAGE.**				
BARNSTABLE, .	32,774	615	359	256	–	493	80	23	19	–
Barnstable, .	4,793	67	40	27	–	59	3	3	2	–
Brewster, . .	1,259	23	15	8	–	20	3	–	–•	–
Chatham, . .	2,411	36	24	12	–	36	–	–	–	–
Dennis, . .	3,269	75	39	36	–	75	–	–	–	–
Eastham, . .	668	9	5	4	–	7	–	2	–	–
Falmouth, . .	2,237	40	22	18	–	37	2	–	1	–
Harwich, . .	3,080	62	36	26	–	59	–	1	2	–
Mashpee, . .	348	11	7	4	–	10	–	1	–	–
Orleans, . .	1,323	25	12	13	–	24	–	1	–	–
Provincetown, .	3,865	115	68	47	–	43	60	5	7	–
Sandwich, . .	3,694	48	28	20	–	36	5	3	4	–.
Truro, . .	1,269	27	19	8	–	19	6	–	2	–.
Wellfleet, . .	2,135	42	22	20	–	35	1	6	–	–
Yarmouth, . .	2,423	35	22	13	–	33	–	1	1	–
BERKSHIRE, .	64,827	1,653	859	793	1	720	708	78	137	10
Adams, . .	12,090	362	184	178	–	116	198	18	27	3
Alford, . .	430	7	1	6	–	5	2	–	–	–
Becket, . .	1,346	23	12	11	–	13	8	1	1	–
Cheshire, . .	1,758	46	33	13	–	17	25	2	2	–
Clarksburg, .	686	16	8	8	–	9	6	–	1	–
Dalton, . .	1,252	44	21	23	–	17	17	2	8	–
Egremont, . .	931	22	15	7	–	18	1	3	–	–
Florida, . .	1,322	54	25	28	1	18	33	–	3	–
Gt. Barrington, .	4,320	94	38	56	–	58	24	5	6	1
Hancock, . .	882	15	11	4	–	12	1	–	2	–
Hinsdale, . .	1,695	59	28	31	–	15	36	1	7	–
Lanesborough, .	1,393	55	26	29	–	19	28	3	5	–
Lee, . .	3,866	94	49	45	–	35	35	11	12	1
Lenox, . .	1,965	51	25	26	–	23	23	–	5	–
Monterey, . .	653	8	5	3	–	6	1	–	1	–
Mt. Washington,	256	4	1	3	–	4	–	–	–	–
New Ashford, .	208	2	1	1	–	2	–	–	–	–
N. Marlborough,	1,855	53	25	28	–	29	18	2	3	1
Otis, . . .	960	10	6	4	–	9	–	–	1	–
Peru, . . .	455	3	1	2	–	2	1	–	–	–
Pittsfield, . .	11,112	337	170	167	–	130	150	17	36	4
Richmond, . .	1,091	16	10	6	–	3	12	1	–	–
Sandisfield, .	1,482	21	9	12	–	14	5	–	2	–
Savoy, . .	861	17	9	8	–	16	–	1	–	–
Sheffield, . .	2,535	45	31	14	–	26	18	1	–	–
Stockbridge, .	2,003	35	24	11	⁘	21	10	3	1	–
Tyringham, .	557	16	8	8	–	11	3	1	1	–
Washington, .	694	10	7	3	–	5	4	–	1	–
W. Stockbridge, .	1,924	56	33	23	–	19	32	3	2	–
Williamstown, .	3,559	63	35	28	–	34	16	3	10	–
Windsor, . .	686	15	8	7	–	14	1	–	–	–

registered during the year 1873—Continued.

	MARRIAGES.						DEATHS.						
Couples.	NATIVITY.						Persons.	SEX.			No. whose ages are registered.	AGE.	
	Am.	For.	Am. M. and For. Fe.	For. M. and Am. Fe.	Unk.			M.	F.	Unk.		Agg'te.	Average.
297	259	27	5	6	–		576	313	255	8	574	21,913	38·18
45	43	1	–	1	–		64	32	30	2	63	2,854	45·30
14	13	–	1	–	–		20	12	8	–	20	970	48·50
22	22	–	–	–	–		28	16	12	–	28	1,446	51·64
34	33	1	–	–	–		58	40	18	–	58	1,922	33·14
4	4	–	–	–	–		18	6	12	–	18	930	51·67
24	23	1	–	–	–		58	31	27	–	58	2,937	50·64
21	20	1	–	–	–		47	24	18	5	47	2,098	44·64
1	1	–	–	–	–		9	5	4	–	9	238	26·44
16	15	–	–	1	–		34	20	14	–	34	1,495	43·97
40	19	15	3	3	–		81	45	36	–	80	2,378	29·73
29	26	3	–	–	–		58	30	28	–	58	2,297	39·60
10	7	2	1	–	–		17	10	7	–	17	747	43·94
22	19	2	–	1	–		38	21	17	–	38	1,407	37·21
15	14	1	–	–	–		46	21	24	1	46	194	40·43
513	320	107	25	61	–		1,111	556	555	–	1,106	38,276	34·61
132	58	44	13	17	–		269	136	133	–	267	7,387	27·66
3	3	–	–	–	–		8	6	2	–	8	389	48·63
9	5	3	1	–	–		22	10	12	–	22	796	36·18
13	13	–	–	–	–		41	17	24	–	41	1,224	29·85
1	1	–	–	–	–		8	4	4	–	8	198	24·75
12	7	2	–	3	–		28	12	16	–	28	1,093	39·04
3	3	–	–	–	–		14	10	4	–	14	640	45·71
3	–	1	1	1	–		27	17	10	–	27	379	14·04
36	22	9	2	3	–		72	35	37	–	72	2,951	40·99
6	5	1	–	–	–		5	4	1	–	5	384	76·80
17	11	4	–	2	–		28	14	14	–	28	861	30·75
11	5	1	1	4	–		31	18	13	–	30	1,089	36·30
36	22	6	–	8	–		77	36	41	–	77	2,857	37·10
4	3	–	1	–	–		19	9	10	–	19	569	29·95
5	3	–	–	*2	–		6	3	3	–	6	217	36·17
1	1	–	–	–	–		1	1	–	–	1	70	70·00
1	1	–	–	–	–		2	2	–	–	2	125	62·50
7	5	–	–	2	–		29	10	19	–	29	1,501	51·76
6	6	–	–	–	–		8	4	4	–	8	348	43·50
1	1	–	–	–	–		4	–	4	–	4	146	38·50
111	66	23	3	19	–		204	106	98	–	203	6,328	31·37
2	2	–	–	–	–		4	2	2	–	4	195	48·75
10	10	–	–	–	–		16	6	10	–	16	863	53·94
5	4	–	1	–	–		8	4	4	–	7	348	49·71
21	19	2	–	–	–		45	25	20	–	45	2,162	48·04
13	8	5	–	–	–		36	18	18	–	36	1,450	40·28
1	·1	–	–	–	–		8	3	5	–	8	274	34·25
6	5	–	1	–	–		11	6	5	–	11	372	33·82
11	7	3	1	–	–		29	15	14	–	29	995	34·31
20	17	3	–	–	–		46	22	24	–	46	1,857	40·37
6	6	–	–	–	–		5	1	4	–	5	208	41·60

TABLE I.—*Births, Marriages, and Deaths,*

Counties and Towns.	Population. United States Census, 1870.	Whole No.	SEX.			PARENTAGE.				
			M.	F.	U.	Am.	For.	Am.Fa. and For. M.	For.Fa. and Am. M.	Unk.
BRISTOL, . .	102,886	3,328	1749	1576	3	1270	1724	128	190	16
Acushnet, . .	1,132	17	7	10	–	16	1	–	–	–
Attleborough,	6,769	208	108	100	–	103	80	7	15	3
Berkley, . .	744	12	1	11	–	12	–	–	–	–
Dartmouth, .	3,367	68	43	25	–	58	7	–	2	1
Dighton, . . .	1,817	47	23	24	–	35	10	1	–	1
Easton, . .	3,668	135	74	61	–	42	81	3	8	1
Fairhaven, .	2,626	38	21	17	–	38	–	–	–	–
Fall River, .	26,766	1,410	740	670	–	223	1049	59	77	2
Freetown, .	1,372	25	13	12	–	23	–	–	2	–
Mansfield, .	2,432	65	36	29	–	41	19	1	4	–
New Bedford,	21,320	473	242	231	–	233	177	25	33	5
Norton, . .	1,821	23	14	9	–	13	6	1	3	–
Raynham, .	1,713	33	18	15	–	24	7	1	1	–
Rehoboth, . .	1,895	36	21	15	–	34	1	–	1	–
Seekonk, . .	1,021	18	6	12	–	16	1	–	–	1
Somerset, .	1,776	55	28	27	–	40	15	–	–	–
Swanzey, . .	1,294	24	10	14	–	20	3	1	–	–
Taunton, .	18,629	576	311	262	3	241	262	28	44	1
Westport, .	2,724	65	33	32	–	58	5	1	–	1
DUKES, . .	3,787	56	29	26	1	47	7	1	–	1
Chilmark, . .	476	5	4	1	–	5	–	–	–	–
Edgartown, .	1,516	19	8	10	1	13	6	–	–	–
Gay Head, .	160	4	2	2	–	4	–	–	–	–
Gosnold, . .	99	*	–	–	–	–	–	–	–	–
Tisbury, . .	1,536	28	15	13	–	25	1	1	–	1
ESSEX, . . .	200,843	5,686	2933	2753	–	2615	2345	339	353	34
Amesbury, . .	5,581	170	83	87	–	68	92	2	8	–
Andover, . .	4,873	84	40	44	–	29	44	6	5	–
Beverly, . .	6,507	167	84	83	–	119	27	12	8	1
Boxford, . .	847	14	6	8	–	9	3	1	1	–
Bradford, .	2,014	41	22	19	–	30	8	2	1	–
Danvers, . .	5,600	128	73	55	–	69	47	7	5	–
Essex, . .	1,614	31	13	18	–	27	1	1	1	1
Georgetown, .	2,088	44	21	23	–	35	7	1	1	–
Gloucester, .	15,389	572	293	279	–	249	214	55	40	14
Groveland, .	1,776	40	19	21	–	27	12	1	–	–
Hamilton, . .	790	23	9	14	–	15	6	1	1	–
Haverhill, . .	13,092	365	188	177	–	192	129	19	24	1
Ipswich, . .	3,720	81	35	46	–	57	16	4	3	1
Lawrence, . .	28,921	850	435	415	–	167	590	33	57	3
Lynn, . . .	28,233	842	440	402	–	435	296	60	45	6
Lynnfield, .	818	16	7	9	–	11	4	–	1	–

* No Births.

registered during the year 1873—Continued.

	MARRIAGES.						DEATHS.						
Couples.	Nativity.					Persons.	Sex.			No. whose ages are registered.	Age.	
	Am.	For.	Am. M and For. Fe.	For. M and Am. Fe.	Unk.		M.	F.	U.		Agg'te.	Average.
1,440	720	540	80	98	2	2,912	1524	1387	1	2,885	77,453	26·85
8	8	–	–	–	–	14	5	9	–	14	565	40·36
63	50	7	1	5	–	180	101	79	–	177	5,077	28·68
7	7	–	–	–	–	12	5	7	.	12	438	36·50
25	22	1	1	1	–	64	31	33	–	64	2,808	43·88
19	14	3	–	2	–	29	12	17	–	28	1,382	49·36
28	18	9	–	1	–	66	32	34	–	64	2,203	34·42
30	25	–	2	3	–	51	22	29	–	51	2,155	42·26
631	169	376	38	47	1	1,264	679	585	–	1,262	21,258	16·84
12	11	–	–	1	–	8	4	3	1	8	333	29·13
20	18	–	1	1	–	55	31	24	–	55	2,309	41·98
276	167	78	14	17	–	470	235	235	–	461	14,907	32·34
17	15	1	–	1	–	20	10	10	–	20	890	44·50
10	10	–	–	–	–	25	13	12	–	25	901	36·04
12	12	–	–	–	–	19	6	13	–	19	1,170	61·58
6	5	1	–	–	–	15	7	8	–	13	755	58·08
17	14	2	1	–	–	35	20	15	–	35	843	24·09
14	13	1	–	–	–	25	14	11	–	25	1,447	57·88
225	123	61	21	19	1	497	262	235	–	492	15,504	31·57
20	19	–	1	–	–	63	35	28	–	60	2,508	41·80
34	28	3	–	3	–	58	32	26	–	58	2,787	48·05
6	6	–	–	–	–	4	1	3	–	4	274	68·50
18	13	2	–	3	–	26	15	11	–	26	911	35·04
*	–	–	–	–	–	2	1	1	–	2	104	52·00
1	1	–	–	–	–	1	1	–	–	1	†	·33
9	8	1	–	–	–	25	14	11	–	25	1,497	59·88
2,200	1280	586	170	163	1	4,429	2270	2149	10	4,300	128,882	29·97
57	32	13	5	7	–	113	54	58	1	113	3,463	30·66
36	19	12	–	5	–	84	42	42	–	83	3,029	36·49
74	52	12	6	3	1	164	79	85	–	164	5,031	30·67
8	7	–	1	–	–	11	6	5	–	11	401	36·45
21	17	2	–	2	–	32	16	16	–	32	1,226	38·31
42	30	4	4	4	–	97	48	49	–	96	2,922	30·44
7	6	–	1	–	–	28	9	19	–	28	1,200	42·86
21	17	1	3	–	–	38	15	23	–	38	1,411	37·13
161	73	63	11	14	–	455	312	141	2	350	8,631	24·95
8	7	1	–	–	–	27	14	12	1	27	880	32·59
8	6	1	–	1	–	17	11	6	–	17	1,004	59·06
216	158	33	12	13	–	303	138	162	3	293	8,936	30·50
28	20	2	3	3	–	75	41	34	–	73	3,485	47·33
382	128	188	30	36	–	670	320	348	2	668	14,042	21·02
380	251	71	32	26	–	679	351	328	–	677	18,956	28·00
4	4	–	–	–	–	9	5	4	–	9	568	63·11

* No Marriages.   † Four months.

TABLE I.—*Births, Marriages, and Deaths,*

Counties and Towns.	Population. United States Census, 1870.	BIRTHS.								
		Whole No.	SEX.			PARENTAGE.				
			M.	F.	U.	Am.	For.	Am.Fa. and For.M.	For.Fa. and Am.M.	Unk.
ESSEX—*Con.*										
Manchester,	1,665	34	19	15	–	21	8	3	2	–
Marblehead,	7,703	242	130	112	–	157	44	26	13	2
Methuen,	2,959	87	38	49	–	36	32	11	8	–
Middleton,	1,010	19	8	11	–	16	1	1	–	1
Nahant,	475	21	9	12	–	13	8	–	–	–
Newbury,	1,430	39	19	20	–	36	1	1	1	–
Newburyport,	12,595	296	165	131	–	135	124	13	23	1
North Andover,	2,549	87	47	40	–	31	46	5	4	1
Peabody,	7,343	268	134	134	–	80	160	11	17	–
Rockport,	3,904	107	55	52	–	56	34	11	5	1
Rowley,	1,157	25	12	13	–	21	3	1	–	–
Salem,	24,117	712	375	337	–	284	323	40	64	1
Salisbury,	3,776	103	57	46	–	71	28	–	4	–
Saugus,	2,247	44	26	18	–	30	6	4	4	–
Swampscott,	1,846	55	27	28	–	33	16	3	3	–
Topsfield,	1,213	26	14	12	–	19	4	1	2	–
Wenham,	985	19	11	8	–	17	2	–	–	–
West Newbury,	2,006	34	19	15	–	20	9	3	2	–
FRANKLIN,	32,635	733	392	340	1	461	217	15	33	7
Ashfield,	1,180	16	11	5	–	16	–	–	–	–
Bernardston,	961	12	8	4	–	10	1	–	1	–
Buckland,	1,946	38	22	16	–	14	21	–	2	1
Charlemont,	1,005	14	8	6	–	14	–	–	–	–
Coleraine,	1,742	23	8	15	–	18	3	1	1	–
Conway,	1,460	26	16	10	–	23	3	–	–	–
Deerfield,	3,632	104	56	48	–	41	51	3	7	2
Erving,	579	13	8	5	–	11	1	–	1	–
Gill,	653	10	5	5	–	10	–	–	–	–
Greenfield,	3,589	89	48	41	–	58	26	3	2	–
Hawley,	672	14	9	4	1	14	–	–	–	–
Heath,	613	13	5	8	–	13	–	–	–	–
Leverett,	877	9	6	3	–	8	1	–	–	–
Leyden,	518	14	4	10	–	12	1	–	1	–
Monroe,	201	4	2	2	–	4	–	–	–	–
Montague,	2,224	141	90	51	–	45	76	6	12	2
New Salem,	987	11	7	4	–	11	–	–	–	–
Northfield,	1,720	32	11	21	–	23	7	–	–	2
Orange,	2,091	46	16	30	–	41	4	–	1	–
Rowe,	581	11	6	5	–	10	–	–	1	–
Shelburne,	1,582	24	12	12	–	16	4	1	3	–
Shutesbury,	614	12	6	6	–	11	–	–	1	–
Sunderland,	832	15	8	7	–	10	5	–	–	–
Warwick,	769	8	5	3	–	7	1	–	–	–
Wendell,	539	8	2	6	–	5	2	1	–	–
Whately,	1,068	26	13	13	–	16	10	–	–	–

registered during the year 1873—Continued.

| | MARRIAGES. | | | | | | DEATHS. | | | | | | |
| | | NATIVITY. | | | | | | SEX. | | | No. whose ages are registered. | AGE. | |
Couples.	Am.	For.	Am. M. and For. Fe.	For. M. and Am. Fe.	Unk.	Persons.	M.	F.	U.			Agg'te.	Average.
6	5	1	–	–	–	37	15	22	–	37		1,387	37·49
70	46	7	12	5	–	171	106	65	–	170		5,092	29·95
46	30	13	2	1	–	45	23	22	–	42		1,298	30·90
7	6	–	–	1	–	15	6	9	–	15		670	44·67
3	3	–	–	–	–	10	3	7	–	10		339	33·90
13	12	–	1	–	–	23	13	10	–	23		1,008	43·82
109	71	22	7	9	–	249	114	135	–	249		9,619	38·63
27	10	9	4	4	–	40	20	20	–	40		1,534	38·35
47	36	6	4	1	–	160	75	85	–	160		4,302	26·89
56	27	14	6	9	–	96	55	41	–	96		3,014	31·40
14	14	–	–	–	–	22	15	7	–	22		1,018	46·28
247	109	104	19	15	–	551	261	290	–	550		17,319	31·49
42	35	4	1	2	–	77	43	34	–	77		1,936	25·14
18	14	1	1	2	–	33	12	21	–	33		1,325	40·15
12	7	1	4	–	–	37	17	19	1	36		994	27·61
12	11	–	1	–	–	22	13	9	–	22		1,198	54·45
7	7	–	–	–	–	13	4	9	–	13		655	50·38
11	10	1	–	–	–	26	14	12	–	26		989	38·04
303	240	30	13	19	1	568	270	298	–	567		22,509	39·79
4	3	1	–	–	–	13	7	6	–	13		474	36·46
8	8	–	–	–	–	14	4	10	–	14		517	36·93
5	4	1	–	–	–	55	27	28	–	55		1,504	27·35
9	9	–	–	–	–	9	6	3	–	9		565	62·77
20	15	2	1	2	–	18	10	8	–	18		689	38·28
15	9	3	2	1	–	31	9	22	–	31		1,327	42·81
31	25	1	2	3	–	76	45	31	–	76		2,895	38·09
2	2	–	–	–	–	9	3	6	–	9		334	37·11
5	4	–	–	1	–	8	5	3	–	8		480	60·00
44	26	9	3	6	–	48	19	29	–	48		2,027	42·23
5	5	–	–	–	–	8	6	2	–	8		463	57·88
7	7	–	–	–	–	10	3	7	–	10		493	49·30
12	12	–	–	–	–	16	8	8	–	16		799	49·94
3	3	–	–	–	–	3	1	2	–	3		249	83·00
1	1	–	–	–	–	4	2	2	–	4		195	48·75
27	15	10	1	1	–	68	40	28	–	68		1,979	49·94
9	9	–	–	–	–	21	9	12	–	21		1,160	55·24
12	11	–	1	–	–	31	16	15	–	31		1,519	49·00
33	30	–	1	2	–	33	16	17	–	33		1,037	31·43
3	3	–	–	–	–	9	7	2	–	9		503	55·89
10	6	2	1	1	–	22	7	15	–	22		804	36·54
12	12	–	–	–	–	12	2	10	–	12		428	35·66
8	8	–	–	–	–	20	9	11	–	20		677	33·85
8	6	–	1	–	1	10	3	7	–	10		595	59·50
6	4	–	–	2	–	7	1	6	–	6		221	36·83
4	3	1	–	–	–	13	5	8	–	13		575	44·23·

TABLE I.—*Births, Marriages, and Deaths,*

Counties and Towns.	Population. United States Census, 1870.	BIRTHS.								
		Whole No.	SEX.			PARENTAGE.				
			M.	F.	U.	Am.	For.	Am.Fa. and For. M.	For.Fa. and Am. M.	Unk.
HAMPDEN, .	78,409	2,527	1316	1208	3	958	1298	109	155	7
Agawam, . .	2,001	64	24	40	–	24	33	4	3	–
Blandford, . .	1,026	22	14	8	–	21	1	–	–	–
Brimfield, . .	1,288	30	13	16	1	13	14	1	2	–
Chester, . .	1,253	29	15	14	–	22	5	–	2	–
Chicopee, . .	9,607	278	159	119	–	69	182	12	14	1
Granville, . .	1,293	29	16	13	–	23	5	–	1	–
Holland, . .	344	2	–	2	–	2	–	–	–	–
Holyoke, . .	10,733	483	247	236	–	72	378	15	18	–
Longmeadow, .	1,342	28	16	12	–	20	7	–	1	–
Ludlow, . .	1,136	35	18	17	–	21	8	4	2	–
Monson, . .	3,204	69	39	30	–	39	23	1	6	–
(St. Prim. Sch'l),	–	1	–	1	–	–	1	–	–	–
Montgomery, .	318	9	5	4	–	8	–	1	–	–
Palmer, . .	3,631	122	76	46	–	51	53	4	14	–
Russell, . .	635	24	14	10	–	13	10	–	–	1
Southwick, . .	1,100	12	11	1	–	11	1	–	–	–
Springfield, .	26,703	872	439	431	2	342	424	40	63	3
Tolland, . .	509	5	3	2	–	4	1	–	–	–
Wales, . .	831	15	7	8	–	8	4	2	1	–
Westfield, . .	6,519	240	117	123	–	122	83	13	20	2
W. Springfield, .	2,606	97	47	50	–	40	43	9	5	–
Wilbraham, .	2,330	61	36	25	–	33	22	3	3	–
HAMPSHIRE, .	44,388	1,111	584	527	–	508	503	36	58	6
Amherst, . .	4,035	79	40	39	–	57	15	4	2	1
Belchertown, .	2,428	56	26	30	–	41	13	1	–	1
Chesterfield, .	811	23	12	11	–	19	1	1	1	1
Cummington, .	1,037	19	9	10	–	17	1	1	–	–
Easthampton, .	3,620	92	47	45	–	28	57	3	4	–
Enfield, . .	1,023	20	12	8	–	10	7	2	1	–
Goshen, . .	368	4	–	4	–	3	–	–	1	–
Granby, . .	863	24	12	12	–	19	4	–	1	–
Greenwich, .	665	11	4	7	–	9	2	–	–	–
Hadley, . .	2,301	67	41	26	–	25	40	–	2	–
Hatfield, . .	1,594	46	26	20	–	18	25	–	3	–
Huntington, .	1,156	18	13	5	–	14	3	1	–	–
Middlefield, .	728	14	7	7	–	4	8	–	2	–
Northampton, .	10,160	300	155	145	–	97	158	15	27	3
Pelham, . .	673	6	4	2	–	6	–	–	–	–
Plainfield, . .	521	8	5	3	–	8	–	–	–	–
Prescott, . .	541	9	5	4	–	9	–	–	–	–
South Hadley, .	2,840	89	44	45	–	28	53	1	7	–
Southampton, .	1,159	26	11	15	–	16	8	1	1	–
Ware, . .	4,259	110	61	49	–	31	74	3	2	–
Westhampton, .	587	19	10	9	–	12	5	1	1	–
Williamsburg, .	2,159	57	32	25	–	24	28	2	3	–
Worthington, .	860	14	8	6	–	13	1	–	–	–

*registered during the year 1873—*Continued.

	MARRIAGES.						DEATHS.						
Couples.		NATIVITY.				Persons.		SEX.			No. whose ages are registered.	AGE.	
	Am.	For.	Am. M. and For. Fe.	For. M. and Am. Fe.	Unk.		M.	F.	Unk.			Agg'te.	Average.
921	480	313	50	78	–	1,915	978	936	1	1,904	48,965	25·72
11	9	–	1	1	–	35	16	19	–	35	770	22·00
6	6	–	–	–	–	21	11	10	–	21	1,014	48·29
8	7	–	–	1	–	20	9	11	–	20	1,042	52·10
12	9	1	–	2	–	16	9	7	–	16	436	27·25
103	51	33	5	14	–	258	128	130	–	255	6,635	26·02
9	9	–	–	–	–	26	15	11	–	26	1,283	49·35
*	–	–	–	–	–	6	4	2	–	6	369	61·50
203	44	124	19	16	–	444	225	219	–	441	6,152	13·95
7	7	–	–	–	–	25	9	16	–	25	864	34·56
11	9	2	–	–	–	21	13	8	–	21	892	42·48
23	20	–	1	2	–	38	25	13	–	38	1,406	37·00
–	–	–	–	–	–	15	11	4	–	15	133	8·87
1	1	–	–	–	–	4	3	1	–	4	140	35·00
41	20	16	1	4	–	79	40	39	–	79	2,193	27·76
3	1	1	–	1	–	12	6	6	–	11	599	54·45
10	10	–	–	–	–	21	11	10	–	21	1,367	65·91'
345	191	106	19	29	–	630	316	313	1	629	15,718	24·99
3	3	–	–	–	–	6	2	4	–	6	296	49·33
12	10	1	1	–	–	14	6	8	–	14	537	38·46
80	57	16	2	5	–	130	70	60	–	128	4,040	31·56
23	7	13	1	2	–	66	35	31	–	65	1,784	27·45
10	9	–	–	1	–	28	14	14	–	28	1,295	46·25
343	230	69	23	21	–	803	400	403	–	800	26,873	33·59
32	27	2	3	–	–	43	25	18	–	43	1,653	38·44
12	10	1	–	1	–	42	19	23	–	42	2,062	49·09
13	13	–	–	–	–	12	5	7	–	12	670	55·80
4	4	–	–	–	–	13	7	6	–	13	670	51·30
25	10	10	2	3	–	57	35	22	–	57	1,367	23·98
13	8	3	1	1	–	11	5	6	–	11	659	59·91
1	1	–	–	–	–	3	2	1	–	3	150	50·00
5	4	–	–	1	–	10	3	7	–	10	429	42·90
7	7	–	–	–	–	14	7	7	–	14	738	52·71
11	6	5	–	–	–	40	18	22	–	39	1,770	45·38
8	3	5	–	–	–	28	12	16	–	28	934	33·36
11	8	1	1	1	–	18	9	9	–	18	795	44·17
1	1	–	–	–	–	4	1	3	–	4	215	53·75
95	61	19	7	8	–	217	107	110	–	216	4,974	23·03
8	7	–	–	1	–	9	5	4	–	9	354	39·33
5	5	–	–	–	–	8	3	5	–	8	375	46·88
3	3	–	–	–	–	10	5	5	–	10	584	58·40
15	7	5	1	2	–	59	28	31	–	59	1,559	26·42
10	10	–	–	–	–	17	8	9	–	16	843	52·69
33	17	10	5	1	–	130	64	66	–	130	3,521	27·08
3	2	• –	1	–	–	19	12	7	–	19	921	48·47
24	12	8	2	2	–	29	14	15	–	29	1,088	37·52
4	4	–	–	–	–	10	6	4	–	10	542	54·20

* No Marriages.

TABLE I.—*Births, Marriages, and Deaths,*

Counties and Towns.	Population. United States Census, 1870.	Whole No.	SEX.			PARENTAGE.				
			M.	F.	U.	Am.	For.	Am.Fa. and For. M.	For.Fa. and Am. M.	Unk.
MIDDLESEX, .	274,353	8,605	4468	4134	3	3174	4370	427	622	12
Acton, . .	1,593	32	16	16	–	20	12	–	–	–
Arlington, . .	3,261	117	64	53	–	34	73	4	6	–
Ashby, . .	994	10	7	3	–	9	1	–	–	–
Ashland, . .	2,186	59	34	25	–	34	18	4	3	–
Ayer, . . .	–	56	28	28	–	23	28	1	4	–
Bedford, . .	849	11	3	8	–	3	6	2	–	–
Belmont, . .	1,513	47	25	22	–	8	34	3	2	–
Billerica, . .	1,833	33	20	13	–	9	18	3	3	–
Boxborough, .	338	2	1	1	–	2	–	–	–	–
Brighton,, . .	4,967	174	84	88	2	61	94	8	10	1
Burlington, .	626	8	2	6	–	3	4	–	1	–
Cambridge, .	39,634	1,335	683	652	–	406	727	79	121	2
Carlisle, . .	569	8	3	5	–	6	1	1	–	–
Charlestown, .	28,323	865	444	421	–	358	377	62	66	2
Chelmsford, .	2,374	43	23	20	–	25	15	1	2	–
Concord, . .	2,412	54	36	18	–	18	29	4	2	1
Dracut, . .	2,078	23	13	10	–	13	4	2	4	–
Dunstable, . .	471	10	6	4	–	9	–	–	1	–
Everett, . .	2,220	87	42	45	–	49	31	4	3	–
Framingham, .	4,968	116	59	57	–	55	48	7	6	–
Groton, . .	3,584	34	17	17	–	16	16	–	2	–
Holliston, . .	3,073	51	26	25	–	23	24	2	2	–
Hopkinton, .	4,419	90	44	46	–	35	43	3	9	–
Hudson, . .	3,389	107	60	47	–	39	52	3	13	–
Lexington,. .	2,277	35	19	16	–	14	16	1	4	–
Lincoln, . .	791	15	11	4	–	5	8	–	2	–
Littleton, . .	983	14	8	6	–	4	8	1	–	1
Lowell, . .	40,928	1,351	710	641	–	364	840	64	82	1
Malden, . .	7,367	261	124	136	1	116	115	14	15	1
Marlborough, ;	8,474	389	187	202	–	113	225	16	35	–
Maynard, . .	–	50	28	22	–	20	26	1	2	1
Medford, . .	5,717	116	62	54	–	58	37	6	15	–
Melrose, . .	3,414	93	46	47	–	53	24	8	8	–
Natick, . .	6,404	226	112	114	–	96	96	13	21	–
Newton, . .	12,825	314	160	154	–	113	160	19	21	1
North Reading, .	942	18	9	9	–	16	2	–	–	–
Pepperell, . .	1,842	31	16	15	–	20	9	–	2	–
Reading, . .	2,664	68	31	37	–	59	4	3	2	–
Sherborn, . .	1,062	22	13	9	–	15	4	–	3	–
Shirley, . .	1,451	26	15	11	–	12	10	3	1	–
Somerville, .	14,685	723	370	353	–	260	401	25	37	–
Stoneham, . .	4,513	112	61	51	–	54	37	6	15	–
Stow, . . .	1,813	16	9	7	–	12	3	1	–	–
Sudbury, . .	2,091	22	9	13	–	19	3	–	–	–
Tewksbury, .	1,944	12	6	6	–	8	4	–	–	–
(St. Almshouse),	–	59	34	25	–	4	48	4	3	–
Townsend,. .	1,962	51	31	20	–	35	14	1	1	–
Tyngsborough, .	629	11	7	4	–	11	–	–	–	–

registered during the year 1873—Continued.

| | MARRIAGES. | | | | | | DEATHS. | | | | | |
| Couples. | Nativity. | | | | | Persons. | Sex. | | | No. whose ages are registered. | Age. | |
	Am.	For.	Am. M. and For. Fe.	For. M. and Am. Fe.	Unk.		M.	F.	Unk.		Agg'te.	Average.
3,106	1637	936	210	320	3	6,539	3236	3299	4	5,840	166,523	28·52
15	14	–	–	1	–	23	13	10	–	23	1,125	48·91
37	19	15	2	1	–	68	33	35	–	68	2,598	38·21
7	5	–	–	2	–	19	11	8	–	19	983	51·74
25	13	5	2	5	–	40	21	19	–	39	1,292	33·13
18	9	7	2	–	–	36	21	15	–	36	1,305	36·25
5	2	–	1	2	–	14	7	7	–	14	639	45·64
8	4	2	–	2	–	37	17	20	–	37	1,240	33·51
11	10	1	–	–	–	28	13	15	–	28	1,054	37·64
1	1	–	–	–	–	4	1	3	–	4	266	66·50
52	23	20	4	5	–	100	54	46	–	96	2,579	26·86
4	2	1	–	1	–	8	5	3	–	8	486	60·75
435	173	179	32	50	1	969	469	497	3	965	23,743	24·60
4	4	–	–	–	–	13	4	9	–	13	682	52·46
374	208	89	36	41	–	794	402	392	–	787	19,783	25·14
17	13	1	1	1	1	46	14	32	–	45	1,662	36·93
32	20	8	3	1	–	55	35	20	–	55	2,269	41·07
9	8	–	1	–	–	38	20	18	–	38	1,140	38·00
*	–	–	–	–	–	3	2	1	–	3	197	65·67
22	21	1	–	–	–	55	21	34	–	53	1,389	26·21
52	33	8	8	3	–	77	33	44	–	77	3,099	38·95
21	19	–	–	2	–	20	12	8	–	20	1,105	55·25
32	26	4	1	1	–	44	20	24	–	44	1,685	38·30
22	14	5	1	2	–	58	36	22	–	58	1,869	32·24
34	25	4	3	2	–	86	44	42	–	86	1,940	22·56
16	9	4	2	1	–	61	32	29	–	61	2,381	39·03
4	4	–	–	–	–	7	2	5	–	7	344	49·14
2	2	–	–	–	–	18	8	10	–	18	805	44·72
709	314	270	44	81	–	1,162	542	620	–	1,160	26,610	22·94
77	46	20	4	7	–	144	70	73	1	144	4,396	30·53
74	32	28	3	11	–	238	117	121	–	238	4,257	17·89
10	4	4	–	2	–	19	12	7	–	19	737	38·79
58	38	12	3	5	–	123	62	61	–	121	4,591	37·94
26	17	5	2	2	–	43	14	29	–	42	1,565	37·26
60	38	14	3	5	–	150	85	65	–	150	4,962	33·08
138	75	40	11	12	–	183	79	104	–	181	5,552	30·67
8	8	–	–	–	–	16	5	11	–	16	643	40·19
15	8	5	–	2	–	39	18	21	–	39	2,064	52·92
26	22	2	1	1	–	48	30	18	–	48	1,947	40·56
4	3	1	–	–	–	17	10	7	–	17	611	35·94
11	8	1	1	1	–	26	13	13	–	26	1,106	42·54
149	71	52	9	16	1	423	201	222	–	422	9,753	23·11
46	28	9	5	4	–	64	29	35	–	64	1,828	28·56
6	4	–	1	1	–	22	11	11	–	22	1,190	54·09
4	4	–	–	–	–	19	12	7	–	19	1,002	52·74
7	6	1	–	–	–	21	11	10	–	21	1,037	49·33
–	–	–	–	–	–	342	192	150	–	338	12,983	38·41
22	18	1	–	3	–	39	21	18	–	39	1,545	39·62
5	5	–	–	–	–	12	7	5	–	12	484	40·33

* No Marriages.

TABLE I.—*Births, Marriages, and Deaths,*

Counties and Towns.	Population. United States Census, 1870.	BIRTHS.								
		Whole No.	SEX.			PARENTAGE.				
			M.	F.	U.	Am.	For.	Am.Fa. and For. M.	For.Fa. and Am. M.	Unk.
MIDDLESEX—*Con.*										
Wakefield, . .	4,135	147	83	64	–	70	64	6	7	–
Waltham, . .	9,065	317	166	151	–	102	182	10	23	–
Watertown, .	4,326	168	100	68	–	63	82	10	13	–
Wayland, . .	1,240	34	23	11	–	22	7	1	4	–
Westford, . .	1,803	47	23	24	–	23	20	2	2	–
Weston. . .	1,261	32	17	15	–	21	8	1	2	–
Wilmington, .	866	24	13	11	–	21	3	–	–	–
Winchester, .	2,645	82	39	43	–	30	37	3	11	1
Woburn, . .	8,560	347	186	161	–	83	218	15	31	–
NANTUCKET, .	4,123	55	27	28	–	46	3	6	–	–
NORFOLK, .	89,443	2,517	1284	1228	5	1061	1111	150	189	6
Bellingham, .	1,282	33	18	15	–	20	9	3	–	1
Braintree, . .	3,948	87	36	48	3	37	30	5	15	–
Brookline, . .	6,650	254	139	115	–	60	169	11	13	1
Canton, . .	3,879	92	48	44	–	23	50	11	8	–
Cohasset, . .	2,130	52	27	25	–	24	17	7	4	–
Dedham, . .	7,342	171	79	90	2	51	102	6	11	1
Dover, . .	645	6	1	5	–	4	2	–	–	–
Foxborough, .	3,057	37	18	19	–	25	9	1	2	–
Franklin, . .	2,512	46	23	23	–	31	12	–	3	–
Holbrook, . .	–	43	24	19	–	31	10	–	2	–
Hyde Park, .	4,136	181	92	89	–	82	75	11	13	–
Medfield, . .	1,142	20	12	8	–	15	2	1	2	–
Medway, . .	3,721	85	33	52	–	42	31	6	6	–
Milton, . .	2,683	70	37	33	–	31	33	3	2	1
Needham, . .	3,607	105	56	49	–	40	45	8	12	–
Norfolk, . .	1,081	32	19	13	–	12	17	1	2	–
Norwood, . .	–	50	33	17	–	15	28	2	5	–
Quincy, . .	7,442	230	111	119	–	114	93	8	14	1
Randolph, . .	5,642	101	58	43	–	41	40	12	8	–
Sharon, . .	1,508	19	7	12	–	13	3	–	3	–
Stoughton, . .	4,914	124	71	53	–	56	55	3	9	1
Walpole, . .	2,137	49	24	25	–	27	14	6	2	–
West Roxbury, .	8,683	291	141	150	–	72	163	29	27	–
Weymouth, .	9,010	290	151	139	–	164	92	14	20	–
Wrentham, .	2,292	49	26	23	–	31	10	2	6	–
PLYMOUTH, .	65,365	1,549	802	746	1	1025	362	52	73	37
Abington, . .	9,308	258	131	127	–	155	88	6	9	–
Bridgewater, .	3,660	57	29	28	–	19	19	4	15	–
(*St. Workhouse*),	–	33	21	12	–	2	–	–	–	31
Brockton,* . .	8,007	289	150	139	–	183	84	8	12	2

* Name changed from North Bridgewater, 1873.

registered during the year 1873—Continued.

| Couples. | MARRIAGES. Nativity. | | | | | Persons. | DEATHS. Sex. | | | No. whose ages are registered. | Age. | |
	Am.	For.	Am. M. and For. Fe.	For. M. and Am. Fe.	Unk.		M.	F.	Unk.		Agg'te.	Average.
61	33	21	2	5	—	93	52	41	—	92	2,172	22·52
123	61	36	10	16	—	176	85	91	—	176	5,049	28·68
50	20	19	4	7	—	77	39	38	—	77	2,123	27·57
14	9	1	2	2	—	29	9	20	—	29	1,025	35·34
9	7	1	-	1	—	21	10	11	—	21	1,144	54·48
9	5	3	1	-	—	18	13	5	—	18	623	34·61
8	5	3	-	-	—	13	6	7	—	13	247	19·00
25	12	11	-	2	—	53	29	24	—	53	1,586	29·92
93	55	22	5	11	—	188	102	86	—	187	5,686	30·41
36	34	1	—	1	—	106	48	58	—	106	6,070	57·26
800	470	209	42	79	—	1,677	808	868	1	1,670	55,000	32·93
14	10	2	-	2	—	26	13	13	—	26	1,128	43·38
32	20	8	1	3	—	62	38	24	—	62	1,899	30·63
77	21	46	3	7	—	132	50	82	—	131	3,352	25·58
31	13	13	-	5	—	44	19	25	—	44	1,137	25·84
20	13	6	1	-	—	43	20	23	—	43	1,667	38·74
63	28	18	4	13	—	96	50	46	—	95	3,385	35·63
4	4	-	-	-	—	9	5	4	—	9	521	57·88
26	22	3	-	1	—	49	22	27	—	49	1,939	39·57
20	15	2	2	1	—	41	19	22	—	41	1,377	33·58
13	12	-	-	1	—	25	13	12	—	25	946	37·84
63	29	26	4	4	—	123	75	48	—	122	2,841	23·29
7	5	1	-	1	—	26	11	15	—	26	1,402	53·92
18	13	-	1	4	—	56	20	36	—	56	2,015	35·98
25	12	6	4	3	—	36	17	19	—	36	1,608	44·66
43	17	17	4	5	—	77	36	41	—	76	2,049	26·96
7	5	1	1	-	—	14	4	10	—	14	657	46·93
7	4	1	-	2	—	33	15	18	—	33	1,528	46·30
69	39	16	6	8	—	184	103	81	—	182	5,453	29·96
30	23	2	5	-	—	75	34	41	—	75	2,336	31·15
11	8	-	1	2	—	26	12	14	—	25	971	38·84
43	32	7	1	3	—	88	41	46	1	88	3,025	34·37
20	17	2	1	-	—	34	13	21	—	34	1,567	46·09
65	30	28	2	5	—	161	67	94	—	161	5,105	31·71
83	69	4	1	9	—	168	87	81	—	168	5,171	30·77
9	9	-	-	-	—	49	24	25	—	49	1,921	39·20
642	506	79	22	35	—	1,235	616	616	3	1,228	46,056	37·50
87	65	13	4	5	—	136	78	58	—	136	3,924	28·85
28	16	5	2	5	—	41	19	22	—	41	1,387	33·83
-	-	-	-	-	—	61	44	17	—	60	1,885	31·41
105	69	24	5	7	—	217	110	105	2	214	5,976	27·93

TABLE I.—*Births, Marriages, and Deaths,*

Counties and Towns.	Population. United States Census, 1870.	BIRTHS.								
		Whole No.	SEX.			PARENTAGE.				
			M.	F.	U.	Am.	For.	Am.Fa. and For. M.	For.Fa. and Am. M.	Unk.
PLYM'TH—*Con.*										
Carver,	1,092	25	14	11	–	21	–	2	2	–
Duxbury,	2,341	32	18	14	–	26	1	1	4	–
E. Bridgewater,	3,017	71	35	36	–	50	20	–	–	1
Halifax,	619	6	2	4	–	5	1	–	–	–
Hanover,	1,628	32	21	11	–	26	5	–	–	1
Hanson,	1,219	22	7	15	–	18	1	2	1	–
Hingham,	4,422	95	55	39	1	56	23	7	7	2
Hull,	261	7	4	3	–	7	–	–	–	–
Kingston,	1,604	27	18	9	–	22	4	–	1	–
Lakeville,	1,159	19	10	9	–	13	1	3	2	–
Marion,	896	18	3	15	–	18	–	–	–	–
Marshfield,	1,659	23	12	11	–	21	2	–	–	–
Mattapoisett,	1,361	12	5	7	–	12	–	–	–	–
Middleborough,	4,687	88	38	50	–	76	9	1	2	–
Pembroke,	1,447	29	12	17	–	26	2	1	–	–
Plymouth,	6,238	162	86	76	–	107	31	11	13	–
Plympton,	804	10	6	4	–	9	–	–	1	–
Rochester,	1,024	18	9	9	–	17	–	–	1	–
Scituate,	2,350	47	28	19	–	29	13	3	2	–
South Scituate,	1,661	31	14	17	–	28	3	–	–	–
Wareham,	3,098	114	68	46	–	63	49	1	1	–
W. Bridgewater,	1,803	24	6	18	–	16	6	2	–	–
SUFFOLK,	270,802	10,254	5168	5085	1	2750	5820	597	894	193
Boston,	250,526	9,672	4887	4785	–	2446	5631	559	844	192
Chelsea,	18,547	552	265	286	1	289	180	36	47	–
Revere,	1,197	22	10	12	–	10	9	–	3	–
Winthrop,	532	8	6	2	–	5	–	2	–	1
WORCESTER,	192,716	5,792	3004	2785	3	2519	2745	178	339	11
Ashburnham,	2,172	53	27	26	–	33	16	2	2	–
Athol,	3,517	79	44	35	–	61	14	1	3	–
Auburn,	1,178	23	15	8	–	9	10	2	2	–
Barre..	2,572	40	22	18	–	24	12	1	3	–
Berlin,	1,016	15	8	7	–	13	2	–	–	–
Blackstone,	5,421	121	66	55	–	29	86	4	2	–
Bolton,	1,014	22	13	9	–	16	2	1	3	–
Boylston,	800	22	11	11	–	14	5	3	–	–
Brookfield,	2,527	68	33	35	–	32	32	–	4	–
Charlton,	1,878	34	20	14	–	22	9	–	3	–
Clinton,	5,429	187	103	84	–	40	122	10	15	–
Dana,	758	7	4	3	–	6	–	–	1	–
Douglas,	2,182	72	44	28	–	19	45	3	5	–
Dudley,	2,388	92	54	38	–	17	67	2	6	–
Fitchburg,	11,260	317	154	163	–	158	131	14	14	–

registered during the year 1873—Continued.

Couples.	Am.	For.	Am. M. and For. Fe.	For. M. and Am. Fe.	Unk.	Persons.	M.	F.	U.	No. whose ages are registered.	Agg'te.	Average.
			NATIVITY.					SEX.			AGE.	
6	3	1	2	—	—	19	7	12	—	19	771	40·58
20	18	—	—	2	—	25	11	14	—	25	1,240	49·60
35	29	4	1	1	—	53	30	22	1	53	2,103	39·68
6	6	—	—	—	—	8	4	4	—	8	421	52·62
11	9	2	—	—	—	44	22	22	—	44	1,566	35·59
11	10	—	—	1	—	22	11	11	—	22	1,393	63·32
55	43	8	1	3	—	90	45	45	—	90	3,801	42·23
*	—	—	—	—	—	5	2	3	—	4	78	19·50
11	9	—	1	1	—	28	12	16	—	28	1,424	50·86
6	4	—	—	2	—	10	6	4	—	9	406	45·11
5	5	—	—	—	—	14	5	9	—	14	720	51·43
29	28	—	—	1	—	31	14	17	—	31	1,631	52·61
12	10	—	1	1	—	21	11	10	—	21	1,029	49·00
50	47	3	—	—	—	62	27	35	—	62	2,521	40·66
10	10	—	—	—	—	25	13	12	—	25	1,334	53·36
60	50	7	—	3	—	120	52	68	—	120	4,030	33·58
9	9	—	—	—	—	12	5	7	—	12	747	62·25
10	10	—	—	—	—	13	6	7	—	12	736	61·33
19	15	2	1	1	—	47	20	27	—	47	1,968	41·87
14	11	1	2	—	—	39	22	17	—	39	1,740	44·61
35	23	9	1	2	—	61	31	30	—	61	2,128	34·88
8	7	—	1	—	—	31	9	22	—	31	1,097	35·39
3,952	1449	1730	352	421	—	8,324	4330	3994	—	8,318	166,432	20·01
3,724	1308	1677	331	408	—	7,868	4097	3771	—	7,684	153,642	19·54
224	139	52	20	13	—	434	223	211	—	432	12,062	27·92
4	2	1	1	—	—	12	5	7	—	12	493	41·08
*	—	—	—	—	—	10	5	5	—	10	235	23·50
1,850	1102	485	87	172	4	3,659	1861	1798	—	3,634	113,979	31·36
27	22	2	1	1	1	38	18	20	—	38	1,553	40·87
42	36	1	4	1	—	73	34	39	—	72	1,902	26·42
9	8	1	—	—	—	11	5	6	—	11	412	37·45
19	16	—	—	3	—	52	24	28	—	52	2,354	45·27
2	2	—	—	—	—	13	7	6	—	13	606	46·61
43	20	12	—	10	1	88	45	43	—	88	2,844	32·32
7	5	1	—	1	—	21	12	9	—	21	752	35·81
7	6	1	—	—	—	11	7	4	—	11	372	33·82
23	13	4	1	5	—	46	24	22	—	46	1,660	36·09
15	13	1	1	—	—	22	8	14	—	22	1,090	49·54
62	22	27	4	9	—	89	45	44	—	89	2,233	25·09
6	6	—	—	—	—	10	2	8	—	10	387	38·70
15	7	6	1	1	—	32	17	15	—	32	691	21·59
10	10	—	—	—	—	69	37	32	—	69	1,932	28·00
121	77	21	8	15	—	216	111	105	—	216	6,854	31·73

3   * No Marriages.

TABLE I.—*Births, Marriages, and Deaths,*

Counties and Towns.	Population. United States Census, 1870.	Whole No.		BIRTHS.						
			SEX.			PARENTAGE.				
			M.	F.	U.	Am.	For.	Am.Fa. and For. M.	For.Fa. and Am. M.	Unk.
WORCES'R—*Con.*										
Gardner,	3,333	102	56	46	~	50	45	1	6	–
Grafton,	4,594	105	53	52	–	41	48	9	7	–
Hardwick,	2,219	41	19	22	–	11	27	–	3	–
Harvard,	1,341	14	5	9	~	9	5	–	–	–
Holden,	2,062	75	42	33	–	27	36	4	8	–
Hubbardston,	1,654	13	6	7	–	13	–	–	–	–
Lancaster,	1,845	34	14	20	–	21	10	2	–	1
Leicester,	2,768	67	29	38	–	22	41	2	2	–
Leominster,	3,894	144	71	73	–	98	36	3	6	1
Lunenburg,	1,121	14	6	8	–	11	2	1	–	–
Mendon,	1,175	37	21	16	–	28	8	1	–	–
Milford,	9,890	278	144	134	–	96	153	10	19	–
Millbury,	4,397	154	79	75	–	48	80	8	17	1
New Braintree,	640	13	8	5	–	6	6	–	1	–
Northborough,	1,504	31	17	14	–	15	11	1	3	1
Northbridge,	3,774	106	51	55	–	31	61	7	7	–
N. Brookfield,	3,343	158	83	75	–	44	96	3	14	1
Oakham,	860	20	13	7	–	13	6	1	–	–
Oxford,	2,669	48	20	28	–	12	32	2	1	1
Paxton,	646	7	4	3	–	6	1	–	–	–
Petersham,	1,335	14	4	10	–	13	1	–	–	–
Phillipston,	693	11	6	5	–	8	–	2	1	–
Princeton,	1,279	15	6	9	–	13	–	–	2	–
Royalston,	1,354	6	1	5	–	4	2	–	–	–
Rutland,	1,024	21	11	10	–	15	6	–	–	–
Shrewsbury,	1,610	37	20	17	–	19	12	3	3	–
Southborough,	2,135	51	24	27	–	24	24	2	1	–
Southbridge,	5,208	206	123	83	–	15	185	4	1	1
Spencer,	3,952	207	111	94	2	38	152	3	14	–
Sterling,	1,670	24	8	16	–	15	7	–	2	–
Sturbridge,	2,101	59	37	21	1	32	22	4	1	–
Sutton,	2,699	69	25	44	–	26	34	3	5	1
Templeton,	2,802	76	40	36	–	47	23	1	5	–
Upton,	1,989	32	15	17	–	23	8	–	1	–
Uxbridge,	3,058	72	41	31	–	29	33	3	7	–
Warren,	2,625	85	39	46	–	36	40	3	6	–
Webster,	4,763	176	92	84	–	26	144	–	6	–
Westborough,	3,601	133	62	71	–	59	66	2	4	2
West Boylston,	2,862	94	50	44	–	30	53	4	7	–
West Brookfield,	1,842	43	23	20	–	22	17	3	1	–
Westminster,	1,770	35	16	19	–	30	–	1	4	–
Winchendon,	3,398	75	40	35	–	46	21	1	7	–
Worcester,	41,105	1,638	851	787	–	854	638	41	104	1

registered during the year 1873—Concluded.

MARRIAGES.						DEATHS.						
Couples.	Nativity.					Persons.	Sex.			No. whose ages are registered.	Age.	
	Am.	For.	Am. M. and For. Fe.	For. M. and Am. Fe.	Unk.		M.	F.	Unk.		Agg'te.	Average.
46	26	14	5	1	–	62	31	31	–	62	2,030	32·74
39	17	16	2	4	–	44	21	23	–	44	1,304	29·64
26	14	11	–	1	–	25	13	12	–	25	1,378	55·12
5	5	–	–	–	–	18	15	3	–	18	1,002	55·66
8	5	3	–	–	–	44	25	19	–	40	1,514	37·85
12	10	1	–	1	–	30	17	13	–	30	1,500	50·00
16	13	2	–	1	–	29	15	14	–	29	1,537	53·00
7	4	2	–	1	–	56	25	31	–	56	1,711	30·55
33	26	6	–	1	–	93	47	46	–	92	3,074	33·41
6	6	–	–	–	–	13	6	7	–	13	837	64·39
10	9	–	1	–	–	14	6	8	–	14	548	39·14
70	42	17	5	6	–	150	74	76	–	150	4,576	30·51
54	26	17	5	6	–	91	48	43	–	89	2,464	27·68
7	6	–	–	1	–	7	1	6	–	7	232	33·14
4	4	–	–	–	–	37	20	17	–	36	1,821	50·58
42	21	12	2	7	–	64	36	28	–	63	2,025	32·14
41	24	10	1	6	–	77	41	36	–	77	1,969	25·57
12	12	–	–	–	–	18	6	12	–	18	1,070	59·44
19*	16	2	–	1	–	28	8	20	–	28	1,036	37·00
3	2	–	–	1	–	9	4	5	–	9	557	61·89
9	9	–	–	–	–	11	6	5	–	11	541	49·18
3	3	–	–	–	–	13	7	6	–	13	663	51·00
6	6	–	–	–	–	17	5	12	–	17	862	50·70
6	6	–	–	–	–	25	7	18	–	25	1,143	45·72
8	6	–	1	1	–	20	14	6	–	20	767	38·35
5	5	–	–	–	–	27	17	10	–	27	985	36·48
15	10	1	1	3	–	37	20	17	–	37	1,065	28·78
61	20	23	5	12	1	109	55	54	–	109	2,649	24·30
26	16	4	1	4	1	104	60	44	–	98	1,892	19·30
14	13	–	1	–	–	29	12	17	–	27	1,345	49·81
21	16	3	–	2	–	32	14	18	–	28	1,169	41·75
41	20	16	2	3	–	40	23	17	–	40	1,292	32·30
22	17	3	2	–	–	35	16	19	–	35	1,575	45·00
10	10	–	–	–	–	32	19	13	–	32	1,384	43·25
13	7	5	1	–	–	35	13	22	–	35	1,492	42·63
22	18	3	–	1	,–	38	18	20	–	38	1,213	31·92
68	15	42	4	7	–	116	67	49	–	116	2,339	20·16
25	16	7	–	2	–	54	26	28	–	54	1,589	29·43
34	14	15	1	4	–	65	32	33	–	65	1,422	21·88
16	14	1	–	1	–	28	14	14	–	28	923	32·96
16	14	1	–	1	–	30	11	19	–	30	1,544	51·47
35	21	7	3	4	–	66	34	32	–	66	2,657	40·26
506	275	164	24	43	–	996	516	480	–	993	25,641	25·82

TABLE II.—BIRTHS.—1873.

Distinguishing by Counties, by Months, and by Sex, the registered Number of Children BORN ALIVE during the year.

Year and Months	S & X.	STATE.	Barnstable.	Berkshire.	Bristol.	Dukes and Nantucket.	Essex.	Franklin.	Hampden.	Hampshire.	Middlesex.	Norfolk.	Plymouth.	Suffolk.	Worcester.
THE YEAR.	Totals,	44,481	615	1,653	3,328	111	5,686	733	2,527	1,111	8,605	2,517	1,549	10,254	5,792
	Males,	22,974	359	859	1,749	56	2,933	392	1,316	584	4,468	1,284	802	5,168	3,004
	Females,	21,485	256	793	1,576	54	2,753	340	1,208	527	4,134	1,228	746	5,086	2,785
	Not stated,	22	-	1	3	1	-	1	3	-	3	5	1	-	3
Jan.	Totals,	3,348	41	130	247	12	448	46	161	75	609	186	114	856	423
	Males,	1,730	23	69	127	7	198	29	87	39	831	87	57	444	232
	Females,	1,615	18	61	120	5	250	17	73	36	278	99	57	412	189
	Unknown,	3	-	-	-	-	-	-	1	-	-	-	-	-	2
Feb.	Totals,	3,230	33	106	248	6	442	44	191	88	636	152	110	740	434
	Males,	1,693	22	60	142	3	245	24	89	48	340	67	54	368	231
	Females,	1,537	11	46	106	3	197	20	102	40	296	85	56	372	203
Mar.	Totals,	3,616	47	128	279	11	470	61	222	80	711	226	128	798	455
	Males,	1,886	30	73	152	9	240	37	114	40	386	106	64	399	296
	Females,	1,729	17	55	126	2	230	24	108	40	325	120	64	399	219
	Unknown,	1	-	-	1	-	-	-	-	-	-	-	-	-	-
Apr.	Totals,	3,177	39	126	226	7	408	50	179	69	616	172	107	672	506
	Males,	1,596	21	54	120	3	228	27	84	31	307	82	61	328	250
	Females,	1,581	18	72	106	4	180	23	95	38	309	90	46	344	256
May.	Totals,	3,384	40	121	241	8	430	62	186	80	598	193	118	857	450
	Males,	1,752	23	66	119	3	232	29	103	44	319	106	62	444	202
	Females,	1,632	17	55	122	5	198	33	83	36	279	87	56	413	248

Month	Category	Total													
June	Totals	3,571	471	746	128	205	675	96	217	65	514	9	251	159	47
	Males	1,867	266	387	64	114	343	49	122	38	263	4	124	67	26
	Females	1,704	205	359	59	91	382	47	95	27	251	5	127	83	21
July	Totals	3,777	485	867	143	188	723	117	240	55	463	9	285	137	65
	Males	1,934	240	436	74	108	367	61	121	32	229	3	157	72	34
	Females	1,841	244	431	69	80	356	56	119	23	234	5	128	65	31
	Unknown	2	1	—	—	—	—	—	—	—	—	1	—	—	—
Aug.	Totals	4,087	532	904	157	255	781	130	226	68	494	10	327	138	65
	Males	2,109	274	477	81	139	382	70	117	36	244	6	166	77	40
	Females	1,972	258	427	75	113	399	60	108	32	250	4	161	60	25
	Unknown	6	—	—	1	3	—	—	1	—	—	—	—	1	—
Sept.	Totals	3,974	534	922	129	212	776	92	229	73	502	12	286	162	45
	Males	2,046	264	470	57	107	421	50	122	34	261	6	147	84	23
	Females	1,927	270	452	72	105	355	42	106	39	241	6	139	78	22
	Unknown	1	—	—	—	—	—	—	1	—	—	—	—	—	—
Oct.	Totals	4,053	519	930	127	232	806	96	209	75	523	10	307	147	72
	Males	2,095	280	465	75	115	399	50	108	38	275	4	164	79	43
	Females	1,956	239	465	52	116	407	46	101	36	248	6	143	68	29
	Unknown	2	—	—	—	1	—	—	—	—	—	—	—	—	—
Nov.	Totals	4,000	499	968	144	223	793	91	242	68	462	11	289	149	61
	Males	2,080	270	469	82	118	420	46	128	34	249	4	148	74	38
	Females	1,917	229	499	62	105	371	45	114	34	213	7	140	75	28
	Unknown	3	—	—	—	—	2	—	—	—	—	—	1	—	—
Dec.	Totals	4,261	484	994	149	273	878	97	225	66	530	6	342	157	60
	Males	2,184	259	481	71	135	451	56	121	34	269	4	183	84	36
	Females	2,073	225	512	78	137	426	41	104	32	261	2	158	73	24
	Unknown	4	—	1	—	1	1	—	—	—	—	—	1	—	—
Not stat'd	Totals	3	—	—	—	—	3	—	—	—	—	—	—	—	—
	Males	2	—	—	—	—	2	—	—	—	—	—	—	—	—
	Females	1	—	—	—	—	1	—	—	—	—	—	—	—	—

SUPPLEMENT A.

PLURALITY BIRTHS—1873.

[Included in Tables I and II.]

Year and Months	SEX.	State.	Barnstable.	Berkshire.	Bristol.	Dukes and Nantucket.	Essex.	Franklin.	Hampden.	Hampshire.	Middlesex.	Norfolk.	Plymouth.	Suffolk.	Worcester.
THE YEAR	Totals, .	832	2	39	79*	6	113*	20	44	14	166*	54	32	147*	116
	Males, .	422	2	25	37	3	63	12	17	6	71	31	18	71	66
	Fem., .	410	–	14	42	3	50	8	27	8	95	23	14	76	50
Jan.	Totals, .	70	–	4	6	2	12	–	–	–	14	6	4	16	6
	Males, .	31	–	2	2	–	5	–	–	–	7	5	2	5	3
	Fem., .	39	–	2	4	2	7	–	–	–	7	1	2	11	3
Feb.	Totals, .	48	–	–	4	–	12	–	6	–	4	2	4	4	12
	Males, .	23	–	–	2	–	9	–	2	–	3	2	1	–	4
	Fem., .	25	–	–	2	–	3	–	4	–	1	–	3	4	8
Mar.	Totals, .	56	–	2	2	2	10	4	–	4	14	4	2	8	4
	Males, .	27	–	2	1	2	2	3	–	1	7	2	–	4	3
	Fem., .	29	–	–	1	–	8	1	–	3	7	2	2	4	1
Apr.	Totals, .	50	–	2	6	–	10	–	2	–	12	2	4	4	8
	Males, .	31	–	2	2	–	9	–	–	–	5	–	4	4	5
	Fem., .	19	–	–	4	–	1	–	2	–	7	2	–	–	3
May.	Totals, .	58	–	4	2	2	8	–	2	–	8	4	–	16	12
	Males, .	34	–	2	2	1	6	–	–	–	3	1	–	12	7
	Fem., .	24	–	2	–	1	2	–	2	–	5	3	–	4	5
June.	Totals, .	90	2	2	10	–	16	2	8	2	12	4	–	14	18
	Males, .	42	2	1	5	–	7	1	4	1	3	2	–	6	10
	Fem., .	48	–	1	5	–	9	1	4	1	9	2	–	8	8
July.	Totals, .	71	–	2	10	–	4	4	4	2	23	2	4	12	4
	Males, .	37	–	1	6	–	3	3	–	1	12	2	2	4	3
	Fem., .	34	–	1	4	–	1	1	4	1	11	–	2	8	1
Aug.	Totals, .	75	–	4	17	–	8	2	8	2	12	4	4	4	10
	Males, .	41	–	3	7	–	4	–	5	1	4	2	4	4	7
	Fem., .	34	–	1	10	–	4	2	3	1	8	2	–	–	3
Sept.	Totals, .	92	–	10	8	–	13	4	4	–	17	2	–	18	16
	Males, .	44	–	7	4	–	6	2	3	–	8	–	–	6	8
	Fem., .	48	–	3	4	–	7	2	1	–	9	2	–	12	8

SUPPLEMENT A.—Concluded.

Months.	SEX.	State.	Barnstable.	Berkshire.	Bristol.	Dukes and Nantucket	Essex.	Franklin.	Hampden.	Hampshire.	Middlesex.	Norfolk.	Plymouth.	Suffolk.	Worcester.
Oct.	Totals, .	68	–	4	6	–	6	2	2	–	10	10	6	14	8
	Males, .	38	–	2	3	–	3	1	–	–	4	7	4	8	6
	Fem., .	30	–	2	3	–	3	1	2	–	6	3	2	6	2
Nov.	Totals, .	75	–	3	–	–	6	–	4	4	26	6	–	18	8
	Males, .	39	–	3	–	–	4	–	1	2	9	6	–	9	5
	Fem., .	36	–	–	–	–	2	–	3	2	17	–	–	9	3
Dec.	Totals, .	79	–	2	8	–	8	2	4	–	14	8	4	19	10
	Males, .	35	–	–	3	–	5	2	2	–	6	2	1	9	5
	Fem., .	44	–	2	5	–	3	–	2	–	8	6	3	10	5

* Five cases of Triplets were registered in the year 1873. One of three females occurred in Bristol County; one of two males and one female in Essex and Middlesex Counties, respectively; and one of one male and two females in Middlesex and Suffolk Counties, respectively. In three of the five cases both parents were Foreign born, in one case both were American, and in the remaining case the father was American and the mother Foreign born.

Supplement B.

ILLEGITIMATE BIRTHS—1873.

[Included in Tables I. and II.]

Year and Months	SEX.	State.	Barnstable.	Berkshire.	Bristol.	Dukes and Nantucket	Essex.	Franklin.	Hampden.	Hampshire.	Middlesex.	Norfolk.	Plymouth.	Suffolk.	Worcester.
THE YEAR	Totals, .	587	11	14	27	2	39	3	13	10	62	12	42	322	30
	Males, .	294	5	10	11	–	17	–	6	6	32	7	24	166	10
	Fem., .	293	6	4	16	2	22	3	7	4	30	5	18	156	20
Jan.	Totals, .	42	3	2	1	–	2	–	1	1	8	2	2	19	1
	Males, .	21	2	1	1	–	–	–	–	–	7	–	1	8	1
	Fem., .	21	1	1	–	–	2	–	1	1	1	2	1	11	–
Feb.	Totals, .	47	–	1	2	–	4	–	1	1	9	2	4	18	5
	Males, .	23	–	1	1	–	–	–	–	1	6	1	1	10	2
	Fem., .	24	–	–	1	–	4	–	1	–	3	1	3	8	3
Mar.	Totals, .	43	–	1	1	–	5	1	1	1	8	–	5	19	1
	Males, .	19	–	1	1	–	2	–	1	–	3	–	2	9	–
	Fem., .	24	–	–	–	–	3	1	–	1	5	–	3	10	1
Apr.	Totals, .	45	2	1	4	1	–	–	2	1	3	1	4	21	5
	Males, .	18	–	1	1	–	–	–	–	–	1	1	3	9	2
	Fem., .	27	2	–	3	1	–	–	2	1	2	–	1	12	3
May.	Totals, .	42	1	2	3	1	2	1	–	–	1	2	7	21	1
	Males, .	24	1	1	2	–	1	–	–	–	–	1	5	13	–
	Fem., .	18	–	1	1	1	1	1	–	–	1	1	2	8	1
June.	Totals, .	38	–	2	2	–	8	–	1	1	3	–	3	17	1
	Males, .	21	–	2	–	–	4	–	–	1	2	–	2	9	1
	Fem., .	17	–	–	2	–	4	–	1	–	1	–	1	8	–
July.	Totals, .	43	–	1	1	–	4	1	1	1	7	–	3	23	1
	Males, .	23	–	–	–	–	2	–	1	1	3	–	2	13	1
	Fem., .	20	–	1	1	–	2	1	–	–	4	–	1	10	–
Aug.	Totals, .	66	3	–	1	–	2	–	–	1	4	3	5	41	6
	Males, .	40	1	–	1	–	1	–	–	–	3	3	3	26	2
	Fem., .	26	2	–	–	–	1	–	–	1	1	–	2	15	4
Sept.	Totals, .	44	1	–	3	–	2	–	–	1	4	–	2	29	2
	Males, .	25	–	–	2	–	1	–	–	1	2	–	2	17	–
	Fem., .	19	1	–	1	–	1	–	–	–	2	–	–	12	2

SUPPLEMENT B.—Concluded.

Months.	SEX.	STATE.	Barnstable.	Berkshire.	Bristol.	Dukes and Nantucket.	Essex.	Franklin.	Hampden.	Hampshire.	Middlesex.	Norfolk.	Plymouth.	Suffolk.	Worcester.
Oct.	Totals, .	55	1	2	2	–	3	–	–	–	5	–	2	38	2
	Males, .	25	1	2	–	–	2	–	–	–	2	–	2	16	–
	Fem., .	30	–	–	2	–	1	–	–	–	3	–	–	22	2
Nov.	Totals, .	62	–	1	3	–	4	–	2	2	4	1	1	42	2
	Males, .	23	–	1	1	–	2	–	1	2	–	1	–	15	–
	Fem., .	39	–	–	2	–	2	–	1	–	4	–	1	27	2
Dec.	Totals, .	60	–	1	4	–	3	–	4	–	6	1	4	34	3
	Males, .	32	–	–	1	–	2	–	3	–	3	–	1	21	1
	Fem., .	28	–	1	3	–	1	–	1	–	3	1	3	13	2

NOTE.—Of the Illegitimate Births registered in the foregoing table, 32 occurred at the State Almshouse at Tewksbury, 32 at the State Workhouse in Bridgewater, and 140 in the city of Boston. There were also 26 Births in Boston (not included in the above table), of which the parentage was entirely unknown.

TABLE III.—STILL-BORN.

Distinguishing by Counties, by Months, and by Sex, the registered Number of Still-Births during the year

1873.

Year and Months	SEX	STATE	Barnstable	Berkshire	Bristol	Dukes and Nantucket	Essex	Franklin	Hampden	Hampshire	Middlesex	Norfolk	Plymouth	Suffolk	Worcester
THE YEAR	Totals, .	1246	13	22	128	1	155	11	35	7	225	63	30	526	30
	Males, .	715	9	11	73	–	83	7	14	4	129	32	17	319	17
	Fem., .	455	4	10	49	–	52	1	17	3	70	23	11	204	11
	Unk., .	76	–	1	6	1	20	3	4	–	26	8	2	3	2
Jan.	Totals, .	103	2	–	7	–	14	1	4	–	19	6	1	48	1
	Males, .	53	2	–	2	–	6	1	2	–	10	4	1	24	1
	Fem., .	44	–	–	4	–	5	–	2	–	7	2	–	24	–
	Unk., .	6	–	–	1	–	3	–	–	–	2	–	–	–	–
Feb.	Totals, .	76	–	1	9	–	14	–	4	–	13	3	1	30	1
	Males, .	55	–	1	6	–	8	–	1	–	9	2	1	26	1
	Fem., .	19	–	–	2	–	5	–	3	–	4	1	–	4	–
	Unk., .	2	–	–	1	–	1	–	–	–	–	–	–	–	–
Mar.	Totals, .	122	–	2	17	–	16	1	3	–	17	4	1	60	1
	Males, .	66	–	1	7	–	9	–	1	–	9	1	1	36	1
	Fem., .	45	–	1	9	–	6	–	1	–	4	1	–	23	–
	Unk., .	11	–	–	1	–	1	1	1	–	4	2	–	1	–
Apr.	Totals, .	117	2	1	11	–	15	2	1	1	23	4	4	49	4
	Males, .	72	2	–	6	–	7	2	–	1	14	1	4	31	4
	Fem., .	38	–	–	5	–	5	–	1	–	7	3	–	17	–
	Unk., .	7	–	1	–	–	3	–	–	–	2	–	–	1	–
May.	Totals, .	76	–	–	8	–	10	–	4	–	14	3	1	35	1
	Males, .	51	–	–	7	–	5	–	2	–	12	3	–	22	–
	Fem., .	21	–	–	1	–	4	–	1	–	–	–	1	13	1
	Unk., .	4	–	–	–	–	1	–	1	–	2	–	–	–	–
June.	Totals, .	99	–	6	8	–	12	1	2	1	17	3	5	39	5
	Males, .	60	–	3	4	–	9	–	1	–	9	3	2	27	2
	Fem., .	37	–	3	4	–	3	–	1	1	7	–	3	12	3
	Unk., .	2	–	–	–	–	–	1	–	–	1	–	–	–	–

TABLE III.—Concluded.

Months	SEX	State	Barnstable	Berkshire	Bristol	Dukes and Nantucket	Essex	Franklin	Hampden	Hampshire	Middlesex	Norfolk	Plymouth	Suffolk	Worcester
July	Totals, .	120	2	1	9	–	9	3	3	2	31	5	4	47	4
	Males, .	73	–	1	2	–	6	2	2	1	18	5	2	32	2
	Fem., .	34	2	–	5	–	2	1	1	1	7	–	–	15	–
	Unk., .	13	–	–	2	–	1	–	–	–	6	–	2	–	2
Aug.	Totals, .	93	2	–	10	1	11	1	6	–	11	4	2	43	2
	Males, .	56	2	–	5	–	5	1	2	–	6	2	1	31	1
	Fem., .	33	–	–	5	–	5	–	3	–	4	2	1	12	1
	Unk., .	4	–	–	–	1	1	–	1	–	1	–	–	–	–
Sept.	Totals, .	96	2	2	8	–	13	–	3	1	16	5	1	44	1
	Males, .	50	1	–	6	–	7	–	1	–	10	2	–	23	–
	Fem., .	42	1	2	2	–	4	–	2	1	5	2	1	21	1
	Unk., .	4	–	–	–	–	2	–	–	–	1	1	–	–	–
Oct.	Totals, .	114	–	4	8	–	17	–	2	2	25	11	4	37	4
	Males, .	52	–	2	6	–	8	–	1	2	10	3	–	20	–
	Fem., .	50	–	2	2	–	4	–	1	–	10	6	4	17	4
	Unk., .	12	–	–	–	–	5	–	–	–	5	2	–	–	–
Nov.	Totals, .	108	2	4	13	–	13	–	1	–	22	5	2	44	2
	Males, .	58	1	3	6	–	7	–	1	–	11	1	2	24	2
	Fem , .	46	1	1	6	–	6	–	–	–	10	2	–	20	–
	Unk., .	4	–	–	1	–	–	–	–	–	1	2	–	–	–
Dec.	Totals, .	122	1	1	20	–	11	2	2	–	17	10	4	50	4
	Males, .	69	1	–	16	–	6	1	–	–	11	5	3	23	3
	Fem., .	46	–	1	4	–	3	–	1	–	5	4	1	26	1
	Unk., .	7	–	–	–	–	2	1	1	–	1	1	–	1	–

TABLE IV.—MARRIAGES.

Distinguishing by Counties, and by Months, the Number of Marriages registered during the year

1873.

YEAR AND MONTHS.	State.	Barnstable.	Berkshire.	Bristol.	Dukes and Nantucket.	Essex.	Franklin.	Hampden.	Hampshire.	Middlesex.	Norfolk.	Plymouth.	Suffolk.	Worcester.
THE YEAR, .	16,437	297	513	1440	70	2200	303	921	343	3106	800	642	3952	1850
January, .	1,532	45	34	145	9	191	24	93	30	273	79	62	368	179
February, .	1,328	24	38	102	4	188	16	91	17	240	60	39	357	152
March, . .	734	18	30	52	5	133	26	43	23	121	34	38	133	78
April, . .	1,208	24	34	93	5	168	31	55	24	223	81	48	287	135
May, . .	1,479	21	56	133	3	182	30	90	43	262	71	62	350	176
June, . .	1,576	12	50	128	3	219	29	84	37	298	87	63	405	161
July, . .	1,188	14	27	109	6	146	21	74	17	255	59	32	295	133
August, .	1,090	15	36	113	6	136	20	62	26	187	43	44	282	120
September, .	1,454	18	50	131	5	188	15	71	24	307	59	51	372	163
October, .	1,637	24	53	150	6	213	35	84	35	310	71	59	410	187
November, .	1,994	50	52	180	10	277	23	117	35	384	94	88	459	225
December, .	1,192	32	36	104	7	158	33	55	32	244	62	55	234	140
Unknown, .	25	–	17	–	1	1	–	2	–	2	–	1	–	1

Table V.—MARRIAGES.

Exhibiting the Social Condition and Ages, respectively, of Parties Married during the year

1873.

Aggregate—Of all Conditions.

Age of Males.	All Ages.	Under 20	20 to 25	25 to 30	30 to 35	35 to 40	40 to 45	45 to 50	50 to 55	55 to 60	60 to 65	65 to 70	70 to 75	75 to 80	Over 80	Unknown.
						Age of Females.										
All Ages,	16,437	3,380	7,232	3,266	1,191	621	352	176	82	42	36	17	1	1	-	40
Und. 20,	313	231	70	8	3	-	-	-	-	-	-	-	-	-	-	1
20 to 25,	6,564	2,270	3,717	504	57	12	1	-	-	-	-	-	-	-	-	3
25 to 30,	4,989	660	2,511	1,538	227	40	8	1	-	-	-	-	-	-	-	4
30 to 35,	2,015	149	652	742	377	77	14	2	-	-	-	-	-	-	-	2
35 to 40,	971	50	188	273	258	157	36	8	-	-	-	-	-	-	-	1
40 to 45,	545	11	54	104	134	113	103	19	1	2	1	-	-	-	-	3
45 to 50,	392	5	26	53	73	109	64	48	11	-	-	-	-	-	-	3
50 to 55,	259	3	10	26	41	59	65	30	17	4	2	-	-	-	-	2
55 to 60,	139	-	4	10	13	33	28	29	11	6	3	2	-	-	-	-
60 to 65,	112	1	-	6	3	15	20	18	26	11	11	-	-	-	-	1
65 to 70,	65	-	-	1	3	3	9	17	9	12	6	5	-	-	-	-
70 to 75,	35	-	-	-	1	3	4	2	4	4	10	7	-	-	-	-
75 to 80,	15	-	-	-	-	-	-	2	3	3	3	2	1	1	-	-
Over 80,	1	-	-	-	-	-	-	-	-	*-	-	-	1	-	-	-
Unk.,	22	-	-	1	1	-	-	-	-	-	-	-	-	-	-	20

(A.)   First Marriage of both Parties.

Age of Males.	All Ages.	Under 20	20 to 25	25 to 30	30 to 35	35 to 40	40 to 45	45 to 50	50 to 55	55 to 60	60 to 65	65 to 70	70 to 75	75 to 80	Over 80	Unknown.
All Ages,	13,136	3,219	6,668	2,503	546	132	39	9	4	-	-	-	-	-	-	16
Und. 20,	311	231	70	7	2	-	-	-	-	-	-	-	-	-	-	1
20 to 25,	6,342	2,238	3,622	436	39	4	1	-	-	-	-	-	-	-	-	2
25 to 30,	4,426	608	2,327	1,327	148	13	-	-	-	-	-	-	-	-	-	3
30 to 35,	1,406	113	509	536	216	24	6	-	-	-	-	-	-	-	-	2
35 to 40,	426	22	108	143	97	46	8	1	-	-	-	-	-	-	-	1
40 to 45,	126	5	21	34	30	23	13	-	-	-	-	-	-	-	-	-
45 to 50,	55	1	7	15	6	16	4	5	1	-	-	-	-	-	-	-
50 to 55,	23	-	3	4	6	5	4	1	-	-	-	-	-	-	-	-
55 to 60,	6	-	1	-	1	-	2	1	1	-	-	-	-	-	-	-
60 to 65,	4	1	-	-	-	1	-	1	1	-	-	-	-	-	-	-
65 to 70,	2	-	-	-	1	-	-	-	1	-	-	-	-	-	-	-
70 to 75,	1	-	-	-	-	-	1	-	-	-	-	-	-	-	-	-
75 to 80,	-	-	-	-	-	-	-	-	-	-	-	-	-	-	-	-
Over 80,	-	-	-	-	-	-	-	-	-	-	-	-	-	-	-	-
Unk.,	8	-	-	1	-	-	-	-	-	-	-	-	-	-	-	7

TABLE V.—Continued.

(B.) First Marriage of Male and subsequent Marriage of Female.

AGE OF MALES	ALL AGES	Under 20	AGE OF FEMALES.													Unknown
			20 to 25	25 to 30	30 to 35	35 to 40	40 to 45	45 to 50	50 to 55	55 to 60	60 to 65	65 to 70	70 to 75	75 to 80	Over 80	
ALL AGES,	752	8	123	251	182	113	48	14	5	3	1	—	—	—	—	4
Und. 20,	2	—	—	1	1	—	—	—	—	—	—	—	—	—	—	—
20 to 25,	150	6	60	59	16	8	—	—	—	—	—	—	—	.	—	1
25 to 30,	259	1	46	118	64	22	6	1	—	—	—	—	—	—	—	1
30 to 35,	158	—	11	51	65	24	7	—	—	—	—	—	—	—	—	—
35 to 40,	89	1	3	18	21	32	12	2	—	—	—	—	—	—	—	—
40 to 45,	47	—	2	4	7	14	13	4	—	2	—	—	—	—	—	1
45 to 50,	29	—	—	—	7	8	6	5	3	—	—	—	—	—	—	—
50 to 55,	9	—	1	—	—	3	2	1	1	1	—	—	—	—	—	—
55 to 60,	2	—	—	—	1	1	—	—	—	—	—	—	—	—	—	—
60 to 65,	3	—	—	—	—	1	2	—	—	—	—	—	—	—	—	—
65 to 70,	2	—	—	—	—	—	—	1	1	—	—	—	—	—	—	—
70 to 75,	1	—	—	—	—	—	—	—	—	—	—	1	—	—	—	—
75 to 80,	—	—	—	—	—	—	—	—	—	—	—	—	—	—	—	—
Over 80,	—	—	—	•	—	—	—	—	—	—	—	—	—	—	—	—
Unk.,	1	—	—	—	—	—	—	—	—	—	—	—	—	—	—	1

(C.) Subsequent Marriage of the Male but First Marriage of the Female.

AGE OF MALES	ALL AGES	Under 20	20 to 25	25 to 30	30 to 35	35 to 40	40 to 45	45 to 50	50 to 55	55 to 60	60 to 65	65 to 70	70 to 75	75 to 80	Over 80	Unknown
ALL AGES,	1,543	148	401	405	277	152	92	32	15	8	5	2	—	—	—	6
Und. 20,	—	—	—	—	—	—	—	—	—	—	—	—	—	—	—	—
20 to 25,	61	25	30	6	—	—	—	—	—	—	—	—	—	—	—	—
25 to 30,	264	50	131	74	8	1	—	—	—	—	—	—	—	—	—	—
30 to 35,	350	34	119	131	57	9	—	—	—	—	—	—	—	—	—	—
35 to 40,	295	26	70	81	83	28	6	1	—	—	—	—	—	—	—	—
40 to 45,	204	6	26	51	58	32	27	2	1	—	—	—	—	—	—	1
45 to 50,	147	4	17	31	41	35	10	5	2	—	—	—	—	—	—	2
50 to 55,	109	3	5	19	18	23	28	8	4	—	—	—	—	—	—	1
55 to 60,	53	—	3	6	7	15	10	7	1	1	1	2	—	—	—	—
60 to 65,	38	—	—	5	3	8	7	4	6	2	3	—	—	—	—	—
65 to 70,	13	—	—	1	1	1	2	4	—	4	—	—	—	—	—	—
70 to 75,	4	—	—	—	1	—	2	—	—	—	1	—	—	—	—	—
75 to 80,	3	—	—	—	—	—	—	1	1	1	—	—	—	—	—	—
Over 80,	—	—	—	—	—	—	—	—	—	—	—	—	—	—	—	—
Unk.,	2	—	—	—	—	—	—	—	—	—	—	—	—	—	—	2

TABLE V.—Concluded.

(D.)　Subsequent Marriage of both Parties.

AGE OF MALES.	ALL AGES.	Under 20	20 to 25	25 to 30	30 to 35	35 to 40	40 to 45	45 to 50	50 to 55	55 to 60	60 to 65	65 to 70	70 to 75	75 to 80	Over 80	Unknown.
ALL AGES,	988	2	39	103	186	224	173	121	57	31	30	15	1	1	–	5
Und. 20,	–	–	–	–	–	–	–	–	–	–	–	–	–	–	–	–
20 to 25,	8	–	4	2	2	–	–	–	–	–	–	–	–	–	–	–
25 to 30,	38	–	7	18	7	4	2	–	–	–	–	–	–	–	–	–
30 to 35,	100	2	13	23	39	20	1	2	–	–	–	–	–	–	–	–
35 to 40,	159	–	7	30	57	51	10	4	–	–	–	–	–	–	–	–
40 to 45,	168	–	5	15	39	44	50	13	–	–	1	–	–	–	–	1
45 to 50,	161	–	2	7	19	50	44	33	5	–	–	–	–	–	–	1
50 to 55,	118	–	1	3	17	28	31	20	12	3	2	–	–	–	–	1
55 to 60,	78	–	–	4	4	17	16	21	9	5	2	–	–	–	–	–
60 to 65,	66	–	–	1	–	5	11	13	18	9	8	–	–	–	–	1
65 to 70,	48	–	–	–	1	2	7	12	7	8	6	5	–	–	–	–
70 to 75,	29	–	–	–	–	3	1	2	4	4	8	7	–	–	–	–
75 to 80,	12	–	–	–	–	–	–	1	2	2	3	2	1	1	–	–
Over 80,	1	–	–	–	–	–	–	–	–	–	–	1	–	–	–	–
Unk.,	2	–	–	–	1	–	–	–	–	–	–	–	–	–	–	1

(E.)　Condition of Parties not stated.

AGE OF MALES.	ALL AGES.	Under 20	20 to 25	25 to 30	30 to 35	35 to 40	40 to 45	45 to 50	50 to 55	55 to 60	60 to 65	65 to 70	70 to 75	75 to 80	Over 80	Unknown.
ALL AGES,	18	3	1	4	–	–	–	–	1	–	–	–	–	–	–	9
Und. 20,	–	–	–	–	–	–	–	–	–	–	–	–	–	–	–	–
20 to 25,	3	1	1	1	–	–	–	–	–	–	–	–	–	–	–	–
25 to 30,	2	1	–	1	–	–	–	–	–	–	–	–	–	–	–	–
30 to 35,	1	–	–	1	–	–	–	–	–	–	–	–	–	–	–	–
35 to 40,	2	1	–	1	–	–	–	–	–	–	–	–	–	–	–	–
40 to 45,	–	–	–	–	–	–	–	–	–	–	–	–	–	–	–	–
45 to 50,	–	–	–	–	–	–	–	–	–	–	–	–	–	–	–	–
50 to 55,	–	–	–	–	–	–	–	–	–	–	–	–	–	–	–	–
55 to 60,	–	–	–	–	–	–	–	–	–	–	–	–	–	–	–	–
60 to 65,	1	–	–	–	–	–	–	–	1	–	–	–	–	–	–	–
65 to 70,	–	–	–	–	–	–	–	–	–	–	–	–	–	–	–	–
70 to 75,	–	–	–	–	–	–	–	–	–	–	–	–	–	–	–	–
75 to 80,	–	–	–	–	–	–	–	–	–	–	–	–	–	–	–	–
Over 80,	–	–	–	–	–	–	–	–	–	–	–	–	–	–	–	–
Unk.,	9	–	–	–	–	–	–	–	–	–	–	–	–	–	–	9

TABLE VI.—DEATHS.

Distinguishing by Counties, by Months, and by Sex, the registered Number of Persons who Died during the year

1873.

Year and Months	SEX.	STATE.	Barnstable.	Berkshire.	Bristol.	Dukes and Nantucket.	Essex.	Franklin.	Hampden.	Hampshire.	Middlesex.	Norfolk.	Plymouth.	Suffolk.	Worcester.
THE YEAR	Totals,	33912	576	1111	2912	164	4429	568	1915	803	6539	1677	1235	8324	3659
	Males,	17242	313	556	1524	80	2270	270	978	400	3236	808	616	4330	1861
	Fem.,	16642	255	555	1387	84	2149	298	936	403	3299	868	616	3994	1798
	Unk.,	28	8	–	1	–	10	–	1	–	4	1	3	–	–
Jan.	Totals,	2,809	37	85	209	10	308	46	138	69	534	127	90	855	301
	Males,	1,470	21	37	113	4	159	21	70	35	281	55	40	480	154
	Fem.,	1,338	16	48	96	6	148	25	68	34	253	72	50	375	147
	Unk.,	1	–	–	–	–	1	–	–	–	–	–	–	–	–
Feb.	Totals,	2,478	36	74	176	10	297	32	125	54	511	123	87	651	302
	Males,	1,225	21	34	90	4	148	12	58	26	256	52	38	337	149
	Fem.,	1,251	15	40	86	6	147	20	67	28	255	71	49	314	153
	Unk.,	2	–	–	–	–	2	–	–	–	–	–	–	–	–
Mar.	Totals,	2,970	49	97	259	9	407	47	159	68	551	166	96	739	323
	Males,	1,489	26	44	142	6	195	20	89	28	264	82	47	386	160
	Fem.,	1,479	23	53	117	3	211	27	70	40	287	83	49	353	163
	Unk.,	2	–	–	–	–	1	–	–	–	–	1	–	–	–
Apr.	Totals,	2,685	42	85	248	20	389	36	142	57	507	148	94	645	272
	Males,	1,349	29	36	126	11	175	15	77	31	277	68	51	319	134
	Fem.,	1,336	13	49	122	9	214	21	65	26	230	80	43	326	138
May.	Totals,	2,520	35	73	205	12	342	51	129	72	498	134	99	592	278
	Males,	1,309	22	37	113	6	180	29	61	28	242	67	54	323	147
	Fem.,	1,207	11	36	92	6	161	22	67	44	256	67	45	269	131
	Unk.,	4	2	–	–	–	1	–	1	–	–	–	–	–	–
June.	Totals,	2,315	48	81	168	21	305	29	127	56	438	126	99	569	248
	Males,	1,231	28	47	106	11	160	11	65	30	215	69	56	299	134
	Fem.,	1,081	19	34	62	10	144	18	62	26	223	57	42	270	114
	Unk.,	3	1	–	–	–	1	–	–	–	–	–	1	–	–
July.	Totals,	3,338	54	99	280	14	432	46	258	74	656	142	105	835	343
	Males,	1,678	26	48	135	3	222	27	130	36	315	69	57	438	172
	Fem.,	1,654	25	51	145	11	209	19	128	38	341	73	46	397	171
	Unk.,	6	3	–	–	–	1	–	–	–	–	–	2	–	–

TABLE VI.—Concluded.

Months	SEX.	State	Barnstable	Berkshire	Bristol	Dukes and Nantucket	Essex	Franklin	Hampden	Hampshire	Middlesex	Norfolk	Plymouth	Suffolk	Worcester
Aug.	Totals,	4,039	69	130	331	12	645	69	237	87	801	206	138	880	434
	Males,	2,141	36	71	178	6	382	36	107	40	402	104	78	472	229
	Fem.,	1,896	33	59	153	6	261	33	130	47	399	102	60	408	205
	Unk.,	2	–	–	–	–	2	–	–	–	–	–	–	–	–
Sept.	Totals,	3,074	58	107	283	20	399	70	176	70	614	153	99	714	311
	Males,	1,573	33	58	148	9	202	29	93	36	308	74	47	375	161
	Fem ,	1,500	24	49	135	11	197	41	83	34	306	79	52	339	150
	Unk.,	1	1	–	–	–	–	–	–	–	–	–	–	–	–
Oct.	Totals,	2,659	54	100	235	14	344	52	140	81	516	129	114	590	290
	Males,	1,315	21	52	124	5	178	25	74	38	253	73	54	279	139
	Fem.,	1,342	33	48	110	9	165	27	66	43	263	56	60	311	151
	Unk.,	2	–	–	1	–	1	–	–	–	–	–	–	–	–
Nov.	Totals,	2,469	39	97	271	8	277	44	148	52	442	112	106	611	262
	Males,	1,219	21	50	132	5	141	20	76	28	216	41	50	307	132
	Fem.,	1,249	18	47	139	3	136	24	72	24	225	71	56	304	130
	Unk.,	1	–	–	–	–	–	–	–	–	1	–	–	–	–
Dec.	Totals,	2,556	55	83	247	14	284	46	136	63	471	111	108	643	295
	Males,	1,243	29	42	117	10	128	25	78	44	207	54	44	315	150
	Fem.,	1,309	25	41	130	4	156	21	58	19	261	57	64	328	145
	Unk.,	4	1	–	–	–	–	–	–	–	3	–	–	–	–

5

TABLE VII.—DEATHS BY AGE AND SEX,

Distinguishing by Age and by Sex, the Number of Deaths registered in each Population, distinguishing Sex, according to the U. S. Census of 1870,—and

STATE AND COUNTIES.	Population. U. S. Census, 1870.		Percentage of Deaths to Pop.	No. of Deaths Regist'd 1873.	Under 1	1 to 2	2 to 3	3 to 4	4 to 5	5 to 10	10 to 15
Massachusetts	1,457,351	Per.	2·33	33,912	7,911	2,195	1,001	715	552	1,328	737
	703,779	Ma.	2·45	17,242	4,377	1,139	491	341	272	720	348
	753,572	Fe.	2·21	16,642	3,507	1,056	509	374	280	608	389
	-	U.	-	28	27	-	1	-	-	-	-
BARNSTABLE,	32,774	Per.	1·76	576	86	14	12	5	5	14	12
	16,035	Ma.	1·95	313	49	8	9	3	5	6	4
	16,739	Fe.	1·52	255	29	6	3	2	-	8	8
	-	U.	-	8	8	-	-	-	-	-	-
BERKSHIRE,	64,827	Per.	1·71	1,111	218	58	29	22	*19	45	25
	32,294	Ma.	1·72	556	130	27	10	12	10	26	13
	32,533	Fe.	1·71	555	88	31	19	10	9	19	12
BRISTOL,	102,886	Per.	2·83	2,912	708	213	98	77	64	151	78
	49,419	Ma.	3·08	1,524	424	111	44	37	30	94	35
	53,467	Fe.	2·59	1,387	283	102	54	40	34	57	43
	-	U.	-	1	1	-	-	-	-	-	-
DUKES,	3,787	Per.	1·53	58	7	1	1	-	-	1	3
	1,819	Ma.	1·76	32	3	-	1	-	-	1	1
	1,968	Fe.	1·32	26	4	1	-	-	-	-	3
ESSEX,	200,843	Per.	2·21	4,429	1,005	280	114	78	60	157	25
	95,498	Ma.	2·38	2,270	569	145	57	36	31	80	43
	105,345	Fe.	2·04	2,149	427	135	56	42	29	77	43
	-	U.	-	10	9	-	1	-	-	-	-
FRANKLIN,	32,635	Per.	1·74	568	83	22	5	10	5	20	13
	16,362	Ma.	1·65	270	51	12	5	5	1	10	7
	16,273	Fe.	1·83	298	32	10	-	5	4	10	6
HAMPDEN,	78,409	Per.	2·44	1,915	473	149	68	35	36	97	48
	37,382	Ma.	2·62	978	250	78	38	15	16	48	22
	41,027	Fe.	2·28	936	222	71	30	20	20	49	26
	-	U.	-	1	1	-	-	-	-	-	-
HAMPSHIRE,	44,388	Per.	1·81	803	168	46	17	6	8	17	17
	21,443	Ma.	1·87	400	92	30	8	2	5	8	9
	22,945	Fe.	1·76	403	76	16	9	4	3	9	8
MIDDLESEX,	274,353	Per.	2·38	6,539	1,593	417	176	144	107	266	126
	131,959	Ma.	2·45	3,236	819	216	80	65	55	135	62
	142,394	Fe.	2·32	3,299	770	201	96	79	52	131	64
	-	U.	-	4	4	-	-	-	-	-	-
NANTUCKET,	4,123	Per.	2·57	106	7	2	1	-	-	2	-
	1,825	Ma.	2·63	48	4	-	1	-	-	2	-
	2,298	Fe.	2·52	58	3	2	-	-	-	-	-
NORFOLK,	89,443	Per.	1·87	1,677	358	88	48	38	26	62	34
	42,944	Ma.	1·88	808	200	46	20	14	6	36	16
	46,499	Fe.	1·87	868	157	42	28	24	20	26	18
	-	U.	-	1	1	-	-	-	-	-	-
PLYMOUTH,	65,365	Per.	1·89	1,235	221	55	33	19	14	45	35
	32,116	Ma.	1·92	616	126	28	16	9	10	23	15
	33,249	Fe.	1·85	616	92	27	17	10	4	22	20
	-	U.	-	3	3	-	-	-	-	-	-
SUFFOLK,	270,802	Per.	3·07	8,324	2,175	621	281	221	150	339	163
	129,482	Ma.	3·34	4,330	1,186	319	144	111	72	189	71
	141,320	Fe.	2·83	3,994	989	302	137	110	78	150	92
WORCESTER,	192,716	Per.	1·90	3,659	809	229	118	60	58	112	92
	95,201	Ma.	1·95	1,861	474	119	58	32	31	62	45
	97,515	Fe.	1·84	1,798	335	110	60	28	27	50	47

AND BY COUNTIES AND TOWNS—1873.

County and Town in the State, during the year 1873,—in connection with the also with the Percentage of the Registered Number of Deaths to the Population.

	15 to 20	20 to 25	25 to 30	30 to 35	35 to 40	40 to 45	45 to 50	50 to 55	55 to 60	60 to 65	65 to 70	70 to 75	75 to 80	80 to 85	85 to 90	90 to 95	95 and over	Unknown
	1341	1,876	1,673	1,484	1377	1112	1108	1146	1073	1248	1386	1385	1222	934	574	226	78	280
	612	980	764	674	628	541	580	589	605	648	712	672	593	410	223	86	19	218
	729	896	909	760	749	571	528	557	468	600	674	713	629	524	551	140	59	62
	24	47	24	26	19	18	20	11	22	28	32	50	45	34	14	8	2	4
	11	27	12	12	8	11	11	5	13	15	23	29	25	15	3	5	1	3
	13	20	12	14	11	7	9	6	9	13	9	21	20	19	11	3	1	1
	40	66	46	36	38	38	35	32	40	54	58	59	47	41	37	13	10	5
	12	31	20	14	17	21	20	20	24	24	29	28	19	19	18	8	2	2
	28	35	26	22	21	17	15	12	16	30	29	81	28	22	19	5	8	3
	116	143	136	102	103	67	85	78	93	100	113	129	89	83	42	18	3	23
	51	78	60	52	52	24	41	43	55	61	58	56	48	34	14	9	1	12
	65	65	76	50	51	43	44	35	38	39	55	73	41	49	28	9	2	11
	1	3	2	–	3	1	3	6	1	4	4	2	6	4	3	2	–	–
	1	1	1	–	3	1	1	1	1	4	4	1	5	2	1	–	–	–
	–	2	1	–	–	1	2	5	–	–	–	1	1	2	2	2	–	–
	189	246	167	179	165	154	127	156	123	161	203	200	178	127	76	41	13	159
	82	114	71	77	68	62	67	86	63	76	94	98	87	61	31	12	2	153
	107	132	96	102	97	72	60	70	60	85	109	102	91	66	45	29	11	6
	30	39	20	23	18	21	14	29	21	33	37	34	32	31	22	5	–	1
	13	19	5	8	7	6	8	16	15	12	18	13	16	15	7	1	–	–
	17	20	15	15	11	15	6	13	6	21	19	21	16	16	15	4	–	1
	108	118	86	69	77	57	42	50	48	56	82	64	46	48	29	13	5	11
	56	76	32	31	40	26	24	24	26	32	36	35	23	27	9	6	1	7
	42	42	54	38	37	31	18	26	22	24	46	29	23	21	20	7	4	4
	33	42	33	38	34	24	26	26	28	35	41	50	49	34	20	6	1	4
	13	27	10	19	16	8	16	16	12	18	26	29	26	9	6	2	1	1
	20	15	23	19	18	16	10	10	16	17	15	30	23	25	14	4	–	3
	239	352	335	287	275	211	221	241	196	262	269	266	215	165	94	34	15	33
	112	161	146	132	119	113	117	130	111	138	136	137	104	76	34	15	6	19
	127	191	189	155	156	98	104	111	85	124	133	129	111	89	60	21	9	14
	1	2	2	4	4	0	1	3	13	8	10	12	11	11	4	3	–	–
	1	–	1	2	2	1	–	1	5	5	3	4	5	7	6	2	–	–
	–	2	1	2	2	4	1	2	8	5	6	7	4	5	2	2	–	–
67	73	83	79	63	52	52	53	66	63	72	93	80	63	43	17	6	7	
31	29	40	32	23	29	27	23	38	29	39	40	48	20	14	4	1	3	
36	44	43	38	40	23	25	30	28	34	33	53	32	43	29	13	5	4	
35	61	60	44	45	33	46	42	40	60	81	77	71	55	44	11	4	4	
15	35	29	16	17	15	19	20	23	31	48	37	37	31	21	4	4	2	
20	26	31	28	28	18	27	22	17	29	33	40	40	29	23	7	4	2	
296	580	498	404	409	328	317	298	265	242	231	187	180	115	64	25	8	7	
146	291	263	207	214	167	164	145	155	129	110	94	70	45	22	12	1	3	
150	209	235	197	195	161	153	153	110	113	121	93	110	70	42	13	7	4	
162	184	181	153	124	123	119	121	117	142	153	162	173	123	82	30	11	22	
68	91	74	72	42	58	65	59	64	76	87	79	84	55	41	9	3	13	
94	93	107	80	82	65	54	62	53	66	66	83	89	68	41	21	8	9	

Table VII.—Continued.

COUNTIES AND TOWNS.	POPULATION—1870.		DEATHS.			Und. 1	1 to 2	2 to 3	3 to 4	4 to 5
	Persons.	Sex.	Per ct. to Pop.	Persons.	Sex.					
BARNSTABLE Co.	32,774	Tot. 32,774 Ma. 16,035 Fe. 16,739 U. .	. 1·76 .	. 576 .	576 313 255 8	86 49 29 8	14 8 6 –	12 9 3 –	5 3 2 –	5 5 – –
Barnstable, .	4,793	Ma. 2,298 Fe. 2,495 U. .	1·34 .	64 .	32 30 2	6 3 2	– 1 –	– – –	– – –	– – –
Brewster, . .	1,259	Ma. 614 Fe. 645	1·59	20	12 8	3 –	– –	– –	– –	2 –
Chatham, . .	2,411	Ma. 1,197 Fe. 1,214	1·16	28	16 12	1 –	– –	– –	– –	– –
Dennis, . .	3,269	Ma. 1,578 Fe. 1,691	1·77	58	40 18	4 2	1 –	4 1	1 –	– –
Eastham, . .	668	Ma. 317 Fe. 321	2·69	18	6 12	– –	2 –	– –	– –	– –
Falmouth, .	2,237	Ma. 1,111 Fe. 1,126	2·59	58	31 27	3 3	– 1	– –	– –	– –
Harwich, . .	3,080	Ma. 1,540 Fe. 1,540 U. .	1·52 .	47 .	24 18 5	– 3 5	– – –	– 1 –	– – –	1 – –
Mashpee, . .	348	Ma. 160 Fe. 188	2·59	9	5 4	1 1	– –	– –	– –	– –
Orleans, . .	1,323	Ma. 630 Fe. 693	2·57	34	20 14	4 –	– –	1 –	– –	– –
Provincetown, .	3,865	Ma. 1,907 Fe. 1,958	2·10	81	45 36	13 9	2 2	3 –	1 –	1 –
Sandwich, .	3,694	Ma. 1,800 Fe. 1,894	1·57	58	30 28	5 3	2 –	– –	1 1	– –
Truro, . .	1,269	Ma. 625 Fe. 644	1·34	17	10 7	3 –	1 –	– –	– –	– –
Wellfleet, .	2,135	Ma. 1,085 Fe. 1,050	1·78	38	21 17	3 3	– –	1 –	– –	1 –
Yarmouth, .	2,423	Ma. 1,143 Fe. 1,280 U. .	1·90 .	46 .	21 24 1	3 2 1	– 2 –	– 1 –	– 1 –	– – –
BERKSHIRE Co.,	64,827	Tot. 64,827 Ma. 32,294 Fe. 32,533	. 1·71	. 1,111	1,111 556 555	218 130 88	58 27 31	29 10 19	22 12 10	19 10 9
Adams, . .	12,090	Ma. 6,063 Fe. 6,027	2·22	269	136 133	37 24	9 11	4 7	5 2	3 5
Alford, . .	430	Ma. 223 Fe. 207	1·86	8	6 2	1 –	– –	– –	– –	– –
Becket, . .	1,346	Ma. 683 Fe. 663	1·63	22	10 12	4 2	– –	– –	– 1	– –

Age and Sex, by Towns.

5 to 10	10 to 15	15 to 20	20 to 25	25 to 30	30 to 35	35 to 40	40 to 45	45 to 50	50 to 55	55 to 60	60 to 65	65 to 70	70 to 75	75 to 80	80 to 85	85 to 90	90 to 95	95 & over	Unknown
14	12	24	47	24	26	19	18	20	11	22	28	32	50	45	34	14	8	2	4
6	4	11	27	12	12	8	11	11	5	13	15	23	29	25	15	3	5	1	3
8	8	13	20	12	12	14	11	7	9	6	9	13	9	21	20	19	11	3	1
–	–	–	–	–	–	–	–	–	–	–	–	–	–	–	–	–	–	–	–
–	–	2	2	–	2	1	1	1	2	–	1	4	3	4	1	–	–	1	1
–	1	–	2	1	1	3	1	1	1	3	2	3	3	1	1	2	–	–	–
–	–	–	–	–	–	–	–	–	–	–	–	–	–	–	–	–	–	–	–
–	–	–	–	–	–	–	–	–	–	–	1	1	3	1	1	–	–	–	–
–	–	1	2	1	–	–	–	–	–	–	–	1	1	1	1	–	–	–	–
–	2	1	2	–	–	1	–	2	–	2	–	–	1	2	1	–	1	–	–
–	1	–	–	1	–	1	1	–	1	1	1	–	1	–	3	1	–	–	–
2	–	2	7	2	4	1	1	1	1	2	1	2	1	1	1	–	1	–	–
–	2	–	2	–	2	1	1	2	–	–	2	–	–	–	2	1	–	–	–
–	–	–	–	1	1	1	1	1	2	–	–	1	–	3	2	–	1	–	–
1	–	–	–	1	1	1	1	1	2	–	–	1	–	2	–	1	1	–	–
–	–	–	4	2	–	–	1	2	–	–	2	4	4	1	5	1	2	–	–
–	–	5	3	–	–	–	–	–	1	–	1	–	4	3	3	1	1	–	1
1	1	2	1	–	1	1	1	–	–	2	1	2	4	4	2	–	–	–	–
–	1	–	1	–	4	–	1	–	–	1	1	–	2	1	2	–	–	–	–
–	–	–	–	–	–	–	–	–	–	–	–	–	–	–	–	–	–	–	–
–	–	–	2	–	–	–	–	–	–	1	–	–	–	1	–	–	–	–	–
–	1	1	–	–	1	–	–	–	–	–	–	–	–	1	–	–	–	–	–
–	–	1	1	–	–	1	–	2	–	1	2	–	5	1	1	–	–	–	–
2	–	1	–	3	1	–	1	–	–	1	1	–	1	2	1	–	–	–	–
1	1	1	2	3	2	1	3	2	–	1	–	3	2	1	–	–	1	–	1
1	1	1	4	1	–	1	1	1	1	1	–	2	5	2	1	1	1	–	–
1	–	–	2	3	–	–	2	1	1	1	1	3	2	3	1	–	–	–	1
–	–	3	5	3	–	2	–	–	–	–	2	1	1	2	2	1	1	1	–
–	–	–	1	–	–	–	–	–	–	1	1	1	1	–	1	–	–	–	–
–	–	–	–	1	–	2	–	–	–	1	1	–	–	1	–	1	–	–	–
1	–	1	2	2	1	1	1	–	–	–	2	2	2	–	1	–	–	–	–
2	1	1	–	–	2	–	–	1	–	–	–	2	2	3	–	–	–	–	–
–	–	1	1	–	2	1	1	–	1	2	4	1	3	1	–	–	–	–	–
2	–	–	1	–	2	–	–	3	–	1	2	–	1	2	3	1	–	–	–
–	–	–	–	–	–	–	–	–	–	–	–	–	–	–	–	–	–	–	–
45	25	40	66	46	36	38	38	35	32	40	54	58	59	47	41	37	13	10	5
26	13	12	31	20	14	17	21	20	20	24	24	29	29	28	19	18	8	2	2
19	12	28	35	26	22	21	17	15	12	16	30	29	31	28	22	19	5	8	3
9	2	3	5	4	7	1	7	7	4	3	5	5	4	5	3	2	1	–	1
5	6	8	8	6	5	5	2	4	3	3	5	5	4	3	4	4	2	2	–
–	–	–	1	–	–	–	–	1	–	1	–	1	–	–	–	1	–	–	–
–	–	–	–	1	–	–	–	–	1	–	–	–	–	–	–	–	–	–	–
–	–	–	3	2	–	–	–	1	–	1	–	–	1	–	2	1	–	–	–
–	–	–	–	–	–	–	–	1	–	1	3	–	1	–	2	1	–	–	–

Table VII.—Continued.

Counties and Towns.	Population—1870.			Deaths.			Und. 1	1 to 2	2 to 3	3 to 4	4 to 5
	Persons.	Sex.		Per ct. to Pop.	Persons.	Sex.					
Berkshire—Con.											
Cheshire, . .	1,758	Ma. Fe.	876 882	2·33	41	17 24	7 1	1 3	– 1	– –	1 –
Clarksburg, .	686	Ma. Fe.	362 324	1·17	8	4 4	2 –	– –	– –	1 –	– –
Dalton, . .	1,252	Ma. Fe.	585 667	2·23	28	12 16	3 –	1 –	– –	1 1	– –
Egremont, .	931	Ma. Fe.	450 481	1·50	14	10 4	1 –	1 –	– –	– –	– –
Florida, . .	1,322	Ma. Fe.	803 519	2·04	27	17 10	5 6	– –	– 2	– –	1 –
Gt. Barrington, .	4,320	Ma. Fe.	2,033 2,287	1·67	72	35 37	4 7	– 4	1 1	– –	– –
Hancock, . .	882	Ma. Fe.	455 427	·57	5	4 1	– –	– –	– –	– –	– –
Hinsdale, .	1,695	Ma. Fe.	800 895	1·65	28	14 14	2 4	1 –	– –	– –	– –
Lanesborough, .	1,393	Ma. Fe.	701 692	2·23	31	18 13	4 3	1 1	1 –	– –	– –
Lee, . . .	3,866	Ma. Fe.	1,816 2,050	1·99	77	36 41	6 4	1 3	1 4	– 1	2 1
Lenox, . .	1,965	Ma. Fe.	1,002 963	·97	19	9 10	1 2	– 1	1 –	1 –	– –
Monterey, . .	653	Ma. Fe.	321 332	·92	6	3 3	– –	1 –	– –	– –	– –
Mt. Washington,	256	Ma. Fe.	122 134	·39	1	1 –	– –	– –	– –	– –	– –
New Ashford, .	208	Ma. Fe.	121 87	·96	2	2 –	– –	– –	– –	– –	– –
New Marlboro',	1,855	Ma. Fe.	954 901	1·56	29	10 19	2 3	– –	– –	– –	– –
Otis, . . .	960	Ma. Fe.	497 463	·83	8	4 4	– –	1 –	– –	– –	– –
Peru, . . .	455	Ma. Fe.	241 214	·88	4	– 4	1 –	– –	– –	1 –	– –
Pittsfield, . .	11,112	Ma. Fe.	5,288 5,824	1·83	204	106 98	33 21	7 6	1 3	2 3	1 1
Richmond, .	1,091	Ma. Fe.	569 522	·37	4	2 2	1 –	– –	– –	– –	– –
Sandisfield, .	1,482	Ma. Fe.	788 694	1·08	16	6 10	– –	– –	– –	1 –	– –
Savoy, . .	861	Ma. Fe.	451 410	·93	8	4 4	– –	– –	– –	1	– –

Age and Sex, by Towns.

5 to 10	10 to 15	15 to 20	20 to 25	25 to 30	30 to 35	35 to 40	40 to 45	45 to 50	50 to 55	55 to 60	60 to 65	65 to 70	70 to 75	75 to 80	80 to 85	85 to 90	90 to 95	95 & over	Unknown
2	-	1	1	1	·	-	2	1	-	1	2	1	2	1	1	-	1	-	-
2	-	1	1	1	2	-	2	1	-	1	2	1	2	1	1	-	1	-	-
-	-	-	-	-	-	-	-	1	-	-	-	2	-	-	-	-	-	-	-
2	-	-	-	-	-	-	-	-	-	-	-	2	-	-	-	-	-	-	-
1	-	-	1	-	-	-	2	-	2	-	1	-	1	-	-	-	-	1	-
1	-	1	-	-	3	1	2	-	-	1	3	1	1	-	-	1	-	-	-
-	-	-	1	2	-	-	-	-	1	1	2	-	-	1	-	-	-	-	-
-	-	-	-	-	-	-	1	-	-	-	-	2	-	-	1	-	-	-	-
-	2	1	2	1	2	1	-	2	-	-	-	-	-	-	-	-	-	-	-
-	-	1	-	-	1	-	-	-	-	-	-	-	-	-	-	-	-	-	-
1	1	1	1	1	1	1	1	3	1	3	-	4	7	2	1	-	1	-	-
1	2	-	3	1	1	1	-	-	1	3	4	3	3	1	1	-	-	-	-
-	-	-	-	-	-	-	-	-	-	-	-	2	-	1	-	1	-	-	-
-	-	-	-	-	-	-	-	-	-	-	-	-	-	-	-	1	-	-	-
2	1	1	-	-	-	1	1	1	1	2	-	-	1	-	-	-	-	-	-
-	-	-	2	1	1	1	-	1	1	-	1	1	1	-	-	-	-	-	-
-	1	-	-	1	1	-	1	-	-	-	-	1	1	1	3	1	-	-	1
-	-	1	3	-	-	-	1	1	-	-	-	-	-	1	2	-	-	-	-
1	-	-	6	1	-	2	3	-	-	1	1	3	3	1	1	1	1	1	-
1	2	5	1	1	1	-	2	2	-	-	1	3	3	2	2	1	1	-	-
1	1	-	-	1	-	-	1	-	1	-	1	-	-	-	-	-	-	-	-
-	-	-	1	2	1	-	-	-	-	-	-	-	-	-	2	1	-	-	-
-	-	-	1	-	-	-	-	-	-	-	-	-	1	-	-	-	-	-	-
-	1	-	-	1	-	-	-	-	-	-	-	-	1	-	-	-	-	-	-
-	-	-	-	-	-	-	-	-	-	-	-	-	1	-	-	-	-	-	-
-	-	-	-	-	-	-	-	-	-	-	-	-	-	-	-	-	-	-	-
-	-	-	-	-	-	-	-	1	-	-	-	-	1	-	-	-	-	-	-
-	-	-	-	-	-	-	-	-	-	-	-	-	-	-	-	-	-	-	-
-	1	-	-	-	-	-	1	1	1	-	-	1	1	-	1	1	-	-	-
-	-	1	1	1	-	1	-	-	-	-	2	2	3	2	-	2	-	1	-
1	-	-	1	1	-	-	-	-	-	-	-	-	-	-	1	-	-	-	-
-	-	-	-	-	1	-	-	-	-	-	-	-	1	-	1	-	-	-	-
-	-	-	-	-	-	-	-	-	-	-	1	-	-	1	-	-	-	-	-
-	-	-	-	-	-	-	-	-	-	-	-	-	-	-	-	-	-	-	-
1	2	3	3	1	7	4	1	4	2	4	11	3	-	6	4	2	-	-	1
-	6	8	4	2	7	2	1	4	4	4	2	4	5	2	3	-	-	2	1
-	-	-	-	1	-	-	-	-	-	-	-	-	1	-	-	-	1	-	-
-	-	1	-	-	-	1	-	-	2	1	1	-	2	2	-	-	-	-	1
-	-	1	-	-	-	1	-	-	1	-	1	1	-	2	2	-	-	-	1
-	-	-	-	2	-	-	-	-	-	-	-	-	2	-	-	-	-	-	-
-	-	-	1	-	-	-	-	-	-	-	-	-	1	-	-	-	-	-	1

TABLE VII.—Continued.

COUNTIES AND TOWNS.	POPULATION—1870.		DEATHS.			Und. 1	1 to 2	2 to 3	3 to 4	4 to 5
	Persons.	Sex.	Per ct. to Pop.	Persons.	Sex.					
Berkshire—Con.										
Sheffield,	2,535	Ma. 1,254 / Fe. 1,281	1·78	45	25 / 20	4 / –	– / 1	– / –	– / –	– / 1
Stockbridge,	2,003	Ma. 964 / Fe. 1,039	1·80	36	18 / 18	4 / 1	– / –	– / –	1 / –	– / –
Tyringham,	557	Ma. 269 / Fe. 288	1·43	8	3 / 5	1 / 2	– / –	– / –	– / –	– / –
Washington,	694	Ma. 373 / Fe. 321	1·59	11	6 / 5	– / –	1 / –	– / 1	– / –	– / 1
W. Stockbridge,	1,924	Ma. 1,009 / Fe. 915	1·51	29	15 / 14	2 / 5	– / 1	1 / –	– / –	1 / –
Williamstown,	3,559	Ma. 1,854 / Fe. 1,705	1·29	46	22 / 24	6 / 1	2 / –	– / –	– / –	1 / –
Windsor,	686	Ma. 367 / Fe. 319	·73	5	1 / 4	– / 1	– / –	– / –	– / –	– / –
BRISTOL CO.,	102,886	Tot. 102,886 / Ma. 49,419 / Fe. 53,467 / U. .	2·83 (Ma)	2,912 (Ma)	Tot. 2,912 / 1,524 / 1,387 / 1	708 / 424 / 283 / 1	213 / 111 / 102 / –	98 / 44 / 54 / –	77 / 37 / 40 / –	64 / 30 / 34 / –
Acushnet,	1,132	Ma. 557 / Fe. 575	1·24	14	5 / 9	2 / 1	1 / –	– / –	– / –	– / –
Attleborough,	6,769	Ma. 3,309 / Fe. 3,460	2·66	180	101 / 79	21 / 15	1 / 6	2 / 4	4 / 2	4 / 3
Berkley,	744	Ma. 368 / Fe. 376	1·61	12	5 / 7	– / –	– / –	– / 1	– / –	– / –
Dartmouth,	3,367	Ma. 1,643 / Fe. 1,724	1·90	64	31 / 33	2 / 8	2 / 1	– / –	– / –	– / –
Dighton,	1,817	Ma. 881 / Fe. 936	1·60	29	12 / 17	4 / 2	– / 1	– / –	– / –	– / –
Easton,	3,668	Ma. 1,911 / Fe. 1,757	1·80	66	32 / 34	11 / 7	2 / –	– / –	– / 2	2 / 1
Fairhaven,	2,626	Ma. 1,240 / Fe. 1,386	1·94	51	22 / 29	4 / 2	– / 1	– / 1	– / –	– / –
Fall River,	26,766	Ma. 12,652 / Fe. 14,114	4·72	1,264	679 / 585	224 / 156	73 / 61	31 / 38	26 / 25	17 / 19
Freetown,	1,372	Ma. 670 / Fe. 702 / U. .	·58	8	4 / 3 / 1	1 / – / 1	– / – / –	– / – / –	– / – / –	– / – / –
Mansfield,	2,432	Ma. 1,196 / Fe. 1,236	2·26	55	31 / 24	7 / 1	– / –	1 / –	– / –	– / –
New Bedford,	21,320	Ma. 9,880 / Fe. 11,440	2·20	470	235 / 235	53 / 49	9 / 12	5 / 1	2 / 3	3 / 2
Norton,	1,821	Ma. 812 / Fe. 1,009	1·10	20	10 / 10	1 / –	– / 1	– / –	– / –	– / 2

Age and Sex, by Towns.

5 to 10	10 to 15	15 to 20	20 to 25	25 to 30	30 to 35	35 to 40	40 to 45	45 to 50	50 to 55	55 to 60	60 to 65	65 to 70	70 to 75	75 to 80	80 to 85	85 to 90	90 to 95	95 & over	Unknown
2 / 1	2 / 1	1 / –	1 / 2	– / 1	– / –	– / 1	– / –	1 / –	2 / 1	– / –	2 / 2	– / –	2 / 3	3 / 4	1 / 1	4 / –	– / –	– / 1	– / –
– / –	1 / –	– / 1	– / 2	1 / 2	2 / 1	1 / –	– / 3	1 / 2	4 / –	1 / –	– / 3	1 / 1	1 / –	1 / –	– / –	– / 1	– / –	– / –	– / –
– / –	– / –	– / –	– / –	– / –	– / 1	– / –	– / –	2 / –	– / –	– / –	– / 1	– / –	– / –	– / –	– / –	– / 1	– / –	– / –	– / –
2 / 1	– / –	– / –	2 / –	– / 1	1 / –	– / –	– / –	– / –	1 / –	– / –	– / –	– / 1	– / –	2 / –	– / –	– / –	– / –		
– / –	– / –	2 / 1	1 / –	1 / 1	1 / 1	– / 1	1 / –	– / –	2 / –	1 / 1	– / 1	1 / 1	1 / –	1 / 1	– / –	1 / –	1 / –		
1 / 1	– / –	– / 2	2 / 1	1 / 3	– / –	2 / 1	1 / 2	– / 1	2 / –	3 / 1	– / 2	2 / 2	1 / 2	1 / 2	1 / –	– / –	1 / –		
– / –	– / –	– / 1	– / –	– / –	– / –	– / –	– / 1	1 / –	– / –	– / –	– / –	– / 1	– / –	– / –	– / –	– / –			
151 / 94 / 57	78 / 35 / 43	116 / 51 / 65	143 / 78 / 65	136 / 60 / 76	102 / 52 / 50	103 / 52 / 51	67 / 24 / 43	85 / 41 / 44	78 / 43 / 35	93 / 55 / 38	100 / 61 / 39	113 / 58 / 55	129 / 56 / 73	89 / 48 / 41	83 / 34 / 49	42 / 14 / 28	18 / 9 / 9	3 / 1 / 2	23 / 12 / 11
1 / –	– / –	– / –	– / –	– / 1	– / –	– / –	2 / –	– / 1	1 / 1	1 / –	– / –	1 / 1	1 / 1	– / –	– / –			
7 / 2	2 / 2	3 / 7	7 / 6	4 / 1	2 / 3	3 / 3	1 / 4	5 / 1	5 / 2	5 / 1	4 / 4	6 / 5	3 / 4	6 / –	1 / 3	1 / –	1 / 1	– / 3	
– / –	– / 1	2 / –	– / 1	1 / 1	1 / –	– / –	– / –	– / –	– / 1	– / –	– / –	1 / 1	1 / –	– / –	– / –	– / –		
4 / 1	– / –	1 / –	2 / 2	3 / 2	1 / –	1 / 1	– / –	– / 1	2 / 1	1 / 1	3 / –	1 / –	1 / 5	4 / 2	3 / 4	– / 1	2 / 1	1 / –	
– / –	– / 1	– / –	– / –	– / –	3 / –	– / –	– / –	1 / –	2 / 2	– / 1	1 / 1	1 / 5	2 / 1	2 / –	– / –	– / –		
1 / –	– / 2	2 / 1	1 / –	2 / 1	– / –	2 / –	– / –	– / 1	2 / 3	1 / 3	2 / 4	2 / 3	1 / 1	1 / 1	2 / –	– / –	– / –	
1 / 1	– / 1	1 / 1	2 / 3	2 / 1	2 / 1	– / 2	1 / 1	1 / 1	– / 3	3 / 1	– / 1	1 / 3	3 / –	– / 3	2 / 1	1 / –		
57 / 32	21 / 24	23 / 30	37 / 30	22 / 27	26 / 24	20 / 20	12 / 11	9 / 18	14 / 10	12 / 6	14 / 9	11 / 8	11 / 14	5 / 8	6 / 9	5 / 6	2 / –	– / –	1
– / –	– / –	1 / –	– / –	– / 1	– / –	– / –	– / –	– / 1	1 / –	– / –	– / –	1 / –	– / 1	– / –	– / –			
1 / 1	– / 1	1 / –	5 / 3	– / 1	1 / 1	1 / 2	2 / –	– / 2	– / –	1 / 1	6 / 2	2 / 2	3 / 2	2 / –	– / 1	– / –	– / –	
10 / 12	5 / 7	11 / 8	12 / 9	12 / 19	9 / 6	13 / 11	3 / 7	9 / 8	6 / 6	13 / 9	14 / 8	14 / 13	13 / 16	3 / 7	4 / 12	3 / 4	2 / 1	1 / –	6 / 5
– / –	– / –	– / –	– / –	– / –	– / –	– / –	1 / 1	– / –	– / –	2 / –	3 / –	– / 3	– / 2	2 / 1	– / 1	– / –		

TABLE VII.—Continued.

COUNTIES AND TOWNS.	POPULATION—1870. Persons.	Sex.		Per ct. to Pop.	DEATHS. Persons.	Sex.	Und. 1	1 to 2	2 to 3	3 to 4	4 to 5
Bristol—Con.											
Raynham, .	1,713	Ma.	842	1·46	25	13	2	–	–	–	
		Fe.	871			12	4	–	–	–	
Rehoboth, .	1,895	Ma.	918	1·00	19	6	2	–	–	–	
		Fe.	977			13	–	–	–	–	
Seekonk, . .	1,021	Ma.	512	1·47	15	7	–	–	–	–	
		Fe.	509			8	–	–	1	–	
Somerset, . .	1,776	Ma.	929	1·97	35	20	8	1	1	–	
		Fe.	847			15	2	3	1	–	
Swanzey, . .	1,294	Ma.	615	1·93	25	14	2	–	–	–	
		Fe.	679			11	–	–	–	–	
Taunton, . .	18,629	Ma.	9,124	2·67	497	262	72	22	5	4	
		Fe.	9,505			235	35	15	5	8	
Westport, .	2,724	Ma.	1,360	2·31	63	35	8	–	–	1	
		Fe.	1,364			28	1	1	1	–	
DUKES COUNTY,	3,787	Tot.	3,787	.	.	58	7	1	1	–	
		Ma.	1,819	1·53	58	32	3	–	1	–	
		Fe.	1,968			26	4	1	–	–	
Chilmark, .	476	Ma.	238	·84	4	1	–	–	–	–	
		Fe.	238			3	–	–	–	–	
Edgartown, .	1,516	Ma.	704	1·72	26	15	1	–	1	–	
		Fe.	812			11	4	1	–	–	
Gay Head, .	160	Ma.	82	1·25	2	1	–	–	–	–	
		Fe.	78			1	–	–	–	–	
Gosnold, . .	99	Ma.	55	1·01	1	1	1	–	–	–	
		Fe.	44			–	–	–	–	–	
Tisbury, . .	1,536	Ma.	740	1·63	25	14	1	–	–	–	
		Fe.	796			11	–	–	–	–	
ESSEX COUNTY,	200,843	Tot.	200,843	.	.	4,429	1005	280	114	78	6
		Ma.	95,498			2,270	569	145	57	36	3
		Fe.	105,345	2·21	4,429	2,149	427	135	56	42	2
		U.	.			10	9	–	1		
Amesbury, .	5,581	Ma.	2,780	2·02	113	54	12	3	2	3	
		Fe.	2,801			58	12	3	3	1	
		U.	.		.	58	1	–	–	–	
Andover, . .	4,873	Ma.	2,304	1·72	84	42	9	3	–	–	
		Fe.	2,569			42	6	1	2	–	
Beverly, . .	6,507	Ma.	3,112	2·52	164	79	8	9	7	4	
		Fe.	3,395			85	10	5	2	6	
Boxford, . .	847	Ma.	432	1·30	11	6	2	–	–	–	
		Fe.	415			5	1	–	–	–	
Bradford, . .	2,014	Ma.	920	1·59	32	16	3	2	–	–	
		Fe.	1,094			16	2	–	–	–	

Age and Sex, by Towns.

5 to 10	10 to 15	15 to 20	20 to 25	25 to 30	30 to 35	35 to 40	40 to 45	45 to 50	50 to 55	55 to 60	60 to 65	65 to 70	70 to 75	75 to 80	80 to 85	85 to 90	90 to 95	95 & over	Unknown
-	-	-	1	1	2	-	-	1	1	2	1	1	-	-	-	-	1	-	-
-	-	-	-	-	1	1	2	-	1	-	-	2	-	-	-	-	-	-	-
-	-	1	-	-	-	-	1	1	1	-	2	2	1	1	2	-	1	1	-
-	-	1	-	-	-	1	-	-	-	1	1	-	1	2	1	-	-	-	2
-	-	2	-	1	-	2	-	1	-	-	-	-	1	3	-	-	-	-	-
1	1	-	-	1	1	-	1	-	1	-	-	-	-	-	2	-	-	-	-
-	-	-	1	1	1	-	-	1	-	-	1	1	-	2	1	2	1	-	-
-	-	-	-	2	-	-	-	-	-	-	-	2	1	1	2	1	1	-	-
10	5	5	11	8	9	8	7	9	10	14	12	12	15	9	7	2	-	-	2
6	3	13	11	16	8	7	13	10	8	10	7	14	13	12	7	6	2	-	4
3	1	-	-	3	-	-	-	2	2	2	3	1	4	2	1	1	1	-	-
2	1	2	1	2	1	1	-	-	-	3	2	-	2	2	1	3	-	-	-
1	3	1	3	2	-	3	1	3	6	1	4	4	2	6	4	3	2	-	-
1	1	1	1	1	-	3	-	1	1	1	4	4	1	5	2	1	2	-	-
-	2	-	2	1	-	-	1	2	5	-	-	-	1	1	2	2	2	-	-
-	-	-	-	1	-	-	-	-	-	-	1	-	-	-	1	-	1	-	-
-	-	-	-	-	-	-	-	-	-	-	-	-	-	-	-	-	-	-	-
1	1	1	-	-	-	2	-	1	-	-	3	2	1	1	-	-	-	-	-
-	1	-	1	-	-	-	-	-	3	-	-	-	-	-	1	-	-	-	-
-	-	-	1	-	-	-	-	-	-	-	-	-	-	-	1	-	-	-	-
-	-	-	-	-	-	-	-	-	-	-	-	-	-	-	-	-	-	-	-
-	-	-	-	-	-	-	-	-	-	-	-	-	-	-	-	-	-	-	-
-	1	-	1	1	-	1	-	-	1	1	1	1	-	4	1	1	-	-	-
-	1	-	-	-	-	-	1	2	2	-	-	-	1	1	-	2	1	-	-
157	91	189	246	167	179	165	134	127	156	123	161	203	200	178	127	76	41	13	159
80	48	82	114	71	77	68	62	67	86	63	76	94	98	87	61	31	12	2	153
77	43	107	132	96	102	97	72	60	70	60	85	109	102	91	66	45	29	11	6
-	-	-	-	-	-	-	-	-	-	-	-	-	-	-	-	-	-	-	-
3	-	1	3	3	2	2	4	1	5	-	-	2	3	2	2	1	-	-	-
3	-	1	4	2	3	3	-	2	1	3	3	2	2	3	2	-	1	2	-
-	-	-	-	-	-	-	-	-	-	-	-	-	-	-	-	-	-	-	-
-	3	-	2	1	2	3	-	1	2	1	2	2	4	4	1	-	-	-	1
1	2	2	2	3	1	1	3	-	4	2	1	2	3	1	1	-	1	1	-
2	1	2	3	4	2	2	4	3	2	3	4	3	4	5	3	2	-	-	-
11	3	5	4	4	6	3	-	-	1	4	3	5	5	2	2	1	1	-	-
-	-	-	1	-	-	-	-	1	-	-	1	-	2	-	-	-	-	-	-
-	-	-	1	1	-	-	-	-	-	-	-	1	-	-	-	-	-	-	1
-	1	-	-	1	-	-	-	1	1	1	-	2	-	2	1	-	-	-	-
1	1	1	-	-	2	1	1	1	1	-	-	1	3	-	1	-	-	-	-

TABLE VII.—Continued.

COUNTIES AND TOWNS	POPULATION—1870.			DEATHS.			Und. 1	1 to 2	2 to 3	3 to 4	4 to 5
	Persons.	Sex.		Per ct. to Pop.	Persons.	Sex.					
Essex—Con.											
Danvers, . .	5,600	Ma. Fe.	2,751 2,849	1·73	97	48 49	11 8	1 1	– –	– –	5 –
Essex, . .	1,614	Ma. Fe.	842 772	1·73	28	9 19	– 1	3 3	– –	– –	– –
Georgetown, .	2,088	Ma. Fe.	995 1,093	1·82	38	15 23	2 4	– –	2 –	– 1	1 1
Gloucester, .	15,389	Ma. Fe. U.	7,878 7,511 .	2·96	455	312 141 2	45 44 2	9 11 –	4 3 –	1 2 –	2 1
Groveland, .	1,776	Ma. Fe. U.	838 938 .	1·52	27	14 12 1	5 2 1	1 1 –	– – –	– – –	– –
Hamilton, .	790	Ma. Fe.	409 381	2·15	17	11 6	1 1	– –	– –	– –	– –
Haverhill,. .	13,092	Ma. Fe. U.	6,393 6,699 .	2·31	303	138 162 3	41 25 2	8 9 –	3 4 1	2 4 –	– 3 –
Ipswich, . .	3,720	Ma. Fe.	1,757 1,963	2·02	75	41 34	8 5	1 1	1 –	– 1	– –
Lawrence,. .	28,921	Ma. Fe. U.	12,618 16,303 .	2·32	670	320 348 2	112 80 2	37 30 –	12 11 –	11 8 –	1 8
Lynn, . .	28,233	Ma. Fe.	13,472 14,761	2·40	679	351 328	102 73	16 23	12 7	7 6	3 7
Lynnfield,. .	818	Ma. Fe.	396 422	1·10	9	5 4	– –	– –	– –	– –	– –
Manchester, .	1,665	Ma. Fe.	783 882	2·22	37	15 22	5 2	– –	1 –	1 2	– –
Marblehead, .	7,703	Ma. Fe.	3,845 3,858	2·22	171	106 65	19 17	4 8	1 2	– –	4 1
Methuen, . .	2,959	Ma. Fe.	1,392 1,567	1·52	45	23 22	5 6	– –	1 –	– –	– –
Middleton, .	1,010	Ma. Fe.	514 496	1·49	15	6 9	2 2	– –	– –	– –	– –
Nahant, . .	475	Ma. Fe.	235 240	2·11	10	3 7	1 4	– –	– –	– –	– –
Newbury,. .	1,430	Ma. Fe.	746 684	1·61	23	13 10	4 3	– –	– –	– –	– –
Newburyport, .	12,595	Ma. Fe.	5,646 6,949	1·98	249	114 135	21 22	6 8	4 7	2 1	– –
North Andover,	2,549	Ma. Fe.	1,270 1,279	1·57	40	20 20	4 2	1 –	– 1	– –	– –
Peabody, . .	7,343	Ma. Fe.	3,732 3,611	2·18	160	75 85	27 20	11 6	1 1	1 2	4 –

Age and Sex, by Towns.

5 to 10	10 to 15	15 to 20	20 to 25	25 to 30	30 to 35	35 to 40	40 to 45	45 to 50	50 to 55	55 to 60	60 to 65	65 to 70	70 to 75	75 to 80	80 to 85	85 to 90	90 to 95	95 & over	Unknown
1	.2	2	5	3	1	2	-	1	2	-	2	2	4	2	-	1	-	-	1
4	2	6	6	2	-	-	6	1	1	1	2	1	2	2	3	-	1	-	-
-	-	-	-	-	-	-	-	-	1	1	-	-	1	1	1	1	-	-	-
-	1	-	1	1	3	-	-	1	2	1	-	-	2	2	-	1	-	-	-
-	-	1	-	3	-	-	1	-	2	-	-	-	1	2	-	-	-	-	-
-	-	-	2	1	1	2	-	-	2	-	3	1	3	-	1	1	-	-	-
8	3	7	16	10	5	11	7	5	2	2	4	11	3	3	5	3	1	-	145
2	3	3	10	2	4	4	10	3	4	2	2	6	5	8	4	7	1	-	-
1	-	-	-	-	2	1	-	-	2	-	-	1	1	-	-	-	-	-	-
-	1	-	-	-	-	1	2	-	-	-	1	-	1	-	2	1	-	-	-
-	-	-	-	-	-	-	-	1	1	1	-	4	-	2	-	-	1	-	-
-	-	-	-	-	-	-	-	-	-	1	-	-	-	1	3	-	-	-	-
8	3	9	7	4	2	4	3	5	7	4	5	9	5	4	5	-	-	-	-
8	4	4	12	12	10	8	8	10	2	2	7	10	10	7	1	2	-	-	-
-	-	1	2	-	2	2	2	-	-	3	5	5	3	5	-	1	-	-	-
-	-	1	1	1	-	2	-	-	4	2	1	5	3	2	1	2	2	-	-
17	9	13	17	6	10	7	7	8	12	8	8	10	5	4	2	2	-	-	2
16	7	22	23	20	18	13	11	15	11	7	9	11	10	9	3	4	1	1	-
17	8	15	20	11	11	10	9	15	14	13	14	11	15	14	8	2	1	1	2
12	6	16	20	19	23	17	8	6	9	10	12	14	13	8	8	6	3	1	1
-	-	-	-	-	1	1	-	1	-	-	-	-	-	1	-	1	-	-	-
-	-	-	-	-	-	-	-	-	1	1	1	1	-	-	-	-	-	-	-
2	-	-	3	1	-	1	2	1	2	2	-	1	3	1	1	1	-	-	-
8	6	4	6	2	7	7	5	3	3	6	5	1	8	4	2	1	-	-	-
-	4	4	2	1	4	3	2	3	2	-	1	1	3	4	3	1	-	-	-
-	-	-	-	3	2	-	-	1	1	-	1	1	3	2	2	-	-	-	2
-	-	2	-	-	-	-	1	1	-	1	-	2	1	3	-	3	1	-	1
-	-	1	-	-	-	1	-	-	-	-	-	-	1	1	-	-	1	-	-
-	-	-	1	-	-	-	-	-	-	1	-	2	-	1	1	-	1	-	-
-	-	-	-	-	-	-	1	-	-	-	-	-	-	-	-	-	1	-	-
-	-	-	1	-	-	1	-	-	-	-	-	-	-	1	-	-	-	-	-
-	-	-	1	-	-	-	-	-	2	1	-	1	-	1	2	1	-	-	-
-	-	1	2	-	-	-	-	1	-	1	-	1	-	1	-	-	-	-	-
3	3	1	6	2	5	3	3	9	7	6	4	5	11	5	3	4	1	-	-
1	1	5	6	7	7	9	3	1	5	5	9	10	5	6	4	4	7	2	-
-	-	-	1	2	1	-	-	-	-	2	1	1	3	-	3	1	-	-	-
1	-	2	3	1	2	3	1	-	1	-	-	1	1	1	-	-	-	-	-
1	1	-	1	-	4	1	3	1	4	2	1	-	6	2	3	1	-	-	-
3	2	2	10	3	5	4	-	4	2	1	3	4	4	3	3	2	-	1	-

Table VII.—Continued.

Counties and Towns	Population—1870 Persons	Sex		Per ct. to Pop.	Deaths Persons	Sex	Und. 1	1 to 2	2 to 3	3 to 4	4 to 5
*Essex—*Con.											
Rockport,	3,904	Ma.	1,980	2·46	96	55	13	1	–	–	2
		Fe.	1,924			41	8	3	1	1	–
Rowley,	1,157	Ma.	571	1·90	22	15	3	–	–	–	–
		Fe.	586			7	1	–	–	–	–
Salem,	24,117	Ma.	10,940	2·28	551	261	84	25	3	3	3
		Fe.	13,177			290	55	17	11	3	2
Salisbury,	3,776	Ma.	1,828	2·04	77	43	9	2	–	1	1
		Fe.	1,948			34	6	2	–	1	–
Saugus,	2,247	Ma.	1,088	1·47	33	12	2	–	–	–	–
		Fe.	1,159			21	2	1	–	1	–
Swampscott,	1,846	Ma.	907	2·00	37	17	5	–	2	–	1
		Fe.	939			19	1	2	–	–	–
		U.	.	.	.	1	1	–	–	–	–
Topsfield,	1,213	Ma.	593	1·81	22	13	–	–	–	–	–
		Fe.	620			9	–	–	1	–	–
Wenham,	985	Ma.	502	1·32	13	4	2	–	–	–	–
		Fe.	483			9	1	–	–	–	–
West Newbury,	2,006	Ma.	1,029	1·30	26	14	2	2	1	–	–
		Fe.	977			12	1	–	–	2	–
FRANKLIN Co.,	32,635	Ma.	32,635	.	.	568	83	22	5	10	5
		Fe.	16,362	1·74	568	270	51	12	5	5	1
		U.	16,273			298	32	10	–	5	4
Ashfield,	1,180	Ma.	592	1·10	13	7	1	–	–	–	–
		Fe.	588			6	–	–	–	1	–
Bernardston,	961	Ma.	472	1·46	14	4	2	–	–	–	–
		Fe.	489			10	1	–	–	1	–
Buckland,	1,946	Ma.	1,027	2·83	55	27	6	1	1	2	1
		Fe.	919			28	2	2	–	1	2
Charlemont,	1,005	Ma.	480	·90	9	6	–	–	–	–	–
		Fe.	525			3	–	–	–	–	–
Colrain,	1,742	Ma.	846	1·03	18	10	1	3	–	–	–
		Fe.	896			8	–	–	–	–	–
Conway,	1,460	Ma.	742	2·12	31	9	3	–	–	–	–
		Fe.	718			22	2	1	–	–	–
Deerfield,	3,632	Ma.	1,847	2·09	76	45	9	1	1	1	–
		Fe.	1,785			31	2	2	–	–	1
Erving,	579	Ma.	311	1·55	9	3	–	–	–	–	–
		Fe.	268			6	1	1	–	–	–
Gill,	653	Ma.	331	1·23	8	5	1	–	–	–	–
		Fe.	322			3	–	–	–	–	–
Greenfield,	3,589	Ma.	1,740	1·34	48	19	3	–	–	–	–
		Fe.	1,849			29	5	1	–	1	1

Age and Sex, by Towns.

5 to 10	10 to 15	15 to 20	20 to 25	25 to 30	30 to 35	35 to 40	40 to 45	45 to 50	59 to 55	55 to 60	60 to 65	65 to 70	70 to 75	75 to 80	80 to 85	85 to 90	90 to 95	95 & over	Unknown.
1	3	4	4	3	4	-	2	1	1	2	-	3	1	5	2	2	1	-	-
1	-	3	6	1	1	2	-	2	-	2	1	4	1	1	1	1	-	-	1
-	-	-	3	1	1	1	-	-	-	-	1	1	-	1	1	-	1	1	-
-	-	1	-	-	-	-	-	1	-	-	1	-	-	1	1	1	-	-	-
7	4	13	12	8	12	9	8	7	8	2	13	11	7	6	10	4	2	-	-
6	1	22	9	12	9	12	12	7	13	11	12	15	14	17	15	6	6	3	-
1	1	1	4	1	-	-	3	-	4	1	2	3	3	3	1	1	1	-	-
2	-	-	1	2	-	4	-	-	3	-	4	3	3	-	2	1	-	-	-
-	-	2	-	-	1	1	-	2	1	-	-	2	1	-	-	-	-	-	-
-	2	1	1	-	1	1	-	1	-	-	1	2	2	3	1	-	-	-	1
1	-	3	1	-	-	-	-	-	-	-	1	1	1	1	-	-	-	-	-
2	2	1	1	-	-	2	1	-	1	-	1	2	-	1	-	-	1	-	1
-	-	1	-	1	1	-	-	-	-	-	2	-	3	3	2	-	-	-	-
1	1	-	-	-	1	1	-	1	-	-	1	-	-	1	-	-	1	-	-
-	-	-	-	-	-	-	-	-	-	-	-	-	-	1	1	-	-	-	-
-	-	1	-	1	-	-	-	-	-	1	1	2	1	1	-	-	-	-	-
1	-	1	-	1	-	-	-	1	-	-	-	1	1	2	1	-	-	-	-
-	-	1	1	-	-	-	-	-	3	3	-	-	1	-	-	-	-	-	-
20	13	30	39	20	23	18	21	14	29	21	33	37	34	32	31	22	5	-	1
10	7	13	19	5	8	7	6	8	16	15	12	18	13	16	15	7	1	-	-
10	6	17	20	15	15	11	15	6	13	6	21	19	21	16	16	15	4	-	1
-	-	2	1	1	-	-	-	-	-	-	1	1	-	-	-	-	-	-	-
-	-	-	1	-	1	-	-	-	1	-	-	1	-	1	-	-	-	-	-
-	-	-	1	-	1	-	-	-	-	1	-	-	-	1	-	-	3	-	-
-	-	1	1	1	1	-	-	-	-	-	-	-	1	-	-	-	3	-	-
3	2	2	-	1	-	1	1	-	1	1	-	1	3	-	-	-	-	-	-
2	3	1	1	-	1	1	1	1	1	2	1	4	2	-	-	-	-	-	-
-	-	1	-	1	-	-	-	-	-	1	-	1	-	1	-	1	-	-	-
-	-	-	-	-	-	-	-	-	-	-	-	-	-	3	-	-	-	-	-
-	-	-	-	-	1	-	-	-	1	2	-	2	-	-	-	-	-	-	-
-	-	1	1	1	1	-	-	1	-	-	-	1	-	-	1	-	-	-	-
-	-	-	-	-	-	-	-	-	1	1	2	1	1	-	1	1	1	-	-
1	-	3	2	-	-	1	2	-	1	1	2	1	2	1	1	1	-	-	-
1	1	3	3	-	3	2	1	5	3	3	-	3	2	3	-	-	-	-	-
2	-	2	-	3	2	1	1	1	2	1	1	2	1	4	1	2	-	-	-

TABLE VII.—Continued.

COUNTIES AND TOWNS.	POPULATION—1870.			DEATHS.			Und 1	1 to 2	2 to 3
	Persons.	Sex.		Per ct. to Pop.	Persons.	Sex.			
Franklin—Con.									
Hawley, . .	672	Ma. Fe.	358 314	1·19	8	6 2	1 –	1 –	– –
Heath, . .	613	Ma. Fe.	302 311	1·63	10	3 7	– 1	– 1	– –
Leverett, .	877	Ma. Fe.	437 440	1·82	16	8 8	1 1	1 –	– –
Leyden, . .	518	Ma. Fe.	265 253	·58	3	1 2	– –	– –	– –
Monroe, . .	201	Ma. Fe.	115 86	1·99	4	2 2	– –	– –	– –
Montague, .	2,224	Ma. Fe.	1,161 1,063	3·06	68	40 28	11 6	3 1	1 –
New Salem, .	987	Ma. Fe.	474 513	2·13	21	9 12	2 –	– –	– –
Northfield, .	1,720	Ma. Fe.	822 898	1·80	31	16 15	1 1	– –	– –
Orange, . .	2,091	Ma. Fe.	1,029 1,062	1·58	33	16 17	4 3	2 –	1 –
Rowe, . .	581	Ma. Fe.	299 282	1·55	9	7 2	– –	– –	– –
Shelburne, .	1,582	Ma. Fe.	767 815	1·39	22	7 15	1 2	– 1	– –
Shutesbury, .	614	Ma. Fe.	292 322	1·95	12	2 10	– 3	– –	– –
Sunderland, .	832	Ma. Fe.	413 419	2·40	20	9 11	2 1	– –	1 –
Warwick, . .	769	Ma. Fe.	389 380	1·30	10	3 7	– –	– –	– –
Wendell, . .	539	Ma. Fe.	280 259	1·29	7	1 6	– 1	– –	– –
Whately, . .	1,068	Ma. Fe.	571 497	1·22	13	5 8	2 –	– –	– –
HAMPDEN CO., .	78,409	Tot. Ma. Fe. U.	78,409 37,382 41,027 ·	· 2·44 · ·	· 1,915 · ·	1,915 978 936 1	473 250 222 1	149 78 71 –	68 38 30 –
Agawam, .	2,001	Ma. Fe.	965 1,036	1·75	35	16 19	3 9	– –	3 1
Blandford, .	1,026	Ma. Fe.	501 525	2·05	21	11 10	2 –	– –	– –
Brimfield, .	1,288	Ma. Fe.	639 649	1·55	20	9 11	1 –	– –	– –

Age and Sex, by Towns.

5 to 10	10 to 15	15 to 20	20 to 25	25 to 30	30 to 35	35 to 40	40 to 45	45 to 50	50 to 55	55 to 60	60 to 65	65 to 70	70 to 75	75 to 80	80 to 85	85 to 90	90 to 95	95 & over	Unknown
-	-	-	-	-	-	-	-	-	-	-	-	1	1	-	2	-	-	-	-
-	-	-	-	-	-	-	-	-	-	-	-	-	-	1	1	-	-	-	-
-	-	-	-	1	-	-	-	-	1	1	-	2	1	-	1	-	-	-	-
-	-	-	1	-	-	-	-	-	-	-	-	1	-	-	1	-	-	-	-
1	-	-	-	-	-	-	-	-	-	-	1	1	1	-	1	2	-	-	-
-	-	1	1	-	-	-	1	-	-	-	-	1	-	1	2	-	-	-	-
-	-	-	-	-	-	-	-	-	-	-	-	-	-	1	1	-	-	-	-
-	-	-	-	-	-	-	-	-	-	-	-	-	-	1	1	-	-	-	-
1	-	-	-	-	-	-	-	-	-	-	-	-	-	1	-	-	-	-	-
-	-	-	-	-	-	1	-	-	-	-	-	-	-	1	-	-	-	-	-
1	1	1	1	2	2	-	2	2	2	-	2	3	-	2	1	1	-	-	-
1	1	3	3	2	-	-	1	-	2	-	3	1	-	1	-	2	-	-	-
1	-	-	-	-	-	-	-	-	1	-	-	2	-	2	-	1	-	-	-
-	-	-	1	-	2	-	1	1	-	-	-	2	1	1	2	1	-	-	-
-	-	2	2	-	1	-	1	-	1	2	-	1	-	1	3	1	-	-	-
-	-	1	-	-	1	1	4	1	1	-	-	2	2	1	-	-	-	-	-
-	1	1	2	-	-	1	-	-	1	1	-	-	1	1	1	-	-	-	-
-	1	1	2	3	-	1	1	-	-	1	2	-	-	1	1	-	-	-	-
-	-	-	2	-	1	-	-	-	-	-	-	-	2	-	1	1	-	-	-
-	-	-	-	1	-	-	-	-	-	-	-	-	-	-	1	-	-	-	-
1	2	1	1	-	3	1	-	1	-	-	1	1	-	1	1	1	-	-	-
-	1	1	1	-	-	-	-	-	-	-	-	-	-	-	1	-	1	-	-
-	-	-	2	1	2	1	-	-	-	-	-	-	-	-	1	-	-	-	-
-	-	-	-	-	-	-	-	-	-	-	-	-	-	-	1	-	1	-	-
2	1	1	-	2	-	1	-	-	1	-	1	-	-	1	-	-	1	-	-
-	2	-	-	-	1	-	-	-	-	-	1	1	-	1	-	-	-	-	-
-	-	1	-	-	1	-	-	1	*2	-	-	-	3	-	1	-	-	-	-
-	-	-	-	-	-	-	-	-	-	-	1	2	-	-	-	1	-	-	1
-	-	2	-	-	-	-	-	1	1	1	-	2	-	3	-	-	-	-	-
97	48	108	118	86	69	77	57	42	50	48	56	82	64	46	48	29	13	5	11
48	22	56	76	32	31	40	26	24	24	26	32	36	35	23	27	9	6	1	7
49	26	52	42	54	38	37	31	18	26	22	24	46	29	23	21	20	7	4	4
2	-	-	1	1	-	1	-	-	-	2	-	-	-	-	-	-	1	-	-
1	-	-	-	-	1	-	1	2	-	2	2	-	-	-	-	-	-	-	-
-	1	1	-	-	1	1	-	-	-	1	-	3	-	2	-	-	-	-	-
-	1	1	-	1	-	-	-	1	-	-	2	1	1	-	1	-	-	-	-
1	-	1	1	-	-	-	4	-	1	2	1	1	-	2	-	2	-	-	-

TABLE VII.—Continued.

Counties and Towns	Persons		Sex	Per ct. to Pop.	Persons	Sex	Und. 1	1 to 2	2 to 3	3 to 4	4 to 5
Hampden—Con.											
Chester,	1,253	Ma.	641	1·28	16	9	4	–	–	–	–
		Fe.	612			7	2	–	–	–	–
Chicopee,	9,607	Ma.	4,284	2·69	258	128	40	11	4	2	1
		Fe.	5,323			130	27	9	7	2	3
Granville,	1,293	Ma.	656	2·01	26	15	5	–	–	–	–
		Fe.	637			11	1	–	–	1	–
Holland,	344	Ma.	178	1·74	6	4	–	–	–	–	–
		Fe.	166			2	–	–	–	–	–
Holyoke,	10,733	Ma.	4,856	4·14	444	225	66	30	8	4	7
		Fe.	5,877			219	67	27	6	6	6
Longmeadow,	1,342	Ma.	632	1·86	25	9	2	–	1	–	–
		Fe.	710			16	5	1	–	1	–
Ludlow,	1,136	Ma.	560	1·85	21	13	–	1	–	–	–
		Fe.	576			8	–	–	–	–	–
Monson,	3,204	Ma.	1,632	1·19	38	25	2	2	2	–	–
		Fe.	1,572			13	1	1	–	–	–
State Almsh'se at Monson,	–	Ma.	–	–	15	11	1	–	2	1	1
		Fe.	–			4	–	–	–	1	1
Montgomery,	318	Ma.	172	1·26	4	3	2	–	–	–	–
		Fe.	146			1	–	–	–	–	–
Palmer,	3,631	Ma.	1,702	2·18	79	40	14	2	1	–	–
		Fe.	1,929			39	7	6	–	1	–
Russell,	635	Ma.	305	1·89	12	6	1	–	–	–	–
		Fe.	330			6	1	–	–	–	–
Southwick,	1,100	Ma.	562	1·91	21	11	–	–	–	–	–
		Fe.	538			10	–	–	–	–	–
Springfield,	26,703	Ma.	12,894	2·36	630	316	83	25	13	6	4
		Fe.	13,809			313	82	21	13	4	6
		U.	.	.	.	1	1	–	–	–	–
Tolland,	509	Ma.	282	1·18	6	2	–	–	–	–	–
		Fe.	227			4	1	–	–	–	–
Wales,	831	Ma.	411	1·68	14	6	–	–	–	–	–
		Fe.	420			8	–	–	–	–	–
Westfield,	6,519	Ma.	3,125	1·99	130	70	15	6	2	–	1
		Fe.	3,394			60	12	1	1	2	2
W. Springfield,	2,606	Ma.	1,229	2·53	66	35	8	1	2	–	1
		Fe.	1,377			31	6	4	2	1	2
Wilbraham,	2,330	Ma.	1,156	1·20	28	14	1	–	–	1	–
		Fe.	1,174			14	1	1	–	–	–
HAMPSHIRE CO.	44,388	Tot.	44,388	.	.	803	168	46	17	6	2
		Ma.	21,443	1·81	803	400	92	30	8	2	2
		Fe.	22,945			403	76	16	9	4	4

Age and Sex, by Towns.

5 to 10	10 to 15	15 to 20	20 to 25	25 to 30	30 to 35	35 to 40	40 to 45	45 to 50	50 to 55	55 to 60	60 to 65	65 to 70	70 to 75	75 to 80	80 to 85	85 to 90	90 to 95	95 & over	Unknown
-	-	1	1	-	-	-	-	-	-	-	1	1	-	-	1	-	-	-	-
1	-	-	-	1	1	-	1	-	-	-	-	1	-	-	-	-	-	-	-
6	3	5	8	1	6	2	4	1	4	3	5	8	5	2	3	1	2	1	-
3	2	9	7	8	9	6	3	3	2	2	2	11	5	1	3	3	-	-	3
-	-	-	-	-	1	-	1	-	-	2	-	-	1	3	1	1	-	-	-
-	-	-	-	1	-	1	-	-	-	-	-	3	-	-	1	1	1	1	-
-	-	-	1	-	-	-	-	1	-	-	1	-	-	-	-	1	-	-	-
-	?	-	-	-	-	-	-	-	-	1	-	-	-	-	-	-	1	-	-
21	9	19	15	3	10	5	5	3	1	5	1	3	3	1	2	-	1	-	3
21	9	22	10	12	6	6	6	2	1	-	2	2	3	1	1	1	1	1	-
-	-	-	-	-	-	-	-	1	1	-	1	-	1	2	-	-	-	-	-
-	1	-	1	1	-	1	1	-	-	-	-	2	1	-	1	-	-	-	-
1	1	1	2	-	-	-	1	-	-	-	1	1	1	-	2	1	-	-	-
-	1	-	2	1	-	1	-	-	-	-	2	-	1	-	-	-	-	-	-
1	-	2	5	-	2	3	1	-	-	-	-	1	1	1	2	-	-	-	-
-	-	1	-	-	-	1	1	1	-	1	1	2	1	-	1	-	1	-	-
3	1	2	-	-	-	-	-	-	-	-	-	-	-	-	-	-	-	-	-
-	1	-	-	-	1	-	-	-	-	-	-	-	-	-	-	-	-	-	-
-	-	-	-	-	-	-	-	-	-	-	-	1	-	-	-	-	-	-	-
-	-	-	-	-	-	-	-	-	-	-	-	-	1	-	-	-	-	-	-
1	1	1	3	3	-	3	2	-	-	2	2	1	1	1	1	1	-	-	-
-	1	2	3	2	1	1	2	1	1	1	3	3	1	2	-	-	1	-	-
-	-	-	1	-	-	-	-	-	-	-	1	-	1	-	-	1	-	-	1
-	-	1	-	-	-	-	-	-	1	-	-	-	1	-	-	-	2	-	-
-	-	1	1	-	1	-	-	-	-	-	2	1	3	-	-	-	2	-	-
-	-	1	-	-	-	-	-	-	-	-	1	-	2	4	1	1	-	-	-
12	6	16	26	16	7	17	8	13	10	4	12	12	10	8	6	2	-	-	-
18	5	11	16	20	17	7	11	5	18	10	7	12	6	6	9	7	1	-	1
-	-	-	-	-	-	-	-	-	-	-	-	-	-	1	1	-	-	-	-
-	1	-	-	-	1	-	-	-	-	-	-	-	-	-	1	-	-	-	-
1	1	2	-	-	-	-	-	-	1	-	-	1	-	-	-	-	-	-	-
1	1	1	-	1	-	-	-	-	-	-	1	-	1	2	-	-	-	-	-
-	-	1	7	5	3	5	2	3	5	4	3	2	3	-	1	-	-	-	2
1	2	2	2	3	1	7	-	5	1	4	-	3	3	3	2	3	-	-	-
-	-	2	2	2	-	3	1	1	1	-	1	2	3	2	2	-	-	-	1
2	1	1	-	3	2	2	-	-	-	-	1	1	1	1	-	-	1	-	-
-	-	1	2	1	1	-	-	2	-	1	-	1	-	1	1	1	-	-	-
-	-	1	-	-	-	2	2	-	-	2	1	-	1	1	1	1	-	-	-
17	17	33	42	33	38	34	24	26	26	28	35	41	50	49	34	20	6	1	4
8	9	13	27	10	19	16	8	16	16	12	18	26	20	26	9	6	2	1	1
9	8	20	15	23	19	18	16	10	10	16	17	15	30	23	25	14	4	-	3

TABLE VII.—Continued.

Counties and Towns.	Persons.	Sex.		Per ct. to Pop.	Persons.	Sex.	Und. 1	1 to 2	2 to 3	3 to 4	4 to 5
Hampshire-Con.											
Amherst, . .	4,035	Ma.	2,042	1·07	43	25	5	2	–	–	–
		Fe.	1,993			18	3	–	–	–	–
Belchertown, .	2,428	Ma.	1,215	1·73	42	19	–	1	–	–	1
		Fe.	1,213			23	4	1	–	–	–
Chesterfield, .	811	Ma.	401	1·48	12	5	1	–	–	–	–
		Fe.	410			7	–	–	–	–	–
Cummington, .	1,037	Ma.	504	1·25	13	7	1	–	–	–	–
		Fe.	533			6	–	–	–	–	–
Easthampton, .	3,620	Ma.	1,640	1·57	57	35	12	4	1	1	1
		Fe.	1,980			22	4	1	1	–	–
Enfield, . .	1,023	Ma.	499	1·08	11	5	1	–	–	–	–
		Fe.	524			6	–	–	–	–	–
Goshen, . .	368	Ma.	190	·82	3	2	–	–	–	–	–
		Fe.	178			1	–	–	1	–	–
Granby, . .	863	Ma.	432	1·16	10	3	1	–	1	–	–
		Fe.	431			7	–	–	–	–	–
Greenwich, .	665	Ma.	319	2·11	14	7	–	–	1	–	–
		Fe.	346			7	–	–	–	–	–
Hadley, . .	2,301	Ma.	1,201	1·74	40	18	4	–	–	–	–
		Fe.	1,100			22	4	1	–	–	–
Hatfield, . .	1,594	Ma.	811	1·13	28	12	–	2	–	–	1
		Fe.	783			16	2	–	1	1	–
Huntington, .	1,156	Ma.	549	1·56	18	9	2	–	–	–	–
		Fe.	607			9	1	–	–	–	–
Middlefield, .	728	Ma.	376	·55	4	1	–	–	–	–	–
		Fe.	352			3	–	–	–	–	–
Northampton, .	10,160	Ma.	4,860	2·14	217	107	34	10	3	1	–
		Fe.	5,300			110	24	6	–	3	1
Pelham, . .	673	Ma.	322	1·34	9	5	–	–	–	–	–
		Fe.	351			4	–	1	–	–	–
Plainfield, . .	521	Ma.	259	1·54	8	3	–	–	–	–	–
		Fe.	262			5	1	–	–	–	–
Prescott, . .	541	Ma.	265	1·85	10	5	–	–	–	–	–
		Fe.	276			5	–	–	–	–	–
South Hadley, .	2,840	Ma.	1,218	2·08	59	28	9	4	–	–	1
		Fe.	1,622			31	6	5	2	–	1
Southampton, .	1,159	Ma.	590	1·47	17	8	–	1	–	–	–
		Fe.	569			9	1	–	–	–	–
Ware, . .	4,259	Ma.	2,006	3·05	130	64	19	6	–	–	1
		Fe.	2,253			66	21	1	3	–	–
Westhampton, .	587	Ma.	281	3·24	19	12	–	–	2	–	–
		Fe.	306			7	1	–	1	–	–

Age and Sex, by Towns.

5 to 10	10 to 15	15 to 20	20 to 25	25 to 30	30 to 35	35 to 40	40 to 45	45 to 50	50 to 55	55 to 60	60 to 65	65 to 70	70 to 75	75 to 80	80 to 85	85 to 90	90 to 95	95 & over	Unknown
–	1	2	2	–	2	3	–	2	–	1	2	–	1	1	–	1	–	–	–
–	1	1	–	1	2	–	–	–	1	1	–	1	2	–	2	3	–	–	–
–	–	2	2	2	–	–	–	–	1	–	2	1	2	1	1	2	–	1	–
–	–	–	2	1	2	–	1	–	–	–	3	–	2	2	2	2	1	–	–
–	–	–	–	–	–	1	1	–	–	–	2	–	2	–	–	1	–	1	–
–	–	–	–	–	–	1	1	–	–	2	–	2	–	–	–	1	–	–	–
–	1	–	–	–	1	1	–	–	–	–	–	1	1	1	1	–	–	–	–
1	–	–	–	–	–	–	–	–	–	–	–	2	1	1	1	–	–	–	–
2	2	–	3	–	–	2	–	2	1	1	–	–	1	2	–	–	–	–	–
1	–	2	–	2	2	1	2	1	1	–	–	–	2	1	–	1	–	–	–
–	–	–	–	–	–	1	–	1	–	–	1	1	–	1	1	–	–	–	–
–	–	–	–	–	–	–	–	–	1	1	1	1	1	1	1	–	–	–	–
–	–	–	–	–	–	–	–	1	–	–	1	–	–	–	1	–	–	–	–
1	–	–	–	–	–	–	–	–	–	–	●	–	–	–	–	–	–	–	–
–	–	–	–	–	1	1	–	–	–	1	–	–	1	–	1	1	–	–	–
1	–	–	–	–	1	1	–	–	–	1	–	–	1	–	1	1	–	–	–
–	–	–	–	1	–	1	1	1	–	–	–	2	–	1	–	1	–	–	–
–	–	1	–	1	–	1	–	–	–	–	–	2	–	–	2	–	–	–	–
–	–	1	–	–	1	–	1	2	2	1	1	–	2	2	1	3	1	–	1
–	1	1	–	1	–	–	1	–	2	–	–	2	3	1	3	1	–	–	1
1	–	–	1	1	1	–	1	2	–	–	–	–	–	2	1	–	1	–	–
–	–	2	2	–	–	2	2	–	–	–	–	–	2	1	1	–	–	–	–
–	1	1	–	–	–	1	1	1	–	–	1	–	2	–	1	–	–	–	–
–	–	–	–	–	2	1	–	–	1	–	–	–	1	1	1	–	1	–	–
–	1	–	–	–	–	–	–	1	–	–	–	–	1	1	–	–	–	–	–
1	1	2	6	5	7	7	1	3	5	4	4	5	–	5	2	–	1	–	–
2	3	5	4	7	6	5	6	2	1	7	5	2	8	7	2	2	–	–	2
–	–	2	–	–	–	–	–	–	–	1	1	–	1	–	–	–	–	–	–
–	–	1	–	–	1	–	–	–	–	1	1	–	–	–	–	–	–	–	–
–	–	–	1	–	–	–	1	–	–	–	–	1	–	–	–	–	–	–	–
–	–	–	–	1	–	–	–	1	–	–	–	–	1	–	–	1	–	–	–
1	1	–	–	–	–	–	–	–	–	1	–	1	–	1	–	–	–	–	–
–	–	–	–	–	–	–	1	1	–	–	–	–	–	2	1	–	–	–	–
1	1	–	3	–	1	–	–	–	1	–	–	1	5	1	–	–	–	–	–
–	–	3	1	2	1	1	–	–	2	–	2	–	1	–	3	1	–	–	–
–	–	–	2	–	–	–	–	–	–	1	–	1	–	2	–	–	–	–	1
–	–	–	–	1	–	1	–	–	–	1	–	–	–	3	1	–	1	–	–
2	–	3	4	1	4	2	1	1	4	2	1	6	7	–	–	–	–	–	–
3	1	5	4	5	3	3	–	–	1	1	4	2	2	5	1	1	–	–	–
–	–	–	–	1	–	–	–	–	–	1	5	1	–	2	–	–	–	–	–
1	–	–	–	1	–	–	1	–	–	1	1	–	–	–	1	–	–	–	–

TABLE VII.—Continued.

COUNTIES AND TOWNS.	POPULATION—1870.			DEATHS.			Und. 1	1 to 2	2 to 3	3 to 4	4 to 5
	Persons.	Sex.		Per ct. to Pop.	Persons.	Sex.					
Hampshire—Con.											
Williamsburg, .	2,159	Ma. Fe.	1,041 1,118	1·34	29	14 15	3 4	– –	– –	– –	– –
Worthington, .	860	Ma. Fe.	422 438	1·16	10	6 4	– –	– –	– –	– –	– 1
MIDDLESEX CO.,	274,353	Tot. Ma. Fe. U.	274,353 131,959 142,394	· 2·38 ·	· 6,539 ·	6,539 3,236 3,299 4	1593 819 770 4	417 216 201 –	176 80 96 –	144 65 79 –	107 55 52 –
Acton, . .	1,593	Ma. Fe.	783 810	1·44	23	13 10	1 –	– –	– –	1 1	– –
Arlington, .	3,261	Ma. Fe.	1,571 1,690	2·08	68	33 35	6 6	– 1	1 2	– –	– 1
Ashby, . .	994	Ma. Fe.	468 526	1·91	19	11 8	– –	– –	– 1	1 –	– –
Ashland, . .	2,186	Ma. Fe.	1,136 1,050	1·83	40	21 19	6 3	1 –	– –	– 1	– –
Ayer,* . .	–	Ma. Fe.	– –	–	36	21 15	4 4	– –	– –	– –	– –
Bedford, . .	849	Ma. Fe.	421 428	1·65	14	7 7	– 2	– –	– –	– –	– –
Belmont, . .	1,513	Ma. Fe.	757 756	2·45	37	17 20	5 7	1 –	– –	– 1	– –
Billerica, . .	1,833	Ma. Fe.	875 958	1·53	28	13 15	3 1	1 2	– –	– 1	– –
Boxborough, .	338	Ma. Fe.	182 156	1·18	4	1 3	– –	– –	– –	– –	– –
Brighton, . .	4,967	Ma. Fe.	2,631 2,336	2·01	100	54 46	11 12	2 4	– 1	2 –	– 1
Burlington, .	626	Ma. Fe.	324 302	1·28	8	5 3	– –	– –	– –	– –	– –
·Cambridge, .	39,634	Ma. Fe. U.	19,356 20,278 ·	2·44	969	469 497 3	143 131 3	41 43 –	14 15 –	6 13 –	5 7 –
Carlisle, . .	569	Ma. Fe.	287 282	2·28	13	4 9	– 2	– –	– –	– 1	– –
Charlestown, .	28,323	Ma. Fe.	13,931 14,392	2·80	794	402 392	101 103	22 27	14 10	10 9	8 11
Chelmsford, .	2,374	Ma. Fe.	1,170 1,204	1·95	46	14 32	4 9	– –	– –	– 2	– –
Concord, . .	2,412	Ma. Fe.	1,190 1,222	2·28	55	35 20	9 3	1 1	– –	– –	1 –
Dracut, . .	2,078	Ma. Fe.	1,050 1,028	1·83	38	20 18	4 1	1 3	1 –	2 –	1 3

* Incorporated 1871.

Age and Sex, by Towns.

5 to 10	10 to 15	15 to 20	20 to 25	25 to 30	30 to 35	35 to 40	40 to 45	45 to 50	50 to 55	55 to 60	60 to 65	65 to 70	70 to 75	75 to 80	80 to 85	85 to 90	90 to 95	95 & over	Unknown
-	1	-	3	-	1	-	-	3	-	-	2	2	-	2	-	-	-	-	-
-	-	-	1	1	-	1	-	3	1	1	1	-	1	-	1	-	-	-	-
-	-	-	-	-	-	-	-	1	-	1	-	1	1	1	1	-	-	-	-
-	1	-	-	-	-	-	-	1	-	-	-	1	-	-	-	-	-	-	-
266	126	239	352	335	287	275	211	221	241	196	262	269	266	215	165	94	34	15	33
135	62	112	161	146	132	119	113	117	130	111	138	136	137	104	76	34	13	6	19
131	64	127	191	189	155	156	98	104	111	85	124	133	129	111	89	60	21	9	14
-	1	-	1	-	-	-	-	-	3	-	-	1	1	3	-	1	-	-	-
1	-	-	2	-	-	1	-	1	-	-	-	-	-	1	2	1	-	-	-
2	1	1	3	1	1	2	2	4	2	-	-	3	2	1	1	-	-	-	-
-	2	-	1	1	1	2	1	2	1	-	1	2	-	3	5	2	1	-	-
-	-	-	1	-	1	-	-	-	-	2	1	2	2	1	-	-	-	-	-
-	-	-	2	-	-	-	-	-	-	1	1	2	-	-	-	1	-	-	-
-	-	-	2	2	2	-	2	-	1	-	1	1	2	-	1	-	-	-	-
-	1	-	3	3	1	1	-	1	-	-	1	-	1	1	1	-	1	-	-
1	-	1	2	2	-	2	-	-	2	1	3	-	2	-	-	1	-	-	-
-	-	-	2	2	1	1	-	1	-	-	-	1	-	1	2	1	-	-	-
-	-	-	-	1	1	-	-	-	2	-	1	2	-	-	-	-	-	-	-
-	-	-	1	1	-	-	-	-	-	-	-	1	1	-	1	-	-	-	-
-	-	-	1	1	-	1	-	-	-	-	2	2	2	1	-	2	-	-	-
2	-	1	2	1	-	1	-	1	-	1	1	-	1	1	-	-	-	-	-
-	-	-	1	1	1	1	-	1	-	1	-	1	-	1	1	1	-	-	-
-	-	1	1	1	1	1	-	-	-	-	1	2	1	2	-	-	-	-	-
-	-	-	-	-	-	-	-	-	1	-	-	-	-	-	-	-	-	-	-
-	-	-	-	-	-	-	-	-	1	-	-	1	1	-	-	-	-	-	-
1	3	7	3	1	2	2	2	4	2	1	4	-	2	3	-	-	-	-	2
1	1	2	3	1	1	4	1	1	2	1	3	-	3	1	1	-	-	-	2
-	-	-	-	1	-	-	-	1	1	1	1	-	-	-	1	-	-	-	-
-	-	-	-	-	-	-	1	-	-	1	1	-	-	-	1	-	-	-	-
16	7	16	29	22	17	10	16	10	19	19	19	22	15	11	5	2	1	-	4
15	8	18	31	22	33	30	11	13	22	8	17	18	16	9	8	5	2	1	1
-	-	-	-	-	1	-	-	-	-	-	-	-	-	3	-	-	-	-	-
-	-	-	-	-	-	-	-	1	-	-	2	-	1	1	-	-	1	-	-
17	4	13	27	22	24	20	15	19	12	17	16	14	9	9	3	2	-	1	3
22	8	16	21	20	19	19	19	6	12	9	6	13	10	8	11	5	3	1	4
1	-	-	1	1	-	-	-	1	-	-	2	-	2	1	-	-	-	-	1
-	1	-	1	1	2	2	-	2	-	-	2	5	1	-	1	2	-	1	-
1	2	-	-	1	1	1	1	-	1	2	2	3	3	3	2	1	-	-	-
-	1	-	1	3	-	-	-	1	2	-	-	1	3	1	2	1	-	-	-
3	1	1	-	-	-	-	1	1	1	-	-	1	-	1	1	-	-	-	-
-	-	-	-	1	-	-	-	-	1	1	-	2	3	-	3	-	-	-	-

TABLE VII.—Continued.

COUNTIES AND TOWNS.	POPULATION—1870.			DEATHS.			Und. 1	1 to 2	2 to 3	3 to 4	4 to 5
	Persons.	Sex.		Per ct. to Pop.	Persons.	Sex.					
Middlesex—Con.											
Dunstable, .	471	Ma. Fe.	244 227	·64	3	2 1	– –	– –	– –	– –	– –
Everett, . .	2,220	Ma. Fe.	1,087 1,133	2·48	55	21 34	6 11	1 1	– –	2 1	2 –
Framingham, .	4,968	Ma. Fe.	2,297 2,671	1·55	77	33 44	6 7	3 –	– 1	– 1	2 1
Groton, . .	3,584	Ma. Fe.	1,723 1,861	·56	20	12 8	– –	1 –	– –	– –	– –
Holliston, .	3,073	Ma. Fe.	1,535 1,538	1·43	44	20 24	4 2	1 1	– –	– –	– –
Hopkinton, .	4,419	Ma. Fe.	2,236 2,183	1·31	58	36 22	8 3	– 2	3 2	– –	1 1
Hudson, .	3,389	Ma. Fe.	1,661 1,728	2·54	86	44 42	13 8	9 3	3 5	– 1	– 2
Lexington, .	2,277	Ma. Fe.	1,123 1,154	2·68	61	32 29	7 4	4 1	1 –	– –	– 1
Lincoln, .	791	Ma. Fe.	392 399	·88	7	2 5	– –	– 1	– –	– –	– –
Littleton, .	983	Ma. Fe.	502 481	1·83	18	8 10	2 –	– –	– –	– –	– –
Lowell, .	40,928	Ma. Fe.	17,494 23,434	2·84	1,162	542 620	151 147	47 53	20 15	15 19	13 8
Malden, .	7,367	Ma. Fe. U.	3,530 3,837 .	1·95	144	70 73 1	18 15 1	4 2 –	– 2 –	4 – –	– 1 –
Marlborough, .	8,474	Ma. Fe.	4,325 4,149	2·81	238	117 121	27 43	17 16	6 9	4 4	3 5
Maynard,* .	–	Ma. Fe.	– –	–	19	12 7	1 2	– –	– 1	– –	– –
Medford, .	5,717	Ma. Fe.	2,906 2,811	2·15	123	62 61	10 9	4 5	3 –	– –	2 –
Melrose, .	3,414	Ma. Fe.	1,589 1,825	1·26	43	14 29	4 5	– –	– 1	– –	1 1
Natick, .	6,404	Ma. Fe.	3,208 3,196	2·34	150	85 65	16 15	4 2	3 1	2 3	1 –
Newton, .	12,825	Ma. Fe.	5,973 6,852	1·43	183	79 104	15 28	3 2	– 2	1 4	2 1
North Reading,	942	Ma. Fe.	462 480	1·70	16	5 11	1 –	– 1	– 1	– 1	– –
Pepperell, .	1,842	Ma. Fe.	889 953	2·12	39	18 21	1 2	2 –	– –	– 1	– –
Reading, .	2,664	Ma. Fe.	1,233 1,431	1·80	48	30 18	7 3	1 1	– 1	– –	– –

* Incorporated 1871.

Age and Sex, by Towns.

5 to 10	10 to 15	15 to 20	20 to 25	25 to 30	30 to 35	35 to 40	40 to 45	45 to 50	50 to 55	55 to 60	60 to 65	65 to 70	70 to 75	75 to 80	80 to 85	85 to 90	90 to 95	95 & over	Unknown
–	–	–	–	–	–	–	–	–	–	–	–	–	–	–	1	1	–	–	–
–	–	–	1	–	–	–	–	–	–	–	–	–	–	–	–	–	–	–	–
2	–	1	–	–	–	1	1	1	–	1	–	2	1	–	–	–	–	–	–
1	1	–	3	1	–	–	1	1	1	1	3	1	4	1	–	–	–	–	2
1	1	2	1	2	1	–	–	1	1	–	1	3	4	2	1	–	–	1	–
1	1	1	3	3	2	1	–	–	2	1	3	1	1	6	4	2	2	–	–
2	–	1	–	–	1	–	–	–	1	1	1	–	2	1	–	1	1	1	–
–	1	1	–	–	–	–	–	1	–	–	–	1	1	1	1	–	1	–	–
–	–	3	–	2	2	1	2	3	1	2	–	2	2	1	1	–	1	–	–
–	1	2	–	2	4	1	2	3	1	–	1	1	1	–	1	1	–	–	–
3	–	–	1	–	1	3	3	2	2	–	2	1	2	2	1	1	–	–	–
1	–	2	–	3	2	–	1	1	1	–	–	–	1	–	1	1	–	–	–
3	–	2	3	–	–	4	–	1	1	–	–	–	–	–	3	1	1	–	–
1	1	2	2	1	3	1	1	–	2	–	1	4	2	–	–	1	–	1	–
1	–	1	–	1	–	–	3	–	4	1	–	2	3	–	4	1	–	–	–
3	–	–	1	1	–	1	2	2	1	1	1	1	2	2	4	1	–	–	–
–	1	–	–	–	1	–	–	–	–	–	–	–	2	2	–	–	–	–	–
–	1	–	–	–	–	–	–	–	–	–	–	–	2	–	–	–	–	–	–
1/2	–	–	–	–	1	–	–	1	–	–	1	–	1	1	–	–	1	–	–
–	1	–	–	1	1	–	–	–	–	2	–	–	1	–	–	2	–	–	–
29	8	25	26	29	22	28	17	17	22	16	14	10	15	7	5	4	–	–	2
33	7	44	45	33	21	32	19	20	19	22	24	18	17	13	3	5	2	1	–
2	–	2	2	5	1	5	2	5	5	2	5	1	2	3	–	1	–	1	–
3	3	3	2	7	3	7	2	3	2	3	4	2	4	3	–	1	1	–	–
12	1	1	5	2	4	5	4	4	3	1	1	4	4	1	3	2	2	1	–
12	–	1	3	5	3	4	3	3	1	1	1	1	–	4	–	2	–	–	–
–	–	–	2	1	–	1	–	–	–	3	2	1	–	1	–	–	–	–	–
–	1	–	–	–	1	–	–	–	–	–	1	–	–	1	–	–	–	–	–
1	2	2	3	3	2	2	1	1	1	3	3	5	8	4	1	–	–	–	1
–	2	2	2	3	6	4	2	1	1	2	3	3	5	3	4	3	–	–	1
–	–	–	1	1	–	1	2	–	–	1	–	–	2	–	–	–	–	–	1
1	–	1	2	2	2	1	2	1	–	–	1	2	1	1	3	1	1	–	–
6	1	8	2	3	5	3	3	4	1	6	3	2	7	3	1	–	–	–	–
4	1	2	3	1	1	2	2	4	3	2	3	5	7	1	1	1	1	–	–
4	6	5	1	3	4	5	4	2	2	5	3	4	2	2	3	2	–	–	1
2	3	1	8	9	4	3	3	4	4	3	3	3	4	6	6	–	–	–	1
–	–	–	1	–	–	–	2	–	–	1	–	–	–	–	–	–	–	–	–
–	1	1	–	1	–	–	1	–	–	–	1	1	1	–	1	1	–	–	–
1/1	–	1	–	–	1	–	–	–	1	–	1	3	1	2	3	1	–	–	–
–	1	–	–	1	1	1	1	–	1	1	1	2	–	2	2	3	1	–	–
–	1	1	1	1	1	1	1	3	1	1	–	2	5	2	–	1	–	–	–
–	–	–	1	1	1	–	1	–	–	2	1	2	1	1	1	–	1	–	–

TABLE VII.—Continued.

COUNTIES AND TOWNS.	POPULATION—1870.			DEATHS.			Und. 1	1 to 2	2 to 3	3 to 4	4 to 5
	Persons.	Sex.		Per ct. to Pop.	Persons.	Sex.					
Middlesex—Con.											
Sherborn, .	1,062	Ma. Fe.	508 554	1·60	17	10 7	4 2	– –	– –	– –	– –
Shirley, . .	1,451	Ma. Fe.	726 725	1·79	26	13 13	1 3	– 1	– –	– –	1 1
Somerville, .	14,685	Ma. Fe.	7,295 7,390	2·88	423	201 222	73 68	16 11	4 9	5 3	4 1
Stoneham, .	4,513	Ma. Fe.	2,205 2,308	1·42	– 64	29 35	4 5	1 3	3 2	2 1	1 1
Stow, . .	1,813	Ma. Fe.	888 925	1·21	22	11 11	1 –	– –	– –	1 1	– –
Sudbury, . .	2,091	Ma. Fe.	1,035 1,056	·91	19	12 7	1 –	1 –	– 1	– –	– –
Tewksbury, .	1,944	Ma. Fe.	926 1,018	1·08	21	11 10	1 1	– –	– –	– –	– –
State Almsh'se at Tewksbury,	–	Ma. Fe.	– –	–	342	192 150	41 31	4 1	– 3	– –	– –
Townsend, .	1,962	Ma. Fe.	989 973	1·99	39	21 18	3 5	4 –	– –	1 –	– –
Tyngsboro', .	629	Ma. Fe.	329 300	1·91	12	7 5	– –	– –	– –	– –	– –
Wakefield, .	4,135	Ma. Fe.	1,994 2,141	2·25	93	52 41	16 13	4 4	– –	1 1	2 –
Waltham, . .	9,065	Ma. Fe.	4,259 4,806	1·94	176	85 91	20 22	4 5	1 3	2 2	2 2
Watertown, .	4,326	Ma. Fe.	2,081 2,245	1·78	77	39 38	6 5	2 –	1 2	– 4	1 1
Wayland, . .	1,240	Ma. Fe.	624 616	2·34	29	9 20	5 6	– –	– 1	– –	– –
Westford, . .	1,803	Ma. Fe.	900 903	1·16	21	10 11	1 –	– –	– –	– –	– –
Weston, . .	1,261	Ma. Fe.	633 628	1·43	18	13 5	5 –	– –	– –	– –	– –
Wilmington, .	866	Ma. Fe.	428 438	1·50	13	6 7	2 3	– –	– 1	– –	– –
Winchester, .	2,645	Ma. Fe.	1,289 1,356	2·00	53	29 24	7 4	2 –	– 2	– 1	– 2
Woburn, . .	8,560	Ma. Fe.	4,309 4,251	2·20	188	102 86	34 14	7 4	2 2	3 2	2 –
NANTUCKET CO.	4,123	Tot. Ma. Fe.	4,123 1,825 2,298	2·57	106	106 48 58	7 4 3	2 – 2	1 1 –	– – –	– – –

Age and Sex, by Towns.

5 to 10	10 to 15	15 to 20	20 to 25	25 to 30	30 to 35	35 to 40	40 to 45	45 to 50	50 to 55	55 to 60	60 to 65	65 to 70	70 to 75	75 to 80	80 to 85	85 to 90	90 to 95	95 & over	Unknown
-	1	1	1	-	-	-	-	-	-	1	1	1	1	1	1	-	-	-	-
-	1	1	1	-	-	-	-	-	-	-	-	2	-	-	-	-	-	-	-
-	1	-	1	-	1	-	1	-	1	-	1	1	1	-	2	1	-	-	-
-	-	1	-	-	1	1	-	-	-	1	1	-	-	1	-	2	-	-	-
8	4	7	8	7	5	4	3	9	8	7	6	4	9	5	2	1	1	-	1
11	6	5	13	13	13	14	1	10	6	6	5	8	8	7	2	-	-	2	-
2	1	1	-	-	2	-	1	1	-	3	-	2	1	1	1	1	1	-	-
2	2	1	2	5	-	2	-	1	2	1	1	2	2	-	-	-	-	-	-
-	-	-	1	-	1	-	-	-	2	1	1	-	-	2	-	1	-	-	-
-	-	-	-	1	1	-	-	-	-	1	1	-	1	4	-	1	-	-	-
-	-	-	-	1	1	-	-	1	1	1	1	-	2	-	-	1	-	1	-
-	1	-	-	-	-	-	-	-	-	-	1	-	1	2	-	1	-	-	-
-	1	-	-	1	1	1	-	-	1	-	1	1	-	-	2	1	-	-	-
-	-	1	-	1	-	-	-	-	3	-	1	1	-	-	2	-	-	-	-
-	4	3	9	12	12	9	11	12	11	6	19	10	14	7	6	-	-	-	2
-	-	2	5	9	9	9	10	10	11	7	6	11	7	3	9	4	-	1	2
1	-	-	-	-	-	-	1	-	-	-	1	2	2	2	4	-	-	-	-
-	-	-	3	1	-	-	-	-	-	4	1	3	-	-	-	1	-	-	-
1	-	3	-	-	-	-	-	1	-	-	1	1	-	-	-	-	-	-	-
1	1	-	-	-	-	-	-	-	-	1	-	-	1	1	-	-	-	-	-
1	2	4	3	4	-	1	-	1	3	-	5	2	2	-	-	1	-	-	-
1	-	2	2	3	1	2	4	-	2	-	1	-	2	-	2	-	-	-	1
4	2	4	4	3	6	3	2	5	4	3	4	3	3	3	1	2	-	-	-
5	2	4	5	7	4	2	1	4	3	1	3	3	6	5	-	1	1	-	-
3	2	2	3	2	3	3	2	2	1	-	-	1	1	-	3	-	1	-	-
1	1	2	3	8	1	1	2	2	1	-	-	1	-	1	-	2	-	-	-
-	-	-	-	-	-	-	1	1	-	-	-	1	-	1	-	-	1	-	-
-	-	1	2	1	-	-	1	1	-	-	1	1	1	1	1	1	-	1	-
1	1	1	-	1	1	1	-	-	-	-	1	-	1	-	1	-	-	-	-
-	-	-	-	-	1	-	-	1	-	1	-	2	-	-	3	1	2	-	-
-	-	-	1	2	-	-	-	-	-	-	2	-	2	-	1	-	-	-	-
1	-	-	1	-	-	-	1	-	1	-	1	-	-	-	-	-	-	-	-
-	-	-	1	-	1	-	1	-	-	-	1	-	-	-	-	-	-	-	-
-	-	1	-	1	-	-	-	-	-	-	1	-	-	-	-	-	-	-	-
1	1	1	1	-	1	1	3	1	1	-	1	4	1	2	1	-	-	-	-
-	1	1	2	3	2	2	1	-	-	1	-	-	1	1	-	-	-	-	-
3	4	3	2	7	3	5	-	2	1	4	4	6	1	1	6	1	-	-	1
3	2	4	5	5	6	3	2	2	2	1	8	2	6	6	3	3	1	-	-
2	-	1	2	2	4	4	5	1	3	13	8	10	12	11	11	4	3	-	-
2	-	1	-	1	2	2	1	-	1	5	3	4	5	7	6	2	1	-	-
-	-	-	2	1	2	2	4	1	2	8	5	6	7	4	5	2	2	-	-

TABLE VII.—Continued.

COUNTIES AND TOWNS.	POPULATION—1870.			Per ct. to Pop.	DEATHS.			Und. 1	1 to 2	2 to 3	3 to 4	4 to 5
	Persons.	Sex.			Per ct. to Pop.	Persons.	Sex.					
NORFOLK CO.,	89,443	Tot.	89,443	·	·	1,677	1,677	358	88	48	38	26
		Ma.	42,944	1·87	1,677		808	200	46	20	14	6
		Fe.	46,499				868	157	42	28	24	20
		U.	·	·	·		1	1	–	–	–	–
Bellingham,	1,282	Ma.	631	2·03	26		13	2	1	–	–	–
		Fe.	651				13	3	–	1	–	–
Braintree,	3,948	Ma.	1,941	1·57	62		38	9	1	3	–	–
		Fe.	2,007				24	3	–	2	1	2
Brookline,	6,650	Ma.	2,984	1·98	132		50	24	2	1	1	–
		Fe.	3,666				82	21	6	1	2	1
Canton,	3,879	Ma.	1,833	1·13	44		19	6	1	–	–	–
		Fe.	2,046				25	4	2	2	–	–
Cohasset,	2,130	Ma.	1,008	2·02	43		20	5	–	–	1	–
		Fe.	1,122				23	4	–	–	1	–
Dedham,	7,342	Ma.	·3,479	1·31	96		50	11	2	–	–	–
		Fe.	3,863				46	10	2	2	–	–
Dover,	645	Ma.	311	1·40	9		5	–	–	–	–	–
		Fe.	334				4	–	–	–	–	–
Foxborough,	3,057	Ma.	1,301	1·60	49		22	3	1	2	–	1
		Fe.	1,756				27	4	–	–	1	2
Franklin,	2,512	Ma.	1,163	1·63	41		19	4	2	1	–	–
		Fe.	1,349				22	5	–	–	–	1
Holbrook,*	–	Ma.	–	–	25		13	4	–	–	1	–
		Fe.	–				12	1	–	–	1	–
Hyde Park,	4,136	Ma.	2,017	2·97	123		75	26	5	–	2	1
		Fe.	2,119				48	12	2	6	2	–
Medfield,	1,142	Ma.	525	2·28	26		11	1	2	–	–	–
		Fe.	617				15	1	1	–	–	–
Medway,	3,721	Ma.	1,823	1·50	56		20	6	1	–	–	–
		Fe.	1,898				36	9	2	1	–	–
Milton,	2,683	Ma.	1,272	1·34	36		17	2	1	1	–	1
		Fe.	1,411				19	3	–	–	–	1
Needham,	3,607	Ma.	1,749	2·13	77		36	5	4	2	1	1
		Fe.	1,858				41	3	2	3	2	3
Norfolk,	1,081	Ma.	566	1·30	14		4	–	–	–	–	1
		Fe.	515				10	1	–	–	–	–
Norwood,*	–	Ma.	–	–	33		15	3	1	–	–	–
		Fe.	–				18	2	–	–	–	1
Quincy,	7,442	Ma.	3,791	2·47	184		103	21	8	3	2	–
		Fe.	3,651				81	23	4	2	3	1
Randolph,	5,642	Ma.	2,782	1·33	75		34	7	2	3	2	–
		Fe.	2,860				41	5	2	–	1	2
Sharon,	1,508	Ma.	729	1·72	26		12	2	–	1	–	–
		Fe.	779				14	1	1	1	–	–

* Incorporated 1873.

Age and Sex, by Towns.

5 to 10	10 to 15	15 to 20	20 to 25	25 to 30	30 to 35	35 to 40	40 to 45	45 to 50	50 to 55	55 to 60	60 to 65	65 to 70	70 to 75	75 to 80	80 to 85	85 to 90	90 to 95	95 & over	Unknown
62	34	67	73	83	70	63	52	52	53	66	63	72	93	80	63	43	17	6	7
36	16	31	29	40	32	23	29	27	23	38	29	39	40	48	20	14	4	1	3
26	18	36	44	43	38	40	23	25	30	28	34	33	53	32	43	29	13	5	4
-	-	-	-	-	-	-	-	-	-	-	-	-	-	-	-	-	-	-	-
1	-	-	-	1	-	-	1	1	-	-	1	-	1	1	2	1	-	-	-
-	-	1	-	-	1	-	-	-	1	1	1	1	1	-	2	-	-	-	-
1	-	3	3	1	1	1	-	3	1	3	2	1	1	1	1	2	-	-	-
2	1	1	3	1	-	1	-	1	-	-	-	1	2	1	2	-	-	-	-
1	-	1	-	1	2	-	-	1	1	4	5	2	3	-	1	-	-	-	-
4	2	4	2	4	5	6	4	-	4	2	1	3	4	-	3	1	1	-	1
-	-	2	1	3	-	-	-	-	1	1	1	1	-	2	-	-	-	-	-
1	1	-	6	2	-	-	2	-	3	-	1	-	-	-	1	-	-	-	-
-	-	1	1	1	1	2	2	-	-	-	-	3	-	2	-	1	-	-	-
-	1	1	-	2	1	2	1	1	-	2	-	-	2	3	-	1	1	-	-
6	1	-	3	3	2	2	2	-	1	3	2	6	2	4	-	-	-	-	-
-	1	3	2	1	1	2	-	2	-	2	2	3	4	2	2	3	1	-	1
-	-	-	-	1	-	-	-	-	-	-	-	3	-	-	-	1	-	-	-
1	-	-	-	-	-	1	-	-	-	-	-	-	-	1	-	-	1	-	-
-	-	1	1	2	-	-	-	-	-	1	-	4	1	4	1	-	-	-	-
-	1	-	4	1	2	1	-	1	-	-	1	2	3	1	2	1	-	-	-
1	-	1	-	1	2	1	-	2	1	1	-	-	1	-	1	-	-	-	-
2	-	1	-	3	1	-	-	-	-	-	-	1	1	3	3	-	1	-	-
1	-	2	-	1	-	-	1	-	-	-	-	-	2	1	1	-	-	-	-
1	-	-	-	3	-	-	-	-	-	2	-	-	2	-	1	1	-	-	-
6	1	2	3	4	2	3	2	5	3	2	1	2	2	3	-	-	-	-	1
2	1	1	2	1	1	1	4	2	-	1	2	1	1	4	1	-	-	-	-
-	-	-	-	1	-	-	2	1	-	1	1	-	1	2	-	4	2	-	-
1	-	2	-	-	1	-	-	-	-	1	3	-	2	2	1	-	-	-	-
-	-	-	1	1	3	5	1	1	3	-	-	1	2	2	-	3	2	1	-
1	-	-	-	-	2	-	1	1	1	-	-	-	1	2	2	1	-	-	-
-	-	-	1	-	3	-	-	-	-	1	3	3	1	1	1	1	-	-	-
4	5	1	1	1	-	-	1	2	2	-	1	1	2	1	-	-	1	-	-
2	1	1	2	3	4	1	1	1	3	1	3	1	-	-	-	2	1	-	1
-	-	-	-	1	-	-	-	-	-	1	-	-	-	-	1	-	-	-	-
-	-	2	1	-	-	-	-	-	2	1	1	-	-	1	-	1	-	-	-
-	-	2	2	1	1	-	1	-	-	1	-	-	2	-	1	2	1	-	-
-	-	1	1	1	1	1	-	-	1	-	3	1	2	-	2	1	-	-
1	1	7	2	6	6	1	6	4	4	7	3	4	3	7	3	1	1	-	2
3	3	4	2	5	2	4	2	2	3	5	3	1	3	2	2	1	1	-	-
1	2	1	1	1	3	-	1	-	-	2	2	1	2	-	1	2	-	-	-
3	1	1	5	2	2	-	-	1	3	-	2	3	3	1	3	-	-	1	-
-	-	2	-	-	1	-	2	-	-	1	-	1	1	-	-	-	-	-	1
-	-	2	2	-	-	1	-	-	-	1	-	-	-	2	-	1	2	1	1	-

TABLE VII.—Continued.

COUNTIES AND TOWNS.	POPULATION—1870.		DEATHS.			Und. 1	1 to 2	2 to 3	3 to 4	4 to 5
	Persons.	Sex.	Per ct. to Pop.	Persons.	Sex.					
Norfolk—Con. Stoughton,	4,914	Ma. 2,449 Fe. 2,465 U. .	1·79	88	41 46 1	9 8 1	2 3 –	– 2 –	1 2 –	– 1 –
Walpole, .	2,137	Ma. 1,021 Fe. 1,116	1·59	34	13 21	1 1	– 1	– 1	– –	– –
West Roxbury,	8,683	Ma. 3,993 Fe. 4,690	1·86	161	67 94	22 15	4 6	1 3	1 5	– 3
Weymouth, .	9,010	Ma. 4,502 Fe. 4,508	1·86	168	87 81	24 13	5 5	2 1	3 3	1 2
Wrentham, .	2,292	Ma. 1,074 Fe. 1,218	2·14	49	24 25	3 5	1 3	– –	– –	– –
PLYMOUTH CO.,	65,365	Tot. 65,365 Ma. 32,116 Fe. 33,249 U. .	1·89	1,235	1,235 616 616 3	221 126 92 3	55 28 27 –	33 16 17 –	19 9 10 –	14 10 4 –
Abington, .	9,308	Ma. 4,688 Fe. 4,620	1·46	136	78 58	27 16	5 4	2 1	1 1	1 1
Bridgewater, .	3,660	Ma. 1,775 Fe. 1,885	1·12	41	19 22	4 5	– 1	2 1	– –	1 –
State Almsh'se at Bridgewater,	–	Ma. – Fe. –	–	61	44 17	11 5	2 1	– –	1 –	– –
Carver, . .	1,092	Ma. 556 Fe. 536	1·74	19	7 12	1 1	– 2	– –	– 1	– –
Duxbury, .	2,341	Ma. 1,153 Fe. 1,188	1·07	25	11 14	3 1	– –	– –	– –	– –
E. Bridgewater,	3,017	Ma. 1,465 Fe. 1,552 U. .	1·76	53	30 22 1	8 2 1	2 1 –	– – –	– – –	– – –
Halifax, . .	619	Ma. 292 Fe. 327	1·29	8	4 4	– –	1 –	– –	– –	– –
Hanover, . .	1,628	Ma. 792 Fe. 836	2·70	44	22 22	7 1	– –	1 –	– 1	– –
Hanson, . .	1,219	Ma. 596 Fe. 623	1·80	22	11 11	– 3	– –	– –	– –	– –
Hingham, .	4,422	Ma. 2,070 Fe. 2,352	2·04	90	45 45	9 8	1 2	1 –	– 2	– 1
Hull, . . .	261	Ma. 134 Fe. 127	1·92	5	2 3	– –	– 1	– –	– –	– –
Kingston, .	1,604	Ma. 765 Fe. 839	1·75	28	12 16	– –	– –	– 1	– –	1 –
Lakeville, .	1,159	Ma. 572 Fe. 587	·86	10	6 4	1 –	1 –	– –	– –	– –
Marion, . .	896	Ma. 431 Fe. 465	1·56	14	5 9	1	1	1	–	–

Age and Sex, by Towns.

5 to 10	10 to 15	15 to 20	20 to 25	25 to 30	30 to 35	35 to 40	40 to 45	45 to 50	50 to 55	55 to 60	60 to 65	65 to 70	70 to 75	75 to 80	80 to 85	85 to 90	90 to 95	95 & over	Unknown
1	1	2	2	2	1	3	2	1	2	1	3	1	3	3	-	1	-	-	-
-	-	3	2	2	1	5	1	1	-	-	2	1	5	3	2	-	1	1	-
1	1	1	-	-	-	1	-	-	1	-	-	1	3	2	1	-	-	-	-
1	-	1	1	1	3	-	-	2	2	-	1	-	2	1	-	3	-	-	-
4	-	1	2	3	3	4	4	1	1	3	3	-	5	3	1	1	-	-	-
1	1	5	6	5	2	3	-	4	2	4	6	3	9	2	6	-	2	1	-
5	2	1	4	5	4	2	2	2	3	3	1	5	2	6	1	1	2	1	-
3	3	4	3	5	3	4	5	4	3	2	1	5	2	3	3	4	-	-	-
-	2	-	3	1	2	-	1	2	-	3	1	2	-	2	1	-	-	-	-
-	1	1	-	-	1	2	-	2	-	2	3	-	-	1	1	2	-	1	-
45	35	35	61	60	44	45	33	46	42	40	60	81	77	71	55	44	11	4	4
23	15	15	35	29	16	17	15	19	20	23	31	48	37	31	26	21	4	-	2
22	20	20	26	31	28	28	18	27	22	17	29	33	40	40	29	23	7	4	2
1	1	1	5	2	2	-	-	2	1	3	9	5	4	6	-	-	-	-	-
2	1	1	4	1	4	5	1	2	1	1	3	3	1	2	1	-	2	-	-
1	-	1	1	1	-	-	1	1	-	-	-	1	1	-	2	1	1	-	-
-	1	-	-	3	2	3	-	2	1	-	-	-	2	-	1	-	-	-	-
-	-	-	2	2	2	1	2	-	6	1	5	3	3	1	-	1	-	-	1
-	-	2	1	4	1	-	-	3	-	-	-	-	-	-	-	-	-	-	-
-	-	-	-	1	-	-	1	-	1	1	-	-	-	1	1	-	-	-	-
-	-	-	1	-	1	-	1	1	1	-	1	1	-	-	-	-	1	-	-
-	1	-	-	-	-	-	1	1	-	1	-	-	2	1	1	-	-	-	-
-	-	1	-	-	1	1	-	1	1	-	-	3	-	1	-	3	1	-	-
1	1	-	2	1	1	1	-	1	2	2	-	-	1	3	4	1	-	-	-
-	2	-	2	1	-	-	1	1	1	2	-	2	2	1	1	2	-	-	-
-	-	-	-	1	-	-	-	-	-	-	-	1	-	1	-	-	-	-	-
-	-	-	1	-	-	-	-	-	-	-	-	1	-	1	1	-	-	-	-
1	1	-	1	2	-	1	-	1	-	1	1	3	-	1	-	-	1	-	-
-	1	3	2	2	1	1	1	1	-	1	2	2	2	-	-	-	-	1	-
-	-	-	-	-	-	-	-	-	1	-	5	2	-	2	2	-	-	-	-
-	-	-	-	-	1	-	-	1	-	1	-	2	3	-	-	-	-	-	-
1	1	2	3	2	1	1	-	1	3	1	1	5	6	3	1	2	-	-	-
1	-	1	-	3	1	1	-	-	3	-	3	6	5	4	3	-	-	1	-
-	-	-	-	-	1	-	-	-	-	-	-	-	-	-	-	-	-	-	1
-	1	1	-	-	1	-	-	-	-	-	-	-	-	-	-	1	-	-	-
1	-	1	-	1	-	-	-	-	1	-	1	1	1	1	2	1	-	-	-
3	-	1	1	1	-	-	-	1	-	1	1	-	-	2	3	1	-	-	-
-	-	-	-	-	-	1	-	-	1	-	-	1	1	-	-	-	-	-	-
-	-	2	-	-	1	-	-	-	-	-	-	1	1	-	-	-	-	-	-
-	-	1	-	-	-	-	-	-	-	-	3	-	-	1	-	-	-	-	-
-	-	-	-	-	1	-	-	-	-	-	1	1	2	1	-	-	-	-	-

TABLE VII.—Continued.

COUNTIES AND TOWNS.	POPULATION—1870. Persons.	Sex.		Per ct. to Pop.	DEATHS. Persons.	Sex.		Und. 1	1 to 2	2 to 3	3 to 4	4 to 5
Plymouth—Con.												
Marshfield,	1,659	Ma.	809	1·87	31	14		1	–	–	–	–
		Fe.	850			17		–	–	–	–	–
Mattapoisett,	1,361	Ma.	631	1·54	21	11		2	–	–	–	–
		Fe.	730			10		–	–	–	–	–
Middleborough,	4,687	Ma.	2,263	1·32	62	27		3	–	–	–	1
		Fe.	2,424			35		6	2	1	1	–
N. Bridgewater,	8,007	Ma.	4,035	2·46	217	110		22	12	5	3	3
		Fe.	3,972			105		19	6	5	–	1
		U.	.	.	.	2		2	–	–	–	–
Pembroke,	1,447	Ma.	748	1·73	25	13		–	–	–	–	1
		Fe.	699			12		2	–	–	–	–
Plymouth,	6,238	Ma.	2,979	1·93	120	52		6	1	3	2	2
		Fe.	3,259			68		8	1	4	4	1
Plympton,	804	Ma.	400	1·49	12	5		–	–	–	–	–
		Fe.	404			7		–	–	–	–	–
Rochester,	1,024	Ma.	497	1·27	13	6		–	–	–	–	–
		Fe.	527			7		–	–	–	–	–
Scituate,	2,350	Ma.	1,164	2·00	47	20		5	–	1	2	–
		Fe.	1,186			27		–	3	1	–	–
South Scituate,	1,661	Ma.	830	2·35	39	22		5	–	–	–	–
		Fe.	831			17		2	2	–	–	–
Wareham,	3,098	Ma.	1,603	1·97	61	31		10	3	1	–	–
		Fe.	1,495			30		6	–	1	–	–
W. Bridgewater,	1,803	Ma.	868	1·72	31	9		1	–	–	–	–
		Fe.	935			22		6	–	1	–	–
SUFFOLK Co.,	270,802	Tot.	270,802	.	.	8,324		2175	621	281	221	150
		Ma.	129,482	3·07	8,324	4,330		1186	319	144	111	72
		Fe.	141,320			3,994		989	302	137	110	78
Boston,	250,526	Ma.	119,917	3·14	7,868	4,097		1120	305	137	107	72
		Fe.	130,609			3,771		942	291	128	108	75
Chelsea,	18,547	Ma.	8,652	2·34	434	223		64	13	7	4	–
		Fe.	9,895			211		47	10	9	2	2
Revere,	1,197	Ma.	652	1·00	12	5		1	1	–	–	–
		Fe.	545			7		–	1	–	–	–
Winthrop,	532	Ma.	261	1·88	10	5		1	–	–	–	–
		Fe.	271			5		–	–	–	–	1
WORCESTER Co.	192,716	Tot.	192,716	.	.	3,659		809	229	118	60	58
		Ma.	95,201	1·90	3,659	1,861		474	119	58	32	31
		Fe.	97,515			1,798		335	110	60	28	27
Ashburnham,	2,172	Ma.	1,102	1·75	38	18		2	2	–	–	–
		Fe.	1,070			20		1	1	–	–	–
Athol,	3,517	Ma.	1,732	2·76	73	34		9	7	–	2	–
		Fe.	1,785			39		6	1	1	–	–

Age and Sex, by Towns.

5 to 10	10 to 15	15 to 20	20 to 25	25 to 30	30 to 35	35 to 40	40 to 45	45 to 50	50 to 55	55 to 60	60 to 65	65 to 70	70 to 75	75 to 80	80 to 85	85 to 90	90 to 95	95 & over	Unknown
1	-	1	1	-	-	2	-	1	1	-	-	1	1	1	1	2	-	-	-
1	-	2	1	-	-	1	1	1	1	1	2	-	-	1	3	2	-	-	-
-	-	-	-	1	2	-	-	1	-	2	1	-	2	-	-	-	-	-	-
-	-	-	-	1	1	-	1	2	-	1	1	-	1	-	-	1	1	-	-
-	-	3	2	2	1	1	1	-	1	-	3	4	3	-	1	1	-	-	-
1	1	-	1	1	4	2	-	2	-	-	2	3	2	3	1	1	-	1	-
10	6	2	7	7	5	4	4	1	2	2	3	2	3	1	3	3	-	-	-
4	4	5	4	7	3	2	7	1	5	4	7	5	7	1	3	4	-	-	1
-	-	-	-	-	-	-	-	-	-	-	-	-	-	-	-	-	-	-	-
-	1	-	-	1	-	-	-	1	-	-	1	3	-	1	2	2	-	-	-
1	-	-	-	-	-	2	-	-	2	-	1	1	-	2	-	1	-	-	-
4	-	-	4	1	-	2	4	2	2	2	4	5	3	2	2	1	-	-	-
6	6	2	2	2	4	3	3	5	1	-	3	3	4	6	-	-	-	-	-
-	-	1	1	1	-	-	-	1	-	-	-	-	1	-	-	-	-	-	-
-	-	-	-	-	-	-	-	-	1	-	-	-	1	1	2	-	1	1	-
-	-	-	2	-	-	-	-	-	-	1	-	1	-	-	2	-	-	-	-
-	-	1	-	-	-	-	-	-	-	-	-	-	3	-	1	1	-	-	1
1	-	1	1	-	1	-	-	2	1	1	1	2	-	1	-	-	-	-	-
1	1	-	1	-	-	3	-	1	-	2	1	1	3	4	3	2	-	-	-
1	1	-	-	2	1	1	-	2	-	1	1	1	1	3	-	2	-	-	-
1	-	-	1	-	-	-	-	2	1	-	1	-	-	2	1	3	1	-	-
1	1	1	1	-	-	2	-	1	-	1	1	1	2	2	1	1	1	-	-
-	2	-	1	2	1	2	1	1	-	3	2	-	-	4	2	1	1	-	-
-	1	1	1	1	-	-	-	-	-	1	-	1	1	-	1	-	-	-	-
-	1	-	-	3	4	-	-	-	-	1	1	-	2	2	1	-	1	-	-
339	153	296	500	498	404	409	328	317	298	265	242	231	187	180	115	64	25	8	7
189	71	146	291	263	207	214	167	164	145	155	129	110	94	70	45	22	12	1	3
150	92	150	209	235	197	195	161	153	153	110	113	121	93	110	70	42	13	7	4
178	66	140	278	252	199	201	158	156	137	143	121	101	87	64	41	20	11	1	2
143	86	140	196	221	186	182	150	145	146	105	108	108	80	105	68	37	13	5	3
10	5	5	13	11	8	12	9	8	8	11	8	9	7	5	3	2	-	-	1
6	5	10	12	13	9	11	11	8	7	5	5	12	12	5	2	5	-	2	1
-	-	-	-	-	-	-	-	-	1	-	-	-	-	1	-	1	-	-	-
-	1	-	-	-	2	1	-	-	-	-	1	1	-	-	-	1	-	-	-
1	-	1	-	-	1	-	-	-	-	-	-	1	-	-	-	-	-	-	-
1	-	-	1	1	-	1	-	-	-	-	-	-	1	-	-	-	-	-	-
112	92	162	184	181	152	124	123	119	121	117	142	153	162	173	123	82	30	11	22
62	45	68	91	74	72	42	58	65	59	64	76	87	79	84	55	41	9	3	13
50	47	94	93	107	80	82	65	54	62	53	66	66	83	89	68	41	21	8	9
2	1	-	2	-	-	1	1	2	1	1	-	2	-	-	1	-	-	-	-
-	-	1	2	1	-	3	-	-	1	1	3	1	1	1	-	3	-	-	-
2	-	1	-	-	4	-	1	1	2	-	-	2	3	-	-	-	-	-	-
2	-	5	3	3	2	2	3	2	1	1	1	1	2	1	-	-	1	-	1

9

TABLE VII.—Continued.

COUNTIES AND TOWNS.	POPULATION—1870.		DEATHS.			Und. 1	1 to 2	2 to 3	3 to 4	4 to 5
	Persons.	Sex.	Per ct. to Pop.	Persons.	Sex.					
Worcester—Con.										
Auburn, . .	1,178	Ma. 596 / Fe. 582	·93	11	5 / 6	1 / –	1 / –	– / 1	– / –	– / –
Barre, . .	2,572	Ma. 1,252 / Fe. 1,320	2·02	52	24 / 28	5 / 2	1 / 1	– / –	– / 1	1 / –
Berlin, . .	1,016	Ma. 491 / Fe. 525	1·28	13	7 / 6	1 / –	– / –	– / –	– / –	– / –
Blackstone, .	5,421	Ma. 2,497 / Fe. 2,924	1·62	88	45 / 43	10 / 6	2 / 1	– / 1	– / –	– / –
Bolton, . .	1,014	Ma. 530 / Fe. 484	2·07	21	12 / 9	5 / 2	– / –	– / –	– / –	– / –
Boylston, . .	800	Ma. 292 / Fe. 408	1·37	11	7 / 4	2 / –	1 / 2	– / –	– / –	1 / –
Brookfield, .	2,527	Ma. 1,250 / Fe. 1,277	1·82	46	24 / 22	4 / –	1 / –	2 / 2	– / 2	1 / –
Charlton, . .	1,878	Ma. 929 / Fe. 949	1·17	22	8 / 14	2 / –	– / –	1 / –	– / –	– / –
Clinton, . .	5,429	Ma. 2,422 / Fe. 3,007	1·64	89	45 / 44	12 / 9	3 / 3	5 / 3	– / 1	– / –
Dana, . .	758	Ma. 369 / Fe. 389	1·32	10	2 / 8	– / –	– / 1	– / –	– / –	– / –
Douglas, . .	2,182	Ma. 1,091 / Fe. 1,091	1·47	32	17 / 15	8 / 4	– / 2	2 / 3	– / 1	– / –
Dudley, . .	2,388	Ma. 1,179 / Fe. 1,209	2·89	69	37 / 32	7 / 9	3 / 3	3 / 2	1 / 1	– / –
Fitchburg, .	11,260	Ma. 5,663 / Fe. 5,597	1·92	216	111 / 105	30 / 24	5 / 6	1 / 1	2 / 1	1 / 1
Gardner, . .	3,333	Ma. 1,657 / Fe. 1,676	1·86	62	31 / 31	9 / 5	1 / 1	1 / 1	1 / –	– / 1
Grafton, . .	4,594	Ma. 2,285 / Fe. 2,309	·96	44	21 / 23	3 / 6	– / 1	2 / 1	2 / 1	1 / 1
Hardwick, .	2,219	Ma. 1,102 / Fe. 1,117	1·13	25	13 / 12	1 / –	– / 1	– / –	– / –	– / –
Harvard, . .	1,341	Ma. 636 / Fe. 705	1·34	18	15 / 3	2 / –	– / –	– / –	– / –	– / –
Holden, . .	2,062	Ma. 1,041 / Fe. 1,022	2·13	44	25 / 19	3 / 3	– / 1	2 / 1	1 / –	– / 1
Hubbardston, .	1,654	Ma. 861 / Fe. 793	1·81	30	17 / 13	2 / –	1 / –	– / –	– / –	– / –
Lancaster, .	1,845	Ma. 812 / Fe. 1,032	1·57	29	15 / 14	1 / –	– / 1	– / 1	– / –	– / –
Leicester, . .	2,768	Ma. 1,337 / Fe. 1,431	2·02	56	25 / 31	5 / 4	1 / 2	1 / 1	– / –	– / –

Age and Sex, by Towns.

5 to 10	10 to 15	15 to 20	20 to 25	25 to 30	30 to 35	35 to 40	40 to 45	45 to 50	50 to 55	55 to 60	60 to 65	65 to 70	70 to 75	75 to 80	80 to 85	85 to 90	90 to 95	95 & over	Unknown
-	-	-	1	-	-	-	-	-	-	-	-	-	1	-	1	-	-	-	-
-	-	-	1	-	-	1	-	2	-	-	-	-	-	1	-	-	-	-	-
-	1	-	-	1	1	-	-	2	-	-	3	2	-	5	1	1	-	-	-
2	1	1	-	1	1	2	1	-	1	-	4	-	5	1	3	-	1	-	-
1	-	-	-	-	1	1	1	-	1	1	-	-	-	-	-	1	-	-	-
-	-	-	1	-	-	-	-	1	1	-	2	-	-	-	1	-	-	-	-
1	2	5	-	2	3	-	3	1	4	3	1	1	2	3	1	1	-	-	-
4	4	2	3	3	2	1	3	2	1	3	-	3	-	2	-	2	-	-	-
1	-	1	-	-	-	2	-	-	-	1	1	2	-	1	-	-	-	-	-
-	-	-	-	1	-	-	-	-	-	-	1	1	-	-	2	-	-	-	-
-	-	-	-	-	-	-	1	-	-	-	-	1	-	1	-	-	-	-	-
-	-	-	-	-	-	-	-	-	-	-	-	-	1	1	-	-	-	-	-
2	-	-	1	1	2	-	-	-	-	-	-	1	1	4	2	2	-	-	-
2	1	1	3	2	-	-	2	1	-	-	3	-	1	1	-	-	1	-	-
-	1	-	-	-	1	-	-	-	-	1	-	-	2	1	-	-	-	-	-
-	1	1	-	1	1	-	2	-	-	1	-	1	-	1	2	1	1	1	-
3	2	1	2	2	2	-	2	-	1	1	3	1	-	5	-	-	-	-	-
-	2	3	5	5	-	3	1	-	-	2	-	-	2	3	2	-	-	-	-
-	-	1	-	-	-	-	-	-	1	-	1	-	-	-	-	-	-	-	-
1	-	1	-	1	-	-	-	1	1	-	-	1	-	1	-	-	-	-	-
-	-	-	1	-	-	2	-	-	1	-	-	1	-	-	1	-	1	-	-
-	-	-	-	-	-	2	-	2	-	-	-	-	-	-	1	-	-	-	-
1	3	1	1	-	1	1	-	1	1	3	2	2	2	1	2	1	-	-	-
-	2	2	1	3	1	1	-	1	-	-	2	-	-	2	-	1	-	1	-
3	1	6	7	4	4	3	4	2	3	3	6	6	6	3	4	-	-	-	-
2	4	7	6	9	6	3	3	3	2	4	3	4	6	3	3	1	-	-	-
2	1	1	2	-	1	1	2	-	1	-	3	1	1	2	-	1	-	-	-
-	2	1	1	1	3	1	1	1	3	1	-	2	3	-	2	-	1	-	-
1	1	1	1	-	1	-	-	1	-	1	1	1	2	1	1	-	-	-	-
1	2	1	-	-	2	-	-	-	1	-	1	-	-	3	1	-	1	-	-
-	-	-	4	-	-	-	-	1	1	-	1	1	-	-	1	3	-	-	-
-	-	-	-	1	1	-	-	-	1	1	1	2	1	3	-	-	-	-	-
-	-	1	-	-	2	1	-	1	-	1	-	2	1	-	1	3	-	-	-
-	-	-	-	-	-	-	-	-	-	-	-	-	2	-	1	-	-	-	-
2	-	2	1	-	-	1	-	-	1	1	-	1	3	1	-	2	1	-	4
-	1	1	1	-	1	-	-	1	1	-	1	1	2	1	1	-	1	-	-
-	-	1	-	1	-	-	-	2	1	-	2	2	1	1	1	1	1	-	-
-	-	1	-	3	-	2	-	-	1	1	1	1	1	1	1	-	-	-	-
1	-	-	-	-	2	-	-	-	-	1	1	-	1	5	1	2	-	-	-
-	-	1	1	2	-	-	-	-	-	1	-	1	2	-	1	2	-	-	-
2	-	2	1	2	1	1	-	1	-	-	-	1	1	2	1	-	1	1	-
2	-	2	4	-	2	1	1	3	-	2	-	-	-	1	2	-	-	-	-

TABLE VII.—Continued.

COUNTIES AND TOWNS.	POPULATION—1870.			DEATHS.			Und. 1	1 to 2	2 to 3	3 to 4	4 to 5
	Persons.	Sex.		Per ct. to Pop.	Persons.	Sex.					
Worcester—Con.											
Leominster,	3,894	Ma.	1,954	2·39	93	47	10	1	–	–	–
		Fe.	1,940			46	8	1	3	2	–
Lunenburg,	1,121	Ma.	541	1·16	13	6	–	–	–	–	–
		Fe.	580			7	1	–	–	–	–
Mendon,	1,175	Ma.	576	1·19	14	6	2	–	–	–	–
		Fe.	599			8	–	1	–	–	–
Milford,	9,890	Ma.	4,970	1·52	150	74	15	9	–	1	2
		Fe.	4,920			76	18	4	2	1	1
Millbury,	4,397	Ma.	2,131	2·07	91	48	16	4	2	–	–
		Fe.	2,266			43	11	5	1	2	1
New Braintree,	640	Ma.	326	1·09	7	1	–	–	–	–	–
		Fe.	314			6	1	–	–	–	–
Northborough,	1,504	Ma.	717	2·46	37	20	4	–	1	–	–
		Fe.	787			17	2	–	–	–	–
Northbridge,	3,774	Ma.	1,869	1·61	64	36	4	4	1	–	–
		Fe.	1,905			28	7	1	1	–	1
No. Brookfield,	3,343	Ma.	1,726	2·30	77	41	8	3	5	2	–
		Fe.	1,617			36	10	2	–	1	–
Oakham,	860	Ma.	423	2·09	18	6	–	1	–	–	–
		Fe.	437			12	–	–	–	–	–
Oxford,	2,669	Ma.	1,293	1·05	28	8	–	1	–	1	–
		Fe.	1,376			20	2	2	1	2	–
Paxton,	646	Ma.	318	1·39	9	4	–	–	–	–	–
		Fe.	328			5	–	–	–	–	–
Petersham,	1,335	Ma.	657	·82	11	6	–	–	–	–	–
		Fe.	678			5	1	–	–	–	–
Phillipston,	693	Ma.	355	1·88	13	7	–	–	–	–	–
		Fe.	338			6	–	–	–	–	–
Princeton,	1,279	Ma.	653	1·33	17	5	–	–	–	–	–
		Fe.	626			12	1	–	1	–	–
Royalston,	1,354	Ma.	674	1·85	25	7	–	–	–	1	–
		Fe.	680			18	1	1	1	–	–
Rutland,	1,024	Ma.	532	1·95	20	14	3	–	–	–	–
		Fe.	492			6	1	–	–	–	–
Shrewsbury,	1,610	Ma.	820	1·67	27	17	8	1	–	–	–
		Fe.	790			10	–	1	–	–	–
Southborough,	2,135	Ma.	1,060	1·73	37	20	4	1	–	–	1
		Fe.	1,075			17	5	–	–	–	–
Southbridge,	5,208	Ma.	2,506	2·09	109	55	21	8	1	–	–
		Fe.	2,702			54	11	1	4	3	1
Spencer,	3,952	Ma.	2,111	2·63	104	60	25	3	3	1	1
		Fe.	1,841			44	7	9	4	1	1

Age and Sex, by Towns.

5 to 10	10 to 15	15 to 20	20 to 25	25 to 30	30 to 35	35 to 40	40 to 45	45 to 50	50 to 55	55 to 60	60 to 65	65 to 70	70 to 75	75 to 80	80 to 85	85 to 90	90 to 95	95 & over	Unknown
3	2	1	8	2	3	1	2	2	1	3	-	1	1	4	1	-	-	-	1
-	-	5	3	-	1	2	1	2	3	2	1	2	3	4	1	1	1	-	-
-	-	-	-	-	-	-	-	1	1	-	-	-	1	-	2	1	-	-	-
-	-	-	1	-	-	-	-	-	-	-	-	1	1	-	3	-	-	-	-
-	1	-	-	-	-	-	-	1	-	-	-	-	1	1	-	-	-	-	-
-	-	-	-	2	-	1	-	1	1	1	-	-	-	-	-	-	1	-	-
1	1	6	3	3	3	2	7	3	5	3	1	2	2	3	1	1	-	-	-
2	1	3	4	3	2	5	4	2	6	1	2	2	4	3	3	2	1	-	-
-	1	1	1	3	1	1	1	1	1	1	2	3	1	2	3	1	-	1	1
1	1	2	1	2	2	4	2	1	-	-	1	-	2	2	-	-	-	-	-
-	-	1	-	-	-	-	-	-	-	-	-	1	-	-	1	-	-	-	-
-	-	1	1	1	-	-	-	-	-	-	1	-	-	1	-	-	-	-	-
-	-	1	-	-	1	1	-	-	2	1	2	-	2	1	3	1	-	-	-
-	-	-	-	-	1	3	-	1	2	1	1	2	1	1	-	1	1	-	-
1	2	-	2	5	1	1	5	2	1	1	1	2	-	1	1	-	-	-	1
-	-	-	1	1	2	2	3	1	1	-	2	-	1	1	2	-	-	1	-
1	2	-	2	-	1	2	3	3	-	2	1	3	1	1	1	-	-	-	-
3	-	1	4	2	1	1	1	-	2	3	-	3	-	2	-	-	-	-	-
-	-	-	-	-	1	2	-	1	-	-	-	1	1	1	1	1	1	-	-
-	-	-	-	-	2	2	-	-	-	-	1	1	1	2	1	1	1	-	-
-	-	-	1	1	-	-	1	-	-	-	1	-	3	-	-	1	1	-	-
-	1	3	-	1	-	-	1	-	-	-	-	3	1	-	1	1	-	1	-
-	-	-	-	-	-	-	1	-	1	-	1	-	1	-	-	-	-	-	-
-	-	-	-	1	-	-	-	-	-	1	2	1	-	-	-	-	-	-	-
-	1	-	-	-	-	-	-	-	-	1	1	-	2	1	-	-	-	-	-
-	-	1	1	-	1	-	-	-	-	-	-	-	-	-	1	-	-	-	-
-	-	3	-	-	-	2	-	-	-	-	-	-	2	1	1	-	-	-	-
-	1	-	-	1	1	1	-	-	-	-	1	-	1	-	-	-	-	-	-
-	-	-	-	-	-	-	-	-	-	1	2	-	-	1	1	-	-	-	-
1	-	-	1	1	-	1	2	1	1	1	-	-	1	-	-	-	-	-	-
-	1	1	-	-	-	1	1	-	-	-	1	-	-	-	-	1	-	-	-
-	1	-	-	3	-	1	2	1	-	-	1	1	3	1	-	1	-	-	-
1	1	-	-	-	-	1	1	1	1	-	4	-	1	-	-	-	-	-	-
-	2	-	1	-	-	1	-	-	-	-	-	-	-	-	1	-	-	-	-
-	-	1	-	-	-	-	1	1	1	1	1	2	-	-	-	-	-	-	-
1	-	-	2	-	-	-	-	-	1	-	-	2	-	1	1	1	-	-	-
2	-	3	-	4	-	-	1	-	-	1	-	1	1	1	-	-	-	-	-
-	1	1	2	3	1	-	1	-	-	-	-	1	1	-	-	1	-	-	-
1	1	1	4	3	2	1	-	1	1	3	2	-	2	-	2	1	-	-	-
1	2	5	1	4	2	4	-	1	3	-	-	2	3	3	2	1	-	-	-
2	3	1	1	2	-	-	1	4	3	-	1	1	2	2	1	-	-	-	3
3	-	1	2	3	1	-	2	-	1	2	-	-	-	2	2	-	-	-	3

TABLE VII.—Concluded.

Counties and Towns.	Population—1870. Persons.	Sex.		Per ct. to Pop.	Deaths. Persons.	Sex.		Und. 1	1 to 2	2 to 3	3 to 4	4 to 5
Worcester—Con.												
Sterling,	1,670	Ma. Fe.	812 858	1·74	29	Ma. Fe.	12 17	– 2	1 –	– –	– –	1 –
Sturbridge,	2,101	Ma. Fe.	985 1,116	1·52	32		14 18	4 1	– 1	– –	– –	– 1
Sutton,	2,699	Ma. Fe.	1,314 1,385	1·48	40		23 17	11 3	– –	1 1	– –	– 1
Templeton,	2,802	Ma. Fe.	1,418 1,384	1·25	35		16 19	2 2	– 1	– 1	1 –	– –
Upton,	1,989	Ma. Fe.	959 1,030	1·61	32		19 13	3 1	1 2	– –	– –	– –
Uxbridge,	3,058	Ma. Fe.	1,475 1,583	1·14	35		13 22	2 3	– 2	– 1	1 1	– –
Warren,	2,625	Ma. Fe.	1,306 1,319	1·45	38		18 20	5 3	– –	1 1	– –	– 1
Webster,	4,763	Ma. Fe.	2,331 2,432	2·44	116		67 49	14 13	10 5	7 1	2 1	1 2
Westborough,	3,601	Ma. Fe.	1,854 1,747	1·50	54		26 28	8 8	2 1	– 1	– –	1 –
W. Boylston,	2,862	Ma. Fe.	1,447 1,415	2·27	65		32 33	13 11	3 3	3 –	– 1	– 1
W. Brookfield,	1,842	Ma. Fe.	884 958	1·52	28		14 14	4 3	1 –	– –	– –	1 1
Westminster,	1,770	Ma. Fe.	865 905	1·69	30		11 19	– 3	– –	– –	– –	– –
Winchendon,	3,398	Ma. Fe.	1,709 1,689	1·94	66		34 32	7 4	1 2	– –	– –	– –
Worcester,	41,105	Ma. Fe.	20,405 20,700	2·42	996		516 480	157 110	35 37	13 17	13 5	17 8

Age and Sex, by Towns.

5 to 10	10 to 15	15 to 20	20 to 25	25 to 30	30 to 35	35 to 40	40 to 45	45 to 50	50 to 55	55 to 60	60 to 65	65 to 70	70 to 75	75 to 80	80 to 85	85 to 90	90 to 95	95 & over	Unknown
-	-	-	-	-	-	-	-	-	-	-	1	4	-	1	1	1	-	-	2
1	-	2	1	1	1	1	-	-	1	-	-	1	3	-	-	2	-	-	1
2	-	1	-	3	-	-	-	-	1	1	1	1	-	-	-	-	-	-	1
-	-	-	-	1	1	1	1	-	1	1	1	1	2	-	2	2	-	-	1
-	-	-	-	-	2	1	-	1	-	-	-	-	3	1	2	1	-	-	-
-	1	-	3	1	-	-	1	-	-	1	-	1	1	2	-	1	-	-	-
1	-	-	1	1	1	-	1	-	-	1	2	3	-	1	1	-	-	-	-
-	1	2	-	1	-	1	-	-	-	1	1	-	1	4	-	-	2	1	-
-	-	-	1	1	1	-	3	-	-	1	1	1	3	-	1	2	-	-	-
-	1	-	-	1	1	1	-	1	-	1	-	1	1	1	1	-	-	-	-
1	-	-	1	-	-	1	1	-	-	-	-	4	1	1	-	1	-	-	-
-	-	1	-	-	1	-	2	-	2	-	1	-	-	4	2	-	1	-	-
1	1	1	1	-	1	1	-	1	-	1	1	4	-	1	-	-	-	-	-
1	-	1	3	1	2	1	-	1	-	1	-	-	2	-	-	2	-	-	-
6	1	1	-	5	4	1	2	-	-	4	2	1	2	1	1	2	-	-	-
2	2	4	-	8	2	3	-	-	-	2	-	2	1	1	-	-	-	-	-
1	1	2	1	2	1	-	1	2	1	-	1	1	-	-	-	1	-	-	-
-	-	-	3	1	1	1	1	-	2	1	-	1	3	1	-	3	-	-	-
1	-	-	3	-	1	-	-	-	1	1	1	-	2	2	1	-	-	-	-
-	2	1	2	2	1	2	1	-	1	1	1	-	-	1	1	-	-	1	-
-	-	-	2	1	-	-	-	1	-	-	-	1	1	1	-	1	-	-	-
-	1	1	-	-	1	1	-	1	2	-	-	1	-	-	-	2	-	-	-
-	1	-	1	-	-	1	-	2	-	1	1	1	1	1	-	-	1	-	-
-	1	2	-	1	-	-	-	1	-	-	2	1	1	4	3	-	-	-	-
3	1	-	2	1	1	1	-	2	1	4	5	-	2	1	1	1	-	-	-
-	-	2	2	3	-	1	1	3	3	1	2	-	2	3	1	2	-	-	-
12	12	22	27	24	22	15	15	17	17	18	21	18	14	12	10	4	-	1	-
19	9	18	31	23	24	20	20	19	11	14	24	20	16	13	12	3	4	-	3

TABLE VIII.—CAUSES OF DEATH.—ALPHABETICAL ARRANGEMENT.

Distinguishing by Months, by Age and by Sex, the registered Number of Deaths from various specified causes (alphabetically arranged), during the year

1873.

[Still-births not included in this Table.]

AGGREGATE.

SEX.	DEATHS. SEX. Males.	Fem.	Unk.	Totals.	January.	February.	March.	April.	May.	June.	July.	August.	September.	October.	November.	December.	Unknown.	Under 5.	5 to 10.	10 to 15.	15 to 20.	20 to 30.	30 to 40.	40 to 50.	50 to 60.	60 to 70.	70 to 80.	Over 80.	Unknown.
Persons,	.	.	.	33,912	2809	2478	2970	2985	2620	2315	3338	4039	3074	2659	2469	2556	—	12422	1313	727	1346	3546	2901	2223	2203	2629	2611	1808	283
Males,	17,242			.	1470	1225	1489	1349	1309	1231	1678	2141	1573	1315	1219	1243	—	6643	712	342	611	1750	1293	1125	1184	1359	1267	737	219
Females,		16,642		.	1338	1251	1479	1336	1307	1081	1654	1896	1500	1342	1249	1309	—	5751	601	385	735	1796	1208	1098	1019	1270	1344	1071	64
Unknown,			28	.	1	2	2	—	4	3	6	2	1	2	1	4	—	28	—	—	—	—	—	—	—	—	—	—	—

TABLE VIII.—Continued.

Cause of Death	Sex	Males	Fem.	Unk.	Totals	Jan.	Feb.	Mar.	Apr.	May	June	July	Aug.	Sept.	Oct.	Nov.	Dec.	Unk.	Under 5	5 to 10	10 to 15	15 to 20	20 to 30	30 to 40	40 to 50	50 to 60	60 to 70	70 to 80	Over 80	Unk.
Abortion,	Fem.,		2		2	1											1							2						
Abscess,	Males,	40			73	2	2	4	2	2	6	3	3	5	5	4	2		13	1	1	1	4	6	5	4	3	1	1	
"	Fem.,		33			2	2	2	2	2	1	1	5	3	4	2	6		6	1	1	1	5	4	4	4	5	2	1	
Abscess, Lumbar,	Males,	4			5									1		1	1		1		1			1	1					
"	Fem.,		1							1									1		1									
Amputation,	Males,	4			4					1	2			1	1		1						1		2 1					
"	Fem.,																													
Anæmia,	Males,	15			79	2	1	2	4	1	1	3	1			2	1		4				1	2	1	2	3	3		
"	Fem.,		64			5	2	5	14	9	6	5	2	4	6	3	3		9		1	3	18	10	8	8	6	1		
Aneurism,	Males,	7			13	2					1		1				3							1	3			1		
"	Fem.,		6			1			1		2	1	1												1	2	1			
Angina Pectoris,	Males,	12			15	1			2			2		1	3	1	1							1	1	3	8	1		
"	Fem.,		3				1					1		1		1	1				1						1			
Apoplexy,	Males,	224			431	15	11	23	27	21	13	22	19	13	19	16	25			1	1	1	4	19	32	38	57	50	20	1
"	Fem.,		207			25	20	17	14	14	12	22	12	13	17	14	27		1		2	2	10	9	21	40	53	41	27	1

TABLE VIII.—Continued.

CAUSES OF DEATH	SEX	Males	Fem.	Unk.	Totals	January	February	March	April	May	June	July	August	September	October	November	December	Unknown	Under 5	5 to 10	10 to 15	13 to 20	20 to 30	30 to 40	40 to 50	50 to 60	60 to 70	70 to 80	Over 80	Unknown
Ascites,	Males,	5			12	1		1	1				1	1	2	1			1				1		1	1		1	1	
"	Fem.,		7			1			1		1	1	2	1	5	1			1						1	5		1		
Asthma,	Males,	44			93	4	4	4	6	5	2		2	4	1	5	7		4					2	6	9	13	5	1	
"	Fem.,		49			6	3	3	3	3	2	2	1	3	5	8	4		1					4	7	11	14	3	3	
Bowels, Disease of,	Males,	19			36	1	3	1	1	2	1	1	2	4	2	1	2		10				2	4	5	1	1	1	1	
"	Fem.,		17						4	3	1	3	1			2	1		4				2	4	1	1	3	1	1	
Brain, Disease of,	Males,	186			329	21	15	15	14	19	6	16	16	21	19	12	12		77	15	4	5	15	12	10	17	16	12	2	1
"	Fem.,		143			16	19	16	12	13	11	11	8	7	9	7	14		64	8	1	6	7	15	9	9	11	10	1	3
Brain, Softening of,	Males,	67			90	9	3	7	4	6	4	7	6	7	5	4	5						1	7	11	8	20	17	3	
"	Fem.,		23			1	2	3	1	1	1	4		4	1	3	2						1		3	3	6	8	3	
Bronchitis,	Males,	171			328	14	12	30	12	13	12	6	6	14	15	15	22		112	6		2	4	7	11	6	10	14	2	
"	Fem.,		157			11	16	16	17	17	11	6	9	8	9	17	20		83	8		1	4	4	3	10	10	20	11	
Burns and Scalds,	Males,	36			88	4	2	1	2	3	1	5	3	3	1	6	5		26	1			1	1	2	1	1	1	1	
"	Fem.,		52			7	5	5	4	5	3	5	2	2	4	4	6		26	5	4	2	8	2	2			1	1	
Cancer,	Males,	146			522	16	12	12	11	12	10	11	13	11	11	17	8		4	1	1		3	11	11	29	41	40	9	5
"	Fem.,		376			33	31	33	26	31	39	35	41	23	28	30	27			1	1		7	38	84	75	92	53	16	

Cause of Death		Total
Cancer of Stomach,	Males,	89
"	Fem.,	52
Carbuncle,	Males,	3
"	Fem.,	5
Casualty,	Males,	416
"	Fem.,	77
Cephalitis,	Males,	400
"	Fem.,	342
Cere. Sp. Meningitis,	Males,	393
"	Fem.,	354
Childbirth,	Fem.,	270
Cholera,	Males,	46
"	Fem.,	60
Cholera Infantum,	Males,	1340
"	Fem.,	1212
"	Unk.,	
Chorea,	Males,	4
"	Fem.,	3
Consumption,	Males,	2543
"	Fem.,	3011
"	Unk.,	
Convulsions,	Males,	328
"	Fem.,	299
"	Unk.,	

TABLE VIII.—Continued.

CAUSES OF DEATH	SEX	Males	Fem.	Unk.	Totals	Jan.	Feb.	Mar.	Apr.	May	June	July	Aug.	Sep.	Oct.	Nov.	Dec.	Unk.	Under 5	5 to 10	10 to 13	13 to 20	20 to 30	30 to 40	40 to 50	50 to 60	60 to 70	70 to 80	Over 80	Unknown
Croup,	Males,	227			435	26	17	33	16	18	12	5	3	9	18	34	26	—	205	21	1	—	—	—	—	—	—	—	—	—
"	Fem.,		208			27	30	21	14	12	11	7	6	11	18	27	29	—	176	26	5	—	—	1	—	—	—	—	—	—
Cyanosis,	Males,	29			45	2	3	4	2	1	4	2	3	—	2	3	3	—	29	—	—	—	—	—	—	—	—	—	—	—
"	Fem.,		16			2	—	1	—	2	1	2	1	2	1	1	4	—	16	—	—	—	—	—	—	—	—	—	—	—
Cystitis,	Males,	23			32	2	2	4	—	—	1	2	1	3	4	2	2	—	—	—	—	—	—	—	—	—	—	—	—	—
"	Fem.,		9			1	1	3	—	—	1	1	1	1	—	—	1	—	—	—	—	—	—	—	—	—	—	—	—	—
Debility,	Males,	367			691	24	22	35	28	26	34	31	37	25	40	31	34	—	271	—	4	2	6	8	7	15	20	38	4	—
"	Fem.,		322			28	35	25	21	25	15	35	35	30	24	20	29	—	200	2	2	1	6	5	13	12	47	31	1	—
"	Unk.,			2											2			—	2											
Delirium Tremens,	Males,	27			30	2	2	2	—	5	1	1	3	4	3	2	2	—	—	—	—	—	5	10	3	6	3	—	—	—
"	Fem.,		3			—	—	—	—	—	1	—	1	—	—	1	—	—	—	—	—	—	—	1	1	—	1	—	—	—
Diabetes,	Males,	36			60	2	4	4	2	5	3	1	4	3	2	1	5	—	1	—	—	—	4	8	6	5	4	3	3	—
"	Fem.,		24			2	1	2	4	—	3	2	1	3	2	3	1	—	2	—	—	—	3	3	2	1	4	2	1	—
Diarrhœa,	Males,	187			353	9	1	5	8	9	9	35	47	28	26	9	7	—	114	4	4	2	5	7	9	11	17	13	5	—
"	Fem.,		166			7	4	7	4	4	9	24	33	33	25	11	5	—	76	—	1	—	9	17	17	8	13	20	6	—
Diphtheria,	Males,	160			310	20	17	6	10	10	9	7	11	16	29	15	10	—	98	31	4	6	6	7	1	2	5	1	1	1
"	Fem.,		150			17	16	21	9	6	6	12	9	21	16	12	6	—	66	43	16	5	3	6	4	1	4	1	—	1

Cause		Males	Fem.	Unk.	Total
Dropsy,	"	245	300		545
Drowned,	"	215	25		240
Dysentery,	"	205	230		435
Dyspepsia,	"	25	19		44
Embolism,	"		1		1
Enteritis,	"	187	191	1	379
Epilepsy,	"	32	34		66
Epistaxis,	"	1			1
Erysipelas,	"	116	119		235
Executed,	"	2			2
Exposure,	"	9	4		13

TABLE VIII.—Continued.

Causes of Death	Sex	Under 5	5 to 10	10 to 15	15 to 20	20 to 30	30 to 40	40 to 50	50 to 60	60 to 70	70 to 80	Over 80	Unk. (age)	Jan.	Feb.	Mar.	Apr.	May	June	July	Aug.	Sept.	Oct.	Nov.	Dec.	Unk. (mo.)	Males	Fem.	Unk.	Totals
Fever, Intermittent,	Males																										10			15
" "	Fem.																											5		
Fever, Remittent,	Males																										10			12
" "	Fem.																													
Fever, Typhus,	Males	72	45	42	98	234	75	55	45	38	30	7	1	44	29	36	38	33	38	55	61	116	101	112	79		742			1406
" "	Fem.	59	43	63	109	155	70	47	33	45	26	11	2	53	29	53	34	18	22	38	55	87	109	94	71			663		
" "	Unk.															1													1	
Fistula,	Males																										7			8
" "	Fem.																											1		
Fits,	Males	6	3		3	1	3	4	4	3	2			1	3	3	1	2		3	2	2	3	1	2		29			57
" "	Fem.	4	2		3	2	2	2	2	1			1	2	3	2	3	2		4	4	1	2	3	2			28		
Fracture,	Males	2	2		3	16	8	9	7		7	4		6	2	7	2		2	4	7	4	4	5	2		57			72
" "	Fem.								1	5	1	3			2	3	1	1	1	1	2	2	1	1				15		
Frozen,	Males						1									1								1			2			2
" "	Fem.																													
Gastritis,	Males	18	3	1	1	3	6	3	15	5	6	1		5	4	4	6	3	3	5	9	4	7	9	3		62			123
" "	Fem.	17	3	1	3	5	9	7	2	7	8			3	6	5	5	3	3	6	6	6	10	6	4			61		

Cause		Totals		
Glanders,	Males,	2	.	1
"	Fem.,	.	.	1
Gout,	Males,	1	.	1
"	Fem.,	.	.	.
Gravel,	Males,	30	4	26
"	Fem.,	.	.	.
Heart Disease,	Males,	1236	610	626
"	Fem.,	.	.	.
Heat,	Males,	22	5	17
"	Fem.,	.	.	.
Hemorrhage,	Males,	75	43	32
"	Fem.,	.	.	.
Hepatitis,	Males,	57	26	31
"	Fem.,	.	.	.
Hernia,	Males,	35	12	23
"	Fem.,	.	.	.
Hip Disease,	Males,	31	14	17
"	Fem.,	.	.	.
Homicide,	Males,	11	1	10
"	Fem.,	.	.	.
Hydrocephalus,	Males,	460	212	248
"	Fem.,	.	.	.

Table VIII.—Continued.

Deaths and Sex

Causes of Death	Sex	Males	Fem.	Unk.	Totals
Hydrothorax	Males, Fem.,	10	11	.	21
Ileus	Males, Fem.,	43	38	.	81
Infanticide	Males, Fem.,	.	4	.	4
Infantile	Males, Fem., Unk.,	256	196	2	454
Inflammation	Males, Fem.,	13	23	.	36
Influenza	Males, Fem.,	17	18	.	35
Inhalat'n of Chlorof.	Males, Fem.,	.	1	.	1
Insanity	Males, Fem.,	39	49	.	88

Months

Causes of Death	Sex	Jan.	Feb.	Mar.	Apr.	May	Jun.	Jul.	Aug.	Sep.	Oct.	Nov.	Dec.	Unk.
Hydrothorax	Males	1	1	1	2	2	–	1	–	2	2	1	1	–
	Fem.	1	2	1	–	1	–	1	–	1	–	2	2	–
Ileus	Males	2	1	3	3	3	3	7	4	4	4	5	3	–
	Fem.	2	2	3	2	2	2	4	8	2	3	2	6	–
Infanticide	Males	–	–	–	–	–	–	–	–	–	–	–	–	–
	Fem.	1	–	1	1	1	–	–	–	–	–	–	–	–
Infantile	Males	14	24	23	13	13	20	30	35	25	23	16	20	–
	Fem.	7	13	18	15	18	11	26	22	15	19	13	19	–
	Unk.	–	–	–	–	–	–	–	1	–	–	–	–	–
Inflammation	Males	–	2	1	1	3	1	1	1	1	1	1	1	–
	Fem.	1	2	3	4	3	2	1	–	2	2	1	2	–
Influenza	Males	–	–	6	2	4	1	–	–	1	1	1	2	–
	Fem.	1	2	7	4	–	–	–	–	2	–	1	1	–
Inhalat'n of Chlorof.	Males	–	–	–	–	–	–	–	–	–	–	1	–	–
	Fem.	–	–	–	–	–	–	–	–	–	–	–	–	–
Insanity	Males	5	4	2	1	5	–	2	6	3	5	3	3	–
	Fem.	6	5	2	5	4	4	2	2	5	5	6	5	–

Ages

Causes of Death	Sex	Under 5	5 to 10	10 to 15	15 to 20	20 to 30	30 to 40	40 to 50	50 to 60	60 to 70	70 to 80	Over 80	Unknown
Hydrothorax	Males	–	–	–	–	1	1	1	2	2	2	2	–
	Fem.	–	–	1	–	–	1	1	1	3	4	–	–
Ileus	Males	13	–	–	–	2	5	3	2	3	1	3	–
	Fem.	6	–	2	2	2	7	4	3	8	4	2	–
Infanticide	Males	–	–	–	–	–	–	–	–	–	–	–	–
	Fem.	4	–	–	–	–	–	–	–	–	–	–	–
Infantile	Males	256	–	–	–	–	–	–	–	–	–	–	–
	Fem.	196	–	–	–	–	–	–	–	–	–	–	–
	Unk.	2	–	–	–	–	–	–	–	–	–	–	–
Inflammation	Males	7	1	1	2	–	–	–	–	–	–	–	–
	Fem.	8	1	1	1	2	–	–	–	–	–	–	–
Influenza	Males	14	1	–	–	–	1	–	–	1	2	–	–
	Fem.	10	–	–	–	–	–	–	–	1	2	1	–
Inhalat'n of Chlorof.	Males	–	–	–	–	–	1	–	–	–	–	–	–
	Fem.	–	–	–	–	–	–	–	–	–	–	–	–
Insanity	Males	–	–	–	–	5	5	6	5	9	7	1	–
	Fem.	–	–	1	–	6	8	10	9	7	7	1	–

Cause of Death	Males	Fem.	Total
Intemperance	47	32	79
Intussusception	1	.	3
Ischuria	4	.	4
Jaundice	21	27	48
Joint Disease	10	4	14
Kidney Disease	122	46	168
Laryngitis	13	10	23
Lightning	2	.	2
Liver Disease	116	118	234
Lost at Sea	192	.	192
Lungs, Disease of	39	27	66

11

Table VIII.—Continued.

Cause	Sex	Males	Fem.	Unk.	Totals	Jan.	Feb.	Mar.	Apr.	May	Jun.	Jul.	Aug.	Sep.	Oct.	Nov.	Dec.	Unk.	Under 5	5 to 10	10 to 15	15 to 20	20 to 30	30 to 40	40 to 50	50 to 60	60 to 70	70 to 80	Over 80	Unk.
Malformation	Males	21	—	—	37	1	2	4	1	4	1	4	1	2	—	—	2	—	21	—	—	—	—	—	—	—	—	—	—	—
	Fem.	—	16	—	—	1	2	2	2	—	—	4	—	2	1	—	2	—	16	—	—	—	1	—	—	—	—	—	—	—
Malignant Pustule	Males	1	—	—	3	—	—	—	1	—	—	—	—	—	—	—	—	—	—	—	—	1	—	—	—	—	—	—	—	—
	Fem.	—	2	—	—	—	—	—	—	—	—	1	—	—	—	—	—	—	—	—	—	1	1	—	—	—	—	—	—
Measles	Males	88	—	—	180	2	4	4	6	11	20	15	8	7	1	5	5	—	66	12	1	5	2	—	—	—	—	—	—	—
	Fem.	—	92	—	—	4	3	3	3	15	17	23	9	5	2	3	5	—	69	6	4	3	5	1	—	—	—	—	—	—
Metria (Puerp. Fev.)	Fem.	—	98	—	98	8	11	16	7	10	3	11	4	8	2	10	8	—	—	—	—	6	46	39	5	—	—	—	—	—
Metritis	Fem.	—	4	—	4	1	—	1	—	—	—	—	—	—	—	—	1	—	—	—	—	—	1	3	—	—	—	—	—	—
Mortification	Males	25	—	—	38	1	4	4	—	1	5	2	3	3	1	1	1	—	—	—	—	1	—	1	2	1	1	14	7	—
	Fem.	—	13	—	—	2	1	—	3	—	—	1	—	2	—	1	1	—	—	—	—	—	—	2	2	1	2	5	2	—
Murder	Males	7	—	—	11	—	—	—	—	—	—	—	1	—	3	—	—	—	—	—	—	1	1	2	1	1	1	—	—	—
	Fem.	—	4	—	—	—	—	—	1	—	—	—	—	—	—	—	—	—	1	—	—	—	1	1	1	—	—	—	—	—
Necrosis	Males	7	—	—	11	—	—	—	1	—	1	—	2	—	—	—	—	—	—	1	—	1	1	2	1	—	—	—	—	—
	Fem.	—	4	—	—	—	—	—	1	—	1	—	2	—	—	—	—	—	—	—	—	1	2	—	1	—	—	—	—	—
Nephria (Bright's Dis.)	Males	149	—	—	271	9	16	16	20	9	17	9	12	7	6	13	15	—	4	3	3	6	20	18	31	23	28	14	—	—
	Fem.	—	122	—	—	9	10	7	16	12	11	6	5	11	7	15	13	—	—	—	2	9	31	23	16	18	14	6	3	—

Cause of Death		Males	Females	Total
Nephritis,	Males	13		22
"	Fem.,		9	
Neuralgia,	Males	7		23
"	Fem.,		16	
Noma (Canker),	Males	68		137
"	Fem.,		69	
Old Age,	Males	668		1672
"	Fem.,		1004	
Ovarian Dropsy,	Fem.,		26	26
Pancreas, Disease of,		1		1
"				
Paralysis,	Males	432		858
"	Fem.,		426	
Paramenia,	Fem.,		4	4
Parotitis,	Males	2		2
"				
Pericarditis,	Males	10		28
"	Fem.,		18	
Peritonitis,	Males	39		102
"	Fem.,		63	
Phlebitis,	Males	3		6
"	Fem.,		3	

TABLE VIII.—Continued.

Causes of Death	Sex	Males	Fem.	Unk.	Totals	Jan.	Feb.	Mar.	Apr.	May	June	July	Aug.	Sep.	Oct.	Nov.	Dec.	Unk.	Under 5	5 to 10	10 to 15	15 to 20	20 to 30	30 to 40	40 to 50	50 to 60	60 to 70	70 to 80	Over 80	Unk.
Pleurisy,	Males	40			69	3	1	3	4	5	6	4	3	3	3	2	3		2			2	5	10	6	5	4	3	3	
"	Fem.,		29			4	3	1	3	2		3	1	1	2	3	2		2			1	2	3	1	4	5	6	5	
Pneumonia,	Males	1126			2097	120	149	138	132	97	86	41	41	51	61	84	126		449	45	15	27	72	78	105	93	90	105	43	4
"	Fem.,		971			110	110	135	105	95	61	38	24	26	54	98	115		356	20	9	31	55	63	53	67	126	135	52	4
Poisoned,	Males	18			29	2		3	3	2		2	1	2	1	4	1		4				2	4	2	3				
"	Fem.,		11			1			3			1	1	1		2	1		3				3	2	1		1			
Premature Births,	Males	163			320	10	9	7	14	16	14	10	17	23	15	16	12		163											
"	Fem.,		151			6	11	22	12	10	12	8	13	23	7	11	16		151											
"	Unk.,			6			1	1		1		2					2		6											
Prostate, Disease of,	Males	13			13	1	1	1	1	2	3	1	3	2	2		3												1	
Puerp. Convulsions,	Fem.		28		28	1	4	1	1	6	2	1	1	2	1	2	4						1	11						
Purpura & Scurvy,	Males	5			11	1		1	1		1	1	1	2		2			1				2				1			
"	Fem.,		6			1		1	1		1	1		1					3				1		1					
Quinsy,	Males	5			5	1		1		1				1					1	1							1			
"	Fem.,		2			1		1		1				1								1			1					
Railroad Accident,	Males	116			126	9	2	10	12	14	14	10	18	7	8	7	5		3	3	2	13	40	20	19	9	5	1	1	1
"	Fem.,		10			1		1	1			2		3	1	1			1	1	2	2		2	2	1	1	2	1	1	

Cause of Death		Total
Rheumatism,	Males,	99
"	Fem.,	96
Scarlatina,	Males,	710
"	Fem.,	762
Scrofula,	Males,	57
"	Fem.,	60
Skin Diseases,	Males,	6
"	Fem.,	1
Small-pox,	Males,	431
"	Fem.,	232
Spina Bifida,	Males,	2
"	Fem.,	5
Spine Disease,	Males,	57
"	Fem.,	56
Spleen, Disease of,	Males,	—
"	Fem.,	1
Stomach Disease,	Males,	25
"	Fem.,	27
Strangulation,	Males,	7
"	Fem.,	1
Strict. of Intestines,	Males,	5
"	Fem.,	5

TABLE VIII.—Concluded.

Causes of Death	Sex	Jan.	Feb.	Mar.	Apr.	May	June	July	Aug.	Sept.	Oct.	Nov.	Dec.	Unk.	Total	Under 5	5 to 10	10 to 15	15 to 20	20 to 30	30 to 40	40 to 50	50 to 60	60 to 70	70 to 80	Over 80	Unk.
Strict. Œsophagus,	Males	–	–	–	–	–	–	–	–	–	–	–	–	–	.	–	–	–	–	–	–	–	–	–	–	–	–
,,	Fem.,	–	–	–	–	–	1	–	–	–	–	1	–	–	1	–	–	–	–	–	–	–	–	–	–	–	–
Strict. of Urethra,	Males,	–	1	–	1	–	–	1	1	1	2	1	–	–	9	–	–	–	–	–	1	–	–	1	–	–	–
Suddenly,	Males,	–	1	–	1	–	2	–	1	1	2	–	–	–	7	–	–	–	–	–	1	–	1	3	2	–	–
,,	Fem.,	2	–	–	–	1	–	2	1	1	–	1	–	–	9	–	–	–	–	–	–	–	3	1	1	–	–
Suffocation,	Males,	1	2	–	–	3	3	–	2	2	2	1	1	–	17	12	1	–	–	–	1	1	–	–	1	–	–
,,	Fem.,	3	2	1	2	–	1	2	–	1	–	2	2	–	12	10	–	–	–	1	–	–	–	–	–	–	–
Suicide,	Males,	6	8	6	4	7	9	9	7	6	8	8	16	–	117	–	–	1	4	15	13	19	18	13	8	1	1
,,	Fem.,	–	3	1	2	1	5	4	–	–	2	5	1	–	.	–	–	–	1	8	5	3	2	3	2	–	–
Syphilis,	Males,	1	2	–	1	3	7	1	2	2	1	2	–	–	35	9	–	–	–	5	2	1	–	2	–	–	–
,,	Fem.,	2	1	3	1	4	1	1	1	1	1	1	–	–	.	12	–	–	1	3	1	1	–	1	–	–	–
Tabes Mesenterica,	Males,	15	15	23	17	12	14	30	45	33	26	16	18	–	522	236	2	–	1	5	3	2	2	4	6	3	–
,,	Fem.,	8	18	14	13	11	19	24	39	43	29	22	18	–	.	224	4	–	2	3	1	2	4	8	6	1	2
Teething,	Males,	6	8	10	11	10	12	24	29	32	21	6	6	–	348	175	–	–	–	–	–	–	–	–	–	–	–
,,	Fem.,	13	4	19	6	7	13	26	28	31	22	5	5	–	.	173	–	–	–	–	–	–	–	–	–	–	–
Tetanus,	Males,	1	–	3	1	1	1	–	–	1	–	1	–	–	12	–	–	2	–	2	–	2	–	–	1	–	–
,,	Fem.,	–	–	–	1	1	–	–	–	1	–	1	–	–	.	1	–	–	1	1	–	–	–	1	–	–	–

DEATHS by Sex

Causes of Death	Males	Fem.	Unk.	Total
Strict. Œsophagus,	.	1	.	.
Strict. of Urethra,	9	.	.	9
Suddenly,	7	9	.	16
Suffocation,	17	12	.	29
Suicide,	93	24	.	117
Syphilis,	21	14	.	35
Tabes Mesenterica,	264	258	.	522
Teething,	175	173	.	348
Tetanus,	8	4	.	12

Cause				Total
Thrush, "	Males,		Fem.,	2
Tumor, "	Males, 18	Fem., 59		77
Ulcers, "	Males, 5	Fem., 6		11
Ulcer of Intestines, "	Males, 3	Fem., 11		14
Unknown, " "	Males, 569	Fem., 518	Unk., 11	1098
Uterus, Disease of,		Fem., 20		20
Vaccination, "	Males, 3	Fem., 2		5
Whooping Cough, "	Males, 126	Fem., 138		264
Worms, "	Males, 5	Fem., 5		10

TABLE IX.—Continued.

CAUSES OF DEATH.	State.	Barnstable.	Berkshire.	Bristol.	Dukes and Nantucket.	Essex.	Franklin.	Hampden.	Hampshire.	Middlesex.	Norfolk.	Plymouth.	Suffolk.	Worcester.
Totals,	9,540	96	290	861	20	1,174	126	707	205	1,861	408	312	2,559	921
DISEASES.														
I.—1. *Miasmatic.*														
1. Small-pox,	668	4	3	10	–	52	1	109	6	115	16	5	315	32
2. Measles,	180	1	7	16	–	18	8	24	5	40	4	6	30	21
3. Scarlatina,	1,472	10	15	219	1	156	8	27	8	294	76	45	494	119
4. Diphtheria,	310	4	33	23	1	40	14	17	6	49	16	14	66	28
5. Quinsy,	7	–	1	2	–	–	–	1	–	1	–	1	1	–
6. Croup,	435	7	22	55	2	49	4	42	11	88	18	8	66	63
7. Whooping Cough,	264	2	14	34	–	37	1	12	12	35	18	14	45	40
8. Typhus (and Infantile Fever),	1,406	32	80	190	4	141	46	171	60	186	53	71	283	149
9. Erysipelas (and Phlebitis)	241	8	5	19	–	21	4	10	2	44	17	10	77	24
10. Metria (Puerperal Fever),	98	–	1	1	–	4	–	6	1	22	2	3	51	7
11. Carbuncle,	8	–	–	1	–	1	–	–	–	2	1	–	2	1
12. Influenza,	35	–	3	6	–	11	–	1	2	6	–	1	4	2
13. Dysentery,	435	5	29	33	4	70	11	17	14	104	20	13	58	57
14. Diarrhœa,	353	3	11	43	–	32	2	9	7	92	16	9	115	15
15. Cholera Infantum,	2,553	8	51	211	5	384	19	210	52	563	93	60	627	270
16. Cholera,	106	–	1	9	–	20	–	5	4	18	4	2	32	11
17. Ague,	15	1	–	5	–	8	–	–	–	1	1	–	–	4
18. Remittent Fever,	12	–	–	1	1	1	–	–	–	2	–	–	6	1
19. Rheumatism,	195	5	8	14	2	28	2	3	10	42	12	3	51	15
20. Cerebro-Spinal Meningitis,*	747	6	6	30	1	106	6	48	5	157.	42	47	236	62

														Totals
I.—2. Enthetic.														
Totals,	—	26	10	2	7	—	2	—	2	—	—	—	—	49
1. Syphilis,	—	16	10	—	7	—	1	—	1	—	—	—	—	35
2. Stricture of Urethra,	—	8	—	—	—	—	1	—	—	—	—	—	—	9
3. Hydrophobia,	—	—	—	—	—	—	—	—	—	—	—	—	—	—
4. Glanders (and Malignant Pustule),	—	2	—	2	—	—	—	—	1	—	—	—	—	5
I.—3. Dietic.														
Totals,	7	65	3	2	15	1	4	1	11	—	6	5	—	·120
1. Privation,	—	—	—	—	—	—	—	—	—	—	—	1	—	1
2. Purpura and Scurvy,	2	4	—	—	1	—	1	—	2	—	—	—	—	11
3. Delirium Tremens, } Alcoholism,	2	14	1	1	8	—	1	—	2	—	1	—	—	30
4. Intemperance,	8	47	2	1	6	1	2	1	7	—	5	4	—	79
I.—4. Parasitic.														
Totals,	—	1	—	1	3	—	2	—	—	—	5	—	—	12
1. Thrush,	—	—	—	—	—	—	—	—	—	—	—	—	—	2
2. Worms,	—	1	—	1	2	—	2	—	—	—	.5	—	—	10
II.—1. Diathetic.														
Totals,	166	249	63	100	274	40	59	29	212	18	126	43	32	1,411
1. Gout,	—	1	—	—	—	—	—	—	—	—	—	—	—	1
2. Dropsy and Anæmia,	79	82	36	37	130	23	29	16	87	11	65	26	4	624
3. Cancer (and Cancer of Stomach),	73	152	16	48	106	13	26	10	76	6	43	17	25	611
4. Noma (Canker),	9	12	11	12	27	3	3	3	44	—	13	—	—	187
5. Mortification,	5	2	—	3	11	1	1	—	5	1	5	1	3	38

* Until the present year Cerebro-Spinal Meningitis has been included with Cephalitis, (III.—1. L.)

TABLE IX.—Continued.

CAUSES OF DEATH.	STATE.	Barnstable.	Berkshire.	Bristol.	Dukes and Nantucket.	Essex.	Franklin.	Hampden.	Hampshire.	Middlesex.	Norfolk.	Plymouth.	Suffolk.	Worcester.
II.—2. *Tubercular.*														
Totals,	6,660	145	184	530	37	837	118	289	143	1,941	309	263	1,737	727
1. Scrofula,	122	–	4	7	1	11	2	4	1	33	3	5	94	17
2. Tabes Mesenterica,	522	6	12	7	2	31	–	18	2	111	11	6	297	19
3. Phthisis (Consumption of Lungs),	5,556	134	155	503	34	722	110	251	128	1,090	279	245	1,268	637
4. Hydrocephalus (Tubercular Meningitis),	460	5	13	•13	–	73	6	16	12	107	16	7	138	54
III.—1. *Nervous System.*														
Totals,	3,332	68	97	333	21	422	51	160	81	616	190	111	856	326
1. Cephalitis,	742	14	21	68	2	67	4	71	16	97	43	16	256	67
2. Apoplexy,	431	10	8	28	5	58	12	22	12	96	21	13	106	40
3. Paralysis,	858	24	34	90	12	134	18	28	19	169	62	47	123	98
4. Insanity,	88	3	–	4	–	11	2	5	2	17	1	2	18	23
5. Chorea,	7	–	1	–	–	1	–	–	–	1	1	–	2	1
6. Epilepsy,	123	5	4	13	1	11	2	8	6	16	4	5	25	23
7. Tetanus,	12	–	1	3	1	–	1	1	1	2	–	–	2	2
8. Convulsions,	629	8	19	82	1	75	6	18	13	115	39	14	199	40
9. *Brain Diseases*, &c.,	442	4	10	45	–	65	6	7	12	103	19	14	125	32
III.—2. *Organs of Circulation.*														
Totals,	1,293	30	45	74	11	183	33	62	46	245	64	57	287	156
1. Pericarditis,	28	–	–	1	–	–	–	1	–	5	–	4	12	4
2. Aneurism,	13	–	–	–	–	–	1	1	–	1	1	3	8	–
3. *Heart Diseases*, &c.,	1,252	30	45	73	11	183	32	61	46	239	63	50	267	152

III.—3. Respiratory Organs.

	Total													
Totals,	2,698	31	97	226	11	324	59	115	57	531	136	71	759	281
1. Epistaxis,	1	—	—	—	—	—	—	—	—	—	1	—	—	—
2. Laryngitis,	23	—	1	—	—	2	—	—	—	5	1	—	12	2
3. Bronchitis,	328	3	4	32	1	14	—	3	1	65	8	4	182	11
4. Pleurisy,	90	2	2	15	3	12	4	2	3	13	4	2	21	7
5. Pneumonia,	2,097	24	84	159	7	267	49	104	53	421	113	64	515	237
6. Asthma,	93	1	3	13	—	18	3	4	—	13	3	1	16	18
7. *Lung Diseases, &c.,*	66	1	3	7	—	11	3	2	—	14	6	—	13	6

III.—4. Digestive Organs.

	Total													
Totals,	1,241	16	31	91	2	158	24	53	33	207	81	48	344	158
1. Gastritis,	123	1	10	6	—	11	1	5	6	21	9	5	38	10
2. Enteritis.	379	5	7	35	—	48	10	26	5	55	28	9	90	61
3. Peritonitis,	102	—	1	4	—	8	1	2	1	30	10	1	40	3
4. Ascites,	12	—	—	—	1	—	—	—	—	3	—	—	8	1
5. Ulceration of Intestines,	14	—	2	2	—	1	—	—	—	4	1	—	1	3
6. Hernia,	35	5	—	4	—	3	1	1	2	6	3	3	9	4
7. Ileus,	81	1	3	7	—	7	1	3	4	12	4	4	14	17
8. Intussusception,	3	—	—	—	—	—	—	—	—	1	—	—	1	—
9. Stricture of Intestines,	11	—	—	1	—	1	—	1	—	—	—	—	4	3
10. Fistula,	8	—	1	—	—	—	—	—	—	2	7	2	3	—
11. *Stomach Diseases, &c.,*	132	2	2	15	1	16	3	3	5	15	—	5	38	21
12. *Pancreas Disease, &c.,*	1	—	—	—	—	—	—	—	—	1	—	—	—	—
13. Hepatitis,	57	—	—	1	—	4	2	2	2	9	5	7	22	3
14. Jaundice,	48	2	2	4	—	11	1	—	7	5	2	—	10	12
15. *Liver Disease, &c.,*	234	—	3	12	—	43	5	10	1	42	12	12	66	20
16. *Spleen Disease, &c.,*	1	—	—	—	—	—	—	—	—	1	—	—	—	—

TABLE IX.—Continued.

CAUSES OF DEATH.	State.	Barnstable.	Berkshire.	Bristol.	Dukes and Nantucket.	Essex.	Franklin.	Hampden.	Hampshire.	Middlesex.	Norfolk.	Plymouth.	Suffolk.	Worcester.
III.—5. *Urinary Organs.*														
Totals,	599	12	20	44	3	66	8	14	16	97	30	40	194	56
1. Nephritis,	22	1	1	–	–	1	–	–	–	7	3	–	9	1
2. Ischuria,	4	–	–	–	–	1	–	–	–	1	1	–	2	–
3. Nephria (Bright's Disease),	271	2	5	15	–	25	–	4	3	41	12	21	121	22
4. Diabetes,	60	2	3	7	–	5	4	3	1	12	3	8	5	7
5. Calculus (Stone, Gravel, &c.),	30	4	1	1	–	–	–	1	3	2	3	–	10	5
6. Cystitis,	32	–	2	1	1	6	1	–	3	2	1	2	9	2
7. *Kidney Diseases, &c.,*	180	3	8	21	3	28	4	5	6	28	8	9	38	19
III.—6. *Generative Organs.*														
Totals,	50	–	2	2	–	9	1	–	–	3	–	3	22	8
1. Ovarian Dropsy,	26	–	2	1	–	3	1	–	–	2	–	1	10	6
2. *Diseases of Uterus, &c.,*	24	–	–	1	–	6	–	–	–	1	–	2	12	2
III.—7. *Organs of Locomotion.*														
Totals,	169	2	7	14	1	19	–	13	1	26	7	4	59	16
1. Arthritis,	–	–	–	–	–	–	–	–	–	–	–	–	–	–
2. *Joint Disease, &c.,**	169	2	7	14	1	19	–	13	1	26	7	4	59	16
III.—8. *Integumentary System.*														
Totals	91	3	1	2	1	10	2	7	3	15	4	2	30	11
1. Phlegmon,	73	2	1	1	1	7	2	6	3	10	4	2	23	11
2. Ulcer,	11	1	–	1	–	3	–	1	–	1	–	–	4	–
3. *Skin Diseases, &c.,*	7	–	–	–	–	–	–	–	–	4	–	–	3	–

	Total												
IV.—1. Dev. Diseases of Children.													
Totals,	2,457	18	36	215	1	311	22	94	21	504	108	62	849	216
1. Stillborn,	1,246	13	22	128	1	155	11	35	7	225	63	30	526	30
2. Infantile, Premature, &c.,†	774	2	5	16	–	90	7	37	9	216	29	22	196	145
3. Cyanosis,	45	–	–	1	–	1	–	1	1	12	1	–	27	1
4. Spina Bifida,	7	–	1	–	–	–	–	–	–	1	–	–	4	1
5. Other Malformations,	37	–	1	–	–	5	–	–	–	9	–	–	17	5
6. Teething,	348	3	7	70	–	60	4	21	4	41	15	10	79	34
IV.—2. Dev. Diseases of Adults.													
Totals,	305	4	16	25	4	42	8	17	5	71	15	4	49	45
1. Paramenia,	4	–	1	–	–	–	–	–	–	–	–	–	1	2
2. Childbirth,‡	301	4	15	25	4	42	8	17	5	71	15	4	48	43
IV.—3. Dev. Diseases of Old People.													
1. Old Age,	1,672	49	95	120	22	220	41	104	65	290	114	114	212	226
IV.—4. Diseases of Nutrition.													
1. Atrophy and Debility,	691	1	15	117	2	64	12	78	10	157	90	13	139	53
V.—I. Accident or Negligence.													
Totals,	828	29	23	37	4	252	8	45	24	91	33	14	185	83
1. Fractures and Contusions,§	198	1	8	5	2	14	4	19	3	17	10	5	85	25
2. Burns and Scalds,	88	2	1	9	1	14	–	10	1	13	5	3	20	9
3. Poison,	30	–	–	1	–	5	1	–	2	3	1	–	15	2
4. Drowning (and Lost at Sea),	432	25	12	19	1	211	3	13	15	37	13	6	40	37
5. Suffocation (and Strangulation),	37	1	1	–	–	4	–	–	2	11	2	–	14	2
6. Otherwise,‖	43	–	1	3	–	4	–	3	1	10	2	–	11	8

* Including Disease of Spine, and Hip Disease.
† See Note on page cv. following.
‡ Not including Metria (Puerperal Fever).
§ Including Railroad Accidents.
‖ Under "Otherwise" (V.—1.—6.) are included Deaths from heat or cold, drinking cold water, exposure, lightning, surgical operations, etc.

TABLE IX.—Concluded.

CAUSES OF DEATH	STATE	Barnstable.	Berkshire.	Bristol.	Dukes and Nantucket.	Essex.	Franklin.	Hampden.	Hampshire.	Middlesex.	Norfolk.	Plymouth.	Suffolk.	Worcester.
V.—2. *Battle.*	—	—	—	—	—	—	—	—	—	—	—	—	—	—
V.—3. *Homicide.*	26	1	2	1	—	2	—	—	—	7	1	—	12	—
V.—4. *Suicide.*	117	—	1	8	—	16	—	4	5	26	5	6	32	14
V.—5. *Execution.*	2	—	—	—	—	—	—	1	—	—	—	—	1	—
V.—6. *Violent deaths, not included above,**	493	6	32	38	3	62	7	30	8	81	25	11	124	66
Sudden, cause unknown, . . .	16	—	—	3	—	—	—	6	—	3	—	—	—	3
Causes not specified,† . . .	1,286	46	90	162	4	194	29	84	46	293	75	54	59	150

* Returned as "Casualty."   † Comprising 75 from "Hemorrhage," 77 from "Tumor," and 36 from "Inflammation," and 1,096 deaths either returned as "Unknown," or of which no cause was stated.

NOTE.—Where a person is "found drowned," the case is classed under "accident or negligence," (V.—1. 4.) Cases of death from cold, heat, drinking cold water, lightning, surgical operation, and exposure, are classed under "accident or negligence," (V.—1. 6.) As "stricture of the urethra" is almost invariably the result of gonorrhœa, it is classed as (I.; 2; 2.)—[DR. FARR.]

TABLE X.—CAUSES OF DEATH.—COMPARATIVE MORTALITY.

Exhibiting the Number of Deaths from Specified Causes (Nosologically Arranged)* during each of the Five Years 1869-70-71-72-73, with the Number of Deaths, annually, to 100,000 of the Population;—also the Number and Percentage of Deaths during the Five Years 1869-73, and during the entire Registration Period of Thirty-two Years and Eight Months, ending December 31, 1873.

[Still-births included.]

CAUSES OF DEATH.	DEATHS 1869.	1870.	1871.	1872.	1873.	Five Yrs. 1869-73.	Thirty-two Years and Eight Mos. end'g Dec. 31, 73.	DEATHS TO 100,000 POPULATION 1869.	1870.	1871.	1872.	1873.	% OF ALL DEATHS Five Yrn. 1869-73.	Thirty-two Years and Eight Mos. end'g Dec. 31, 72.
All Causes,	27,148	28,348	29,333	36,302	35,158	156,289	691,720	1,814.79	1,945.11	2,015.72	2,410.95	2,412.46	–	–
Specified Causes,†	25,713	26,998	28,043	34,845	33,856	149,455	663,269	1,775.63	1,852.61	1,924.29	2,309.98	2,325.12	100·00	100·00
(CLASSES.)														
I.—ZYMOTIC DISEASES,	6,898	6,916	6,544	10,792	9,721	40,871	187,496	476·96	474·56	449·02	740·52	667·02	27·35	28·27
II.—CONSTITUTIONAL DIS.,	6,569	7,185	7,272	8,042	8,071	37,139	181,650	453·64	493·02	494·98	561·82	553·82	24·85	27·39
III.—LOCAL DISEASES,	7,177	7,556	8,160	9,617	9,473	41,983	157,890	495·63	518·47	559·91	669·90	650·02	28·09	23·80
IV.—DEVELOPMENTAL DIS.,	4,027	4,206	4,771	5,103	5,125	23,232	109,863	278·09	288·61	327·36	350·15	351·67	15·54	16·56
V.—VIOLENT DEATHS,	1,042	1,135	1,296	1,291	1,466	6,230	26,370	71·96	77·88	88·93	88·59	100·59	4·17	3·98
(ORDERS.)														
I.—1. Miasmatic Diseases,	6,724	6,770	6,395	10,591	9,540	40,020	182,728	464·35	464·54	438·80	726·72	654·61	26·78	27·55
2. Enthetic Diseases,	39	47	38	37	49	210	688	2·69	3·22	2·61	2·54	3·36	·14	·10
3. Dietic Diseases,	122	90	98	154	120	584	3,242	8·42	6·18	6·72	10·57	8·23	·39	·49
4. Parasitic Diseases,	13	9	13	10	12	57	838	·90	·62	·89	·69	·82	·04	·13
II.—1. Diathetic Diseases,	1,173	1,306	1,313	1,449	1,411	6,652	29,250	81·00	89·62	90·09	99·43	96·82	4·45	4·41
2. Tubercular Diseases,	5,396	5,879	5,959	6,593	6,660	30,487	152,400	372·64	403·40	408·88	462·39	457·00	20·40	22·98

* See "Statistical Nosology," in Appendix, p. cvii. † Including Stillborn.

TABLE X.—Continued.

CAUSES OF DEATH.	DEATHS.							DEATHS TO 100,000 POPULATION.					PERCENTAGE OF ALL DEATHS.	
	1869.	1870.	1871.	1872.	1873.	Five Yrs. 1869-73.	Thirty-two Years and Eight Mos. end'g Dec. 31, 73.	1869.	1870.	1871.	1872.	1873.	Five Yrs. 1869-73.	Thirty-two Years and Eight Mos. end'g Dec. 31, 73.
Diseases of—														
III.—1. Nervous System,	2,576	2,776	2,855	3,618	3,332	15,157	57,641	177·89	190·48	195·90	248·26	228·64	10·14	8·69
2. Organs of Circulation,	940	1,001	1,180	1,249	1,293	5,663	19,861	64·91	68·69	80·97	85·70	88·72	3·79	2·99
3. Respiratory Organs,	2,291	2,185	2,356	2,634	2,698	12,304	46,123	154·07	149·93	161·66	194·46	185·13	8·23	6·95
4. Digestive Organs,	870	987	1,069	1,182	1,241	5,349	23,555	60·08	67·73	73·35	81·11	85·16	3·58	3·55
5. Urinary Organs,	351	392	470	467	599	2,279	6,733	24·24	26·90	32·25	32·04	41·10	1·52	·87
6. Generative Organs,	29	40	40	48	50	207	608	2·00	2·74	2·74	3·29	3·43	·14	·09
7. Organs of Locomotion,	90	97	93	114	169	563	2,190	6·22	6·66	6·38	7·82	11·60	·38	·33
8. Integumentary System,	90	78	97	105	91	461	2,179	6·22	5·35	6·66	7·21	6·24	·31	·33
Dev. Diseases of—														
IV.—1. Children,	2,065	2,118	2,465	2,594	2,457	11,699	63,529	142·61	145·33	169·14	177·99	168·59	7·83	9·58
2. Adults,	254	259	233	271	305	1,322	5,634	17·54	17·77	15·98	18·59	20·93	·88	·85
3. Old People,	1,375	1,444	1,554	1,664	1,762	7,709	35,332	94·95	99·09	106·63	114·18	114·73	5·16	5·33
4. Nutrition,	333	385	519	574	691	2,502	5,368	22·99	26·42	35·61	39·39	47·42	1·67	·81
V.—1. Accid't or Negligence,	615	687	757	732	828	3,619	14,063	42·47	47·14	51·94	50·23	56·81	2·42	2·12
2. Battle,							1,246							·19
3. Homicide,	25	29	25	27	26	132	462	1·73	1·99	1·72	1·86	1·78	·09	·07
4. Suicide,	92	91	122	117	117	539	2,404	6·35	6·24	8·37	8·02	8·02	·36	·36
5. Execution,	1			2		3	11	·07				·14		
6. Viol't D'ths, not class'd,	309	328	392	415	493	1,937	8,184	21·34	22·51	26·90	28·48	33·84	1·30	1·23
Sudden (cause unascertained),	23	26	16	12	16	93	695	1·59	1·78	1·10	·82	1·10		
Causes not specified,	1,412	1,324	1,274	1,445	1,286	6,741	27,756	97·51	90·85	87·42	99·15	88·24		

I.—1. Miasmatic.

Disease														
1. Small-pox,	·78	1·46	46·04	70·61	20·24	8·99	4·07	5,185	2,182	668	1,029	296	131	59
2. Measles,	·91	·82	12·35	29·37	8·99	18·46	15·83	6,017	1,290	180	428	131	269	222
3. Scarlatina,	4·26	3·88	101·00	94·49	59·49	46·87	97·03	28,248	5,804	1,472	1,377	867	683	1,405
4. Diphtheria,	1·10	·92	21·27	18·73	18·80	16·60	20·44	7,279	1,896	310	273	274	242	296
5. Quinsy,	·10	·03	·48	·75	·75	·55	1·04	656	52	7	11	8	8	15
6. Croup,	2·11	1·54	29·85	32·94	32·46	29·78	32·66	13,996	2,295	435	480	473	434	473
7. Whooping Cough,	1·13	1·02	18·12	24·91	16·68	22·64	22·10	7,478	1,520	264	363	243	330	320
8. Typhus (and Inf. Fever),	5·18	4·53	96·48	116·86	76·57	91·47	88·22	34,918	6,763	1,406	1,703	1,116	1,388	1,205
9. Erysipelas (& Phlebitis),	·73	·66	16·54	14·89	14·20	9·06	12·64	4,831	980	241	217	207	132	188
10. Metria (Puerp. Fever),	·19	·22	6·72	4·46	3·37	4·53	4·21	1,243	339	98	65	49	66	61
11. Carbuncle,	·01	·02	·55	·94	·55	·27	·14	111	27	8	5	8	4	2
12. Influenza,	·22	·13	2·40	2·33	2·26	2·47	3·38	1,415	187	35	94	33	36	49
13. Dysentery,	4·10	1·56	29·85	38·70	26·69	33·92	33·22	27,202	2,340	435	564	389	471	481
14. Diarrhœa,	1·25	1·29	24·22	31·84	23·60	21·06	21 06	8,293	1,928	353	464	344	457	305
15. Cholera Infantum,	4·29	7·27	175·18	223·28	117·88	191·33	98·34	28,456	10,863	2,653	3,254	1,718	1,914	1,424
16. Cholera,	·65	·36	7·27	9·40	6·59	7·34	6·56	4,318	541	106	137	96	107	95
17. Ague,	·08	·04	1·03	·82	·48	·76	·35	228	50	15	12	7	11	5
18. Remittent Fever,	·04	·04	·82	1·03	·48	·41	·76	283	51	12	15	7	6	11
19. Rheumatism,	·36	·49	13·38	10·97	8·72	9·93	7·80	2,424	781	195	160	127	136	113
20. Cerebro Spinal Meningitis,	·11	·50	51·26	—	—	—	—	747	747	747	—	—	—	—

I.—2. Enthetic.

Disease														
1. Syphilis,	·09	·11	2·40	1·85	2·20	2·54	2·34	559	165	35	27	32	37	34
2. Stricture of Urethra,	—	·01	·62	·21	·07	·20	—	80	16	9	3	1	3	—
3. Hydrophobia,	—	—	—	—	—	·14	—	28	2	—	—	—	2	—
4. Glanders (& Mal. Pustule),	·01	·02	·34	·48	·94	·94	·35	71	27	5	7	5	5	5

Table X.—Continued.

CAUSES OF DEATH	DEATHS							DEATHS TO 100,000 POPULATION.					PERCENTAGE OF ALL DEATHS.	
	1869.	1870.	1871.	1872.	1873.	Five Yrs. 1869-73.	Thirty-two Years and Eight Mos. end'g Dec. 31, 72.	1869.	1870.	1871.	1872.	1873.	Five Yrs. 1869-73.	Thirty-two Years and Eight Mos. end'g Dec. 31, 72.
I.—3. Dietic.														
1. Privation,	22	2	1	1	—	26	200	1·52	·14	·07	·07	—	·02	·03
2. Purpura and Scurvy,	19	13	9	19	11	71	270	1·40	·89	·61	1·30	·75	·05	·04
3. Del. Trem., } Alcoholism,	27	27	30	45	30	159	874	1·78	1·85	2·06	3·10	2·06	·10	·13
4. Intemp'ce, }	54	48	58	89	79	328	1,898	3·97	3·30	3·98	6·10	5·42	·22	·29
I.—4. Parasitic.														
1. Thrush,	4	1	1	1	2	9	341	·28	·07	·07	·07	·14	·01	·05
2. Worms, &c.,	9	8	12	9	10	48	497	·62	·55	·82	·62	·69	·03	·08
II.—1. Diathetic.														
1. Gout,	2	4	1	—	1	8	67	·14	·27	·07	—	·07	·01	·01
2. Dropsy and Anæmia,	525	568	610	697	624	3,024	14,874	36·25	38·98	41·86	47·81	42·82	2·02	2·24
3. Cancer (and Can. of Stom.),	492	516	551	542	611	2,712	9,107	33·98	35·41	37·80	37·18	41·92	1·82	1·37
4. Noma (Canker),	115	172	102	154	137	680	3,905	7·94	11·80	7·00	10·56	9·40	·45	·60
5. Mortification,	39	46	49	66	38	228	1,297	2·69	3·16	3·36	3·84	2·61	·15	·18
II.—2. Tubercular.														
1. Scrofula,	115	105	149	121	122	612	3,304	7·94	7·20	10·22	8·30	8·37	·41	·50
2. Tabes Mesenterica,	263	363	333	470	522	1,951	6,891	18·17	24·91	22·85	32·25	35·82	1·31	1·04
3. Phthisis (Cons of Lungs),	4,659	5,003	5,070	5,556	5,556	25,844	130,096	321·74	343·29	347·24	381·24	381·56	17·29	19·61
4. Hydrocephalus (Tub. Men.),	359	408	407	446	460	2,080	12,109	24·79	28·00	27·93	30·60	31·56	1·39	1·83

572	601	620	1,081	742	3,566	19,968	**III.—1. Nervous System.** 1. Cephalitis,	39·50	41·24	42·54	70·75	50·92	2·89	2·02
331	394	390	409	431	1,355	6,817	2. Apoplexy,	22·86	27·04	26·76	28·06	29·57	1·31	1·03
607	630	714	791	858	3,600	12,026	3. Paralysis,	41·92	43·23	48·99	54·28	58·88	2·41	1·81
87	103	89	103	88	470	1,782	4. Insanity,	6·01	7·07	6·11	7·07	6·04	·31	·26
1	1	3	6	7	18	60	5. Chorea,	·07	·07	·21	·41	·48	·01	·01
180	134	121	146	123	654	3,927	6. Epilepsy,	8·97	9·19	7·30	10·02	8·44	·44	·59
18	19	18	18	12	85	381	7. Tetanus,	1·24	1·30	1·23	1·24	·82	·06	·06
479	527	522	658	629	2,815	12,069	8. Convulsions,	33·08	36·16	35·82	45·14	43·16	1·88	1·82
351	367	378	456	442	1,994	7,261	9. *Brain Diseases, &c.,*	24·24	25·18	25·94	31·29	30·33	1·33	1·09
19	15	19	16	28	97	322	**III.—2. Organs of Circulation.** 1. Pericarditis,	1·31	1·03	1·31	1·10	1·92	·06	·04
10	8	12	15	13	58	142	2. Aneurism,	·69	·55	·83	1·03	·89	·05	·02
911	978	1,149	1,218	1,252	5,508	19,897	3. *Heart Diseases, &c.,*	62·91	67·11	78·83	83·57	85·91	3·68	2·93
1	—	—	—	2	10		**III.—3. Respiratory Organs.** 1. Epistaxis,	·07	—		—	·07	—	—
13	12	17	16	23	81	262	2. Laryngitis,	·90	·82	1·17	1·10	1·58	·05	·04
239	259	272	287	328	1,385	3,630	3. Bronchitis,	16·51	17·77	18·66	19·69	22·51	·93	·55
93	75	90	81	90	429	3,125	4. Pleurisy,	6·42	5·15	6·18	5·56	6·18	·29	·47
1,736	1,718	1,858	2,295	2,097	9,704	36,298	5. Pneumonia,	119·88	117·89	127·48	157·48	143·89	6·49	5·47
67	66	61	96	93	383	1,165	6. Asthma,	4·63	4·58	4·19	6·58	6·38	·26	·17
82	65	58	59	66	320	1,633	7. *Lung Diseases, &c.,*	5·66	3·77	3·98	4·05	4·53	·21	·25
54	90	93	109	123	469	1,507	**III.—4. Digestive Organs.** 1. Gastritis,	3·73	6·18	6·38	7·48	8·44	·32	·23
225	288	334	358	379	1,584	7,176	2. Enteritis,	15·54	19·76	22·92	24·58	26·01	1·06	1·08
72	86	69	100	102	429	1,178	3. Peritonitis,	4·97	5·90	4·73	6·86	7·00	·29	·18
18	13	11	45	12	69	286	4. Ascites,	1·24	·89	·76	1·03	·82	·05	·03
25	14	20	27	14	100	298	5. Ulceration of Intestines,	1·73	·96	1·37	1·85	·96	·07	·04
45	39	34	36	35	189	706	6. Hernia,	3·11	2·68	2·33	2·47	2·40	·13	·10
64	89	97	94	81	425	1,742	7. Ileus,	4·41	6·11	6·66	6·45	5·56	·29	·26

TABLE X.—Continued.

CAUSES OF DEATH	DEATHS 1869	1870	1871	1872	1873	Five Yrs 1869-73	Thirty-two Years and Eight Mos. endg Dec. 31, 72	DEATHS TO 100,000 POPULATION 1869	1870	1871	1872	1873	PERCENTAGE OF ALL DEATHS Five Yrs 1869-73	Thirty-two Years and Eight Mos. endg Dec. 31, 72
III.—4. Digest. Organs—Con.														
8. Intussusception,	9	3	3	4	8	22	148	·62	·21	·20	·27	·21	·01	·02
9. Stricture of Intestines,	7	11	5	8	11	42	53	·48	·75	·84	·55	·75	·02	·01
10. Fistula,	2	4	5	5	8	24	55	·14	·27	·34	·34	·55	·01	·01
11. Stomach Diseases, &c.,	93	89	119	123	132	556	4,650	6·42	6·11	8·17	8·44	9·06	·37	·70
12. Pancreas Disease, &c.,	—	—	—	—	1	1	4	—	—	—	—	·07	—	—
13. Hepatitis,	37	33	38	56	57	221	687	2·56	2·27	2·61	3·84	3·91	·15	·11
14. Jaundice,	45	34	41	42	48	210	1,014	3·11	2·33	2·81	2·88	3·29	·14	·15
15. Liver Diseases, &c.,	173	194	200	205	234	1,006	4,075	11·95	13·31	13·73	14·07	16·06	·67	·62
16. Spleen Disease, &c.,	1	—	—	—	1	2	26	·07	—	—	—	·07	—	—
III.—5. Urinary Organs.														
1. Nephritis,	13	19	14	23	22	91	278	·90	1·30	·96	1·58	1·61	·06	·04
2. Ischuria,	8	3	5	5	4	25	102	·56	·21	·34	·34	·27	·01	·02
3. Nephria (Bright's Dis.),	125	140	199	223	271	958	1,264	8·63	9·61	13·66	15·30	18·60	·64	·19
4. Diabetes,	50	55	33	53	60	251	988	3·45	3·78	2·27	3·64	4·12	·17	·15
5. Calculus (Gravel, &c.),	30	20	23	11	30	114	622	2·07	1·37	1·68	·75	2·06	·08	·09
6. Cystitis,	18	19	21	13	32	103	298	1·24	1·30	1·44	·89	2·20	·07	·04
7. Kidney Diseases, &c.,	107	136	175	139	180	737	2,181	7·39	9·33	12·01	9·54	12·35	·49	·33
III.—6. Generative Organs.														
1. Ovarian Dropsy,	15	17	27	27	26	112	297	1·03	1·16	1·85	1·86	1·78	·07	·04
2. Uterus Disease, &c.,	14	23	13	21	24	95	311	·97	1·58	·89	1·44	1·65	·06	·04

Deaths (numbers)

Cause of Death	Total						
III.—7. Organs of Locomotion.							
1. Arthritis,	168	6	2	9	9	13	18
2. Joint Diseases, &c.,*	2,022	85	95	90	111	169	550
III.—8. Integumentary System.							
1. Phlegmon,	1,141	66	60	70	82	73	351
2. Ulcer,	289	11	10	13	14	11	59
3. Skin Diseases, &c.,	749	13	8	14	9	7	61
IV.—1. Dev. Dis. of Children.							
1. Stillborn,	22,296	1,094	1,019	1,390	1,283	1,246	6,082
2. Infantile, premature, &c.,†	32,131	665	737	741	876	774	3,793
3. Cyanosis,	424	20	24	30	40	45	159
4. Spina Bifida,	106	6	5	9	10	7	37
5. Other Malformations,	473	26	25	35	18	37	141
6. Teething,	8,099	254	308	260	367	348	1,587
IV.—2. Dev. Dis. of Adults.							
1. Paramenia,	71	3	7	4	4	4	22
2. Childbirth,‡	5,563	251	252	229	267	301	1,800
IV.—3. Dev. Diseases of Old People.							
1. Old Age,	35,332	1,375	1,444	1,554	1,664	1,672	7,709
IV.—4. Dev. Dis. of Nutrition.							
1. Atrophy and Debility,	5,368	333	385	519	574	691	2,502

Rates

Cause of Death							
III.—7. Organs of Locomotion.							
1. Arthritis,	·02	·01	—	·21	·21	·14	·94
2. Joint Diseases, &c.,*	·31	·37	11·60	7·61	6·18	6·52	5·86
III.—8. Integumentary System.							
1. Phlegmon,	·17	·24	5·00	5·62	4·80	4·12	4·56
2. Ulcer,	·04	·04	·76	·96	·89	·68	·76
3. Skin Diseases, &c.,	·12	·03	·48	·62	·96	·55	·90
IV.—1. Dev. Dis. of Children.							
1. Stillborn,	3·86	4·04	85·50	88·04	95·87	69·92	75·55
2. Infantile, premature, &c.,†	4·85	2·54	53·11	60·11	50·84	50·57	45·92
3. Cyanosis,	·06	·11	3·09	2·75	2·06	1·65	1·38
4. Spina Bifida,	·01	·02	·48	·69	·62	·84	·42
5. Other Malformations,	·07	·09	2·54	1·23	2·41	1·72	1·80
6. Teething,	1·22	1·03	23·88	25·17	17·84	21·18	17·54
IV.—2. Dev. Dis. of Adults.							
1. Paramenia,	·01	·01	·27	·27	·27	·48	·21
2. Childbirth,‡	·84	·87	20·66	18·32	15·71	17·29	17·84
IV.—3. Dev. Diseases of Old People.							
1. Old Age,	5·33	5·16	114·79	114·18	106·63	99·09	94·95
IV.—4. Dev. Dis. of Nutrition.							
1. Atrophy and Debility,	·81	1·67	47·42	39·39	35·61	26·42	22·99

* Including Disease of Spine, and Hip Diseases. † See Note on page cv. following. ‡ Not including Metria (Puerperal Fever).

TABLE X.—Concluded.

CAUSES OF DEATH.	DEATHS 1869.	1870.	1871.	1872.	1873.	Five Yrs. 1869-73.	Thirty-two Years and Eight Mos. end'g Dec. 31, 73.	DEATHS TO 100,000 POPULATION 1869.	1870.	1871.	1872.	1873.	PERCENTAGE OF ALL DEATHS Five Yrs. 1869-73.	Thirty-two Years and Eight Mos. end'g Dec. 31, 73.
V.—1. Accident or Negligence.														
1. Fractures and Contusions,*	168	178	224	180	198	948		11·60	12·21	15·37	12·35	13·58	·64	
2. Burns and Scalds,	83	89	101	93	88	454		5·73	6·11	6·98	6·38	6·04	·30	
3. Poison,	26	26	29	26	30	187	} 14063	1·80	1·78	1·99	1·78	2·06	·09	} 2·12
4. Drowning,	283	306	346	299	432	1,666		19·54	21·00	23·74	20·51	29·64	1·11	
5. Suffocation,	30	27	25	39	37	158		2·07	1·85	1·71	2·67	2·54	·11	
6. Otherwise,	25	61	32	95	43	256		1·73	4·19	2·20	6·52	2·95	·17	
V.—2. Battle.	—	—	—	—	—	—	1,246	—	—	—	—	—	—	·19
V.—3. Homicide.	25	29	25	27	26	132	462	1·73	1·99	1·72	1·85	1·78	·09	·07
V.—4. Suicide.†	92	91	122	117	117	589	2,404	6·35	6·24	8·37	8·02	8·02	·36	·36
V.—5. Execution.	1	1	—	2	3	11	11	·07	—	—	—	·14	—	—
V.—6. Viol't D'ths, not classed,	309	328	392	415	493	1,937	8,184	21·34	22·51	26·90	28·47	33·84	1·30	1·23
Sudden, cause unascertained,	23	26	16	12	16	93	695	1·59	1·78	1·10	·82	1·10	—	—
Causes not specified,‡	1,412	1,324	1,274	1,445	1,286	6,741	27,756	97·51	90·85	87·42	99·12	88·24	—	—

* Including "Railroad Accidents."   † Totals; *manner* not stated.   ‡ Including deaths from "Hemorrhage," "Tumor," and "Inflammation."

NOTE.

Previously to the adoption, in the Registration Report of 1855, of the present NOSOLOGICAL ARRANGEMENT of Tables IX. and X., the term "Infantile" in those Tables included under a single designation, not only all deaths returned under the several heads, "Infantile," "Premature," or "Premature Births," but also all ascribed to "Debility" or "Unknown" causes, if under two years of age.

This plan was continued until the Registration Report of 1868, in which, to secure greater accuracy, the method now employed was adopted, by which Deaths returned under the head of "Premature," "Premature Births," or "Infantile," are stated *separately* in Table VIII., and *combined* in Tables IX. and X. Deaths of children under two years, from "Debility" or "Unknown" cause, are no longer classed as "Infantile."

See Registration Report of 1868, p. cv., for a fuller explanation.

14

TABLE XI.—OCCUPATIONS.

Distinguishing by Occupations (statistically classified) the Number, with their Average and Aggregate Ages, of Persons in the State (in two geographical divisions) whose Occupations were specified, and whose Deaths were registered, during the year 1873;—also in the State (entire) during the period of Thirty Years and Eight Months, ending with Dec. 31, 1873.

[This Table includes only persons over twenty years of age.*]

OCCUPATIONS.	NINE EASTERN COUNTIES, 1873.			FIVE WESTERN COUNTIES, 1873.			WHOLE STATE, Thirty Years and Eight Months. From May 1, 1843, to Dec. 31, 1873.		
	Number of Persons.	Ages. Aggregate.	Average.	Number of Persons.	Ages. Aggregate.	Average.	Number of Persons.	Ages. Aggregate.	Average.
ALL CLASSES AND OCCUPATIONS,	6,078	297,565	48·96	1,981	100,956	51·00	138,229	7,023,795	50·81
I. CULTIVATORS OF THE EARTH,	654	44,427	67·93	575	36,129	62·83	30,700	2,001,586	65·19
II. ACTIVE MECHANICS ABROAD,	553	28,109	50·83	154	8,296	53·87	10,349	543,247	52·49
III. ACTIVE MECHANICS IN SHOPS,	722	31,817	44·07	298	14,001	46·98	15,658	745,577	49·19
IV. INACTIVE MECHANICS IN SHOPS,	775	34,464	44·47	204	9,154	44·87	16,414	718,004	43·74
V. LABORERS—NO SPECIAL TRADES,	1,384	66,564	48·10	328	15,373	46·87	26,749	1,265,652	47·31
VI. FACTORS LABORING ABROAD,	301	11,575	38·45	74	2,724	36·81	6,749	242,425	35·92
VII. EMPLOYED ON THE OCEAN,	402	19,525	48·57	6	984	64·00	8,505	393,944	46·32
VIII. MERCHANTS, FINANCIERS, AGENTS, ETC.,	927	43,755	47·21	204	8,990	44·07	15,098	738,719	48·93
IX. PROFESSIONAL MEN,	221	11,369	51·44	62	3,127	50·44	4,917	250,448	50·93
X. FEMALES,	139	5,960	42·88	76	2,778	36·55	3,090	124,193	40·19

I. CULTIVATORS OF THE EARTH,	654	44,427	67·93	575	36,129	62·83	30,700	2,001,586	65·19
II. ACTIVE MECHANICS ABROAD,	553	28,109	50·83	154	8,296	53·87	10,349	543,247	52·49
Brickmakers,	3	99	33·00	2	101	50·50	100	4,799	47·99
Carpenters and Joiners,	316	16,609	52·56	102	5,425	53·19	5,859	312,364	53·31
Caulkers and Gravers,	7	361	51·57	–	–	–	175	10,257	58·61
Masons,	90	3,955	48·39	20	1,056	52·80	1,568	79,145	50·48
Millwrights,	4	298	59·50	5	324	64·80	115	6,747	58·67
Riggers,	5	311	62·22	–	–	–	155	8,130	52·45
Ship-carpenters,	46	2,912	63·30	1	74	74·00	838	49,087	58·52
Slaters,	11	499	45·36	1	28	28·00	74	2,973	40·18
Stone-cutters,	63	2,673	42·43	22	1,208	54·91	942	43,618	46 30
Tanners,	8	452	56·50	1	80	80·00	528	26,177	50·05
III. ACTIVE MECHANICS IN SHOPS,	722	31,817	44·07	298	14,001	46·98	15,658	745,577	49·19
Bakers,	20	912	45·60	1	38	38·00	447	20,883	46·76
Blacksmiths,	83	4,085	49·22	31	1,786	57·61	2,287	121,922	53·31
Brewers,	1	63	63·00	–	–	–	27	1,276	47·26
Cabinet-makers,	51	2,317	45·04	2	149	74·50	734	35,707	48·65
Calico-printers,	–	158	–	–	–	–	9	469	52·11
Card-makers,	2	158	79·00	1	38	38·00	39	1,881	48·23
Carriage-makers and trimmers,	13	510	39·23	3	114	38·00	255	12,338	48·38
Chair-makers,	3	117	39·00	14	632	45·14	131	5,449	41·59
Clothiers,	2	55	27·50	–	–	–	81	4,619	57·02
Confectioners,	8	391	48·87	–	–	–	82	3,567	43·50
Cooks,	2	114	57·00	1	46	46·00	97	3,934	40·56
Coopers,	34	1,734	51·00	–	–	–	896	53,171	59·29
Coppersmiths,	6	241	40·17	–	–	–	93	4,285	46·07

* Soldiers and females excepted.

TABLE XI.—Continued.

OCCUPATIONS.	NINE EASTERN COUNTIES, 1873.			FIVE WESTERN COUNTIES, 1873.			WHOLE STATE, Thirty Years and Eight Months, From May 1, 1843, to Dec. 31, 1873.		
	Number of Persons.	Aggregate.	Average.	Number of Persons.	Aggregate.	Average.	Number of Persons.	Aggregate.	Average.
Curriers,	37	1,440	38·92	1	44	44·00	319	13,036	40·87
Cutlers,	—	—	—	9	361	40·11	124	4,865	39·23
Distillers,	—	—	—	—	—	—	27	1,585	58·71
Dyers,	4	240	60·00	7	358	51·14	137	6,213	45·35
Founders,	23	895	38·91	12	508	42·33	330	14,121	42·73
Furnace-men,	3	101	33·67	—	—	—	123	5,295	43·05
Glass-blowers,	5	178	35·60	2	70	35·00	129	4,888	37·81
Gunsmiths,	1	35	35·00	2	96	48·00	246	11,949	48·57
Hatters,	10	498	49·80	2	73	36·50	345	18,821	54·55
Leather-dressers,	17	845	49·70	1	63	63·00	162	7,680	47·41
Machinists,	99	3,765	38·03	41	1,611	39·29	1,960	79,975	40·80
Millers,	3	139	46·33	8	434	54·25	270	15,506	57·43
Musical Instrument-makers,	3	138	46·00	3	102	34·00	28	1,325	47·32
Nail-makers,	—	—	—	—	—	—	166	6,773	40·80
Pail and Tub-makers,	121	5,264	43·50	23	832	36·17	4	158	39·50
Painters,	1	87	87·00	16	861	53·81	1,739	78,434	45·05
Paper-makers,	—	—	—	—	—	—	274	13,262	48·40
Pianoforte-makers,	12	389	32·42	1	31	31·00	98	4,169	42·50
Plumbers,	3	180	60·00	—	—	—	115	4,077	35·43
Potters,	1	49	49·00	1	89	89·00	39	2,202	56·41
Pump and Block-makers,	—	—	—	—	—	—	83	4,671	56·25
Reed-makers,	—	—	—	—	—	—	9	385	42·78
Rope-makers,	5	245	49·00	—	—	—	242	14,058	58·09
Tallow-chandlers,	—	—	—	—	—	—	64	3,553	55·52

Tinsmiths,	15	40·67	610	1	43	43·00	355	14,541	40·96
Trunk-makers,	1	19·00	19	1	–	–	43	1,709	39·74
Upholsterers,	11	34·90	884	–	–	35·33	115	4,506	39·18
Weavers,	20	42·50	850	24	848	66·43	433	19,385	44·65
Wheelwrights,	19	58·63	1,114	7	465	72·40	489	27,695	56·63
Wood-turners,	4	50·50	202	5	362	49·96	73	3,836	52·55
Mechanics (trade not specified),	79	43·71	3,453	79	3,947	–	1,939	87,503	45·13
IV. INACTIVE MECHANICS IN SHOPS,	775	44·47	34,464	204	9,154	44·38	16,414	718,004	43·74
Barbers,	26	33·81	879	4	165	41·25	367	14,597	39·77
Basket-makers,	1	24·00	24	–	–	–	66	4,096	62·06
Book-binders,	9	47·77	430	–	–	–	146	5,832	39·94
Brush-makers,	3	39·67	119	–	–	–	52	2,257	43·40
Carvers,	7	27·86	195	1	20	20·00	86	2,910	33·84
Cigar-makers,	3	33·33	100	3	90	30·00	145	5,555	38·31
Clock and Watch-makers,	6	47·67	286	1	22	22·00	86	4,681	54·43
Comb-makers,	2	70·00	140	5	235	47·00	127	6,526	51·38
Engravers,	7	45·28	317	1	68	68·00	108	4,490	41·57
Glass-cutters,	8	34·00	272	–	–	–	70	2,967	42·39
Harness-makers,	16	43·88	702	5	262	52·40	404	19,537	48·36
Jewellers,	35	38·97	1,364	–	–	–	446	17,970	40·29
Operatives,	126	35·48	4,470	54	2,177	40·31	2,003	77,966	38·92
Printers,	40	46·87	1,875	7	272	38·86	673	25,956	38·57
Sail-makers,	9	62·56	563	–	–	–	206	10,886	52·84
Shoe-cutters,	40	48·55	1,942	1	70	70·00	333	14,192	42·62
Shoemakers,	362	45·35	16,417	101	4,851	48·03	9,393	417,561	44·45
Silversmiths or Goldsmiths,	1	23·00	23	1	49	49·00	79	3,614	45·76
Tailors,	65	60·98	3,964	10	497	49·70	1,344	63,418	47·19
Tobacconists,	2	56·00	112	–	–	–	43	2,165	50·35
Whip-makers,	1	54·00	54	6	224	37·33	95	4,076	42·91
Wool-sorters,	6	36·00	216	4	152	38·00	142	6,752	47·55

TABLE XI.—Continued.

OCCUPATIONS.	NINE EASTERN COUNTIES, 1878.			FIVE WESTERN COUNTIES, 1878.			WHOLE STATE, Thirty Years and Eight Months. From May 1, 1843, to Dec. 31, 1878.		
	Number of Persons.	Aggregate.	Average.	Number of Persons.	Aggregate.	Average.	Number of Persons.	Aggregate.	Average.
V. LABORERS—No Special Trades,	1,384	66,564	48·10	328	15,373	46·84	26,749	1,265,652	47·31
Laborers,	1,346	64,806	48·15	320	15,135	47·90	26,127	1,238,100	47·39
Servants,	19	744	39·15	5	111	22·20	354	14,227	40·19
Stevedores,	3	161	53·67	–	–	–	75	3,903	52·00
Watchmen,	16	858	53·31	3	127	42·33	175	8,708	49·76
Workmen in powder-mills,	–	–	–	–	–	–	18	714	39·67
VI. FACTORS LABORING ABROAD, ETC.,	301	11,575	38·45	74	2,724	36·81	6,749	242,425	35·92
Baggage-masters,	–	–	–	2	68	34·00	32	1,019	31·84
Brakemen,	20	508	25·40	20	461	23·05	229	6,095	26·35
Butchers,	24	1,148	47·83	10	423	42·30	409	25,095	50·29
Chimney-sweepers,	–	–	–	–	–	–	4	138	34·50
Drivers,	39	1,065	27·31	2	109	54·50	306	11,890	38·86
Drovers,	1	57	57·00	–	–	–	17	838	49·29
Engineers and Firemen,	35	1,357	38·77	10	339	33·90	517	19,756	38·21
Expressmen,	18	761	42·28	–	–	–	203	8,310	40·94
Ferrymen,	1	73	73·00	–	–	–	9	484	53·78
Light-house keepers,	1	–	–	–	–	–	10	604	60·40
Peddlers,	30	1,351	45·03	7	374	54·57	393	17,620	44·83
Sextons,	2	142	71·00	1	20	20·00	75	4,428	59·04

Stablers,	24	852	35·50	3	144	48·00	329	13,843	**42·08**
Teamsters,	104	4,116	39·58	18	760	46·66	1,200	48,162	40·13
Weighers and Gaugers,	1	80	80·00	—	—	—	24	1,456	60·67
Wharfingers,	—	—	—	—	—	—	22	1,100	50·00
VII. EMPLOYED ON THE OCEAN,	402	19,525	48·57	6	384	64·00	8,505	393,944	46·32
Fishermen,	48	2,039	42·48	1	64	64·00	400	17,128	42·82
Marines,	—	—	—	—	—	—	4	165	41·25
Naval Officers,	3	156	52·00	—	—	—	53	2,636	49·74
Pilots,	1	58	58·00	—	—	—	80	4,843	60·54
Seamen,	350	17,272	49·35	5	320	64·00	7,968	369,172	46·33
VIII. MERCHANTS, FINANCIERS, AGENTS, ETC.	927	43,755	47·21	204	8,990	44·41	15,098	738,719	48·93
Agents,	61	2,247	36·83	8	314	39·25	339	15,555	45·89
Bankers,	1	32	32·00	—	—	—	44	2,501	56·84
Bank Officers,	8	521	65·12	1	—	—	135	7,316	54·19
Boarding-house keepers,	9	454	50·45	1	46	46·00	72	3,410	47·36
Booksellers,	—	—	—	2	117	58·50	72	3,840	53·33
Brokers,	6	378	63·00	4	218	54·50	185	9,191	49·68
Clerks and Bookkeepers,	242	7,607	31·43	56	1,568	28·00	3,210	115,791	36·07
Druggists and Apothecaries,	20	909	45·45	4	113	28·25	234	9,903	42·32
Gentlemen,	85	5,810	68·35	15	1,069	71·27	1,458	99,544	68·27
Grocers,	33	1,520	46·06	5	239	47·80	480	22,791	47·48
Innkeepers,	12	583	48·58	4	210	52·50	435	21,644	49·76
Manufacturers,	66	3,627	54·95	23	1,309	56·91	1,310	66,909	51·14
Merchants,	191	11,040	57·80	47	2,171	46·19	3,736	201,815	54·02
News-dealers or Carriers,	3	93	31·00	2	67	33·50	27	1,113	41·22
Railroad Agents or Conductors,	19	730	38·42	11	449	40·82	298	11,720	39·33
Saloon and Restaurant keepers,	90	1,054	35·13	5	221	44·20	268	10,981	40·98

TABLE XI.—Concluded.

OCCUPATIONS.	NINE EASTERN COUNTIES, 1873.			FIVE WESTERN COUNTIES, 1873.			WHOLE STATE, Thirty Years and Eight Months. From May 1, 1843, to Dec. 31, 1873.		
	Number of Persons.	Aggregate.	Average.	Number of Persons.	Aggregate.	Average.	Number of Persons.	Aggregate.	Average.
Stove-dealers,	–	–	–	–	–	–	12	543	45·25
Telegraphers,	–	–	–	–	–	–	5	144	28·80
Traders,	141	7,150	50·71	17	879	51·71	2,778	134,008	48·24
IX. PROFESSIONAL MEN, ETC.,	221	11,369	51·44	62	3,127	50·44	4,917	250,448	50·93
Architects,	5	183	36·60	–	–	–	27	1,273	47·15
Artists,	8	484	60·50	3	139	46·33	172	7,664	44·56
Civil Engineers,	2	109	54·50	3	113	37·66	116	4,911	42·34
Clergymen,	35	2,119	60·54	13	734	56·46	926	54,338	58·68
Comedians,	2	80	40·00	–	–	–	30	1,086	36·20
Dentists,	6	232	38·67	1	69	69·00	107	4,429	41·39
Editors and Reporters,	6	343	57·17	1	62	62·00	78	3,559	45·63
Judges and Justices,	1	62	62·00	–	–	–	17	1,111	65·35
Lawyers,	25	1,547	61·88	7	434	62·00	641	36,285	56·67
Musicians,	18	735	40·83	3	104	34·66	242	9,968	41·19
Photographers,	–	–	–	–	–	–	10	368	36·80
Physicians,	50	2,793	59·46	12	706	58·83	1,120	62,364	55·68
Professors,	3	180	60·00	2	136	68·00	42	2,356	56·10
Public Officers,	8	485	60·62	2	144	72·00	411	22,699	55·23
Sheriffs, Constables, and Policemen,	13	548	42·15	–	–	–	137	7,326	53·48
	19	415	21·84	8	161	20·13	281	6,538	23·27
	6	302	50·33	2	84	42·00	81	4,214	52·02
	14	752	53·71	5	241	48·20	479	19,959	41·67

X. FEMALES.	139	5,960	42·88	76	2,778	36·55	3,090	124,193	40·19
Domestics,	56	2,601	46·45	8	940	46·19	938	43,611	46·49
Dressmakers,	19	968	50·95	7	309	44·14	229	9,774	42·24
Milliners,	2	99	49·50	5	152	30·40	129	5,070	39·30
Nurses,	4	244	61·00	2	128	61·50	112	6,808	60·78
Operatives,	19	556	29·26	22	658	29·68	664	18,579	27·98
Seamstresses,	10	416	41·60	7	272	38·86	276	12,853	46·57
Shoe-binders,	3	190	49·33	1	—	—	44	1,918	43·59
Straw-workers,	1	21	21·00	1	31	31·00	68	2,345	34·49
Tailoresses,	4	182	45·50	8	474	59·25	223	10,588	47·48
Teachers,	21	743	35·38	16	415	25·94	405	12,605	31·12
Telegraphers,	—	—	—	—	—	—	2	42	21·00

15

TABLE XII.—GENERAL ABSTRACT

*Exhibiting the Number of Births, Marriages, and Deaths, registered
Years, 1865–73,—in connection with the Population, according to the
Persons who died;—also showing the Ratios of the annual average*

THE STATE AND COUNTIES.	Population. U.S. Census 1870.	BIRTHS.					
			SEX.			RATIO.	
		Persons.	Males.	Females.	Unk.	Births to 100 Persons living.	Persons living to one Birth.
MASSACHUSETTS,	1,457,351	337,496	173,259	163,844	393	2·57	39
BARNSTABLE, . .	32,774	6,406	3,319	3,060	27	2·17	46
BERKSHIRE, . .	64,827	14,300	7,456	6,821	23	2·45	41
BRISTOL, . . .	102,886	23,588	12,237	11,305	46	2·55	39
DUKES, . . .	3,787	559	284	270	5	1·64	61
ESSEX, . . .	200,843	44,107	22,898	21,150	59	2·44	41
FRANKLIN, . .	32,635	5,762	2,975	2,778	9	1·96	51
HAMPDEN, . .	78,409	18,241	9,279	8,939	23	2·58	39
HAMPSHIRE, . .	44,388	9,007	4,701	4,297	9	2·26	44
MIDDLESEX, . .	274,353	62,581	32,087	30,427	67	2·54	39
NANTUCKET, . .	4,123	480	274	205	1	1·29	77
NORFOLK, . .	89,443	19,381	9,850	9,490	41	2·44	41
PLYMOUTH, . .	65,365	13,362	6,909	6,434	19	2·27	44
SUFFOLK, . . .	270,802	75,264	38,193	37,061	10	3·09	32
WORCESTER, . .	192,716	44,458	22,797	21,607	54	2·56	39

FOR THE NINE YEARS—1865-73.

*in the several Counties and Towns of Massachusetts, for the Nine
U.S. Census of 1870,—distinguishing the Sex of Children Born and of
number of Births, Marriages, and Deaths, to the given Population.*

MARRIAGES.			DEATHS.					
	RATIO.			SEX.			RATIO.	
Couples.	Marriages to 100 Persons.	Persons living to one Marriage.	Persons.	Males.	Females.	Unk.	Deaths to 100 Persons living.	Persons living to one Death.
133,658	1·02	98	248,421	124,327	123,749	345	1·89	53
2,945	1·00	100	4,796	2,473	2,288	35	1·62	62
4,978	·85	117	8,941	4,520	4,384	37	1·54	65
9,493	1·02	97	17,659	8,903	8,729	27	1·92	52
310	·91	110	582	324	258	–	1·71	59
18,644	1·03	97	32,778	16,245	16,481	52	1·82	55
2,603	·88	114	4,798	2,282	2,503	13	1·64	61
7,547	1·07	93	13,542	6,807	6,717	18	1·92	52
3,680	·92	109	6,527	3,169	3,339	19	1·63	61
23,737	·96	104	46,172	22,660	23,472	40	1·87	53
357	·96	104	864	420	444	–	2·34	43
5,903	·74	136	12,497	6,200	6,282	15	1·55	64
5,236	·89	112	10,231	5,140	5,065	26	1·74	58
31,943	1·31	76	58,049	29,652	28,381	16	2·38	42
16,282	·94	106	30,985	15,532	15,406	47	1·78	56

TABLE XII.—*General Abstract*

COUNTIES AND TOWNS.	Population. United States Census, 1870.	BIRTHS.					
		Persons.	SEX.			RATIO.	
			Males.	Females.	Unk.	Births to 100 Persons living.	Persons living to one Birth.
BARNSTABLE CO.,	32,774	6,406	3,319	3,060	27	2·17	46
Barnstable,	4,793	677	314	352	11	1·57	64
Brewster,	1,259	228	128	100	–	2·01	50
Chatham,	2,411	522	255	267	–	2·40	42
Dennis,	3,269	690	344	346	–	2·35	43
Eastham,	668	114	69	45	–	1·89	53
Falmouth,	2,237	301	159	141	1	1·49	67
Harwich,.	3,080	688	363	323	2	2·48	40
Mashpee,*	348	35	20	15	–	2·63	38
Orleans,	1,323	252	119	133	–	2·12	47
Provincetown,	3,865	1,000	539	460	1	2·87	35
Sandwich,	3,694	782	421	361	–	2·50	40
Truro,	1,269	281	142	139	–	2·38	42
Wellfleet,	2,135	416	205	199	12	2·17	46
Yarmouth,	2,423	420	241	179	–	1·91	52
BERKSHIRE CO.,	64,827	14,300	7,456	6,821	23	2·45	41
Adams,	12,090	3,182	1,658	1,518	6	2·92	34
Alford,	430	78	34	44	–	2·02	50
Becket,	1,346	231	118	111	2	1·91	52
Cheshire,	1,758	351	187	163	1	2·22	45
Clarksburg,	686	127	63	64	–	2·06	49
Dalton,	1,252	280	140	140	–	2·49	40
Egremont,	931	131	62	69	–	1·56	64
Florida,	1,322	348	175	171	2	2·92	34
Great Barrington,	4,320	855	438	416	1	2·20	46
Hancock,	882	101	55	46	–	1·27	79
Hinsdale,	1,695	477	237	240	–	3·12	32
Lanesborough,	1,393	434	220	214	–	3·46	29
Lee,	3,866	870	455	415	–	2·50	40
Lenox,	1,965	458	254	204	–	2·59	39
Monterey,	653	101	45	55	1	1·72	58
Mt. Washington,	256	23	10	13	–	1·00	100
New Ashford,.	208	40	22	18	–	2·13	47
New Marlborough,	1,855	436	245	191	–	2·63	38
Otis,	960	120	72	48	–	1·39	72
Peru,	455	77	40	37	–	1·89	53
Pittsfield,	11,112	2,704	1,391	1,311	2	2·70	37
Richmond,	1,091	192	85	107	–	1·96	51
Sandisfield,	1,482	165	81	84	–	1·23	81
Savoy,	861	149	83	66	–	1·92	52
Sheffield,	2,535	582	334	246	2	2·56	39
Stockbridge,	2,003	295	165	129	1	1·64	61
Tyringham,	557	156	75	81	–	3·12	32

* Four years only; incorporated 1870.

for *Nine* Years—Continued.

| | MARRIAGES. | | | DEATHS. | | | | | |
| | | RATIO. | | | SEX. | | | RATIO. | |
Couples.	Marriages to 100 Persons.	Persons living to one Marriage.	Persons.	Males.	Females.	Unk.	Deaths to 100 Persons living.	Persons living to one Death.
2,945	1·00	100	4,796	2,473	2,288	35	1·62	62
387	·90	111	508	241	263	4	1·18	85
116	1·02	98	193	96	96	1	1·70	59
212	·98	102	353	179	173	1	1 62	61
320	1·09	92	486	264	219	3	1·65	65
51	·85	118	106	56	50	–	1·76	57
155	·77	130	341	186	155	–	1·69	59
369	1·33	75	419	213	193	13	1·51	66
12	·89	112	35	15	20	–	2·63	38
144	1·19	84	275	138	137	–	2 30	43
430	1·24	81	587	320	266	1	1·69	59
307	·98	102	591	321	269	1	1·88	53
98	·83	121	197	107	90	–	1·65	60
178	·93	108	354	174	176	4	1·85	54
166	·76	131	351	163	181	7	1·61	62
4,978	·85	117	8,941	4,520	4,384	37	1·54	65
1,191	1·09	91	1,755	909	846	–	1·61	62
26	·67	149	78	42	36	–	2·01	50
81	·67	149	158	60	98	–	1·30	77
124	·79	128	191	93	95	3	1·21	83
25	·40	247	65	37	28	–	1·05	95
101	·90	111	211	100	110	1	1·87	53
76	·91	110	104	58	46	–	1·24	81
39	·33	305	207	132	73	2	1·74	57
357	·92	109	623	284	338	1	1·60	62
24	·30	331	75	38	37	–	·94	106
156	1·02	98	282	138	144	–	1·85	54
85	·68	147	177	95	81	1	1·41	71
364	1·04	96	733	353	380	–	2·10	48
92	·52	192	203	104	97	2	1·15	87
53	·90	111	108	53	55	–	1·85	54
9	·39	256	22	16	6	–	·95	105
11	·59	170	16	11	5	–	·85	117
92	·55	181	222	111	111	–	1·33	75
71	·82	122	130	67	63	–	1·51	66
27	·66	152	72	28	43	1	1·75	57
991	·99	101	1,587	815	761	11	1 59	63
36	·37	273	91	50	40	1	·92	108
109	·82	122	148	75	73	–	1·11	90
80	1·03	97	127	62	65	–	1·64	61
183	·80	125	412	203	208	1	1·82	55
159	·88	113	239	123	116	–	1·33	75
47	·93	107	107	45	61	1	2·12	47

TABLE XII.—*General Abstract*

COUNTIES AND TOWNS.	Population. United States Census, 1870.	BIRTHS.					
		Persons.	SEX.			RATIO.	
			Males.	Females.	Unk.	Births to 100 Persons living.	Persons living to one Birth.
Berkshire—Con.							
Washington, . .	694	75	43	32	–	1·23	83
West Stockbridge, .	1,924	499	260	238	1	2·85	35
Williamstown, .	3,559	675	359	312	4	2·13	47
Windsor, . .	686	88	50	38	–	1·43	70
BRISTOL Co., .	102,886	23,588	12,237	11,305	46	2·55	39
Acushnet, .	1,132	207	112	95	–	2·04	49
Attleborough, .	6,769	2,322	1,179	1,136	7	3·84	26
Berkley, . .	744	81	37	44	–	1·20	83
Dartmouth, .	3,367	612	319	293	–	2·04	49
Dighton, .	1,817	414	208	198	8	2·56	39
Easton, . .	3,668	916	492	424	–	2·78	36
Fairhaven, .	2,626	361	194	167	–	1·54	65
Fall River, .	26,766	7,413	3,834	3,564	15	3·08	33
Freetown, .	1,372	176	88	85	3	1·43	70
Mansfield, .	2,432	489	239	250	–	2·22	45
New Bedford, .	21,320	4,072	2,061	2,009	2	2·13	47
Norton, . .	1,821	254	144	109	1	1·55	65
Raynham, .	1,713	363	187	176	–	2·35	43
Rehoboth, .	1,895	294	158	136	–	1·70	58
Seekonk, .	1,021	128	73	54	1	1·39	72
Somerset, .	1,776	462	245	217	–	2·89	35
Swanzey, .	1,294	250	136	114	–	2·15	47
Taunton, .	18,629	4,269	2,255	2,010	4	2·54	39
Westport, .	2,724	505	276	224	5	2·06	48
DUKES Co., .	3,787	559	284	270	5	1·64	61
Chilmark, .	476	92	45	44	3	2·14	47
Edgartown, .	1,516	234	112	120	2	1·71	58
Gay Head,* .	160	20	12	8	–	1·39	72
Gosnold, . .	99	11	3	8	–	1·23	81
Tisbury, . .	1,536	202	112	90	–	1·47	68
ESSEX Co., . .	200,843	44,107	22,898	21,150	59	2·44	41
Amesbury, .	5,581	1,367	701	658	8	2·72	37
Andover, .	4,873	978	511	467	–	2·23	45
Beverly, .	6,507	1,361	702	659	–	2·32	43
Boxford, .	847	115	54	61	–	1·51	66
Bradford, .	2,014	333	177	155	1	1·85	54

* Four years only; incorporated 1870.

for Ten Years—Continued.

MARRIAGES.			DEATHS.					
	RATIO.			SEX.			RATIO.	
Couples.	Marriages to 100 Persons.	Persons living to one Marriage.	Persons.	Males.	Females.	Unk.	Deaths to 100 Persons living.	Persons living to one Death.
33	·55	183	78	42	36	–	1·29	77
125	·63	158	338	177	159	2	1·71	59
203	·55	181	422	220	192	10	1·14	87
74	1·19	84	85	45	40	–	1·36	73
10,793	·83	121	20,166	10,195	9,943	28	1·54	65
100	·94	106	173	82	91	–	1·63	61
638	·69	145	1,318	677	639	2	1·43	70
66	·84	119	112	58	53	1	1·43	70
263	·76	131	630	326	304	–	1·83	55
192	1·09	91	282	118	161	3	1·61	62
187	·48	209	558	286	272	–	1·43	70
206	·75	134	464	215	245	4	1·68	60
3,464	·76	131	6,858	3,516	3,342	–	1·51	66
112	·80	125	191	100	87	4	1·37	73
165	·62	161	430	205	225	–	1·62	62
2,659	1·02	97	4,067	2,017	2,044	6	1·57	64
114	·71	140	224	101	123	–	1·40	71
127	·75	133	252	136	116	–	1·49	67
156	·85	117	272	131	141	–	1·49	67
59	·50	198	149	84	65	–	1·28	78
142	·74	137	340	179	161	–	1·75	57
104	·79	126	235	124	111	–	1·80	56
1,834	·90	111	3,214	1,632	1,574	8	1·57	64
205	·70	142	397	208	189	–	1·36	73
343	·84	119	671	378	293	–	1·65	61
52	1·02	98	59	36	23	–	1·16	86
173	1·01	99	286	143	143	–	1·68	60
4	1·85	54	23	14	9	–	1·06	94
7	·61	164	15	8	7	–	1·30	77
107	·70	142	288	177	111	–	·58	173
20,755	·93	108	36,833	18,240	18,533	60	1·65	61
488	·81	123	1,008	497	508	3	1·68	59
401	·79	127	897	430	466	1	1·76	57
645	·88	113	1,067	520	547	–	1·47	68
66	·79	126	117	56	61	–	1·40	71
122	·52	192	300	138	162	–	1·28	78

TABLE XII.—*General Abstract*

COUNTIES AND TOWNS.	Population. State Census, 1875.	BIRTHS.					
			SEX.			RATIO.	
		Persons.	Males.	Females.	Unk.	Births to 100 Persons living.	Persons living to one Birth.
Essex—Con.							
Danvers,	6,024	1,441	766	669	6	2·39	42
Essex,	1,713	291	146	141	4	1·70	59
Georgetown,	2,214	326	161	165	–	1·47	68
Gloucester,	16,754	5,023	2,594	2,420	9	3·00	33
Groveland,	2,084	466	233	233	–	2·24	45
Hamilton,	797	143	70	73	–	1·79	56
Haverhill,	14,628	3,102	1,598*	1,501	3	2·12	47
Ipswich,	3,674	657	334	322	1	1·79	56
Lawrence,	34,916	8,674	4,415	4,255	4	2·49	40
Lynn,	32,600	7,128	3,700	3,419	9	2·19	46
Lynnfield,	769	149	75	74	–	1·94	52
Manchester,	1,560	373	207	166	–	2·39	42
Marblehead,	7,677	2,203	1,168	1,035	–	2·87	35
Methuen,	4,205	671	322	349	–	1·59	63
Middleton,	1,092	187	101	86	–	1·71	58
Nahant,	766	151	80	71	–	1·97	51
Newbury,	1,426	321	162	158	1	2·25	44
Newburyport,	13,323	3,041	1,663	1,374	4	2·28	44
North Andover,	2,981	663	343	319	1	2·22	45
Peabody,	8,066	2,209	1,126	1,083	–	2·74	37
Rockport,	4,480	1,148	562	584	2	2·56	39
Rowley,	1,162	219	104	114	1	1·88	53
Salem,	25,958	3,971	2,105	1,865	1	1·53	65
Salisbury,	4,078	1,012	510	501	1	2·48	40
Saugus,	2,578	407	212	192	3	1·58	63
Swampscott,	2,128	466	254	212	–	2·19	46
Topsfield,	1,221	221	130	91	–	1·81	55
Wenham,	911	205	98	107	–	2·25	44
West Newbury,	2,021	381	210	171	–	1·89	53
FRANKLIN CO.,	33,696	6,497	3,373	3,114	10	1·93	52
Ashfield,	1,190	196	105	90	1	1·65	61
Bernardston,	991	192	94	98	–	1·94	52
Buckland,	1,921	511	265	245	1	2·66	38
Charlemont,	1,029	131	70	61	–	1·27	76
Coleraine,	1,699	286	150	136	–	1·68	59
Conway,	1,452	309	175	134	–	1·43	70
Deerfield,	3,414	987	520	466	1	2·89	35
Erving,	794	98	49	49	–	1·23	81
Gill,	673	81	42	39	–	1·20	83
Greenfield,	3,540	810	404	406	–	2·29	44
Hawley,	588	150	82	67	1	2·55	39
Heath,	545	94	45	49	–	1·73	58
Leverett,	831	134	74	60	–	1·61	62

for Ten Years—Continued.

	MARRIAGES.			DEATHS.				
		RATIO.			SEX.			RATIO.
Couples.	Marriages to 100 Persons.	Persons living to one Marriage.	Persons.	Males.	Females.	Unk.	Deaths to 100 Persons living.	Persons living to one Death.
494	·82	122	948	465	476	7	1·57	64
108	·63	158	259	134	124	1	1·51	66
153	·69	145	255	130	125	–	1·15	87
1,798	1·07	93	3,344	2,013	1,327	4	2·00	50
134	·65	155	284	136	145	3	1·36	73
63	·79	126	131	76	54	1	1·64	61
1,642	1·12	89	2,007	932	1,064	11	1·37	73
313	·85	117	678	322	356	–	1·84	54
3,861	1·11	90	5,417	2,587	2,825	5	1·55	64
3,148	·96	104	5,200	2,528	2,664	8	1·59	63
69	·90	111	122	66	56	–	1·59	63
133	·85	117	282	131	151	–	1·81	55
749	·98	102	1,701	887	814	-	2·22	45
302	·72	139	495	248	246	1	1·18	85
77	·70	142	141	62	79	–	1·29	77
22	2·87	348	63	34	29	–	·83	121
91	·64	157	237	109	128	–	1·66	60
1,348	1·01	99	2,385	1,142	1,240	3	1·79	56
204	·68	146	398	205	193	–	1·35	75
452	·56	179	1,257	590	667	–	1·56	64
490	1·09	92	786	405	381	–	1·75	57
94	·81	124	214	106	108	–	1·84	54
2,326	·90	111	4,812	2,308	2,494	10	1·86	54
408	1·00	100	745	353	392	–	1·83	55
150	·58	172	354	181	172	1	1·37	73
105	·49	203	279	140	138	1	1·31	76
86	·70	142	180	92	88	–	1·47	63
93	1·02	98	137	58	79	–	1·50	67
120	·59	169	333	159	174	–	1·65	61
2,873	·85	117	5,402	2,595	2,791	16	1·60	62
77	·65	155	156	69	87	–	1·31	76
103	1·04	96	143	72	71	–	1·44	69
145	·75	133	370	193	177	–	1·93	52
79	·77	130	132	62	70	–	1·28	78
168	·99	101	249	120	129	–	1·47	68
133	·92	109	282	123	159	–	1·94	52
210	·62	162	604	292	309	3	1·77	57
51	·64	156	114	65	49	–	1·44	70
47	·70	143	89	49	39	1	1·32	76
439	1·24	81	592	281	311	–	1·69	59
35	·60	168	96	49	47	–	1·63	61
56	1·03	97	74	31	42	1	1·36	74
64	·77	130	130	63	66	1	1·56	64

TABLE XII.—*General Abstract*

COUNTIES AND TOWNS.	Population. State Census, 1875.	BIRTHS.					
		Persons.	Males.	Females.	Unk.	Births to 100 Persons living.	Persons living to one Birth.
Franklin—Con.							
Leyden,	524	109	50	59	–	2·08	48
Monroe,	190	35	22	13	–	1·84	54
Montague,	3,380	519	277	241	1	1·54	65
New Salem,	923	195	113	81	1	2·11	47
Northfield,	1,641	281	134	145	2	1·71	58
Orange,	2,497	318	154	164	–	1·27	79
Rowe,	661	78	44	34	–	1·18	85
Shelburne,	1,590	279	150	128	1	1·75	57
Shutesbury,	558	98	47	51	–	1·76	57
Sunderland,	860	168	85	83	–	1·95	51
Warwick,	744	147	76	71	–	1·98	51
Wendell,	503	64	28	36	–	1·27	79
Whately,	958	227	118	108	1	2·37	42
HAMPDEN CO.,	94,304	20,859	10,627	10,208	24	2·22	45
Agawam,	2,248	503	245	257	1	2·24	45
Blandford,	964	212	101	111	–	2·20	46
Brimfield,	1,201	236	111	122	3	1·96	51
Chester,	1,396	220	113	107	–	1·57	64
Chicopee,	10,335	2,431	1,240	1,190	1	2·35	43
Granville,	1,240	237	115	121	1	1·91	52
Holland,	334	72	40	31	1	2·16	46
Holyoke,	16,260	3,485	1,792	1,692	1	2·14	47
Longmeadow,	1,467	309	170	139	–	2·11	48
Ludlow,	1,222	264	129	134	1	2·16	46
Monson,	3,733	575	305	269	1	1·54	65
(*Primary School*),	–	159	80	79	–	–	–
Montgomery,	304	76	42	34	–	2·50	40
Palmer,	4,572	1,039	524	515	–	2·27	44
Russell,	643	163	87	75	1	2·56	39
Southwick,	1,114	205	106	99	–	1·84	54
Springfield,	31,053	7,313	3,679	3,631	3	2·35	43
Tolland,	452	101	61	39	1	2·24	45
Wales,	1,020	163	93	70	–	1·60	63
Westfield,	8,431	1,827	957	861	9	2·17	46
W. Springfield,	3,739	782	377	405	–	2·09	48
Wilbraham,	2,576	487	260	227	–	1·89	53
HAMPSHIRE CO.,	44,821	10,055	5,234	4,812	9	2·24	45
Amherst,	3,937	844	446	398	–	2·15	47
Belchertown,	2,315	459	235	224	–	1·98	50
Chesterfield,	746	150	79	71	–	2·01	50

for Ten Years—Continued.

| | MARRIAGES. | | | DEATHS. | | | | | |
| | | RATIO. | | | SEX. | | | RATIO. | |
Couples.	Marriages to 100 Persons.	Persons living to one Marriage.	Persons.	Males.	Females.	Unk.	Deaths to 100 Persons living.	Persons living to one Death.
44	·84	119	71	33	37	1	1·36	74
26	1·37	73	23	10	13	–	1·21	83
195	·58	173	441	235	206	–	1·31	77
95	1·03	97	162	78	84	–	1·75	57
124	·76	132	262	112	149	1	1·60	63
255	1·02	98	375	181	190	4	1·50	67
35	·53	189	78	33	45	–	1·18	85
136	·85	117	273	125	145	3	1·72	58
67	1·20	83	115	49	66	–	2·06	49
62	·72	139	161	68	93	–	1·87	53
78	1·05	95	150	74	75	1	2·02	50
67	1·33	75	89	45	44	–	1·77	57
82	·85	117	171	83	88	–	1·79	56
8,481	·90	111	15,303	7,670	7,609	24	1·62	62
118	·53	190	271	145	125	1	1·21	83
75	·78	128	177	86	91	–	1·83	55
84	·70	143	196	98	98	–	1·63	61
95	·68	147	120	63	57	–	·86	116
1,096	1·06	94	2,045	1,005	1,040	–	1·98	51
87	·70	143	176	78	98	–	1·42	71
20	·60	167	65	28	37	–	1·95	51
1,661	1·02	98	2,697	1,335	1,361	1	1·66	60
104	·71	141	249	115	134	–	1·70	59
107	·88	114	189	98	88	3	1·55	65
207	·56	180	440	235	204	1	1·18	85
–	–	–	424	258	166	–	–	–
28	1·25	80	67	37	30	–	2·20	45
514	1·12	89	620	307	312	1	1·36	74
51	·80	125	105	57	46	2	1·64	61
91	·82	122	171	90	79	2	1·54	65
3,023	·97	103	5,042	2,496	2,539	7	1·62	62
39	·86	116	* 62	37	23	2	1·37	73
89	·87	115	125	61	64	–	1·22	82
667	·79	126	1,237	613	621	3	1·47	68
158	·42	237	494	255	239	–	1·32	76
167	·65	154	331	173	157	1	1·28	78
4,052	·90	111	7,515	3,630	3,865	20	1·68	60
299	·76	132	610	292	318	–	1·55	65
206	·89	112	353	173	176	4	1·53	66
75	1·00	99	141	76	65	–	1·89	53

TABLE XII.—*General Abstract*

COUNTIES AND TOWNS.	Population. State Census, 1875.	BIRTHS.					
		Persons.	SEX.			RATIO.	
			Males.	Females.	Unk.	Births to 100 Persons living.	Persons living to one Birth.
Hampshire—Con.							
Cummington, . .	916	190	92	98	–	2·07	48
Easthampton, .	3,972	829	440	388	1	2·09	48
Enfield, . . .	1,065	220	114	106	–	2·07	48
Goshen, . . .	349	73	36	36	1	2·09	48
Granby, . .	812	182	94	88	–	2·24	45
Greenwich, .	606	91	47	44	–	1·50	67
Hadley, . .	2,125	577	291	286	–	2·72	37
Hatfield, . .	1,600	566	290	276	–	3·50	29
Huntington, . .	1,095	187	96	91	–	1·71	58
Middlefield, . .	603	148	75	73	–	2·46	41
Northampton, .	11,108	2,661	1,404	1,251	6	2·40	42
Pelham, . .	633	71	35	36	–	1·12	89
Plainfield, .	481	92	43	48	1	1·91	52
Prescott, . .	493	83	44	39	–	1·68	59
South Hadley, .	3,370	717	387	330	–	2·13	47
Southampton, .	1,050	219	113	106	–	2·09	48
Ware, . .	4,142	877	457	420	–	2·12	47
Westhampton, .	556	158	80	78	–	2·84	35
Williamsburg, .	2,029	502	248	254	–	2·47	40
Worthington, .	818	159	88	71	–	1·95	51
MIDDLESEX CO., .	284,112	62,814	32,322	30,432	60	2·21	45
Acton, . . .	1,708	340	180	159	1	1·99	50
Arlington, . .	3,906	909	460	449	–	2·33	43
Ashby, . . .	962	144	73	70	1	1·50	67
Ashland, . .	2,211	538	284	251	3	2·43	41
Ayer,* . . .	1,872	234	115	119	–	3·12	32
Bedford, . . .	900	160	99	61	–	1·79	56
Belmont, . .	1,937	385	188	197	–	1·99	50
Billerica, . .	1,881	318	154	164	–	1·69	59
Boxborough, . .	318	50	19	31	–	1·57	64
Burlington, . .	650	100	54	46	–	1·54	65
Cambridge, . .	47,838	11,880	6,035	5,838	7	2·48	40
Carlisle, . .	548	79	41	38	–	1·44	69
Chelmsford, . .	2,372	539	274	265	–	2·27	44
Concord, . .	2,676	501	272	229	–	1·87	53
Dracut, . .	1,116	395	191	204	–	3·53	28
Dunstable, . .	452	62	30	32	–	1·37	73
Everett,† . .	3,651	351	172	179	–	1·92	52
Framingham, . .	5,167	1,006	520	486	–	1·94	51
Groton, . . .	1,908	645	313	331	1	3·38	29
Holliston, . .	3,399	697	360	336	1	2·05	49
Hopkinton, . .	4,503	1,191	610	580	1	2·64	38
Hudson,‡ . .	3,493	804	418	385	1	2·30	43

* Four years only; incorporated 1871. † Five years only; incorporated 1870.
‡ Nine years only; incorporated 1866.

for Ten Years—Continued.

| | MARRIAGES. | | | DEATHS. | | | | | |
| | RATIO. | | | | SEX. | | | RATIO. | |
Couples.	Marriages to 100 Persons.	Persons living to one Marriage.	Persons.	Males.	Females.	Unk.	Deaths to 100 Persons living.	Persons living to one Death.
85	·93	108	155	71	84	–	1·69	59
272	·68	146	587	272	310	5	1·48	68
120	1·13	89	167	71	96	–	1·57	64
24	·70	145	59	34	25	–	1·69	59
53	·65	153	126	53	73	–	1·55	64
45	·74	135	129	67	62	–	2·13	47
148	·69	144	399	188	211	–	1·88	53
92	·57	174	280	133	147	–	1·75	57
122	1·11	90	203	100	102	1	1·86	54
36	·60	167	111	54	56	1	1·84	54
1,256	1·13	88	1,899	953	944	2	1·71	59
73	1·15	87	78	43	35	–	1·23	81
45	·93	107	84	37	47	–	1·74	57
48	·97	103	76	35	41	–	1·54	65
247	·73	136	447	224	219	4	1·33	75
94	·89	112	193	88	105	–	1·84	54
429	1·04	97	790	393	395	2	1·91	52
35	·63	159	114	55	59	–	2·05	49
170	·84	119	361	159	201	1	1·78	56
78	·95	105	153	59	94	–	1·87	54
22,943	·81	124	45,279	22,188	23,052	39	1·59	63
123	·72	139	278	130	148	–	1·63	61
248	·64	157	618	332	286	–	1·58	63
63	·65	153	186	85	100	1	1·93	52
201	·91	110	354	178	175	1	1·60	63
74	·99	101	117	66	51	–	1·61	62
59	·66	152	149	76	72	1	1·66	60
89	·46	218	219	100	116	3	1·13	88
121	·65	155	315	169	146	–	1·67	60
21	.66	151	48	20	28	–	1·51	66
35	·54	186	93	43	50	–	1·43	70
3,969	·83	121	7,714	3,798	3,905	11	1·61	62
50	·91	110	104	41	63	–	1·90	53
160	·68	148	372	158	214	–	1·57	64
234	·88	114	377	207	170	–	1·41	71
95	·85	117	322	138	183	1	2·88	35
27	·60	167	70	27	43	–	1·57	64
86	·47	212	218	99	118	1	1·22	82
459	·89	112	740	344	396	–	1·43	70
290	1·52	66	454	217	237	–	2·38	42
312	·92	109	445	220	225	–	1·31	76
298	·66	151	591	293	297	1	1·29	78
260	·75	134	479	224	255	–	1·37	73

TABLE XII.—*General Abstract*

COUNTIES AND TOWNS.	Population. State Census, 1 8 7 5.	BIRTHS.					
			SEX.			RATIO.	
		Persons.	Males.	Females.	Unk.	Births to 100 Persons living.	Persons living to one Birth.
MIDDLESEX—*Con.*							
Lexington, . .	2,505	384	199	185	–	1·53	65
Lincoln, . . .	834	153	83	70	–	1·83	54
Littleton, . .	950	169	93	75	1	1·78	56
Lowell, . . .	49,688	9,611	4,973	4,636	2	1·93	52
Malden, . . .	10,843	2,193	1,115	1,077	1	2·02	49
Marlborough,. .	8,424	3,345	1,711	1,634	–	3·97	25
Maynard,* . .	1,965	193	100	93	–	2·45	40
Medford,. . .	6,627	1,064	543	516	5	1·61	62
Melrose, . . .	3,990	742	393	348	1	1·86	54
Natick, . . .	7,419	2,108	1,053	1,046	9	2·84	35
Newton, . . .	16,105	2,793	1,402	1,391	–	1·65	61
North Reading, .	979	185	94	91	–	1·89	53
Pepperell, . .	1,927	368	199	169	–	1·91	52
Reading,. . .	8,186	467	228	239	–	1·47	68
Sherborn, . .	999	159	83	75	1	1·60	62
Shirley, . . .	1,352	236	122	114	–	1·75	57
Somerville, . .	21,868	5,196	2,720	2,470	6	2·37	42
Stoneham, . .	4,984	986	520	466	–	1·98	51
Stow, . . .	1,022	328	175	153	–	3·20	31
Sudbury,. . .	1,177	335	171	164	–	2·85	35
Tewksbury, . .	1,997	192	100	92	–	·96	104
(State Almshouse), .	–	581	298	283	–	–	–
Townsend, . .	2,196	441	241	200	–	2·01	50
Tyngsborough, .	665	83	45	38	–	1·25	80
Wakefield, . .	5,349	1,130	591	536	3	2·11	47
Waltham, . .	9,967	2,508	1,331	1,174	3	2·52	40
Watertown, . .	5,099	1,158	589	565	4	2·27	44
Wayland, . .	1,766	276	141	135	–	1·56	64
Westford, . .	1,933	424	207	211	6	2·19	46
Weston, . . .	1,282	188	94	94	–	1·47	68
Wilmington, . .	879	153	75	77	1	1·74	57
Winchester, . .	3,099	696	377	319	–	2·25	45
Woburn, . . .	9,568	2,641	1,394	1,246	1	2·76	36
NANTUCKET CO.,	3,201	540	302	237	1	1·68	59
NORFOLK CO., .	88,321	19,604	9,994	9,567	43	2·44	41
Bellingham, . .	1,247	249	127	121	1	2·10	50
Braintree, . .	4,156	870	434	432	4	2·10	48
Brookline, . .	6,675	1,992	1,034	950	8	2·99	33
Canton, . . .	4,192	868	441	425	2	2·07	48
Cohasset, . .	2,197	498	259	239	–	2·27	44
Dedham,. . .	5,756	1,818	944	870	4	3·16	32

* Four years only; incorporated 1871.

for Ten Years—Continued.

| | MARRIAGES. | | | DEATHS. | | | | |
| | RATIO. | | | | SEX. | | RATIO. | |
Couples.	Marriages to 100 Persons.	Persons living to one Marriage.	Persons.	Males.	Females.	Unk.	Deaths to 100 Persons living.	Persons living to one Death.
179	·71	140	438	202	236	–	1·75	57
34	·41	245	91	47	44	–	1·09	92
61	·64	156	178	79	99	–	1·87	53
5,862	1·18	85	8,955	4,212	4,741	2	1·80	56
681	·63	159	1,217	593	621	3	1·12	89
768	·91	110	1,505	745	760	–	1·79	56
54	·68	146	75	44	31	–	·95	105
493	·75	134	911	424	487	–	1·38	73
264	·66	151	532	249	280	3	1·33	75
564	·76	132	1,120	561	559	–	1·51	66
964	·60	167	1,439	685	753	1	·89	112
83	·85	118	156	75	81	–	1·59	63
158	·82	122	351	178	172	1	1·82	55
223	·70	143	445	216	229	–	1·40	72
84	·84	119	163	73	89	1	1·63	61
111	·82	122	213	99	114	–	1·57	64
862	·39	254	3,072	1,562	1,509	1	1·40	71
340	·68	147	661	323	338	–	1·33	75
114	1.11	90	210	110	99	1	2·05	49
92	·78	128	229	108	121	–	1·94	51
73	·36	274	159	78	81	–	·79	126
–	–	–	2,739	1,508	1,231	–	–	–
188	·85	117	380	181	199	–	1·73	58
49	·73	136	126	63	63	–	1·89	53
485	·91	110	788	388	398	2	1·47	68
1,033	1.04	96	1,536	746	788	2	1·55	65
521	1·02	98	680	315	364	1	1·33	75
91	·52	194	201	106	95	–	1·14	88
145	·75	133	313	157	155	1	1·62	62
74	·58	173	173	83	90	–	1·35	74
66	·75	133	157	82	75	–	1·79	56
214	·69	145	377	197	180	–	1·22	82
739	·78	129	1,426	734	692	–	1·49	67
397	1·24	84	951	455	496	–	2·97	34
6,161	·75	134	12,908	6,421	6,473	14	1·58	63
85	·68	146	182	95	85	2	1·46	68
278	·67	149	651	327	324	–	1·58	64
589	·88	113	1,024	501	523	–	1·53	65
294	·70	143	590	273	316	1	1·41	71
173	·79	127	343	172	171	–	1·56	64
556	·97	103	1,095	560	534	1	1·90	53

TABLE XII.—*General Abstract*

COUNTIES AND TOWNS.	Population. State Census, 1875.	BIRTHS.					
		Persons.	SEX.			RATIO.	
			Males.	Females.	Unk.	Births to 100 Persons living.	Persons living to one Birth.
Norfolk—Con.							
Dover, . . .	650	94	52	42	–	1·44	69
Foxborough, . .	3,168	480	235	242	3	1·51	66
Franklin, . .	2,983	439	215	224	–	1·47	68
Holbrook,* . .	1,726	127	69	58	–	2·45	41
Hyde Park,† . .	6,316	1,112	546	563	3	2·51	40
Medfield, . .	1,163	185	94	91	–	1·59	63
Medway, . .	4,242	783	387	395	1	1·84	54
Milton, . .	2,738	625	331	293	1	2·28	44
Needham, . .	4,548	957	464	491	2	2·11	48
Norfolk,‡ . .	920	150	74	76	–	3·26	31
Norwood,* . .	1,749	140	81	59	–	2·79	36
Quincy, . .	9,155	1,895	975	917	3	2·07	48
Randolph, . .	4,064	1,368	704	658	1	3·35	30
Sharon, . .	1,330	268	136	130	2	2·02	50
Stoughton, . .	4,842	1,217	627	590	–	2·51	40
Walpole, . .	2,290	434	224	208	2	1·90	53
Weymouth, . .	9,819	2,598	1,335	1,259	4	2·64	38
Wrentham, . .	2,395	442	206	234	2	1·84	54
PLYMOUTH CO., .	69,362	14,883	7,710	7,151	22	2·15	47
Abington,** . .	3,241	2,339	1,214	1,125	–	2·36	42
Bridgewater, . .	3,969	740	394	343	3	1·86	54
(*State Workhouse*), .	–	385	206	179	–	–	–
Brockton,§ . .	10,578	2,245	1,138	1,103	4	2·12	47
Carver, . .	1,127	219	122	97	–	1·94	52
Duxbury, . .	2,245	408	223	182	3	1·82	55
East Bridgewater, . .	2,808	571	287	284	–	2·03	49
Halifax, . .	568	102	47	55	–	1·79	56
Hanover, . .	1,801	370	191	179	–	2·05	49
Hanson, . .	1,265	249	127	122	–	1·97	51
Hingham, . .	4,654	903	486	412	5	1·94	52
Hull, . .	316	47	24	23	–	1·49	67
Kingston, . .	1,569	272	137	134	1	1·73	58
Lakeville, . .	1,061	219	103	116	–	2·07	48
Marion, . .	862	165	65	100	–	1·91	52
Marshfield, . .	1,817	286	144	140	2	1·57	64
Mattapoisett, . .	1,361	214	101	112	1	1·57	64
Middleborough, .	5,023	842	440	402	–	1·68	60
Pembroke, . .	1,399	286	145	141	–	2·04	49
Plymouth, . .	6,370	1,584	799	782	3	2·49	40
Plympton, . .	755	142	77	65	–	1·88	53
Rochester, . .	1,001	209	105	104	–	2·09	48
Rockland,†† .	4,203	80	55	25	–	1·90	53

* Three years only; incorporated 1872.   † Seven years only; incorporated 1868.
‡ Five years only; incorporated 1870.   § Name changed from N. Bridgewater, 1874.

for Ten Years—Continued.

| MARRIAGES. | | | DEATHS. | | | | | |
| | RATIO. | | | SEX. | | | RATIO. | |
Couples.	Marriages to 100 Persons.	Persons living to one Marriage.	Persons.	Males.	Females.	Unk.	Deaths to 100 Persons living.	Persons living to one Death.
44	·67	148	90	39	51	–	1·38	72
238	·75	133	421	192	228	1	1·33	75
177	·59	169	412	190	220	2	1·38	72
44	·85	118	75	38	37	–	1·45	69
306	·69	144	605	305	299	1	1·37	73
80	·69	145	162	76	86	–	1·39	72
263	·63	160	559	268	291	–	1·32	76
233	·85	117	418	204	214	–	1·53	66
259	·57	176	578	292	286	–	1·27	79
30	·65	153	88	48	40	–	1·93	52
24	·48	209	85	34	51	–	1·69	59
604	·66	151	1,337	711	626	–	4·86	69
388	·95	105	943	467	472	4	2·32	43
108	·81	123	271	142	129	–	2·04	49
352	·72	138	785	387	396	2	1·62	62
145	·34	295	350	172	178	–	·81	123
705	·72	139	1,416	729	687	–	1·44	69
186	·78	129	428	199	229	–	1·78	56
5,859	·85	118	11,358	5,677	5,654	27	1·64	61
758	·76	131	1,234	625	605	4	1·25	80
282	·71	141	463	242	220	1	1·17	86
–	–	–	810	470	340	–	–	–
856	·81	124	1,350	683	654	13	1·27	78
95	·84	119	174	92	82	–	1·54	65
181	·81	124	358	183	174	1	1·59	63
284	1 01	99	500	261	238	1	1·78	56
54	·95	105	108	46	61	1	1·90	53
168	·93	107	296	164	131	1	1·64	61
121	·96	104	180	92	88	–	1·42	70
364	·78	128	766	359	406	1	1·64	61
14	·44	228	48	33	15	–	1·52	66
118	·75	133	275	118	157	–	1·75	57
86	·81	123	173	77	96	–	1·63	61
77	·89	112	168	83	85	–	1·95	51
125	·69	145	268	123	144	1	1·47	68
130	·95	105	271	135	135	1	1·99	50
419	·83	120	710	332	378	–	1·41	71
128	·92	109	259	130	128	1	1·85	54
636	1·00	100	1,159	543	616	–	1·82	55
82	1·08	92	143	67	75	1	1·89	53
95	·95	105	170	85	85	–	1·70	59
17	4·03	248	40	20	20	–	·95	105

** Ratios based upon the joint population of Abington, South Abington, and Rockland.
†† Incorporated March 9, 1874.

TABLE XII.—*General Abstract*

COUNTIES AND TOWNS.	Population. State Census, 1875.	BIRTHS.					
		Persons.	SEX.			RATIO.	
			Males.	Females.	Unk.	Births to 100 Persons living.	Persons living to one Birth.
Plymouth—Con.							
Scituate, . . .	2,463	518	282	236	–	2·11	47
South Abington, .	2,456	–	–	–	–	–	–
South Scituate, .	1,818	294	165	129	–	1·62	62
Wareham, . .	2,874	845	455	390	–	2·94	3½
West Bridgewater, .	1,758	349	178	171	–	2·00	50 ·
SUFFOLK CO., .	364,886	97,246	49,396	47,830	20	2 40	42
Boston,* . . .	341,919	92,197	46,896	45,287	14	2·41	41
Chelsea, . . .	20,737	4,672	2,302	2,365	5	2·26	44
Revere, . . .	1,603	236	127	108	1	1·47	68
Winthrop, . .	627	141	71	70	–	2·13	47
WORCESTER CO.,	210,295	50,152	25,784	24,311	57	2·39	42
Ashburnham, . .	2,141	479	248	230	1	2·24	45
Athol, . . .	4,134	578	308	270	–	1·40	72
Auburn, . .	1,233	209	106	103	–	1·69	59
Barre, . . .	2,460	429	217	212	–	1·75	57
Berlin, . . .	987	228	117	111	–	2·31	43
Blackstone, . .	4,640	1,427	744	679	4	3·08	33
Bolton, . . .	987	226	101	125	–	2·29	44
Boylston, . .	895	170	90	80	–	1·90	53
Brookfield, . .	2,660	624	303	321	–	2·35	43
Charlton, . .	1,852	267	157	110	–	1·44	69
Clinton, . . .	6,781	1,623	837	782	4	2·39	42
Dana, . . .	760	109	49	60	–	1·43	70
Douglas, . .	2,202	741	387	354	–	3·37	30
Dudley, . . .	2,653	772	396	376	–	2·91	34
Fitchburg, . .	12,289	2,584	1,293	1,290	1	2·10	48
Gardner, . .	3,780	827	438	389	–	2·22	45
Grafton, . .	4,442	987	515	472	–	2·22	45
Hardwick, . .	1,992	489	249	240	–	2·46	41
Harvard, . .	1,304	198	96	102	–	1·52	66
Holden, . . .	2,180	415	203	211	1	1·90	53
Hubbardston, . .	1,440	237	124	113	–	1·64	61
Lancaster, . .	1,957	234	117	116	1	1·20	84
Leicester, . .	2,770	654	334	320	–	2·36	42
Leominster, . .	5,201	928	480	444	4	1·79	56
Lunenburg, . .	1,153	170	97	73	–	1·47	68
Mendon, . .	1,176	309	165	144	–	2·63	38
Milford, . . .	9,818	3,147	1,621	1,526	–	3·21	31
Millbury, . .	4,529	1,440	724	715	1	3·17	32
New Braintree, .	606	95	51	41	3	1·57	64
Northborough, .	1,398	311	141	170	–	2·23	45

* Charlestown, Brighton and West Roxbury annexed to Boston, Jan. 1, 1874.

for Ten Years—Continued.

| MARRIAGES. | | | | DEATHS. | | | | |
| | RATIO. | | | SEX. | | | RATIO. | |
Couples.	Marriages to 100 Persons.	Persons living to one Marriage.	Persons.	Males.	Females.	Unk.	Deaths to 100 Persons living.	Persons living to one Death.
185	·76	133	393	213	180	–	1·59	63
–	–	–	–	–	–	–	–	–
161	·88	113	278	124	154	–	1·53	65
307	1·07	94	512	260	252	–	1·78	56
116	·67	150	252	117	135	–	1·44	69
39,816	·99	101	73,895	37,640	36,228	27	1·81	55
37,847	1·00	100	70,403	35,876	34,512	15	1·83	55
1,886	·92	109	3,305	1,676	1,618	11	1·60	63
47	2·93	34	135	67	68	–	·84	119
36	·54	184	52	21	30	1	·79	127
18,034	·85	117	34,552	17,269	17,233	50	1·64	61
229	1·07	94	398	216	182	–	1·86	54
370	·85	118	581	289	292	–	1·41	71
79	·64	156	132	71	61	–	1·07	93
217	·88	113	457	223	233	1	1·86	54
93	·94	106	167	75	90	2	1·69	59
504	1·08	92	917	463	451	3	1·98	51
81	·82	122	233	107	126	–	2·36	42
67	·75	134	150	75	75	–	1·67	60
222	·83	120	396	184	212	–	1·49	67
136	·74	136	293	135	157	1	1·58	63
592	·87	115	903	431	470	2	1·33	75
80	1·05	95	126	62	63	1	1·66	60
207	·94	106	416	202	214	–	1·89	53
93	·35	285	534	267	265	2	2·01	50
1,166	·95	105	1,847	939	908	–	1·50	67
290	·78	129	458	229	229	–	1·23	81
368	·83	120	602	291	309	2	1·36	74
189	75	105	205	94	111	–	1·03	97
64	·49	204	225	100	125	–	1·73	58
181	·83	120	346	170	176	–	1·59	63
133	·93	108	258	116	139	3	1·79	56
159	·81	123	249	127	122	–	1·27	79
185	·67	149	476	255	221	–	1·72	58
233	·45	223	735	356	379	–	1·41	71
79	·68	146	212	100	112	–	1·84	54
77	·65	153	182	85	97	–	1·55	65
886	·90	111	2,012	1,032	979	1	2·05	49
442	·98	102	835	421	412	2	1·84	54
50	·83	120	93	45	47	1	1·54	65
102	·73	137	265	125	140	–	1·90	53

TABLE XII.—*General Abstract*

COUNTIES AND TOWNS.	Population. State Census, 1875.	BIRTHS.					
		Persons.	SEX.			RATIO.	
			Males.	Females.	Unk.	Births to 100 Persons living.	Persons living to one Birth.
Worcester—Con.							
Northbridge, . .	4,030	939	477	462	–	2·33	43
N. Brookfield,. .	3,749	1,081	582	499	–	2·88	35
Oakham, . .	▸873	130	65	65	–	1·49	67
Oxford, . .	2,938	584	304	280	–	1·99	50
Paxton, . .	600	▪84	43	41	–	1·38	72
Petersham, . .	1,203	191	95	96	–	1·59	63
Phillipston, . .	666	111	57	53	1	1·66	60
Princeton, . .	1,063	184	92	92	–	1·73	58
Royalston, . .	1,260	192	103	84	5	1·52	66
Rutland, . .	1,030	208	116	92	–	2·02	49
Shrewsbury, . .	1,524	382	221	160	1	2·51	40
Southborough, .	1,986	472	251	221	–	2·37	42
Southbridge, . .	5,740	1,514	766	748	–	2·64	38
Spencer, . .	5,451	1,632	844	784	4	2·99	33
Sterling, . .	1,569	294	156	136	2	1·87	53
Sturbridge, . .	2,213	326	176	149	1	1·47	68
Sutton, . .	3,051	653	333	320	–	2·14	47
Templeton, . .	2,764	624	333	291	–	2·26	44
Upton, . .	2,125	425	206	219	–	2·00	50
Uxbridge, . .	3,029	713	357	354	2	2·35	43
Warren, . .	3,260	705	370	335	–	2·16	46
Webster,. .	5,064	1,403	709	694	–	2·77	36
Westborough,. .	5,141	1,020	528	492	–	1·98	50
West Boylston, .	2,902	846	417	429	–	2·92	34
West Brookfield, .	1,903	440	238	202	–	2·31	43
Westminster, . .	1,712	272	133	139	–	1·59	63
Winchendon, . .	3,762	745	386	343	16	1·98	51
Worcester, . .	49,317	13,075	6,718	6,352	5	2·65	38

NOTE. The Census of the table above is corrected from official data supplied since Tables I. and VII. were printed, and differs from that given in those tables in the following particulars : *Additions* have been made, viz. : to Mt Washington, 5 ; New Bedford, 19 ; Taunton, 16 ; Beverly, 8 ; Lawrence, 9 ; Salem, 3 ; Chicopee, 4 ; Russell, 5 ; Westfield, 2 ; Easthampton, 8 ; Bedford, 4 ; Lowell, 11 ; Pepperell, 3 ; Waltham, 22 ; Bellingham, 3 ; Norwood, 76 ; Randolph, 3 ; West Bridgewater, 10 ; Chelsea, 42 ; New Braintree, 3 ; Webster, 5 ; Westborough, 1 ; Worcester, 52. Total, 314. *Subtractions* have occurred, viz. : from Rockport, 10 ; from Winthrop, 36 ; from Paxton, 8. Total, 54. Net increase for the State, 260. The population of each county is changed accordingly.

for Ten Years—Concluded.

| | MARRIAGES. | | | | DEATHS. | | | | |
| Couples. | RATIO. | | Persons. | SEX. | | | RATIO. | | |
	Marriages to 100 Persons.	Persons living to one Marriage.		Males.	Females.	Unk.	Deaths to 100 Persons living.	Persons living to one Death.	
322	·80	125	522	257	265	–	1·29	77	
289	·77	130	652	334	316	2	1·74	58	
65	·75	134	156	74	81	1	1·79	56	
212	·72	139	457	220	236	1	1·53	64	
40	·66	152	121	62	59	–	1·99	60	
109	·91	110	208	107	101	–	1·73	58	
67	1·01	99	113	50	63	–	1·70	59	
86	·81	124	204	94	110	–	1·92	52	
120	·95	105	244	109	135	–	1·94	52	
77	·75	134	170	78	92	–	1·65	61	
118	·77	129	316	158	158	–	2·07	48	
156	·79	127	323	159	164	–	1·63	62	
605	1·05	95	1,053	499	552	2	1·83	55	
303	·55	180	727	373	350	4	1·33	75	
117	·75	134	267	125	141	1	1·70	59	
173	·78	128	304	155	149	–	1·37	73	
245	·80	125	407	211	195	1	1·33	75	
258	·93	107	428	208	220	–	1·55	65	
146	·69	145	289	140	149	–	1·36	73	
256	·85	118	447	217	230	–	1·47	68	
254	·78	128	392	188	204	–	1·20	83	
683	1·35	74	815	422	391	2	1·61	62	
271	·53	189	637	341	296	–	1·24	81	
267	·92	109	476	235	241	–	1·64	61	
141	·74	135	299	154	143	2	1·57	64	
144	·84	119	301	151	150	–	1·76	57	
351	·93	107	611	319	285	7	1·62	62	
4,585	·93	107	8,910	4,544	4,360	6	1·81	55	

TABLE XIII.—BIRTHS.—TEN YEARS—1865–74.

Distinguishing by Counties, by Months, and by Sex, the registered Number of Children BORN ALIVE during the Ten Years, 1865–74; also, for the entire State, the Percentage of the Numbers in each Month (distinguishing Sex), to the Total Number.

10 Years. Months.	SEX.	Percentage.	STATE.	Barnstable.	Berkshire.	Bristol.	Dukes and Nantucket.	Essex.	Franklin.	Hampden.	Hampshire.	Middlesex.	Norfolk.	Plymouth.	Suffolk.	Worcester.
10 Years	Totals,	100·00	383,127	7,111	15,988	26,840	1,151	49,927	6,497	20,859	10,055	70,575	25,646	14,883	83,443	50,152
	Males,	51·40	196,916	9,701	8,367	13,922	615	25,871	3,373	10,627	5,294	36,251	13,040	7,710	42,421	25,784
	Females,	48·49	185,802	3,383	7,597	12,870	530	23,997	3,114	10,208	4,812	34,254	12,560	7,151	41,015	24,311
	Unknown,	·11	409	27	24	48	6	59	10	24	9	70	46	22	7	57
Jan.	Totals,	7·50	28,751	495	1,185	1,995	81	3,698	427	1,484	746	5,100	1,881	1,126	6,710	3,823
	Males,	3·83	14,675	244	618	1,058	44	1,928	236	722	382	2,596	941	551	3,357	1,998
	Females,	3·66	14,048	251	566	932	35	1,768	190	759	363	2,501	937	573	3,353	1,820
	Unknown,	·01	28	—	1	5	2	2	1	3	1	3	3	2	—	5
Feb.	Totals,	7·10	27,197	419	1,110	1,990	75	3,446	415	1,417	667	4,956	1,793	1,067	6,252	3,590
	Males,	3·68	14,087	217	571	1,046	32	1,811	217	710	373	2,587	889	530	3,181	1,923
	Females,	3·41	13,075	201	535	940	42	1,630	198	706	292	2,361	900	537	3,071	1,662
	Unknown,	·01	35	1	4	4	1	5	—	2	2	8	4	—	1	5
Mar.	Totals,	8·11	31,068	471	1,294	2,178	78	4,097	517	1,720	794	5,710	2,080	1,219	6,925	3,985
	Males,	4·20	16,077	240	704	1,141	50	2,124	275	875	417	2,933	1,049	641	3,575	2,053
	Females,	3·91	14,975	231	589	1,034	28	1,973	242	843	376	2,775	1,029	576	3,349	1,980
	Unknown,	—	16	—	1	3	—	—	—	2	1	2	2	2	1	2
Apr.	Totals,	7·50	28,760	436	1,264	2,062	98	3,704	499	1,588	806	5,125	1,911	1,148	6,173	3,946
	Males,	3·83	14,679	220	634	1,044	50	1,934	262	779	412	2,589	987	605	3,140	2,023
	Females,	3·67	14,063	216	629	1,016	47	1,767	236	808	394	2,534	924	541	3,032	1,919
	Unknown,	—	18	—	1	2	1	3	1	1	—	2	—	2	1	4
May.	Totals,	7·82	29,991	450	1,311	2,061	93	3,793	568	1,594	808	5,426	1,943	1,166	6,602	4,176
	Males,	4·01	15,370	235	694	1,071	49	2,003	293	808	411	2,809	1,010	610	3,328	2,049
	Females,	3·81	14,606	213	616	990	44	1,786	275	783	397	2,617	932	555	3,274	2,124
	Unknown,	—	15	2	1	—	—	4	—	3	—	—	1	1	—	8

Month	Category													Total	Rate
June	Totals	4,081	6,568	1,174	2,014	5,882	801	1,609	535	4,022	108	2,066	1,345	513	30,418	7·94
	Males	2,106	3,348	592	1,085	2,873	432	865	283	2,042	67	1,101	713	266	15,723	4·10
	Females	1,972	3,220	580	977	2,703	369	743	252	1,977	41	962	629	246	14,671	3·83
	Unknown	3	—	—	2	·	—	—	—	3	—	3	1	1	24	·01
July	Totals	4,499	7,290	1,298	2,172	5,924	881	1,876	597	4,320	102	2,313	1,439	705	33,416	8·72
	Males	2,274	3,741	670	1,128	3,069	444	936	321	2,162	55	1,217	748	366	17,131	4·47
	Females	2,221	3,549	626	1,039	2,851	436	939	276	2,149	46	1,089	689	338	16,248	4·24
	Unknown	—	—	2	5	6	1	1	—	9	—	7	2	1	37	·01
Aug.	Totals	4,702	7,456	1,315	2,304	6,543	941	2,007	625	4,795	108	2,416	1,443	775	35,430	9·25
	Males	2,387	3,725	704	1,194	3,367	478	1,023	316	2,475	60	1,254	745	419	18,147	4·74
	Females	2,311	3,730	609	1,106	3,170	462	980	307	2,320	48	1,160	696	353	17,252	4·50
	Unknown	4	—	1	5	6	1	4	2	—	—	2	2	3	31	·01
Sept.	Totals	4,900	7,095	1,342	2,279	6,383	900	1,848	615	4,496	95	2,407	1,490	744	33,994	8·88
	Males	2,208	3,616	701	1,156	3,338	450	933	319	2,327	46	1,220	783	403	17,500	4·57
	Females	2,087	3,478	689	1,121	3,038	449	911	295	2,162	49	1,186	705	338	16,458	4·30
	Unknown	6	1	2	2	7	1	4	2	7	—	1	2	3	36	·01
Oct.	Totals	4,457	7,522	1,344	2,365	6,565	929	1,895	607	4,666	104	2,473	1,442	728	35,097	9·16
	Males	2,305	3,883	690	1,182	3,312	481	992	336	2,392	63	1,280	768	352	18,036	4·71
	Females	2,145	3,638	651	1,179	3,250	447	902	269	2,270	41	1,190	673	372	17,027	4·44
	Unknown	7	1	3	4	3	1	1	2	4	—	3	1	4	34	·01
Nov.	Totals	4,247	7,320	1,331	2,368	6,346	856	1,885	539	4,353	110	2,347	1,305	685	33,692	8·80
	Males	2,206	3,734	725	1,170	3,251	437	973	260	2,323	51	1,182	687	367	17,966	4·53
	Females	2,040	3,586	605	1,195	3,090	419	911	278	2,020	58	1,160	616	311	16,289	4·26
	Unknown	1	—	1	3	5	—	1	2	10	1	5	2	7	37	·01
Dec.	Totals	4,311	7,523	1,349	2,517	6,883	917	1,905	551	4,526	97	2,486	1,341	681	35,087	9·16
	Males	2,243	3,792	689	1,292	3,514	515	997	254	2,345	47	1,292	694	370	18,044	4·71
	Females	2,063	3,729	657	1,211	3,351	402	907	295	2,170	50	1,186	646	308	16,975	4·43
	Unknown	—	—	1	14	18	—	1	2	11	—	8	1	3	68	·06
Not stated	Totals														226	·02
	Males														81	·03
	Females														115	·01
	Unknown														30	

SUPPLEMENT TO TABLE XIII.

PLURALITY BIRTHS.—TEN YEARS—1865-74.

[Included in Tables XII and XIII.]

10 Years. Months.	SEX.	STATE.	Barnstable.	Berkshire.	Bristol.	Dukes and Nantucket.	Essex.	Franklin.	Hampden.	Hampshire.	Middlesex.	Norfolk.	Plymouth.	Suffolk.	Worcester.
10 YEARS	Totals, .	7,237	138	424	463	42	1053	135	399	180	1340	514	329	1327	893
	Males, .	3,691	66	224	242	24	549	67	212	87	671	292	157	662	438
	Fem., .	3,544	72	200	221	16	504	68	187	93	669	222	172	665	455
	Unk., .	2	-	-	-	2	-	-	-	-	-	-	-	-	-
Jan.	Totals, .	559	14	33	31	4	93	12	14	14	102	36	22	115	69
	Males,	267	6	15	14	-	53	3	4	7	45	22	10	59	29
	Fem., .	290	8	18	17	2	40	9	10	7	57	14	12	56	40
	Unk., .	2	-	-	-	2	-	-	-	-	-	-	-	-	-
Feb.	Totals, .	461	6	22	30	4	55	8	30	6	86	44	20	82	68
	Males, .	235	2	10	14	1	31	4	16	5	35	28	9	43	37
	Fem., .	226	4	12	16	3	24	4	14	1	51	16	11	39	31
Mar.	Totals, .	481	2	30	18	2	77	11	30	20	90	42	22	76	61
	Males, .	249	1	22	7	2	36	9	16	8	49	24	10	35	30
	Fem., .	232	1	8	11	-	41	2	14	12	41	18	12	41	31
Apr.	Totals, .	561	4	36	32	6	86	8	18	16	96	48	26	109	76
	Males, .	285	2	21	14	4	55	3	8	7	46	25	14	53	33
	Fem., .	276	2	15	18	2	31	5	10	9	50	23	12	56	43
May.	Totals, .	544	12	38	37	4	69	13	38	16	99	24	30	84	80
	Males, .	291	7	15	22	3	30	5	20	7	56	13	20	50	43
	Fem., .	253	5	23	15	1	39	8	18	9	43	11	10	34	37
June	Totals, .	666	10	40	54	4	94	12	48	12	110	57	32	115	78
	Males, .	331	5	19	28	1	45	8	30	8	54	35	14	52	32
	Fem , .	335	5	21	26	3	49	4	18	4	56	22	18	63	46
July.	Totals, .	595	20	36	42	2	100	16	24	14	125	30	24	82	80
	Males, .	317	11	21	22	1	45	7	14	6	75	15	11	43	46
	Fem., .	278	9	15	20	1	55	9	10	8	50	15	13	39	34

Supplement to Table XIII.—Concluded.

Months	SEX	STATE	Barnstable	Berkshire	Bristol	Dukes and Nantucket	Essex	Franklin	Hampden	Hampshire	Middlesex	Norfolk	Plymouth	Suffolk	Worcester
Aug.	Totals, .	718	16	48	43	4	112	14	46	20	134	38	18	134	91
	Males, .	367	10	25	22	1	55	5	27	11	73	21	7	69	41
	Fem., .	351	6	23	21	3	57	9	19	9	61	17	11	65	50
Sept.	Totals, .	653	22	48	50	2	86	16	44	12	108	28	41	124	72
	Males, .	347	13	27	30	2	48	10	25	6	58	13	23	53	39
	Fem., .	306	9	21	20	–	38	6	19	6	50	15	18	71	33
Oct.	Totals, .	711	12	34	56	4	94	7	32	16	132	63	40	148	73
	Males, .	350	4	21	33	4	51	5	15	7	52	36	15	68	39
	Fem., .	361	8	13	23	–	43	2	17	9	80	27	25	80	34
Nov.	Totals, .	579	14	33	22	2	78	6	36	14	116	52	28	113	65
	Males, .	292	4	18	13	1	38	2	21	5	59	28	13	59	31
	Fem., .	287	10	15	9	1	40	4	15	9	57	24	15	54	34
Dec.	Totals, .	709	6	26	48	4	109	12	39	20	142	52	26	145	80
	Males, .	360	1	10	23	4	62	6	16	10	69	32	11	78	38
	Fem., .	349	5	16	25	–	47	6	23	10	73	20	15	67	42

18

TABLE XIV.—STILL–BORN.—TEN YEARS—1865–74.

Distinguishing by Counties, by Months, and by Sex, the registered Number of Still-births during the Ten Years, 1865–74.

10 Years. Months.	SEX.	State.	Barnstable.	Berkshire.	Bristol.	Dukes and Nantucket.	Essex.	Franklin.	Hampden.	Hampshire.	Middlesex.	Norfolk.	Plymouth.	Suffolk.	Worcester.
TEN YEARS.	Totals, .	11,463	169	150	831	30	1386	72	336	119	1629	596	270	5059	816
	Males, .	6,419	88	76	478	16	739	38	178	55	890	291	131	2979	460
	Fem., .	4,342	57	53	293	7	532	26	116	59	588	230	100	1984	297
	Unk , .	702	24	21	60	7	115	8	42	5	151	75	39	96	59
Jan.	Totals, .	864	12	4	71	4	108	1	21	1	124	39	17	407	55
	Males, .	494	9	2	37	2	56	1	9	–	72	20	10	241	35
	Fem., .	326	1	–	27	2	42	–	11	1	44	14	5	160	19
	Unk., .	44	2	2	7	–	10	–	1	–	8	5	2	6	1
Feb.	Totals, .	853	6	6	59	4	109	3	25	9	121	56	19	376	60
	Males, .	463	4	3	33	4	54	3	12	4	67	26	7	214	32
	Fem., .	343	2	3	22	–	43	–	8	5	49	22	10	156	23
	Unk., .	47	–	–	4	–	12	–	5	–	5	8	2	6	5
Mar.	Totals, .	1,037	12	15	100	1	126	3	37	17	130	59	18	455	64
	Males, .	581	8	7	58	1	69	2	20	7	67	28	8	266	40
	Fem., .	385	3	7	35	–	45	–	13	10	47	21	6	178	20
	Unk., .	71	1	1	7	–	12	1	4	–	16	10	4	11	4
Apr.	Totals, .	968	8	12	58	2	131	12	18	10	148	40	22	440	67
	Males, .	576	5	6	34	1	74	5	9	5	88	22	12	271	44
	Fem., .	342	3	5	20	1	43	7	8	4	46	14	6	163	22
	Unk., .	50	–	1	4	–	14	–	1	1	14	4	4	6	1
May.	Totals, .	923	8	11	67	3	112	8	23	10	144	38	18	425	56
	Males, .	516	4	6	36	1	57	4	16	3	78	18	9	251	33
	Fem., .	361	2	3	23	2	51	3	5	7	57	17	6	164	21
	Unk., .	46	2	2	8	–	4	1	2	–	9	3	3	10	2
June.	Totals, .	958	11	13	59	4	112	5	21	12	134	68	25	421	73
	Males, .	544	5	6	34	3	64	3	9	5	81	37	14	248	35
	Fem., .	357	4	7	21	–	42	1	8	7	42	28	9	162	26
	Unk., .	57	2	–	4	1	6	1	4	–	11	3	2	11	12
July.	Totals, .	980	15	13	78	4	96	7	23	12	146	50	24	442	70
	Males, .	556	4	9	43	2	58	4	14	5	75	26	12	266	38
	Fem., .	362	7	3	28	1	34	3	5	5	56	17	6	169	28
	Unk., .	62	4	1	7	1	4	–	4	2	15	7	6	7	4

TABLE XIV.—Concluded.

Months.	SEX.	State.	Barnstable.	Berkshire.	Bristol.	Dukes and Nantucket.	Essex.	Franklin.	Hampden.	Hampshire.	Middlesex.	Norfolk.	Plymouth.	Suffolk.	Worcester.
Aug.	Totals, .	945	17	9	53	1	125	3	29	7	115	43	30	443	70
	Males, .	535	8	6	33	–	63	1	14	5	59	19	11	274	42
	Fem., .	352	8	2	16	–	55	2	8	2	44	19	10	161	25
	Unk., .	58	1	1	4	1	7	–	7	–	12	5	9	8	3
Sept.	Totals, .	883	19	9	53	3	104	6	33	12	144	43	14	381	62
	Males, .	475	11	4	35	1	53	2	18	4	73	22	8	215	29
	Fem., .	341	6	3	17	–	40	4	12	8	54	13	4	156	24
	Unk., .	67	2	2	1	2	11	–	3	–	17	8	2	10	9
Oct.	Totals, .	924	15	18	63	1	119	5	22	10	114	46	23	417	71
	Males, .	511	7	10	38	–	72	1	10	7	55	22	8	246	35
	Fem., .	337	5	5	21	–	36	3	9	2	38	16	12	161	29
	Unk., .	76	3	3	4	1	11	1	3	1	21	8	3	10	7
Nov.	Totals, .	965	24	24	78	1	107	9	34	10	144	45	30	387	72
	Males, .	531	14	10	46	1	54	5	23	6	74	26	14	218	40
	Fem., .	379	9	9	27	–	42	2	11	3	58	13	15	163	27
	Unk., .	55	1	5	5	–	11	2	–	1	12	6	1	6	5
Dec.	Totals, .	1,144	22	15	89	2	135	10	50	9	159	65	29	465	94
	Males, .	630	9	7	50	–	63	7	24	4	99	25	17	269	56
	Fem., .	449	7	6	35	1	59	1	18	5	50	32	11	191	33
	Unk., .	65	6	2	4	1	13	2	8	–	10	8	1	5	5
Not stated.	Totals, .	19	–	1	3	–	2	–	–	–	6	4	1	–	2
	Males, .	7	–	–	1	–	2	–	–	–	2	-	1	–	1
	Fem., .	8	–	–	1	–	–	–	–	–	3	4	–	–	–
	Unk., .	4	–	1	1	–	–	–	–	–	1	–	–	–	1

TABLE XV.—MARRIAGES.—TEN YEARS—1865-74.

Distinguishing by Counties, and by Months, the Number of Marriages registered during the Ten Years, 1865-74.

TEN YEARS. MONTHS.	STATE.	Barnstable.	Berkshire.	Bristol.	Dukes & Nantucket.	Essex.	Franklin.	Hampden.	Hampshire.	Middlesex.	Norfolk.	Plymouth.	Suffolk.	Worcester.
TEN YEARS,	149,222	3,246	5,469	10,793	740	20,755	2,873	8,481	4,052	26,306	7,785	5,859	34,829	18,034
January,	13,653	428	433	990	69	1,815	260	877	346	2,285	676	544	3,224	1,706
February,	11,205	253	431	758	50	1,474	193	774	275	1,880	523	364	2,968	1,262
March,	7,336	209	288	509	49	1,141	220	440	241	1,192	335	358	1,466	888
April,	11,403	214	380	697	37	1,529	257	613	327	2,022	665	434	2,795	1,433
May,	12,804	218	491	896	52	1,670	259	825	378	2,208	652	468	3,014	1,673
June,	13,265	194	414	989	50	1,925	227	684	352	2,457	720	529	3,116	1,608
July,	10,787	180	360	844	69	1,594	164	611	252	1,918	522	376	2,630	1,267
August,	10,014	142	332	740	61	1,376	162	531	261	1,735	511	349	2,592	1,222
September,	12,733	166	534	891	53	1,740	196	691	339	2,495	657	463	3,044	1,464
October,	14,804	243	568	1,069	94	1,982	280	803	391	2,617	827	504	3,643	1,783
November,	18,650	570	620	1,411	76	2,656	368	991	519	3,296	1,039	873	4,031	2,200
December,	12,290	424	463	991	77	1,847	276	616	370	2,175	657	580	2,302	1,512
Unknown,	278	5	155	8	3	6	11	25	1	26	1	17	4	16

TABLE XVI.—MARRIAGES.—TEN YEARS—1865–74.

Exhibiting the Social Condition and Ages of Parties Married during the Ten Years, 1865–74.

AGGREGATE—Of all Conditions.

| AGE OF MALES. | ALL AGES. | AGE OF FEMALES. | | | | | | | | | | | | |
		Under 20	20 to 25	25 to 30	30 to 35	35 to 40	40 to 45	45 to 50	50 to 55	55 to 60	60 to 65	65 to 70	70 to 75	Over 75	Unknown.
ALL AGES,	149,222	29,797	65,805	30,029	10,635	5,760	2,874	1,605	911	474	288	164	52	21	807
Und. 20,	2,791	1978	736	55	13	3	–	–	–	–	–	–	–	–	6
20 to 25,	56,854	19197	32271	4692	485	110	11	3	2	–	–	–	–	–	83
25 to 30,	46,527	6718	23547	13713	1981	377	64	21	4	2	–	–	–	1	99
30 to 35,	18,434	1380	6271	6697	3185	696	125	29	4	2	1	–	–	–	44
35 to 40,	9,364	351	1980	2865	2282	1458	318	67	12	1	4	–	–	–	26
40 to 45,	5,108	90	597	1097	1308	1145	656	151	33	6	2	–	–	–	23
45 to 50,	3,599	39	251	569	772	939	573	354	73	13	1	1	–	–	14
50 to 55,	2,314	18	81	216	351	550	494	315	220	39	15	6	–	–	9
55 to 60,	1,479	10	32	78	163	287	310	275	177	104	24	7	–	1	11
60 to 65,	1,095	3	15	23	62	123	216	223	198	133	72	16	4	1	6
65 to 70,	623	–	9	9	23	42	60	109	115	97	75	66	11	–	7
70 to 75,	357	–	2	5	5	21	32	43	53	56	64	43	25	7	1
75 to 80,	125	–	–	1	1	2	9	12	14	20	28	21	10	6	1
Over 80,	42	–	2	2	–	2	5	2	5	1	1	4	2	2	14
Unk.,	510	13	11	7	4	5	1	1	1	–	1	–	–	3	463

(A.)   First Marriage of both Parties.

AGE OF MALES.	ALL AGES	Under 20	20 to 25	25 to 30	30 to 35	35 to 40	40 to 45	45 to 50	50 to 55	55 to 60	60 to 65	65 to 70	70 to 75	Over 75	Unknown.
ALL AGES,	117076	28440	59896	22271	4477	1177	287	89	38	12	6	2	2	1	378
Und. 20,	2,736	1971	708	44	7	2	–	–	–	–	–	–	–	–	4
20 to 25,	54,608	18912	31317	4001	276	38	1	–	–	–	–	–	–	–	63
25 to 30,	40,989	6212	21746	11635	1179	136	13	6	1	1	–	–	–	1	59
30 to 35,	12,576	1079	4774	4738	1699	227	28	4	–	–	–	–	–	–	27
35 to 40,	3,926	191	1056	1355	847	399	60	8	1	–	–	–	–	–	9
40 to 45,	1,228	44	203	326	322	214	85	21	7	1	–	–	–	–	5
45 to 50,	474	13	61	122	103	95	49	23	4	–	1	–	–	–	3
50 to 55,	187	4	15	33	37	47	26	12	8	3	–	–	–	–	2
55 to 60,	76	2	6	10	4	15	17	9	7	4	–	–	–	–	2
60 to 65,	30	1	1	1	1	4	6	5	5	1	4	–	1	–	–
65 to 70,	12	–	2	–	2	–	1	–	4	1	1	1	–	1	–
70 to 75,	5	–	–	1	–	–	1	1	–	1	–	–	1	–	–
75 to 80,	2	–	–	1	–	–	–	–	–	–	–	1	–	–	–
Over 80,	–	–	–	–	–	–	–	–	–	–	–	–	–	–	–
Unk.,	227	11	7	4	–	–	–	–	1	–	–	–	–	–	204

Table XVI.—Continued.

(B.) First Marriage of Male and Second Marriage of Female.

AGE OF MALES.	ALL AGES.	Under 20	20 to 25	25 to 30	30 to 35	35 to 40	40 to 45	45 to 50	50 to 55	55 to 60	60 to 65	65 to 70	70 to 75	Over 75	Unknown.
ALL AGES,	7,694	109	1382	2531	1874	1048	425	167	69	19	15	3	1	-	51
Und. 20,	50	5	27	11	6	1	-	-	-	-	-	-	-	-	-
20 to 25,	1,548	71	627	572	191	66	9	3	2	-	-	-	-	-	7
25 to 30,	2,536	28	484	1156	604	193	41	10	3	-	-	-	-	-	17
30 to 35,	1,660	4	157	524	619	265	66	15	3	2	-	-	-	-	5
35 to 40,	968	1	57	190	299	278	99	29	8	1	3	-	-	-	3
40 to 45,	457	-	18	51	93	130	112	38	10	3	1	-	-	-	1
45 to 50,	248	-	8	17	35	69	61	37	18	3	-	-	-	-	-
50 to 55,	121	-	2	8	16	26	21	22	16	5	3	-	-	-	2
55 to 60,	40	-	1	2	5	12	9	5	1	3	1	-	-	-	1
60 to 65,	33	-	-	-	4	4	6	5	6	2	4	2	-	-	-
65 to 70,	9	-	-	-	-	-	1	3	2	-	2	1	-	-	-
70 to 75,	4	-	-	-	1	1	-	-	-	-	1	-	1	-	-
75 to 80,	-														
Over 80,	1	-	-	-	-	-	-	-	-	-	-	-	-	-	1
Unk., .	19	-	1	-	1	3	-	-	-	-	-	-	-	-	14

(C.) Second Marriage of the Male but First Marriage of the Female.

AGE OF MALES.	ALL AGES.	Under 20	20 to 25	25 to 30	30 to 35	35 to 40	40 to 45	45 to 50	50 to 55	55 to 60	60 to 65	65 to 70	70 to 75	Over 75	Unknown.
ALL AGES,	14889	1185	4065	3988	2541	1595	771	370	158	76	36	17	1	2	84
Und. 20,	-														
20 to 25,	538	190	260	76	6	3	1	• -	-	-	-	-	-	-	2
25 to 30,	2,463	461	1181	706	96	12	2	1	-	1	-	-	-	-	3
30 to 35,	3,225	283	1239	1101	500	87	7	1	-	-	-	-	-	-	7.
35 to 40,	3,015	156	788	1012	680	311	52	6	1	-	-	-	-	-	9
40 to 45,	2,015	45	332	556	528	378	140	24	3	1	-	-	-	-	8
45 to 50,	1,529	24	167	332	401	359	159	73	7	3	-	-	-	-	4
50 to 55,	910	14	57	131	181	232	163	79	46	4	-	2	-	-	1
55 to 60,	548	8	21	44	97	128	120	81	29	12	4	2	-	-	2
60 to 65,	333	2	11	16	32	56	83	62	33	19	14	2	-	1	2
65 to 70,	164	-	4	8	15	20	25	28	26	24	5	7	-	-	2
70 to 75,	66	-	2	4	3	4	13	11	9	9	8	2	-	1	-
75 to 80,	21	-	-	-	-	2	3	3	2	3	5	2	1	-	-
Over 80,	7	-	-	-	-	2	2	1	2	-	-	-	-	-	-
Unk., .	55	2	8	2	2	1	1	-	-	-	-	-	-	-	44

TABLE XVI.—Concluded.

(D.)   Subsequent Marriage of both Parties.

AGE OF MALES.	AGE OF FEMALES.													
	ALL AGES.	Under 20	20 to 25	25 to 30	30 to 35	35 to 40	40 to 45	45 to 50	50 to 55	55 to 60	60 to 65	65 to 70	70 to 75	Over 75	Unknown.
ALL AGES,	9,141	33	400	1174	1720	1927	1388	977	644	363	231	141	48	18	77
Und. 20,	–	–	–	–	–	–	–	–	–	–	–	–	–	–	–
20 to 25,	96	7	42	33	10	3	–	–	–	–	–	–	–	–	1
25 to 30,	451	11	108	185	97	36	8	4	–	–	–	–	–	–	2
30 to 35,	940	11	95	324	359	115	24	9	1	–	1	–	–	–	1
35 to 40,	1,443	2	78	303	454	469	107	24	2	–	1	–	–	–	3
40 to 45,	1,392	1	44	160	361	418	318	68	13	1	1	–	–	–	7
45 to 50,	1,339	1	15	97	231	413	304	221	44	7	–	1	–	–	5
50 to 55,	1,090	–	7	43	117	244	283	201	149	27	12	3	–	–	4
55 to 60,	814	–	4	22	57	131	164	180	140	85	19	5	–	1	6
60 to 65,	695	–	3	6	25	59	120	151	153	109	50	12	3	–	4
65 to 70,	436	–	3	1	6	22	33	77	83	71	67	57	11	–	5
70 to 75,	281	–	–	–	1	16	18	31	44	45	55	41	23	6	1
75 to 80,	102	–	–	–	1	–	6	9	12	17	23	18	9	6	1
Over 80,	18	–	–	–	–	–	3	1	3	1	1	4	2	2	1
Unk., .	44	–	1	–	1	1	–	1	–	–	1	–	–	3	36

(E.)   Conditions of Parties not stated.

	ALL AGES.	Under 20	20 to 25	25 to 30	30 to 35	35 to 40	40 to 45	45 to 50	50 to 55	55 to 60	60 to 65	65 to 70	70 to 75	Over 75	Unknown.
ALL AGES,	422	30	62	65	23	13	3	2	2	4	–	1	–	–	217
Und. 20,	5	2	1	–	–	–	–	–	–	–	–	–	–	–	2
20 to 25,	64	17	25	10	2	–	–	–	–	–	–	–	–	–	10
25 to 30,	88	6	28	31	5	–	–	–	–	–	–	–	–	–	18
30 to 35,	33	3	6	10	8	2	–	–	–	–	–	–	–	–	4
35 to 40,	12	1	1	5	2	1	–	–	–	–	–	–	–	–	2
40 to 45,	16	–	–	4	4	5	1	–	–	–	–	–	–	–	2
45 to 50,	9	1	–	1	2	3	–	–	–	–	–	–	–	–	2
50 to 55,	6	–	–	1	–	1	1	1	1	–	–	1	–	–	–
55 to 60,	1	–	–	–	–	1	–	–	–	–	–	–	–	–	–
60 to 65,	4	–	–	–	–	–	1	–	1	2	–	–	–	–	–
65 to 70,	2	–	–	–	–	–	–	1	–	1	–	–	–	–	–
70 to 75,	1	–	–	–	–	–	–	–	–	1	–	–	–	–	–
75 to 80,	–	–	–	–	–	–	–	–	–	–	–	–	–	–	–
Over 80,	–	–	–	–	–	–	–	–	–	–	–	–	–	–	–
Unk., .	181	–	1	3	–	–	–	–	–	–	–	–	–	–	177

TABLE XVII.—DEATHS.—TEN YEARS.—1865–74.

Distinguished by Counties, by Months, and by Sex, the registered Number of Persons who have died during the Ten Years, 1865–74; also for the entire State, the Percentage of the Numbers in each Month (distinguishing Sex) to the Total Number.

Months. 10 Years	SEX	Percentage	State	Barnstable	Berkshire	Bristol	Dukes and Nantucket	Essex	Franklin	Hampden	Hampshire	Middlesex	Norfolk	Plymouth	Suffolk	Worcester
10 Years	Totals,	100·00	280,308	5,339	10,136	20,166	1,622	36,833	5,402	15,303	7,515	51,856	16,628	11,358	69,598	34,552
	Males,	50·03	140,239	2,756	5,125	10,195	833	18,240	2,595	7,670	3,630	25,522	8,181	5,677	32,546	17,269
	Females,	49·83	139,684	2,544	4,970	9,943	789	18,533	2,791	7,609	3,865	26,287	8,426	5,654	31,040	17,233
	Unknown,	·14	385	39	41	28	–	60	16	24	20	47	21	27	12	50
Jan.	Totals,	7·71	21,624	382	751	1,640	124	2,772	411	1,114	541	4,034	1,268	875	5,117	2,595
	Males,	3·89	10,908	201	368	854	63	1,400	196	535	260	2,032	628	421	2,646	1,304
	Females,	3·82	10,700	180	383	786	61	1,368	215	579	281	1,998	638	462	2,470	1,289
	Unknown,	–	16	1	–	–	–	4	–	–	–	4	2	–	1	2
Feb.	Totals,	7·35	20,609	409	730	1,429	116	2,736	354	1,104	488	3,876	1,241	853	4,685	2,588
	Males,	3·67	10,289	224	363	714	55	1,373	174	563	237	1,905	596	422	2,408	1,255
	Females,	3·67	10,295	183	364	712	61	1,359	178	540	251	1,969	644	429	2,276	1,329
	Unknown,	·01	25	2	3	3	–	4	2	1	–	2	1	–	1	4
Mar.	Totals,	8·37	23,451	467	833	1,590	140	3,127	456	1,277	682	4,253	1,426	995	5,346	2,859
	Males,	4·08	11,419	250	391	788	64	1,444	224	630	315	1,982	696	501	2,714	1,420
	Females,	4·28	12,000	214	437	801	76	1,678	230	645	366	2,269	727	492	2,632	1,434
	Unknown,	·01	32	3	5	1	–	5	2	2	2	2	3	2	–	5
Apr.	Totals,	7·79	21,850	409	819	1,594	154	2,873	386	1,169	603	3,858	1,311	975	4,965	2,734
	Males,	3·88	10,887	217	415	809	79	1,447	192	570	287	1,892	620	496	2,511	1,352
	Females,	3·90	10,939	190	401	783	75	1,424	194	595	314	1,964	690	478	2,454	1,377
	Unknown,	·01	24	2	3	2	–	2	–	4	2	2	1	1	–	5
May.	Totals,	7·71	21,620	359	730	1,481	151	2,773	447	1,122	794	3,857	1,305	929	4,947	2,725
	Males,	3·90	10,938	201	357	771	75	1,366	221	563	373	1,917	641	453	2,575	1,425
	Females,	3·80	10,657	156	371	710	76	1,403	219	556	421	1,937	663	476	2,372	1,297
	Unknown,	·01	25	2	2	–	–	4	7	3	–	3	1	–	–	3

Month	Category														Total	%
June	Totals	2,333	4,299	800	1,141	3,527	471	1,040	367	2,400	109	1,201	648	390	18,721	6·68
	Males	1,167	2,211	421	688	1,753	238	522	182	1,203	56	638	336	190	9,505	3·39
	Females	1,164	2,086	377	550	1,768	231	516	185	1,192	53	561	306	197	9,186	3·28
	Unknown	—	2	2	—	6	1	—	—	5	—	2	1	3	30	·01
July	Totals	3,810	6,615	870	1,505	5,006	682	1,703	434	3,258	119	1,755	855	431	26,543	5·46
	Males	1,728	3,435	468	747	2,511	338	883	208	1,629	62	866	433	223	13,531	4·82
	Females	1,572	3,179	398	756	2,492	341	820	224	1,619	57	888	417	202	12,965	4·62
	Unknown	10	1	2	2	3	3	—	2	10	—	1	5	6	47	·02
Aug.	Totals	4,065	6,796	1,187	1,898	6,122	818	1,795	632	4,548	145	2,300	1,182	566	32,054	11·44
	Males	2,048	3,523	601	961	3,079	389	890	288	2,316	82	1,188	631	292	16,288	5·81
	Females	2,011	3,269	584	936	3,038	428	900	343	2,225	63	1,108	547	268	15,720	5·61
	Unknown	6	4	2	1	5	1	—	1	7	—	4	4	6	46	·02
Sept.	Totals	3,359	5,704	1,122	1,651	5,052	737	1,453	570	3,812	171	2,096	1,014	572	27,813	9·75
	Males	1,639	2,911	536	788	2,453	365	731	259	1,927	90	1,055	531	283	13,568	4·84
	Females	1,718	2,791	584	860	2,596	365	719	311	1,876	81	1,039	476	287	13,703	4·89
	Unknown	2	2	2	3	3	7	3	—	9	—	2	7	2	42	·02
Oct.	Totals	2,890	5,023	970	1,412	4,297	683	1,227	504	3,141	145	1,777	931	478	23,428	8·36
	Males	1,455	2,516	489	708	2,096	296	626	247	1,561	72	898	468	225	11,657	4·16
	Females	1,430	2,507	480	703	2,197	335	600	257	1,576	73	874	463	247	11,742	4·19
	Unknown	5	—	1	—	3	2	1	—	9	—	5	7	6	29	·01
Nov.	Totals	2,427	4,921	868	1,188	3,803	552	1,154	426	2,674	112	1,669	823	407	21,024	7·50
	Males	1,185	2,507	415	561	1,836	279	571	205	1,280	57	813	403	203	10,315	3·68
	Females	1,240	2,414	447	627	1,964	273	581	220	1,392	55	853	416	202	10,684	3·81
	Unknown	2	—	6	—	3	—	2	—	2	—	3	4	2	25	·01
Dec.	Totals	2,662	5,180	907	1,273	4,160	505	1,136	414	2,705	128	1,611	805	457	21,943	7·83
	Males	1,289	2,589	450	642	2,061	248	584	199	1,280	71	790	418	238	10,859	3·88
	Females	1,369	2,590	454	628	2,092	257	552	214	1,421	57	817	382	217	11,050	3·94
	Unknown	4	1	3	9	7	—	—	1	4	—	4	5	2	94	·01
Not stated	Totals	5	—	9	9	11	9	9	1	14	8	23	20	12	128	·05
	Males	2	—	7	5	5	5	2	1	14	7	11	11	9	75	·03
	Females	3	—	4	4	3	3	6	1	—	1	11	7	1	43	·02
	Unknown	—	—	—	—	3	1	1	—	—	—	1	2	2	10	—

TABLE XVIII.—DEATHS.—TEN YEARS—1865–74.

Distinguishing by Counties, by Age, and by Sex, the registered Number of Persons who have died during the Ten Years, 1865–74; also, for the entire State, the Percentage of the Numbers in each specified Age (distinguishing Sex) to the Total Number.

Age	Sex	Percentage	State	Barnstable	Berkshire	Bristol	Dukes and Nantucket	Essex	Franklin	Hampden	Hampshire	Middlesex	Norfolk	Plymouth	Suffolk	Worcester
All Ages	Totals	100·00	280,308	5,339	10,196	20,166	1,622	36,833	5,402	15,903	7,515	51,856	16,628	11,358	63,598	34,552
	Males	50·33	140,239	2,756	5,125	10,195	833	18,240	2,595	7,670	3,630	25,522	8,181	5,677	32,546	17,269
	Females	49·83	139,684	2,544	4,970	9,943	789	18,533	2,791	7,609	3,865	26,287	8,426	5,654	31,040	17,233
	Unknown	·14	385	39	41	28	—	60	16	24	20	47	21	27	12	50
Under 1	Totals	21·81	61,112	733	1,792	4,912	188	8,061	747	3,530	1,267	11,527	3,494	1,913	16,400	7,258
	Males	11·90	33,340	403	1,027	2,435	77	4,381	417	1,897	687	6,229	1,848	1,055	8,850	4,040
	Females	9·78	27,425	293	731	1,852	61	3,625	315	1,614	565	5,263	1,666	831	7,538	3,171
	Unknown	·13	347	37	34	25	—	55	15	19	15	41	20	27	12	47
1 to 2	Totals	7·16	20,073	213	614	1,460	29	2,492	240	1,256	406	3,722	1,109	588	5,380	2,564
	Males	3·71	10,400	116	339	744	15	1,308	116	629	201	1,937	573	311	2,777	1,334
	Females	3·45	9,667	97	274	716	14	1,183	123	625	205	1,785	636	277	2,603	1,229
	Unknown	—	6	—	1	—	—	1	1	2	—	—	—	—	—	1
2 to 3	Totals	3·22	9,042	140	339	649	19	1,104	118	568	202	1,642	507	259	2,241	1,254
	Males	1·66	4,654	76	183	335	8	562	57	294	108	836	242	131	1,165	657
	Females	1·56	4,380	64	154	313	11	541	61	273	94	804	265	128	1,076	596
	Unknown	—	8	—	2	1	—	1	—	1	—	2	—	—	—	1
3 to 4	Totals	2·15	6,033	71	287	409	15	802	82	370	144	1,099	355	182	1,511	756
	Males	1·08	3,027	37	135	192	6	410	38	172	71	549	169	83	777	388
	Females	1·07	3,002	34	102	217	9	391	44	197	73	649	185	99	734	368
	Unknown	—	4	—	—	—	—	1	—	1	—	1	1	—	—	—

4 to 5 Totals	562	1,044	113	251	826	86	260	62	573	16	321	171	56	4,341	1·55
Males	266	530	55	130	416	46	134	30	289	8	161	72	29	2,166	·77
Females	296	514	58	121	410	40	126	32	284	8	160	99	27	2,175	·78
Under 5 Totals	12,394	26,576	3,055	5,656	18,816	2,105	5,984	1,249	13,032	217	7,151	3,153	1,213	100,601	35·89
Males	6,685	14,099	1,635	2,962	9,961	1,113	3,126	658	6,950	114	3,867	1,756	661	53,587	19·12
Females	5,660	12,465	1,393	2,673	8,811	977	2,835	575	6,024	103	3,258	1,360	515	46,649	16·64
Unknown	49	12	27	21	44	15	23	16	58	-	26	37	37	365	·13
5 to 10 Totals	1,360	2,351	349	730	2,230	296	703	210	1,436	51	794	472	162	11,144	3·98
Males	684	1,225	176	380	1,141	147	364	117	718	24	434	252	89	5,751	2·05
Females	675	1,126	173	350	1,089	149	339	93	718	27	360	219	73	5,391	1·93
Unknown	1	-	-	-	-	-	-	-	-	-	-	1	-	2	-
10 to 15 Totals	873	1,095	245	359	1,112	175	362	134	775	30	475	277	111	6,023	2·15
Males	401	541	112	174	538	84	210	56	349	11	221	135	53	2,885	1·08
Females	472	554	133	185	574	91	152	78	426	19	254	142	58	3,138	1·12
15 to 20 Totals	1,365	2,235	416	602	1,955	340	691	221	1,476	38	748	412	234	10,733	3·83
Males	603	1,053	170	291	844	132	297	97	637	23	299	180	122	4,748	1·69
Females	762	1,182	246	311	1,111	207	394	124	839	15	449	232	112	5,984	2·14
Unknown	-	-	-	-	-	1	-	-	-	-	-	-	-	1	-
20 to 30 Totals	3,345	7,395	1,101	1,596	5,417	697	1,598	552	3,780	151	1,917	976	634	29,159	10·40
Males	1,531	3,726	528	722	2,408	303	754	228	1,664	93	905	453	336	13,651	4·87
Females	1,814	3,669	573	874	3,009	394	844	324	2,116	58	1,012	523	297	15,507	5·53
Unknown	-	-	-	-	-	-	-	-	-	-	-	-	1	1	-
30 to 40 Totals	2,510	6,069	832	1,300	4,446	625	1,163	380	2,866	112	1,480	732	416	22,931	8·18
Males	1,093	3,102	354	559	2,012	274	513	166	1,260	66	698	318	194	10,609	3·78
Females	1,417	2,967	478	741	2,434	351	650	214	1,606	46	782	414	222	12,322	4·40

Table XVIII.—Concluded.

Age	SEX	Percentage	STATE	Barnstable	Berkshire	Bristol	Dukes and Nantucket	Essex	Franklin	Hampden	Hampshire	Middlesex	Norfolk	Plymouth	Suffolk	Worcester
40 to 50	Totals,	6·82	19,107	351	644	1,309	86	2,277	357	953	515	3,564	1,073	718	5,028	2,232
	Males,	3·45	9,652	184	317	679	40	1,127	165	494	240	1,782	523	347	2,663	1,091
	Females,	3·37	9,454	167	326	630	46	1,150	192	459	275	1,782	550	371	2,365	1,141
	Unknown.	—	1	—	—	—	—	—	—	—	—	—	—	—	—	—
50 to 60	Totals,	6·62	18,562	374	688	1,383	133	2,325	422	897	538	3,491	1,091	798	4,209	2,213
	Males,	3·56	9,977	194	379	754	63	1,222	217	462	283	1,862	584	452	2,347	1,158
	Females,	3·06	8,585	180	309	629	70	1,103	205	435	255	1,629	507	346	1,862	1,055
60 to 70	Totals,	7·74	21,694	561	926	1,678	219	2,868	599	1,041	717	4,004	1,387	1,169	3,784	2,741
	Males,	4·00	11,215	300	473	896	129	1,461	299	529	367	2,057	717	615	1,907	1,465
	Females,	3·74	10,479	261	453	782	90	1,407	300	512	350	1,947	670	554	1,877	1,276
70 to 80	Totals,	7·89	22,103	715	927	1,716	295	3,041	667	1,059	841	3,760	1,541	1,460	3,020	3,061
	Males,	9·72	10,422	355	445	807	153	1,385	315	530	404	1,729	749	754	1,269	1,527
	Females,	4·16	11,681	360	482	909	142	1,656	352	529	437	2,031	792	706	1,751	1,534
80 to 90	Totals,	4·93	13,828	441	671	1,119	229	1,941	486	644	526	2,300	999	1,000	1,531	1,941
	Males,	2·03	5,683	209	299	459	100	761	229	302	232	892	398	451	507	844
	Females,	2·90	8,145	232	372	660	129	1,180	257	342	294	1,408	601	549	1,024	1,097
90 to 100	Totals,	·86	2,410	74	127	217	45	337	86	111	61	434	191	160	227	340
	Males,	·28	790	27	48	78	10	107	29	43	17	140	62	56	77	96
	Females,	·58	1,620	47	79	139	35	230	57	68	44	294	129	104	150	244

Over 100.	Totals,	23	24	3	8	37	3	5	3	14	2	11	12	2	147	·06
	Males,	11	7	1	2	14	—	1	—	3	—	6	5	1	51	·02
	Females,	12	17	2	6	23	3	4	3	11	2	5	7	1	96	·03
Not stated.	Totals,	154	54	52	95	290	76	92	36	665	14	168	119	51	1,866	·67
	Males,	80	23	26	58	142	34	45	19	596	7	92	65	31	1,218	·43
	Females,	74	31	26	37	145	38	46	17	67	7	74	52	19	633	·23
	Unknown,	—	—	—	—	3	4	1	—	2	—	2	2	1	15	·01

APPENDIX.

LAWS

CONCERNING THE REGISTRATION OF BIRTHS, MARRIAGES AND DEATHS.

[General Statutes—Chapter 21.]

OF THE REGISTRY AND RETURNS OF BIRTHS, MARRIAGES, AND DEATHS.

SECTION

1. City and Town Clerks to obtain, record, and index facts concerning Births, Marriages, and Deaths.
2. Parents and others to give notice of Births, and Deaths.
3. Physicians to give Certificate of Cause of Death, when requested. Penalty.
4. Sextons, Undertakers, &c., to make returns to Clerks of Cities and Towns. Clerks to give Certificate of Registry of Death to the Person having charge of funeral rites *preliminary* to Interment, for delivery, &c. If Interment takes place without such Certificate, notice thereof to be given, under penalty of twenty dollars.
5. Clerk annually to transmit certified Copies of Records to Secretary.

SECTION

6. Record or Certificate of Clerk to be *prima facie* evidence in Legal Proceedings.
7. Clerks—Fees of, payable by City or Town; Accounts of, to be certified by Secretary. Penalty for neglect of duty.
8. Superintendents of State Almshouses to record and return to Secretary, births and deaths therein.
9. Secretary to furnish Blank Books for Records and forms for Returns, with Instructions. Clerks to distribute the Blank Forms for Returns.
10. Secretary,—to cause Returns to be bound &c.; to Report annually to Legislature,&c.; to do all other acts necessary to secure the execution of the provisions of this chapter.
11. Registrars may be chosen, in certain cases, in place of Town Clerks.

SECTION 1.   The clerk of each city and town shall receive or obtain, and record, and index, the following facts concerning the births, marriages, and deaths, therein, separately numbering and recording the same in the order in which he receives them, designated in separate columns:

In the record of births, the date of the birth, the place of birth, the name of the child (if it have any), the sex and color of the child, the names and the places of birth of the parents, the occupation of the father, the residence of the parents, and the date of the record;

In the record of marriages, the date of the marriage, the place of marriage, the name, residence and official station of the person by whom married, the names and places of birth of the parties, the residence of each, the age and color of each, the condition of each (whether single or widowed), the occupation, the names of the parents and the date of the record.

In the record of deaths, the date of the death, the name of the deceased, the sex, the color, the condition (whether single, widowed, or married), the age, the residence, the occupation, the place of death, the place of birth, the names and places of birth of the parents, the disease or cause of death, the place of burial, and the date of the record.

SECTION 2. Parents shall give notice to the clerk of their city or town of the births and deaths of their children; every householder shall give like notice of every birth and death happening in his house; the eldest person next of kin shall give such notice of the death of his kindred; the keeper of a workhouse, house of correction, prison, hospital, or almshouse, except the state almshouses at Tewksbury, Bridgewater, and Monson, and the master or other commanding officer of any ship shall give like notice of every birth and death happening among the persons under his charge. Whoever neglects to give such notice for the space of six months after a birth or death, shall forfeit a sum not exceeding five dollars.

SECTION 3. Any physician having attended a person during his last illness, shall—when requested within fifteen days after the decease of such person—forthwith furnish for registration a certificate of the duration of the last sickness, the disease of which the person died, and the date of his decease, as nearly as he can state the same. If any physician refuses or neglects to make such certificate, he shall forfeit and pay the sum of ten dollars to the use of the town in which he resides.

SECTION 4.* Every sexton, undertaker, or other person having charge of a burial-ground, or the superintendent of burials having charge of the obsequies or funeral rites preliminary to the interment of a human body, shall forthwith obtain and return to the clerk of the city or town in which the deceased resided or the death occurred, the facts required by this chapter to be recorded by said officer concerning the deceased, and the person making such return shall receive from his city or town the fee of ten cents therefor.

The clerk, upon recording such facts, shall forthwith give to the person making such return, a certificate that such return has been made, which certificate such person shall deliver to the person having charge of the interment, if other than himself, before the burial when practicable, otherwise within seven days thereafter. When a burial takes place and no certificate is delivered as aforesaid, the sexton, undertaker, or other person having charge of the interment, shall forthwith give notice thereof to the clerk under penalty of twenty dollars.

SECTION 5. The clerk of each city and town shall annually on or before the first day of February, transmit to the secretary of the Commonwealth, certified copies of the records of the births, marriages, and deaths, which have occurred therein during the year ending on the last day of the preceding December.

SECTION 6. The record of the town clerk relative to any birth, marriage, or death, shall be *primâ facie* evidence, in legal proceedings,

---

* See chap. 202, on page clvi., following.

of the facts recorded. The certificate signed by the town clerk for the time being shall be admissible as evidence of any such record.

SECTION 7.* The clerk shall receive from his city or town for obtaining, recording, indexing, and returning to the, secretary of the Commonwealth, the facts in relation to a birth, twenty cents ; a marriage, ten cents ; a death, twenty cents for each of the first twenty entries, and ten cents for each subsequent entry, as the same shall be certified by the secretary of the Commonwealth ; but a city or town containing more than ten thousand inhabitants may limit the aggregate compensation allowed to their clerk. He shall forfeit a sum not less than twenty nor more than one hundred dollars for each refusal or neglect to perform any duty required of him by this chapter.

SECTION 8. The superintendents of the state almshouses at Tewksbury, Bridgewater, and Monson, shall obtain, record, and make return of the facts in relation to the births and deaths which occur in their respective institutions, in like manner as is required of town clerks. The clerks of said towns shall, in relation to the births and deaths of persons in said almshouses, be exempt from the duties otherwise required of them by this chapter.

SECTION 9. The secretary shall, at the expense of the Commonwealth, prepare and furnish to the clerks of the several cities and towns, and to the superintendents of the state almshouses, blank books of suitable quality and size to be used as books of record under this chapter, blank books for indexes thereto, and blank forms for returns, on paper of uniform size ; and shall accompany the same with such instructions and explanations as may be necessary and useful. City and town clerks shall make such distribution of blank forms of returns furnished by the secretary as he shall direct.

SECTION 10. The secretary shall cause the returns received by him for each year to be bound together in one or more volumes with indexes thereto. He shall prepare from the returns such tabular results as will render them of practical utility, make report thereof annually to the legislature, and do all other acts necessary to carry into effect the provisions of this chapter.

SECTION 11. Any city or town containing more than ten thousand inhabitants, may choose a person other than the clerk to be registrar, who shall be sworn, and to whom all the provisions of this chapter concerning clerks shall apply. The returns and notices required to be made and given to clerks shall be made and given to such registrar under like penalties.

SECTION 12. The secretary of this Commonwealth shall prosecute, by an action of tort, in the name of the Commonwealth, for the recovery of any penalty or forfeiture imposed by this chapter.

SECTION 13. Any city or town may make rules and regulations to enforce the provisions of this chapter, or to secure a more perfect registration of births, marriages, and deaths, therein.

* See chaps. 138, 145 and 341, on pp. clv. and clvi., following.

[General Statutes—Chapter 106.]

OF MARRIAGE.

SECTIONS 1, 2 and 3. [Marriage between certain relatives prohibited.]

SECTION 4. [Polygamy forbidden.]

SECTION 5. [Marriage contracted by insane persons or idiots, void.]

SECTION 6. [Marriage of persons marrying out of the state in order to evade, &c., void.]

SECTION 7. Persons intending to be joined in marriage, shall, before their marriage cause notice thereof to be entered in the office of the clerk, or registrar of the city or town in which they respectively dwell, if within the State. If there is no such clerk or registrar in the place of their residence, the entry shall be made in an adjoining city or town.

SECTION 8. The clerk or registrar shall deliver to the parties a certificate under his hand, specifying the time when notice of the intention of marriage was entered with him, together with all facts in relation to the marriage required by law to be ascertained and recorded, except those respecting the person by whom the marriage is to be solemnized. Such certificate shall be delivered to the minister or magistrate in whose presence the marriage is to be contracted, before he proceeds to solemnize the same.

SECTION 9. If a clerk or registrar issues such certificate to a male under the age of twenty-one years, or a female under the age of eighteen years, having reasonable cause to suppose the person to be under such age, except upon the application or consent in writing of the parent, master, or guardian, of such person, he shall forfeit a sum not exceeding one hundred dollars; but if there is no parent, master, or guardian, in this State, competent to act, a certificate may be issued without such application or consent.

SECTION 10. The clerk or registrar may require of any person applying for such certificate, an affidavit sworn to before a justice of the peace for the county where the application is made, setting forth the age of the parties; which affidavit shall be sufficient proof of age to authorize the issuing of the certificate.

SECTION 11. Whoever applying for such certificate wilfully makes a false statement in relation to the age or residence, parent, master,

20

or guardian, of either of the parties intending marriage, shall forfeit a sum not exceeding two hundred dollars.

Section 12. When a marriage is solemnized in another State between parties living in this State, and they return to dwell here, they shall, within seven days after their return, file with the clerk or registrar of the city or town, where either of them lived at the time, a certificate or declaration of their marriage, including the facts concerning marriages required by law, and for every neglect they shall forfeit ten dollars.

Section 13. No magistrate or minister shall solemnize a marriage, having reasonable cause to suppose either of the parties to be under the age mentioned in section nine, without the consent of the parent or guardian having the custody of the minor, if there is any in the State competent to act.

Section 14. Marriages may be solemnized by a justice of the peace in the county for which he is appointed, when either of the parties resides in the same county; and throughout the State by any minister of the gospel ordained according to the usage of his denomination, who resides within the State and continues to perform the functions of his office; but all marriages shall be solemnized in the city or town in which the person solemnizing them resides, or in which one or both of the persons to be married reside.

Section 15. Marriages among the people called Friends or Quakers may be solemnized in the manner heretofore used and practised in their societies.

Section 16. Every justice of the peace, minister, and clerk, or keeper of the records of the meeting wherein any marriages among the Friends or Quakers are solemnized, shall make a record of each marriage solemnized before him, together with all facts relating to the marriage required by law to be recorded. He shall also between the first and tenth days of each month return a copy of the record for the month next preceding, to the clerk or registrar of the city or town in which the marriage was solemnized, and shall when neither of the parties to a marriage resides in the city or town in which the marriage is solemnized, return a copy of the record of such marriage to the clerk or registrar of the city or town in which one or both parties reside. All marriages so returned shall be recorded by the clerk or registrar.

Section 17. Every person neglecting to make the returns required by the preceding section, shall forfeit for each neglect not less than twenty nor more than one hundred dollars.

Section 18. A justice of the peace or minister who joins persons in marriage contrary to the provisions of this chapter, knowing that the marriage is not duly authorized, shall forfeit not less than fifty nor more than one hundred dollars.

Section 19. Whoever undertakes to join persons in marriage knowing that he is not authorized so to do, shall be imprisoned in the jail or confined to hard labor for a term not exceeding six months, or pay a fine of not less than fifty nor more than two hundred dollars.

Section 20. [Unintentional informality does not invalidate marriage in other respects lawful.]

Section 21. The record of a marriage, made and kept as prescribed by law by the person before whom the marriage is solemnized, or by the clerk or registrar of any city or town, or a copy of such record duly certified, shall be received in all courts and places as presumptive evidence of such marriage.

Section 22. [Admission of respondent, general repute, &c., competent evidence to prove the fact of marriage.]

Section 23. [Marriage in foreign countries by a consul or diplomatic agent valid, and certificate of such consul or agent presumptive evidence thereof.]

[General Statutes—Chapter 29.]
OF THE PUBLIC RECORDS.

Section 10. County, city and town records and files may be inspected and copied.]

Section 13. [Penalties; . . . . . . for altering or mutilating any record, paper, or written document, a sum not exceeding fifty dollars,—for wrongfully detaining records, and other documents, fifty dollars.]

[General Statutes—Section 1 of Chapter 174.]
SENTENCE WHEN NO PUNISHMENT IS PROVIDED.

Section 1. In cases of legal conviction, where no punishment is provided by statute, the court shall award such sentence as is conformable to the common usage and practice in this State, according to the nature of the offence, and not repugnant to the constitution.

[Chapter 138.]
AN ACT CONCERNING THE REGISTRY AND RETURN OF MARRIAGES, BIRTHS AND DEATHS.

Section 1. The clerk of each city and town (except in such cities and towns as choose a registrar, under the eleventh section of the twenty-first chapter of the General Statutes, in which cases the provisions of this act shall apply to the registrar), for receiving or obtaining, recording, indexing, and returning the facts relating to marriages, births and deaths occurring therein, shall be entitled to receive therefrom the sums following, viz.: for each marriage, fifteen cents; for each birth, thirty cents; for each death returned to him by the persons specified in sections two, three and four of chapter twenty-one of the General Statutes, twenty cents for each of the first twenty entries, and ten cents for each subsequent entry; for each death not so returned but by him obtained and recorded, twenty cents.

Section 2. Chapter ninety-six of the acts of the year eighteen hundred and sixty-five, and so much of section seven of the twenty-first chapter of the General Statutes as is inconsistent herewith, are hereby repealed.

Section 3. This act shall take effect upon its passage.

[*Approved April* 7, 1866.

[Chapter 58.]

AN ACT RELATING TO THE MARRIAGE OF NON-RESIDENT PARTIES.

SECTION 1. Persons living without the Commonwealth and intending to be joined in marriage within the Commonwealth, shall, before their marriage, cause notice of their intention to be entered in the office of the clerk or registrar of the city or town in which they propose to have the marriage solemnized; and no marriage between such parties shall be solemnized until they have delivered to the justice of the peace or minister, in whose presence the marriage is to be contracted, a certificate from such clerk or registrar, specifying the time when notice of the intention of marriage was entered with him, together with all facts in relation to the marriage required by law to be ascertained and recorded, except those respecting the person by whom the marriage is to be solemnized.

SECTION 2. Marriages may be solemnized by a justice of the peace in the county for which he is appointed.

SECTION 3. A justice of the peace or minister who joins persons in marriage contrary to the provisions of this act shall forfeit not less than fifty nor more than one hundred dollars.

[*Approved March* 11, 1867.

[Chapter 145.]

AN ACT FIXING THE FEES OF CLERKS AND REGISTRARS FOR THE REGISTRY AND RETURN OF BIRTHS.

SECTION 1. The clerk or registrar of a city or town shall receive the sum of fifty cents for receiving or obtaining, recording, indexing and returning the facts relating to each birth; but a city or town containing more than ten thousand inhabitants may limit the aggregate compensation allowed to their clerk or registrar.

SECTION 2. This act shall take effect upon its passage.

[*Approved April* 2, 1873.

[Chapter 202.]

AN ACT RELATING TO THE FEES OF SEXTONS AND OTHERS.

SECTION 1. Section four of chapter twenty-one of the General Statutes is amended by striking out the word "ten" after the words "fee of," and inserting instead thereof, the words "twenty-five."

SECTION 2. This act shall take effect upon its passage.

[*Approved April* 16, 1873.

[Chapter 341.]

AN ACT CONCERNING FEES OF TOWN CLERKS FOR OBTAINING AND RECORDING THE FACTS RELATING TO DEATHS.

Chapter one hundred and thirty-eight of the acts of the year eighteen hundred and sixty-six is amended by striking out the words "twenty cents," at the close of section one, and substituting therefor the words "thirty-five cents."

[*Approved June* 6, 1873.

[Chapter 21.]

AN ACT TO AMEND SECTION FIVE OF CHAPTER TWENTY-ONE OF THE GENERAL STATUTES, IN RELATION TO THE REGISTRY AND RETURN OF BIRTHS, MARRIAGES AND DEATHS.

SECTION 1. Section five of chapter twenty-one, of the General Statutes, is hereby amended by striking out the word " February " in the second line of said section, and inserting in place thereof the word " March."

SECTION 2. This act shall take effect upon its passage.

[*Approved February* 19, 1875.

STATISTICAL NOSOLOGY

ADOPTED FOR REGISTRATION IN MASSACHUSETTS.

The following plan of a Nomenclature and Classification of Diseases does not essentially differ from that authorized by the Registrar-General of England, to be used in the preparation of the "Weekly Return of Births and Deaths in London," and is also, with slight modifications, identical with that embodied in a report drawn up by William Farr, Esq., M. D., of London, for the consideration of the International Statistical Congress which met at Paris in September, 1855; which report was printed in the Appendix to the Sixteenth Registration Report of the Registrar-General, England.

[NOTE.—This page and those that follow contain two lists of causes of death. The first,—that on the left side,—may be called the TABULAR LIST, and comprises all the heads which it is proposed to admit into the complete tables (IX. and X.) and under which ALL deaths, from whatever cause are finally distributed. It represents those diseases which, under the same terms, or terms strictly synonymous with them, are found in practice to occur most frequently.

The SUPPLEMENTAL LIST is *subordinate* to the first, and contains the principal *special diseases* which it may be considered desirable to note. The figures in this list indicate the corresponding numbers of the tabular list under which such diseases are ultimately arranged.

Table VIII. includes both the Tabular and Supplemental lists; Tables IX. and X. the Tabular list only.]

CAUSES OF DEATH.

TABULAR LIST.	SUPPLEMENTAL LIST.
CLASS I. ZYMOTIC DISEASES.	*Of Diseases of Special Character (or Synonymes).*
ORDER I.—*Miasmatic.*	
I. 1.—1. Smallpox,	I. 1.—1. Vaccination not stated.
2. Measles,	Smallpox (2d attack).
3. Scarlatina,	After vaccination.
4. Diphtheria,	Erysipelas, &c., after vaccination.
5. Quinsy,	Chickenpox.
6. Croup,	Miliaria.
7. Whooping Cough,	2. Rubeola.
	3. Angina maligna.
8. Typhoid (and Infantile) Fever,	5. Mumps.
9. Erysipelas,	Tonsillitis.
10. Metria (Puerperal Fever),	8. Typhus fever.
11. Carbuncle,	9. Phlebitis.
12. Influenza,	Pyemia.
	Hospital gangrene.
	Erythema.
13. Dysentery,	10. Childbed fever.
14. Diarrhœa,	11. Anthrax.
15. Cholera Infantum,	
16. Cholera,	
17. Ague,	17. Intermittent fever.
18. Remittent Fever,	18. Yellow fever.
19. Rheumatism,	19. Rheumatism with pericarditis, or disease of heart.
20. Cerebro-spinal Meningitis,	20. "Spotted fever."

CAUSES OF DEATH—(Continued).

TABULAR LIST.	SUPPLEMENTAL LIST.
CLASS I.—(Continued).	
ORDER 2.—*Enthetic.*	
I. 2.—1. Syphilis, ...	I. 2.—1. Gonorrhœa.
2. Stricture of Urethra, . . .	Purulent ophthalmia.
3. Hydrophobia, ...	4. Malignant pustule.
4. Glanders, ...	Necusia (usually from dissection wounds).
ORDER 3.—*Dietic.*	
I. 3.—1. Privation, ...	I. 3.—1. Want of breast milk.
2. Purpura and Scurvy, . . .	2. Rickets.
3. Delirium tremens, } (Alcoholism),	Bronchocele.
4. Intemperance, }	
ORDER 4.—*Parasitic.*	
I. 4.—1. Thrush, ...	I. 4.—2. Porrigo.
2. Worms, &c., ...	Scabies.
	Tape-worm.
	Hydatids.
	Trichiniasis.
CLASS II. CONSTITUTIONAL DISEASES.	
ORDER 1.—*Diathetic.*	
II. 1.—1. Gout, ...	II. 1.—3. Soft cancer.
2. Dropsy and Anæmia, . . .	Sweep's cancer.
3. Cancer, ...	Melanosis.
4. Noma (or Canker), . . .	Other kinds of cancer.
5. Mortification, ...	Polypus (part not stated).
	Lupus.
	5. Bed-sore.
	Dry gangrene.
ORDER 2.—*Tubercular.*	
II. 2.—1. Scrofula, ...	II. 2.—1. Psoas (lumbar) abscess.
2. Tabes Mesenterica, . . .	White swelling.
3. Phthisis (Consumption of Lungs),	Cretinism.
4. Hydrocephalus, ...	2. Tubercular peritonitis.
	3. Hæmoptysis.
	4. Tubercular meningitis
CLASS III. LOCAL DISEASES.	
ORDER 1.—*Nervous System.*	
III. 1.—1. Cephalitis, ...	III. 1.—1. Phrenitis. Myelitis.
2. Apoplexy, ...	4. Monomania.
3. Paralysis, ...	Fright.
4. Insanity, ...	Grief.
5 Chorea, ...	Melancholia.
6. Epilepsy, ...	Rage.
7. Tetanus, ...	6. Hysteria.
8. Convulsions, ...	8. Laryngismus stridulus.
9. *Brain Diseases,* &c., . . .	9. Neuralgia.
	Ophthalmia.
	Otitis.
	Dis. of spinal marrow.
	Necrencephalus. (Softening of Brain. Ramollisement.)

* Other diseases of the brain, or diseases of the nervous system, *not otherwise distinguished,* are referred to this head. *Mutatis mutandis,* the note applies to the corresponding heads in other Orders of this Class.

CAUSES OF DEATH—(Continued).

TABULAR LIST.	SUPPLEMENTAL LIST.

CLASS III.—(Continued).

ORDER 2.—*Organs of Circulation.*

III. 2.—1. Pericarditis,†	III. 2.—1. Carditis.
2. Aneurism, ...	Endocarditis.
3. *Heart Diseases,** &c., . . .	3. Hypertrophia.
	Angina pectoris.
	Syncope.
	Arteritis.
	Hydropericardium.

ORDER 3.—*Respiratory Organs.*

III. 3.—1. Epistaxis, ...	III. 3.—2. Œdema glottidis.
2. Laryngitis, ...	4. Empyema.
3. Bronchitis, ...	Hydrothorax.
4. Pleurisy, ...	Diaphragmitis.
5. Pneumonia, ...	Pneumothorax.
6. Asthma, ...	5. Pulmonary apoplexy.
7. *Lung Diseases, &c.,** . . .	Pleuro pneumonia.
	6. Grinders' asthma.
	Miners' asthma.
	Emphysema.

ORDER 4.—*Digestive Organs.*

III. 4.—1. Gastritis, ...	III. 4.—1. Glossitis.
2. Enteritis, ...	Stomatitis.
3. Peritonitis, ...	Pharyngitis.
4. Ascites, ...	Œsophagitis.
5. Ulceration of Intestines, .	5. Perforation of—
6. Hernia, ...	6. Congenital.
7. Ileus, ...	Femoral.
8. Intussusception, . .	Inguinal.
9. Stricture of Intestines, .	Scrotal.
10. Fistula, ...	Umbilical.
11. *Stomach Diseases,** &c.,	Ventral,
12. *Pancreas Disease,** &c.,	7. Constipation.
13. Hepatitis, ...	11. Dyspepsia.
14. Jaundice, ...	Pyrosis.
15. *Liver Disease,** &c., . .	Gastralgia.
16. *Spleen Disease,** &c., .	Hæmatemesis.
	Melæna.
	Hæmorrhoids.
	14. Gall-stones.
	15. Cirrhosis.

ORDER 5.—*Urinary Organs.*

III. 5.—1. Nephritis, ...	III. 5.—3. Albuminuria.
2. Ischuria, ...	6. Cystirrhœa.
3. Nephria (Bright's disease),	7. Diuresis.
4. Diabetes, ...	Hæmaturia.
5. Calculus (Gravel, &c.),	Dis. of prostate.
6. Cystitis, ...	Dis. of bladder.
6. *Kidney Disease,** &c., .	

ORDER 6.—*Generative Organs.*

III. 6.—1. Ovarian Dropsy, . . .	III. 6.—1. Ovarian tumor.
2. *Disease of Uterus,** &c., .	2. Hysteritis (inflammation
	of womb). Metritis.
	Uterine tumor.
	Polypus uteri.
	Orchitis.
	Hydrocele.

---

* See Note under III. 1.—9. † [See also I. 1.—19.]

CAUSES OF DEATH—(Continued).

TABULAR LIST.	SUPPLEMENTAL LIST.
CLASS III.—(Continued).	
ORDER 7.—*Organs of Locomotion.*	
III. 7.—1. Arthritis,	III. 7.—1. Ostitis.
2. *Joint Disease,* &c.,	Periostitis.
	2. Fragilitas ossium.
	Mollities ossium.
	Caries.
	Necrosis.
ORDER 8.—*Integumentary System.*	Exostosis.
III. 8.—1. Phlegmon,	III. 8.—1. Abscess (part not stated).
2. Ulcer,	Boil.
3. *Skin Diseases,* &c.,	Whitlow.
	3. Roseola.
	Urticaria.
	Eczema.
	Herpes.
	Pemphigus.
	Ecthyma.
	Impetigo.
	Psoriasis.
	Ichthyosis.
	Tumor (part not stated).
CLASS IV. DEVELOPMENTAL DISEASES.	
ORDER 1.—*Developmental Diseases of Children.*	
IV. 1.—1. Stillborn,	IV. 1.—2. Atelectasis.
2. Premature Birth and Infantile Debility,	5. Anus imperforatus.
3. Cyanosis,	Cleft palate.
4. Spina Bifida,	Idiocy.
5. Other Malformations,	
6. Teething,	
ORDER 2.—*Developmental Diseases of Women.*	
IV. 2.—1. Paramenia,	IV. 2.—1. Chlorosis.
2. Childbirth. (*See* Metria I. 1.—9.)	Climacteria.
	Menorrhagia.
	2. Miscarriage.
	Abortion.
	Puerperal mania.
	Puerperal convulsions.
	Phlegmasia dolens.
	Cæsarian operation.
	Extra-uterine fœtation.
	Flooding.
	Retention of placenta.
	Presentation of placenta.
	Deformed pelvis.
ORDER 3.—*Developmental Diseases of Old People.*	Breast abscess.
IV. 3.—1. Old Age,	
ORDER 4.—*Diseases of Nutrition.*	
IV. 4.—1. Atrophy and Debility,	

* See Note under III. 1.—9.

CAUSES OF DEATH—(Concluded).

TABULAR LIST.	SUPPLEMENTAL LIST.
CLASS V. VIOLENT DEATHS.	
ORDER 1.—*Accident or Negligence.*	V. 1.—1. Railroad accidents.
V. 1.—1. Fractures and Contusions,* . .	5. Lost at sea.
2. Wounds, ...	6. Asphyxia.
3. Burns and Scalds, . . .	Strangulation.
4. Poison, ...	7. Exposure.
5. Drowning, ...	Cold water.
6. Suffocation, ...	Frozen.
7. Otherwise, ...	Heat.
	Lightning.
ORDER 2.—*In Battle.*	Surgical operation.
	Neglect.
ORDER 3.—*Homicide.*	
ORDER 4.—*Suicide.*	
V. 4.—1. Wounds, ...	
2. Poison, ...	
3. Drowning, ...	
4. Hanging, ...	
5. Otherwise, ...	
ORDER 5.—*Execution.*	
V. 5.—1. Hanging, ...	
V. 6.—Violent Deaths, not classed, ("casualty,")	
Sudden, cause unascertained, . .	

* Including "Railroad Accidents."

NOTE.—Cases of "infantile fever" are classed with typhus, relapsing, and other continued fevers, under one name "typhoid fever." Cases of "rheumatic fever" are classed with "rheumatism;" of "hemorrhage," and "abscess," with the diseases of the organs affected. Cases of death from cold, heat, drinking cold water, lightning, surgical operation, and exposure, are placed under "Otherwise" [V. 7]. As "stricture of the urethra" is almost invariably the result of gonorrhœa, it is classed as I. 2.—2.

Milton Keynes UK
Ingram Content Group UK Ltd.
UKHW040928180224
437992UK00003B/106

9 783382 831745